CARNELIAN

BY

ANTHONY B BRYANT

All proceeds from this book go to charity.

By the same author , Six Kippers, an Orcadian adventure. 2016

Some comments on Six Kippers.
It's a page -turner from the flight onwards, with an interesting Orkney /archaeological theme, exciting incident and romance. Murdo Grant, Rosemarkie

Just to let you know I've just finished reading your book and I really enjoyed it. A real adventure with plenty of tension, an attractive hero and heroine, and a believably horrible villain. Plus some interesting asides on sailing, Orkney, ancient remains and flying from Inverness, not to mention a personal take on the opening of the Mozart Requiem. I was reminded briefly of Erskine Childers, Biggles, Tommy and Tuppence and John Buchan, but with a much more enlightened, non-bigoted and light touch. So thank you and please get on with the next one. Jon Hall

Finished your book on my bus ride to Edinburgh. Well written, great characters and interesting plot. Can't wait for the next one. Judy Harvey. The Emporium, Cromarty.
I have just finished your book. It has stopped me from doing anything useful since after lunch when I picked it up again! It is a wonderful story, and the settings in Orkney and Edinburgh were all well known to me. It is a wonderful story. Dr Kitty Campbell, Strathpeffer.
I want to say how much I enjoyed this romp through Edinburgh and Orkney………. This is an impressive first novel. It's strengths lie in its pacey action the credibility of the narrative. Its humour and topicality are huge assets. Well done. Elizabeth Sutherland, author.

Copyright 2018

Anthony B Bryant

ISBN: 978-1-912270-17-0

Carnelian

Anthony Bryant

Dedication

To the crew, once upon a time, of *Freyja* and other small boats, and now my companions, more sedately and a great deal more comfortably, on cruise ships.

My thanks to:

- William Mather for the painting which forms the cover.

- The late Jimmy Fraser for help on intellectual property rights, and other legal and practical issues.

- Alexander Bennett, my erstwhile colleague in The National Trust for Scotland for a modern job specification on which mine is based.

- Sheena Munro for correcting my nearly nonexistent French and Italian.

- Alison Brough for the Arabic phrases.

- Murdo Grant for going over the draft and ensuring everything fits together properly, makes sense and that I don't wander too far from the basic plot!

- Elizabeth Sutherland, who originally encouraged me to write and is still in so many ways my mentor, for similarly reading over the draft and making good suggestions.

- Sonia Cameron Jacks, for her dedicated hard work proofing the book.

PREFACE

This story is fiction, so all the people in this book are my invention, as are the *Carnelian*, the *Camel Prince* and the small North African country of Albysia, Qariat and all, never mind Treasures of Scotland.

You may ask if the Edinburgh museum that plays a part herein is the Chambers Street museum, or if the University is one of the city's establishments. I'll leave the reader to decide, but I have the feeling these places would deny anything such as this story describes could ever happen within their hallowed institutions.

For regular cruisers, you may think you recognize the *Carnelian*. I could not possibly comment!

The Ness of Brodgar is an amazing find. It adds much to the other sites nearby, including Skara Brae, which together make up the World Heritage Site called 'The Heart of Neolithic Orkney'. All the references to them are as factual as such things can be within a story like this, but cannot be anywhere near adequate for those who want to study them properly. Life on Orkney 6000 years ago is increasingly being understood as sophisticated and astonishing. Incidentally The Hurlers at Minions and Trethevy Quoit in Cornwall are real too although I last saw them over fifty years ago.

The real Ness of Brodgar project is led by The Archaeology Institute at the University of the Highlands and Islands (often simply called UHI), and there are other participants including the Ness of Brodgar Trust. However my participants are entirely fictional. Apologies to the real folk involved, I hope at least you find my references positive and amusing!

For those who do not already know about both the places and the work in progress, there is plenty of published material, and some recent TV programmes that gave a good sense of the work in progress on the Ness of Brodgar.

Equally I have researched Pompeii sufficiently for the purposes of the story, and we visited the site some years ago. Please remember that the story is about an adventure, not a serious study of archeological sites.

If you know where Si'pelium is, please let me know!

* * * *

Perhaps I should say that this book is another adventure for Ellis Mackenzie and Vaila Flett (later Mr. & Mrs. Mackenzie), who were the leading characters in Six Kippers. I don't think it matters if you haven't read Six Kippers, but you will know them and some other characters better if you have.

CONTENTS

The Prelude

Treasures of Scotland
Invites applications for a new post

Archaeologist, Orkney

Treasures of Scotland is the leading NGO caring for Scotland's archaeological and historic sites. Our archaeologists are involved in almost every aspect of archaeology, including survey and excavation, research, conservation and interpreting sites for visitors. We contribute in partnership with others in projects to care for Scotland's historic and archaeological environment, working closely with neighbours, universities, government agencies, museums and local authorities.

The purposes and scope of this new post are, within Orkney.
To deliver Treasures of Scotland's contribution to the team researching the Ness of Brodgar archaeological site.
To deliver ToS' operational policies for all other sites in which Treasures of Scotland has an interest.
To advise on professional, technical and practical issues.
The role covers the following key areas:
1) He/she will assist the Archaeological Institute of UHI team with fieldwork, research, interpretation and in other ways, on the Ness of Brodgar site.
2) Negotiate permission from landowners for access, as required.
3) Develop good public relations, which will interpret this World Heritage site for visitors on behalf of the partnership and Treasures of Scotland.
4) Ensure Treasures of Scotland is seen to be a competent professional conservation organisation.
5) Will actively manage all other sites in which ToS has an interest and will initiate proposals and submit them to ToS as recommendations for further projects.

Line management. The post holder will report to the Chief Archaeologist, with a functional management relationship to the Site Manager, Orkney, and the Regional Director North.

Qualifications, experience and skills. Applicants must be professionally qualified with a record of practical experience.
He/she should be able to work on their own, or in a team, show initiative and be a good communicator, with an ability to manage a budget and ensure value for money.

The post is based at the Orkney office, The Vennel, Kirkwall, KW17 2TH

General requirements. Applicants must hold a clean driving licence and be sufficiently fit to carry out the duties described.

Remuneration. Salary; Band C, £33,300 p.a. The terms of employment are set out in the ToS standard conditions of employment.

Applications on the form attached to be received no later than Monday 12^(th) July to _employment@tos.org.uk_
Or by post; Treasures of Scotland, Charlotte Square, Edinburgh EH1 4SG

The Interview

The train stopped outside Perth for no apparent reason. 'Come on, come on', Ellis Mackenzie said to himself anxiously wanting to urge the train to move. He mustn't be late for the interview. It mattered so much to him.

He had a timetable for the journey and had been checking the train's progress at each station. The train had been ten minutes late leaving Inverness. It still was. It hadn't caught up even a single minute. He now wished he had travelled to Edinburgh the previous day.

Phil Sanderson, his manager in Inverness had been so kind and supportive. He had offered to introduce him to the key people in the Archaeological Institute of the University of the Highlands and Islands, at their open evening yesterday. He would work with them if he got the job. He could not have missed that opportunity, it was important, and the six fifty early train should get him to Edinburgh in time, but it mustn't be late.

The train jerked to life again to his relief. The Perth platform was crowded. He noted that the train lost another minute while they all boarded. As the train crossed the Tay and started travelling through Fife he calmed down. Ten minutes late should be just soon enough as the train was due at Haymarket at three minutes past ten. If it arrived at thirteen minutes past he would have seventeen minutes to walk to Charlotte Square.

He thought about Vaila. What would she be doing? She'd be in the office, perhaps sorting out the post. A picture of her formed in his mind and made him smile.

He had met her only a couple of months before when on a business trip to Orkney. Shortly afterwards he had taken a three week holiday to the islands. It had been quite an adventure, and now they were engaged. Thinking about her always calmed him and when they crossed the Forth Bridge he was able to enjoy the view without fretting about the time.

He wondered what he would be asked at the interview. He had been to the Ness of Brodgar, read all he could about it, but was it enough? He had been around a number of Orkney's other archaeological sites with Vaila and had now met some of the key people involved. But he knew that his chances rested on how good other candidates were.

Then the train stopped by the Murrayfield Stadium. Time started ticking by. His anxiety grew again. When would it move? He felt the tension. He had never found it easy to wait for anything. The only thing he could do was to put on his coat, pick up his briefcase and stand by the train door so that he would waste no time at Haymarket station.

Vaila was not the only reason the job was so important to him. The chance to work on the Ness of Brodgar could not be missed. He was only twenty four and this new job would really boost his career. It was one of the most important sites in Britain just now. He was fascinated by it. Working on such an important site and living so near the girl he loved was as near perfect as he could imagine.

But it all depended on being on time and he was stuck in a stationary train, unable to do anything about it. They were now fifteen minutes late.

He wondered if he should take a taxi from the station. Would that really be quicker? It might get delayed by traffic. No, he decided. At least by walking he would feel a little more in control of his destiny, but he did not really know how long the walk would be.

At last the train started to move again. He was first out of it at Haymarket. He ran up the steps gave up his ticket and walked into sunshine. If the station clock was right, his watch was ten minutes fast. He still had twenty five minutes after all.

But was it?

He concentrated on the walk, risked crossing roads dodging traffic. He passed others on the pavement, he came close to running, but he did not want to arrive out of breath and covered in sweat.

To his relief when he arrived at the Office the clock on the receptionist's desk said he had ten minutes to spare. His watch really was ten minutes fast. She smiled at him and told him to go straight into the Boardroom as soon as he was ready.

Three other shortlisted candidates were already seated. Ellis was the last to arrive, and he took the vacant seat awaiting him at the large table in the Board Room of Treasures of Scotland's Edinburgh headquarters, an elegant room in Charlotte Square. They were to be together for the first part of the selection process, although they had not yet been told what they would be asked to do. After lunch they would be interviewed separately.

Feeling slightly nervous, he was at least able to relax from his anxious journey, and get his breath back from his dash from the station. He was not quite sure whether to introduce himself or at least to break the silence. No one else spoke, so he looked at a large painting dominating the wall at the end of the room showing a wappenshaw, where potential army recruits were mustered, and shown how to shoot muskets. Although these events began in some form in the thirteenth century, he thought the picture must be from the seventeenth century. It was a magnificent painting which drew the eye whenever one had a spare moment. There were a large number of people shown all doing something busily. It was well lit by the three large windows overlooking Charlotte Square.

He wondered what the others felt, and took short glances at each of them. He thought he detected the same uncertainty as himself, except for the young lady sitting next to him, who was giving the impression of complete confidence, smiling like a cat that has already enjoyed the cream. He had met her before, of course. She was Rosemarie McRaven, the Chief Archaeologist's assistant in HQ. He knew she was a qualified archaeologist, and had a vague memory that she specialised in ceramics.

His mind turned back to the job specification which he knew by heart, having read it through dozens of times. He had a copy of his application form in front of him too, but did not really need either of them.

His present job as Archaeological Surveyor for the North Region of Treasures of Scotland, based in Inverness, was one he really enjoyed. Whilst this new post offered something better still, there was a sting in the tail because, if there was to be an archaeologist in Orkney, his present job would either be redundant, or at least the area he covered would change. He would no longer be needed in Orkney and the number of times he could get to the islands would be severely limited. He felt he had more at stake than any of the other candidates, not that it made much difference to his chances.

At 10.30 precisely the door opened and three people came in. Two took seats one each end of the long table and the third sat by the right hand window.

"Good morning," said the man who had taken the seat to Ellis' right. "I am Chairman of the selection committee today. We will start by introducing ourselves. My name is William Collard, and I am Chief Archaeologist to Treasures of Scotland, as most of you know." Ellis, did indeed know him, as would the internal candidates, although he had never found him to have a particularly warm personality. In fact he had not talked to him one to one since the interview for his current job. Collard was a man of medium height, with mid brown hair yet to show any signs of grey, and he wore a smart plain blue suit. He looked to Ellis more used to working in an office than conducting a dig, not someone who would enjoy exploring a trial trench in the cold on a Scottish island.

The Chairman turned to the man on his right, indicating that he should introduce himself.

"I am James MacRobert, 43 years old, and I am currently the Archaeological Surveyor in Aberdeenshire, a post I have held for eight years. Before joining Treasures of Scotland I worked in England for ten years, giving me wide experience. I now want to broaden my experience still further." Ellis had met him at the regular staff meetings Collard had held for all Treasures of Scotland's archaeologists. He remembered him as rather a serious man. Quite tall and wearing a tweed suit, he not only looked the part but as the oldest and possibly the most experienced candidate he stood a reasonable chance.

The second candidate, a small man in a neat grey suit, said,

"I am an external candidate, not having worked for Treasures of Scotland before. My name is Hamish Stewart. I too have been working in England and long to return north. It is now twelve years since I qualified." Again he did not give anything away about himself. He seemed nervous but his slight Glaswegian accent betrayed his origins and his quiet air of interest in the proceedings suggested he was someone who the panel might like as a safe pair of hands.

The Director of Human Resources, Anna Robertson, gave her name and title next, as she was sitting at the opposite end of the table to the Chairman, between Hamish Stewart and the third candidate. She did not need to explain her role, but she did introduce the Assessor, the man sitting by the window.

"You may call him Alastair, but otherwise he remains anonymous. He is here to help the Selection Panel with any factual information, to make any observations they may request and to review the results of this morning's exercises." She indicated that the next candidate should introduce herself.

"I'm Rosemarie McRaven, I have been Assistant to Mr Collard for three years and before that I worked abroad." She smiled confidently. Ellis saw her as a smartly dressed attractive woman, about his own age. She wore a blood red suit, with a large brooch of Celtic knot work. With short hair well groomed, she had the advantage of knowing Collard well, so maybe she had cause to be confident, but Ellis wondered how she'd go down in Orkney.

Ellis was last to introduce himself. He had debated whether to add something about his Orcadian connections, but they were personal, and this did not seem the moment anyway, so he merely gave his name and present job title.

Anna Robertson then explained that they would next be given a psychometric test. It would only take fifteen minutes. She handed out a five page form to each of them, explained what they were to do and that they should understand that there were no right or wrong answers. The test was just designed to give the selection panel an idea of each candidate's approach to those with whom they would work and in the negotiations the job would entail. Once the appointment had been made the test papers would be destroyed. They would not be told the result.

Ellis looked quickly through the whole form before starting to provide answers, all of which just required ticking boxes. He could not think of how it would tell the panel anything, but wondered, none the less, what sort of man it would suggest he was.

When they had finished, the papers were gathered in by the Assessor and he put them in his case. He was to sort them out in the lunch break.

Collard then divided them into two teams of two, just called team A and Team B, who were to act the part of independent archaeological partnerships bidding for a contract. The Assessor would act the part of the client. A single A4 sheet gave a description of a fictional project, and some details of the work for which the client was seeking bids. The teams were to write a tender report explaining how they would carry out the dig and organise the research the project required. The practical implications and tender were to be given, as they would be in a real bid for a contract, in so far as they could be in an exercise. They were told that it was accepted that it must be hand written, and that they only had an hour to complete the exercise, so presentation was not relevant. Ellis found himself in team B with Rosemarie McRaven. He was starting to think of her as his most serious opponent for the job, because she knew Collard so well, and was not sure whether to be pleased or dismayed to be drawn as her partner.

As they worked on the presentation he grew more concerned, because Rosemarie just wanted to do things her own way. When he pointed out that she was ignoring the question of the costs a client would have to meet she simply said,

"If the client wants the best they must pay. We must show we do things better than the other team. If we do that, nothing else matters."

She simply would not take Ellis' points concerning the practical issues involved in the brief. He said that their proposals must be realistic, and should show that they would be responsible in their management of costs, and in how they would work with landowners, the authorities and the public. Ideally, he had said, they should insert a tender figure as well, as would be the case if this was a genuine bid. Then there was the question of using volunteers as was the case for the Ness of Brodgar.

Rosemarie dismissed everything he said and just continued writing her report without reference to him, so he spent the time writing a paper of his own covering the practical issues he thought should be part of their submission.

When she finished she smiled at Ellis

"That should ensure only you and I remain in the hunt!" She pushed her report towards him and continued "The exercise demands we both sign it at the bottom." She pointed at the small space she had left for him to do so.

"I can't sign that without the inclusion of the practical points I made earlier. While you have been writing, I have completed the sort of assessment of the practical details and costs I believe not only to be essential to this exercise, but are always an important part of a bid for a contract. We have to address the questions a client would want a tenderer to answer."

"*Tiens, c'est impossible!*" she muttered and turned to Ellis to argue, when the Assessor, acting the part of the client came to their team.

"I am to ask you some questions which a commissioning body would want to see in a tender report."

He then asked whether they would use volunteers, and if so, how they would be recruited, fed and housed.

Rosemarie started to say that she did not think volunteers were the answer, when Ellis chipped in   "We intend to submit a two part report, Alasdair. Rosemarie deals with the issues of approach, method, integrity, and best practice, and I am supplying the practical details including those you request", and he quickly outlined what he had written about the use of volunteers speaking as if to a client, and using his knowledge of Orkney. He added in the same vein, "The tender our team is submitting is of course a ball park figure at this stage. Again it is in my part of the report. Once we can address the detail with the client we would of course produce a fixed tender figure."

At that moment they were told there was only five minutes left to complete the exercise, and the Assessor said

"Thank you. That is what we need." He left them to it.

"There's no time to change anything." Rosemarie said. "It's my report and I know how HQ like these things done better than you. Leave it to me." She pushed Ellis' draft aside without looking at it. "Just sign my report here." She pointed to the small space below her signature again.

 "It's to be a team effort, Rosemarie. I can only sign if my part is included. I have gone to the trouble of writing it, because it's what's wanted, as the Assessor said."

She shrugged her shoulders "If you must. Now will you sign?"

Ellis could see that she was hoping to impress the panel by showing that she was the one who wrote the report, with Ellis' contribution only a sop to keep him happy. He remained calm and started to read extracts from Rosemarie's report, to allow time to pass.

When they were told there was only a minute to go, he took the report, now with his part attached. He saw she had written 'By Rosemarie McRaven', on her report. So he added 'and Ellis Mackenzie,' and signed it. Rosemarie looked triumphant. She was so confident that she did not watch what he was doing. She took the report and handed it in as requested, without noticing that he had also signed his part whilst she had only signed the first part.

As Alastair gathered in the reports, Collard said   "Thank you. You have all done remarkably well to produce a report in so short a time, and I have little doubt that both will impress the panel. The Assessor will read your submissions so that the panel can take his observations into account at the end of the individual interviews.

"A sandwich lunch will now be available in the office next door. There are the usual facilities at the end of the corridor. If you would please stay in that office after lunch. It will serve as a waiting room during the individual interviews, starting at 2pm. Each candidate will be seen for approximately half an hour. The order is as you have sat in this room. James MacRobert, Hamish Stewart, Rosemarie McRaven, and Ellis Mackenzie. There is one further point of clarification I must make. Rosemarie McRaven is my assistant, and Magnus Ericson the Property Manager on Orkney, has worked with Ellis Mackenzie in his current post. We are both on the panel, I, as Chairman of course, and Mr Ericson as an observer. Unfortunately he has been delayed by transport difficulties, but is on his way. I shall speak to him on the phone during the lunch break to discuss the process so far with him.

"I must naturally take part in the discussion and decision, as the chosen candidate will be working to me. Mr Ericson may take part in discussion, especially to advise on any specifically Orcadian issues, but has no vote, even if he is with us in time, as he is not an archaeologist. He is doing his best to get here as soon as possible and I hope he can be with us for at least some of the interviews.

"Other candidates may appear to be at a disadvantage. But the panel is quite able to put these connections aside. None the less, to be seen as being as fair as we can be, I will not vote either, if the panel is not unanimous. You should bear in mind that Treasures of Scotland's priority has to be to choose the best candidate for this new role."

During lunch Ellis tried to relax, but found it impossible. He hoped Magnus would arrive in time. There was a small book case in the corner of the room. But he did not see anything that could take his mind off the nervousness he felt. So he just ran through in his mind how he came to be there.

On the Monday, his first day back in the Inverness office after his holiday in Orkney, he remembered coming in a couple of minutes late.

Morag had greeted him with

"See the conquering hero comes. Great to see you back."

"Good to see you too, Morag, whom have I conquered?" He had replied, although he didn't find it hard to guess who she meant.

Someone had sent the office a copy of the Orcadian newspaper. Brenda had waved it at him pointing to an article and a picture. Of course he had already seen it – it reported that Harold and Vaila Flett, son and daughter of Mr and Mrs Ronald Flett, and Ellis Mackenzie had been picked up by the Pentland ferry after escaping from Sir Frank Malloss' yacht, and that most of the crew had been arrested, including Sir Frank himself for attempting to hold them on the yacht against their will. The article explained that the three were not on the yacht willingly, but tantalisingly did not really explain what had happened.

"There must be much more to it than that. Do tell us all about it."

"I'll be a witness when all that goes to court, so I have been asked to say nothing about it until all the legal stuff is over' he had replied. Brenda had said her Dad would think him a hero if Malloss was jailed.

Ellis smiled to himself. The girls' questioning had been kindly meant so he had just got to work on the pile of paper awaiting him on his office desk.

At the Monday meeting and coffee break, while Ellis discussed some of the issues in his in-tray with Phil Sanderson and Morag, he saw Brenda reading the rest of the Orcadian. He wondered if she would look at the personal column. She suddenly broke into a discussion on a site in Caithness.

"Ellis! There's something here you're keeping very quiet about, a little personal announcement!"

"I thought you might spot that."

Brenda read aloud

"Mr and Mrs Ronald Flett are delighted to announce the engagement of their daughter Vaila Ingrid to Ellis Charles Mackenzie of Inverness."

"You are a dark horse." said Morag "I thought you had the look of a man walking on air! Vaila must be the secretary in the Orkney office unless there are two Vaila Fletts. Congratulations to you both. I think I'll have to ring the Orkney office a bit more often to keep up with your adventures! Come on spill the beans, tell us more!" So he had happily told them about Vaila, and how wonderful she was.

As he had got up to return to his office, Morag had said

"I presume you'll be applying for the Orkney job then?"

He had been stunned, and supposed his reaction had been obvious. She had chided him for not looking through the emails from HQ, and told him there was an emailed memo to all staff inviting applications for a new job. He could not wait to return to his office to see it.

He had quickly found it, read it three times with mounting excitement and had filled in the on line form and sent it straight away. He had been lucky. If Morag had not mentioned it he might not have seen it until the next day. That would have been too late as the deadline was that very evening. It was, of course, the reason he was now waiting to be interviewed.

"What are you dreaming about?" Rosemarie jerked him back to the present. "I don't think you should raise your hopes by dreaming of the Orkney job. I've heard the rumours of your affair with the Orkney Secretary. What's her name – something odd? The whole organisation has by now, but it doesn't amount to you knowing Orkney. I think you'll find Mr Collard doesn't like staff indulging in that sort of thing, too."

"Rosemarie, Vaila is my fiancée. It's no secret, it's in the local paper, but I object to our engagement being described as an affair, whether it has anything to do with the job or not."

"Don't be so touchy. It hardly matters anyway because I will be appointed. Maybe I'll find a handsome Orcadian and we can all be friends."

Ellis laughed. He couldn't help thinking of Vaila's former boyfriend. He would meet his match in Rosemarie. But he kept the thought to himself.

After that they waited in silence, until Rosemarie went in for her interview, after Hamish Stewart.

Ellis, now by himself, thought about Vaila which cheered him up. His irritation with Rosemarie faded away as he considered plans for the wedding and for their life together. Whilst they could both live in his little flat in Inverness, he thought they really should look for something a bit better, so he had had a look at a few properties and shown the details to Vaila via Skype. But until he knew whether he would get this new post, it was difficult to take their plans much further. If someone else got the job, he could not see his current work remaining as it was, although how the job might change was hard to say. He hoped that at least he might be able to go to Shetland from time to time.

When Rosemarie came out of the Board room, she said brightly

"Your turn, I don't suppose you'll be in there long, they have already more or less made their decision."

She looked so pleased with herself that for a moment he nearly believed her. Then he realised that she was merely trying to undermine his confidence, so he smiled too, got up and said

"Then I must go straight in. I must not leave them unaware of my brilliance any longer!" He went to the Board room, knocked and went in.

Mr Collard introduced the panel. The way he spoke suggested to Ellis that something was wrong. Collard turned to the man on his right, a very smart gentleman,

"Chairman of the Finance and Staff committee, Mr Graham Stroud." Mr Stroud appeared as if he was irritated by something, if not quite cross.

Next to him, sat a lady, Mrs Vera MacDonald, a member of Council. As she looked at Ellis, he felt she was curious, and she had the hint of a smile. He had met the next panel member at a meeting a few months ago. His name was James Maclean and he was a member of Council as an archaeologist. His face gave nothing away.

There was a knock on the door, and in walked Magnus.

"My apologies Mr Chairman. As you know I should have been here last night but the flight was cancelled due to problems with the aircraft, and I had to come on the overnight ferry, trains and so on."

"How very difficult for you, but you are here just in time to hear Mackenzie's interview. We have not started."

Magnus sat at the end of the table. He at least looked as if he was glad to see Ellis. But his face, behind his magnificent beard, seemed a little troubled to Ellis. Mr Collard said,

"First, before we consider your application, Mr Mackenzie there is a matter we must clear up. We have been told that it is all around The Treasures of Scotland staff that you have been having a very public torrid affair with the secretary in the Orkney Office, Vaila Flett. I, and indeed all the panel, are deeply shocked to hear about it. Such behaviour reflects very badly on the whole organisation. I think you had better explain yourself."

Ellis forgot where he was and why for a moment, so angry was he.

"Rubbish. That's totally untrue and deeply offensive. Vaila would be badly hurt if she ever heard that nonsense. If I do nothing else I must defend her. She is not that sort of girl, whatever you may think of me." He told himself to calm down, but he couldn't. "The truth is that Vaila Flett and I are engaged to be married, with her parents blessing, they have announced it publicly in the Orcadian. Nor have we done anything of which we need be the slightest ashamed. Our engagement may well be known to most staff, it's no secret, and I'm naturally proud of being engaged to such a wonderful girl. We have been congratulated by everyone. To describe it as a torrid affair is an undeserved insult to Vaila."

Before Collard could respond, Magnus spoke, calmly but firmly.

"Chairman, I have known Vaila Flett and her family for many years. Vaila has been my secretary and assistant for four years or so. I have known Ellis Mackenzie since he started his present job. I have watched their love grow and seen it as a genuine, heart-warming story, just as it should be for two fine young people. In any event no one in a place like Orkney can have an affair without everyone knowing about it, especially as it would have involved the daughter of one of the most respected island families, and yet no such story is circulating in the islands. I do not know what you have heard but I will vouch for both of them. Is someone trying to destroy Mr Mackenzie's chances for this post?"

There was a moment's silence. Then Mrs MacDonald said

"I am glad to hear what Mr Ericson tells us, and although we might feel Mr Mackenzie's outburst rather intemperate, it is understandable. I am pleased and impressed that his first reaction was to defend his fiancée rather than himself. I am therefore happy to consider his application without further reference to the rumour, as it is clearly false."

The others nodded and Collard said

"Very well. You all appear agreed." He looked around the table and then turned to Ellis, and started by asking him about the post he currently held.

Various members of the panel asked him questions about his experience, interests and how he would approach the job if he were given it. He felt he gave reasonable replies, and certainly felt he did well when it came to his knowledge of Orkney's archaeology. He even managed to display his knowledge and enthusiasm for the Ness of Brodgar site and that he knew the UHI people involved which interested several panel members.

The final questions came from Mr Stroud.

"You will have to relocate to Orkney, should you be offered this post. In your case I presume you will be pleased to do so?"

"Yes. After the archaeology, it's one of the attractions of the post for me."

"But you will appreciate that if you do not get it, your present post will need to change. Are you prepared to be flexible, to take on different duties perhaps in that event?"

"Yes Sir, I understand your point. But I am very keen to get the Orkney post so I have concentrated on that."

"Thank you."

The Chairman looked round the panel members and as none had further questions, he turned back to Ellis.

"Lastly do you want to ask us about any aspect of the post?"

"Thank you Sir. Can I just apologise for my outburst at the start. It was quite wrong of me, my only excuse being that the rumour story took me by surprise and deeply shocked me. Vaila would be upset and deeply hurt if she heard that rumour, especially if it spreads to Orkney. I hope it is now behind us. I am really keen on this post, the Ness of Brodgar is so important, a very exciting project."

Collard nodded and concluded

"The panel will now consider all the interviews, and we will let candidates know our decision as soon as we can. Thank you, Mr Mackenzie.

Ellis got up and left the room.

To work out his anger at hearing about the rumour, Ellis decided to walk to his mother's house although he thought it would take him at least forty five minutes. About thirty minutes into the walk his phone rang. It was Magnus.

"Ellis I wanted to say how sorry I was to hear of that outrageous rumour. However you convinced the panel of your innocence, and two of them were especially impressed by your concern for Vaila."

"Thank you for what you said too, I doubt if they would have been impressed by me without it."

"Are you going to tell Vaila?"

"I think I'll have to. It would be twice as bad if she heard it from someone else. But I dread it. She'll be furious. She might blame me and probably want me to resign from Treasures of Scotland altogether."

"Don't do that. When I get home I'll have a word with her. She won't blame you Ellis. Now, I can't tell you about the panel discussion or decision, that would be wrong. But I could offer some advice on a different subject."

"Just at the moment I need all the advice I can get."

"OK. Don't buy a house in Inverness!" and Ellis heard Magnus' familiar chuckle.

"Thank you. I'll certainly take your advice!"

Ellis was right about Vaila's reaction to the rumour. He had started his call to her by saying there was good news and bad. First a not so little bird had hinted that he had the job. Vaila must have sensed that all was not as well as it might be, as she made no comment, but asked for the bad news. As he had anticipated, when he told her about the rumour Vaila was furious. Ellis told her he was afraid he may have spoilt his chances of the job by saying how offended he was, especially for her, and he had told the panel that she wasn't that type of girl. He had only managed to reassure her by telling her that between his outburst and Magnus calm reassurance and support, the panel had accepted that the rumour was untrue. He had ended by suggesting she should not worry about it, because the story would die once everyone knew who had been appointed and they were married. That thought calmed her down, but she still asked if he knew who had started the rumour.

"I have my suspicions, but perhaps it's best not to name names just yet."

Edinburgh

A few days later Ellis received the letter he had been waiting for, the formal offer of the new post. It confirmed all the details which had been spelt out in the job specification.

He was asked to accept the post formally by letter, and assuming he did so, to make an appointment with Collard's secretary to spend a day at Treasures of Scotland's Edinburgh office, so he could be briefed, and to finalise the working arrangements. The starting date for the job would then be settled.

Collard had already agreed in outline what Treasures of Scotland would offer to the project. Now Ellis was to develop his specific role with the Archaeology Institute of the University of the Highlands and Islands, usually just called UHI, whilst he was still in Inverness. Ellis then needed to make a start with those in the University who would be carrying out the work on Orkney. Ellis was excited by all he read, and could hardly wait to start work on this extremely important site in Orkney. On top of that Vaila and he would begin their married life there. It all seemed too good to be true, but he had only to re-read the letter to know he was not imagining it.

As soon as he got into work he rang Kirkwall.

"Treasures of Scotland, Orkney Office. How can I help you?" A familiar voice answered.

"The Loch Ness monster here, all the way from Loch Ness, Inverness, Inverness-shire, all ready to eat you up!"

"You wouldn't want to do that, my silly darling! You sound very pleased with yourself."

Ellis told her of the letter and that Collard wanted him to go to Edinburgh on a date to be arranged, to be briefed. He said nothing to her about a small omission in the letter which concerned him. There was no word of congratulation, or welcome, the letter seemed cold. He wondered if the rumour might still be a problem for Collard.

"Well done. I have been holding my breath waiting to hear you had the official appointment. I hardly dared believe you really had got the job, and that you'll actually be living here. It's just wonderful. When I told Mum that you had had a hint that you'd be living and working in Orkney she was over the moon. I don't think she was keen that I should be moving to the big sinful city Inverness! You really are a Magic Monster! How soon can you move?"

"I hope to discover that when in HQ with Collard. I'm wondering Vaila, if this is an opportunity for us both to go to Edinburgh? If I can get a Monday or Friday appointment we could stay with Mum for the weekend. Will Magnus mind you having a couple of days off for that? My Mum has been nagging me for ages to bring you down so you can get to know each other better. I'd also like to see Jeff, as I would like him to be my best man. Apparently he's been telling all our friends how famous you are, so now they all want to meet you too. You know what Jeff's like! I hope you're up for my boasting about the marvellous girl I'm marrying!"

"I'd love to, any opportunity to be with my Magic Monster, never mind my boasting of capturing such a famous monster! I'll ask Magnus but I expect he'll agree. How about the Bank Holiday weekend, that would give us an extra day?"

"Good idea. I'll ring Collard's secretary straight away." That agreed Ellis rang off, and between them the arrangements were completed. Vaila would fly to Dalcross, Inverness Airport, on the Thursday, where Ellis would meet her, and they would drive straight to Edinburgh. He would meet Collard at 10.30 on the Friday prior to the holiday weekend. On the holiday Monday they would have to drive to Inverness for Vaila to catch the flight home.

When Ellis met her at Dalcross airport, they hugged and he kissed her before taking her case.

"Is that a suitably torrid public kiss I wonder?"

"Darling, please don't joke about that. I still feel cross about it."

"Sorry, of course you do. But it gives me an idea. I'll tell you in the car."

As they drove down the A9 they discussed the rumour. Ellis suggested that she came into the office with him when he went for his meeting with Collard.

When she asked why, he told her that he had been wondering how those who had heard the rumour and especially the person who started it would react when they met her.

"If I introduce you to everyone I can, starting with the three secretaries in the main office, who usually know everything that goes on, you might learn something. After that you can meet Collard, his secretary Christine and even his glamorous assistant, Rosemarie McRaven, who was a candidate for the Orkney job. You might just discover something. Are you up for a bit of sleuthing?"

"Of course, but you may have to stop me doing something nasty to whoever started it if we find out who they are. Are you up for that?" Ellis laughed,   "Why else would I have asked you?"

The next morning they arrived at the Charlotte Square office not long after 9 o'clock, and as he was not due to see Collard for an hour or so they went straight to the main office where Ellis introduced Vaila to Claire, Lesley and Alison. They welcomed Vaila, and congratulated them on their engagement. Ellis listened to Vaila's conversation with them, until the accounts office rang Alison to take some letters, and shortly afterwards the Chief Executive, James Chisholm, came in to speak to Claire.

Ellis introduced Vaila to him both as the Orkney office secretary and as his fiancée. James congratulated them, and especially Ellis for getting the new post, and asked when and where they were getting married. Vaila told Ellis later that she thought him a very pleasant man. When he and Claire left, Ellis suggested they went to the archaeology department's office which was in a different building across the road.

Collard's secretary Christine greeted them both warmly, but gave them a momentary fright when Ellis introduced Vaila,

"That's wonderful. I heard all about you both on the office grapevine, so it's good to meet you, Vaila. Now I know what a lucky man Ellis is! Let's see the ring then!" As she admired Vaila's engagement ring she asked them to send some photos when the great day arrived.

As with the main office secretaries, neither Vaila nor Ellis got the slightest hint in their conversation that a 'torrid affair' story had reached Christine.

Collard walked into the office as they were talking.

"Ah. Good Morning. Very good Mackenzie, commendably early."

"Good morning. Can I introduce you to Vaila Flett, my fiancée, and of course the Orkney Office secretary?" And turning to Vaila

"Darling, this is Mr Collard, the Chief Archaeologist."

"Congratulations to both of you. I expect you are looking forward to Ellis moving north, Vaila." Ellis looked for any hint in Collard's reaction to Vaila that would give away whether the rumour still persisted in his mind. He saw none. Perhaps the coldness in the letter was just because he was a rather cold sort of man.

"I am," she replied. "Then we can plan our wedding in earnest. My parents want to make a big thing of it, as we are to have a double wedding with my brother Hal and his fiancée Inga, in St Magnus Cathedral. I expect half Orkney will be there."

Ellis was full of admiration for her quick thinking. Surely if Collard had any lingering thoughts about the rumour they must have ended now. The hint that her family was important enough in Orkney that everyone would take an interest in the wedding surely must have impressed him, never mind that her parents wanted to give them a memorable day.

"That sounds like quite a party! Once you've settled on a date, we must fit in Ellis' duties around it, as I expect you'll go on honeymoon straight afterwards."

"Thank you, yes. Now I should leave you to your meeting. I'll have a look around the shops and perhaps the gardens. When should I come back?"

"We should be finished by noon or so."

Once in his office, Collard started their meeting without any preliminaries.

"So we understand each other, I should tell you that I preferred another candidate at the interviews, but I was the only one on the panel with that view. I believe in being open about these things, which is also why I also felt I had to ask about the rumour, as the whole panel had been told about it. Between Mr Ericson and yourself you reassured them that it was untrue. I'm also glad to have met your fiancée. If she had been present she would, I'm sure, have impressed the panel too. Ironically the rumour probably did you more good than harm in the end. Anyway we must now put these issues behind us, and I'm sure we'll get on well enough."

"Do you by any chance know who started that rumour?"

"I doubt if you'll ever discover that. As you said at the interview, staff did know the two of you were an item, as is I believe the modern expression. Maybe all that happened was a game of Chinese whispers; the story just changed in the telling?"

Ellis felt it best to leave it at that, though he was not convinced by Collard's suggested explanation. To him the timing of the rumour was a bit too coincidental; as if the intention was to spoil his chances of being appointed to the post, just as Magnus had suggested at the interview. But he had the job, so perhaps it no longer mattered. He also wondered if he would ever find Collard a congenial colleague, he seemed rather too conscious of being the Chief Archaeologist. He certainly liked formality, unlike the other staff, including James Chisholm. Ellis hoped their working relationship would at least be professionally helpful in carrying out his work.

Otherwise Ellis felt the meeting went satisfactorily. He would start full time work in Orkney in the New Year, after he had established himself with the folk from UHI, whilst still in Inverness. Collard had also told Ellis that he wanted him to spend a week on Orkney during October, as part of the development of his role, described in his letter of appointment. It would enable him to meet the UHI, team there. This idea naturally delighted Ellis and also meant he could look for accommodation in good time. It would give him a flying start when he took up his new post in the New Year.

Collard asked him to provide a monthly report to himself, copied to UHI in Inverness. Beyond that he would remember later how Collard had said he particularly wanted Ellis to play a part in publicising the work on Ness of Brodgar. This would ensure Treasures of Scotland's role was recognised.

Lastly, Collard had arranged his new contract of employment. He gave it to him and suggested he would be wise to take it away and read it before signing it. It would seal his appointment.

Promptly at noon, Vaila had returned to the office. Christine told her that Ellis was still with Collard. "They will be finished any moment, I should think."

Vaila thought she was very friendly and asked who else worked in the department.

"Just three of us, Mr Collard, Rosemarie McRaven and me. All the other archaeologists, like Ellis, work from the regional offices."

"Ellis has met Rosemarie McRaven of course, and I gather she was a candidate for the Orkney post too. He thought she would have been very disappointed not to get the job."

"You might meet Rosemarie yourself. Her meeting at the Museum should be over by now." Christine paused. "Perhaps I should warn you about her..." and laughed but did not elaborate. She continued, changing the subject, "I hear the wedding is to be in late March. That's great. But to tell the truth I don't think Ellis' ever realised that several of the girls in ToS fancied him themselves! They'll be a bit disappointed." Vaila laughed,

"Then I am a lucky girl!"

"Why are you lucky?" a voice said from behind Vaila. She turned round to see a very smart and glamorous young woman about her own age, wearing an expensive bright blue suit. Somehow Vaila did not like what she saw. Christine said,

"Rosemarie, this is Vaila Flett, Ellis Mackenzie's fiancée. Vaila - Rosemarie McRaven, Mr Collard's assistant."

"Ah, I see why you think you are lucky, both in work and play." Vaila felt she was being inspected.

"I'm afraid you'll think yourself not so lucky Rosemarie – I gather you wanted the Orkney job too? I expect it was a close contest."

"I was certainly surprised that I didn't get it, I put in a special effort too. Even played my trump card. Never mind, I didn't especially want to be isolated from civilisation up there, and it was only to be a stepping stone so I'm now working on an alternative sort of promotion." She smiled, a bit of a crocodile smile to Vaila.

Ellis then came out of Collard's office.

"Hello, darling. Good shopping?"

"Not really, I just looked, I didn't buy anything."

"I see you've met Rosemarie." And turning to Rosemarie he said,

"I trust you are not too cross with me for getting the job."

"She isn't." Vaila interjected "she was worried about being banished from civilisation on Orkney." Vaila had a mischievous grin on her face.

Rosemarie was not at all put out by Vaila's comment, and had her own repost

"Ellis darling, the worst of it is that you are deserting me for your little island maid – or should I say piddie maid? But you will come and see me won't you? We can still have cosy evenings together as we always have had when work brought you here to the centre of Scottish culture?"

"Oh dear! My memory fails me. So sorry, Rosemarie. How terrible, I just can't recall our dates, how dreadful of me!" and he laughed.

"All you need do is come, you darling man. Surely Vaila, you wouldn't mind my keeping him warm for you in Auld Reekie? I might even teach him some moves he can use to please you on honeymoon."

"He doesn't seem to me to need any tuition! Even if he did, Rosemarie, you would have to join the queue of girls volunteering to teach him, from the sounds of it!"

"This man doesn't want to be passed around, if you two don't mind." He laughed again. "Anyway, *Ultima Thule*, is the centre of my universe, it's where the famous girls live! Good to see you again, Rosemarie, but Vaila and I have a lunch date, a real one, so we'd better go."

"Goodbye Rosemarie. I'm sure you'll get another job and another man with your wit, talent and experience!" Vaila's mischievous grin was more in evidence than ever.

Without waiting for Rosemarie's reply, Ellis took Vaila's arm, smiled and winked at Christine, who had clearly enjoyed their little exchange, and left.

As they walked to the Balmoral Hotel where they had arranged to meet Janet, Ellis' Mum, they discussed what they had done during the morning. Ellis was happy with his meeting with Collard on the whole, and he now felt he understood why Collard had not been very warm towards him. He told Vaila that Collard had said that he had favoured another candidate, and that he suspected Collard preferred Rosemarie for the job. Vaila wondered if Collard would want to move her away from his office, because she might be a trouble maker.

"I'm surprised that Rosemarie even applied."

"She told your Piddie Maid that it was to be a stepping stone, though to what she didn't say."

"Perhaps because the Ness of Brodgar is becoming well known, she thought it would be good to be associated with it. Never mind, what else did you discover?"

"One little thing about Collard will amuse you, Ellis. Some of the staff in the main office call him 'Holy Willie' as in Burns' Holy Willie's Prayer" and she quoted.

'That I am here before thy sight
For gifts an' grace
A burning and a shining light
To a' this place.'"

He laughed and she continued "They think he believes himself to be the shining light, uncovering their immorality. For a start he strongly disapproves of those who live together before they marry. He insists on being called Collard when everyone else uses Christian names. They don't like Rosemarie much either, and I certainly agree with them about her."

"If he's 'Holy Willie', perhaps that's why he reacted as he did when told of the rumour."

Ellis then told her Collard had arranged that he should take up the post in Orkney officially on the 3nd January. Collard also wanted him to go to Orkney for a week in October. She was delighted with this news. He added that with a bit of careful planning he should get two weekends in Kirkwall as well.

He then asked Vaila if she had been successful in her sleuthing.

"Perhaps, but I don't know for sure. However what I have heard suggests your girlfriend Rosemarie is the most likely suspect."

He laughed, and teased her about being jealous.

"Are you serious?"

"Of course not. That dragon scares the daylights out of your Magic Monster, my Piddie Maid." And they both burst out laughing to the surprise of several passers-by. "So why do you suspect the dragon?"

Vaila explained that Christine had said she should warn her about Rosemarie, although she didn't get round to saying why. No one had accused Rosemarie of anything specifically, but Vaila had got the impression that she was not popular.

"You wouldn't understand Ellis, a girl senses these things."

"If you mean that she was not popular because she's a man eater, a sort of preying mantis of a girl, I can easily understand. She's the sort that collects men's scalps to display in her hallway, like stalkers hang stags heads, if I can mix my similes!"

"Just make sure she doesn't collect you."

"Me? No fear, I have a fiancée that's worth a million of her."

"Flatterer! Anyway Rosemarie spoke of having played a trump card at the interviews. I can't think what it could be unless she was the one to tell tales of a torrid affair. No one else seems to know anything about it."

Ellis confirmed that the only reference to a rumour he had heard, other than in the interview itself, was from Rosemarie herself. She had told him, as they waited to be interviewed, that she had heard the rumour. He had replied that he resented their engagement being called an affair and she had just said he should not to be so touchy.

"So if no one else had heard of it or anything that even faintly suggested that a rumour existed, then it could not have been something everyone knew about."

Although they might never be able to prove it, it looked as if there had never been any such rumour. It was likely that Rosemarie had invented it and told the panel, perhaps during her own interview, held immediately before Ellis had been before the panel. In the end they had the last laugh, as he had the Orkney post, and that was what mattered to both of them.

They were a few minutes late meeting Janet, but they soon found her as arranged in the Balmoral Hotel. The hotel had a restaurant and a couple of bars but Janet had chosen the Palm Court because it was the ideal informal meeting place. It was an elegant room with a large domed glass roof that made it light and spacious. A number of very large potted palm trees justified its name. Janet pointed out to Ellis and Vaila several well-known Edinburgh folk amongst those in the busy room, whose presence doubtless pleased the management by giving the hotel the air of being appreciated by the best of Edinburgh society. The room certainly had an ambiance of old world elegance.

They soon decided what they would like from the light lunch menu, and Janet ordered it.

They were enjoying talking about plans for the wedding, so did not notice that, as the young waitress approached them with their lunch on her tray, a man was coming in from the lobby carrying a large bundle of music. As he reached their table he stumbled on the rug, knocked into the waitress, and dropped his music on the floor, where it scattered over a large area. The lunch tray followed it with a loud crash of breaking crockery. Ellis jumped up, ensured the waitress and the musician were unhurt and started helping to pick up the music. The waitress stood looking at the mess with such distress on her face that Vaila and Janet also got up to comfort and help her. A moment later a man in formal clothes came bustling over, said he was the duty manager, apologised profusely and reassured Janet that all would be put right and the meal replaced. Then, to their astonishment, turned to the waitress, and berated her fiercely for being so careless. She looked near to tears when the musician intervened.

"Mr Grantly, Mhaire is not to blame. I stumbled on the rug, and knocked into her."

"Don't contradict me in front of the girl and especially in front of guests. Pick up the music and get on with your work, between you, you have spoilt the calm atmosphere of this room." He then told the waitress to go back to the kitchen, arrange for the mess to be cleared up and then to bring a fresh meal, and walked away.

The musician, having recovered all the music turned to them

"I'm really sorry about that. I only came to take this music into the function suite and have a little practice, as I am playing at a wedding reception there tomorrow."

"Don't worry, these things happen." Ellis smiled at him.

"Thank you. It's great for me to play here, quite an accolade. I'm only sorry I don't get the chance to play in this room, the acoustics are excellent, but the hotel has a tradition of a harpist, playing from that special gallery high above the guests." He waved in its direction. "I have to admit it creates a unique backdrop in here. I know Frances, the girl playing now, she's very good. Anyway, I'd better go and practice before Grantly comes back. Thank you."

When they had finished lunch and Janet had paid the bill they got up and were moving to the door just as the pianist was also leaving. They greeted each other, and he again thanked them for being so understanding.

"That's all right. Pleased to help."

"The manager is far too hard on the waitresses. That poor girl comes from somewhere in the Western Isles and is terribly home sick, but he doesn't notice, and blames the girls for anything that goes wrong."

"You were very kind to her. If you play with such sympathy I'm sorry we didn't hear you play."

"Well I really enjoy playing. It's great when folk appreciate it. I've been lucky get a few jobs here. I play in all sorts of places and a wide range of music. The piano in the function suite is an excellent instrument, a real pleasure to play. But I wish my engagements were more regular. Never mind, I may not need to worry for long. I've applied for a job as a pianist on a cruise ship. My wife isn't too keen on my being away so much, but we need a better income, with a little boy to bring up. But I mustn't bore you with my troubles. My name is Peter Keise. If you ever need a musician, I have a Facebook page. It should be easy to find with my funny name!"

He gave them a card with his name phone number and Facebook tag, wished them good afternoon and, as he left the room Vaila said

"What a nice man, though I'm tempted to say Keise by name and keys by nature!"

After dinner that evening at Janet's house, Ellis broached a matter with his Mother that Vaila and he had discussed on their drive to Edinburgh.

"Mum, I expect you know that kilts are not usually worn in the Northern Isles but Vaila and I think if I wore Dad's kilt, it would be something of him with us. I would love to wear it, but don't want to upset you. We wondered how you would feel about it?"

"Does Vaila know what happened?"

"Yes, Janet. Ellis told me about the crash at Rome airport. I'm so sorry, he was clearly a wonderful man. I really wish I had met him."

Janet was silent for a moment as if trying to avoid becoming emotional, then said

"Ellis, I thought you might ask me about that, I've had it cleaned, and it's laid out on my bed for you to try on.

When Ellis came downstairs wearing it, Vaila noticed that he had put it on complete in every detail. Janet smiled.

"You look just like your Father dressed in his kilt. He wore it when we were married and at your christening apart from other special occasions."

"Then at least I now know what he looked like." Vaila said. "I hope Ellis can persuade Jeff to wear the kilt too. That would be very special for us."

When Ellis came down again now in his own clothes, Janet and Ellis spent a happy hour reminiscing, and telling Vaila stories about Ellis' father Charles. It helped her feel closer to Janet.

On the Saturday morning, Vaila encouraged Ellis to ring Jeff.

"I didn't get much chance to talk to him last time, but he made me laugh!"

Jeff was delighted to hear that Ellis was in town and enthusiastic about their going out with as many of their old friends as were available that evening.

"I hope you've brought your famous Orcadian fiancée. If she's with you everyone will want to meet the girl who actually managed to make you think of something other than archaeology!"

"Yes Jeff, Vaila is with me, prepared to be the talk of the town." Vaila leant over and spoke into Ellis' phone.

"Of course I'm here Jeff, I couldn't let Ellis loose alone in Edinburgh with you lot! Just bring Liz; I'd love to meet her and it sounds as if I might need backup!"

Jeff laughed and suggested meeting in the 'Cambridge' and after a drink they could go for a meal somewhere.

"It calls itself a gastro pub, but good as it is for a drink I prefer Browns in George Street."

"Sounds good to me Jeff, see you at six."

"Okay, I'll do the phoning round and I'll book a table."

The Cambridge was a small pub in Young Street, just off Charlotte Square, mainly used by office workers for lunch. Typical of such places it was good as a meeting place if a bit dark. As each of Ellis' friends arrived he introduced Vaila. She revelled in being the centre of attention and when teased about distracting Ellis from archaeology, or anything else, she had no difficulty responding to their banter. Ellis felt very proud of her. She particularly hit it off with Liz, and they were in the middle of a long conversation when the last of the group came in, Ritchie.

After she had been introduced, Ritchie said to Ellis,

"How often do Treasures of Scotland bring you to Edinburgh?" and without waiting for his reply asked Vaila if she'd been into the office with Ellis.

"We spent the morning there. Ellis had a meeting with his boss, so I met a number of the staff."

"Did he introduce you to the siren Rosemarie?"

"Oh yes, glamorous, clever, and dangerous!"

Ritchie roared with laughter.

"She certainly is, and she swears in French too. I went out with her a few times once. It was exciting, but I was never sure what she'd do next. Funnily enough I saw her in the distance at lunch time with an older man. Knowing her, probably someone rich. She always was a gold digger! I felt she only went out with me for practice! You'll need to keep Ellis out of her clutches!"

"When we met her this morning, she did her best to drop hints to Ellis, but I'm not worried about her. Ellis doesn't like her much. Nor, to be honest, do I."

At Jeff's suggestion they then walked to Browns Restaurant. The restaurant was fairly full and they were asked to wait in an area where customers could have a drink while their table was prepared. It was quite small, only just big enough for the ten of them.

On a low table there were a few magazines and newspapers, including a 'Scotsman' which Jeff picked up looking for the rugby results, whilst some of the others were talking to Vaila, keen to know more about Orkney. Liz sat next to Vaila. Kenny teased Vaila by asking why she said Orkney was in the Northern Isles when it was off Aberdeen.

"It must be, I've several maps that prove it." Which led to Vaila happily describing Orkney as the undisputable centre of Britain. When they said she was boasting, she explained that the Stone Age village of Skara Brae and the excavation of the Ness of Brodgar, which Ellis was to work on, looked likely to prove it.

"Some archaeologists have already suggested it may prove Orkney to have been the cultural centre of Britain before Edinburgh or almost everywhere else, had been invented!" Jeff interrupted their conversation.

"Hey, look at this." He read out an advertisement for a competition. "It's a fund raiser for a new hospice. They have to raise over a million pounds so it is a big effort. The first prize is a fortnight's cruise for two to the Mediterranean, on the *Carnelian*."

"Let's see it." Liz took the paper and read aloud.

`"'The Roman World' Cruise is on the *Carnelian* which is a very popular ship. It's not hard to see why. She is small enough to take you to fantastic destinations which larger ships cannot reach. With a choice of restaurants, and comfortable cabins a great library and many other facilities, there is never a dull moment on board. She has a variety of venues where you can meet up with friends, and evening entertainment for every taste. Carnelian Cruises are especially renowned for their expert lecturers who will make the cruise adventurous, enjoyable and instructive.

On this cruise an experienced practical archaeologist will give several talks on British World Heritage sites and of course on the major Roman sites the cruise features, and will lead visits to them.

The cruise sails from Dover to Lisbon, Gibraltar, Ajaccio, Civitavecchia (for Rome) Naples, (for Pompeii and Herculaneum), Qariat (for Si'pelium), Cartagena, Corunna (for Santiago de Compostela) and Dover. On this cruise you will see some of the most interesting Roman settlements both in Italy and on the North African coast." Liz turned to Vaila,

"How about that for your honeymoon? Lots of archaeology!" Jeff smiled at Vaila

"I have a funny feeling that you'll be distracting Ellis so much that he'll forget all about archaeology for once!"

"Is that possible? But if I can't beat it I can always join it. Where can I get an outfit for a vestal virgin?"

"Really? A virgin on honeymoon, vestal or otherwise, doesn't sound quite right!

"Oh trust you to think of that!"Liz came to her defence.

"Jeff, behave!" Ellis laughed.

"Of course I shall only think of my beautiful bride, well, and perhaps a little archaeology too. Anyway we have more or less decided where we're going. Don't ask, we're not telling!"

Vaila took the paper and read the advertisement and returned it to Liz.

"No good to us anyway, we are getting married in March and the Cruise is in September. How about for you?"

Some of the others looked at it, but none took much interest. As Hannah, Kenny's girlfriend, put it   "Cruises are for old folk. Not for me thanks."

When Ellis looked at it himself he thought it was certainly an interesting itinerary, with Pompeii, Herculaneum and especially Si'pelium being included. He was just trying to remember where it was as a waiter came to tell them their table was ready, and he forgot about it.

When they had ordered, Ellis turned to Jeff and asked him if he'd like to be best man.

"Why not? Someone will have to stop you running away in fright at the last minute! Seriously though, I'd be honoured. Can Liz come too?"

"Of course, someone has to ensure you behave – just as seriously!"

Orkney

Ellis drove to Scrabster to catch the ferry arriving in Stromness at 2.20pm on the Friday before the week he was to spend with the Ness of Brodgar team as they closed the site for the winter. This gave him a weekend with Vaila and her family before his working week began.

The forecast for the following day, Saturday, was to be dull and cold but dry, at least until the afternoon according to the forecast, so Vaila suggested they went for a walk up to the Kitchener memorial on Marwick Head.

They set out shortly after breakfast, parked in the Marwick Bay carpark and walked behind the buttressed wall which protects the adjacent farmland from winter storms, through the RSPB reserve until they reached the monument, around a mile from the car. The wind was a sharp breeze from the east, which had discouraged other out of season visitors so they had the path and the monument to themselves.

Certainly the temperature encouraged them to keep walking, but in spite of it they naturally enjoyed simply being together planning and speculating on all their lives would be once they were married.

When they reached the monument Vaila suggested they took a short rest. So Ellis took out a spare waterproof he had in his rucksack and spread it out for them on the ground so that they could sit against the leeward side of the square monument out of the wind and facing the sea.

"Thank you, Sir Monster."

"Anything for my Piddie Lady!"

The monument, which had looked from a distance like a small tower, or even an ancient castle, close by was revealed as a twentieth century monument to the loss of General Kitchener, hence its name. Before he sat down, Ellis had read the plaque on it.

This tower was raised by the people of Orkney in memory of Field Marshall Earl Kitchener of Khartoum on that corner of his country which he had served so faithfully nearest to the place where he died on duty. He and his staff perished along with the officers and nearly all the men of HMS Hampshire on 5th June, 1916.

Vaila told Ellis about it. General Kitchener, who had been famous not only for his leading part in the story of Britain's role in Sudan and the Boer war, but also mainly for a dramatic first world war recruitment poster, showing him pointing out from it saying 'Your country needs you.' He had drowned when on his way to Russia in HMS Hampshire, for secret negotiations related to the World War. The ship was blown up and sunk by a mine, at least that was the official explanation.

But not everyone believed it, Vaila told him, especially many of the Orcadians living nearby at the time. Their stories, together with some unexplained events and Government intense secrecy, cast doubt on the official reports, and encouraged speculation. Consequently there was no shortage of conspiracy theories put forward for the loss of the cruiser and its important passenger, but to this day no one had disproved the official explanation. Whatever the reason however, HMS Hampshire had certainly blown up and sunk, and lay on the bottom roughly where they now saw a ship passing the headland some way offshore.

Neither of them took much notice of it. Ellis was enjoying hearing Vaila's enthusiastic description of a small house in Kirkwall that might suit them. She had already arranged for them to see it during the week and as he would need somewhere to stay when his new job started, it would be a great help to him to settle everything during this visit. He could then live in it when his new job started and she could simply move in once they were married.

Ellis thought that between them they could make the improvements and repairs, and redecorate it by the time of their wedding in their spare time.

As Vaila described it to him, Ellis took out his binoculars to watch the seabirds, and especially kittiwakes and fulmars as they flew about their business around the cliffs. In a pause in their conversation he pointed out one fulmar in particular that was gliding in a figure of eight pattern, apparently without moving a muscle. As he followed its flight with the binoculars to the bird's turn furthest from the cliff, the passing ship filled the binocular's lenses behind the fulmar just at the moment a distress flare shot into the air.

"That's a red rocket flare, did you see it?"

"Were you listening to what I was saying?"

"Of course, but I was distracted by that ship firing a flare."

"What was I saying then?"

"About the kitchen. You don't like the colour."

"Sorry darling, you're forgiven! Just one flare?"

"So far. Yet the ship does not appear to be in trouble. It's still steaming along as if nothing has happened. Didn't you see the flare?"

"I'm afraid not, anyway you're the one with the binoculars."

"I really didn't dream it!"

"But if they were in trouble wouldn't they fire several?"

"I don't know, but I think I'd better ring the coastguard."

"Do you have the number?"

"No but I think 999 works."

When Ellis got through he was asked several questions about the ship and could describe it.

"It looks to me like a smallish cargo ship. The bridge and accommodation block is amidships. There are two masts, one in front of the bridge and one behind it. There's a sort of yard arm, presumably a derrick, on each. Its one distinctive feature is that the bridge and accommodation decks are painted orange, instead of the usual white and so is the funnel."

They asked him about its position, speed and course.

"I'm not much good at judging distance or speed" he told them "but I'd say it must be about two or three miles offshore. It's steaming north, but not very fast. There's no smoke from the funnel that I can see. In fact even through the binoculars I can't see any sign of activity on it at all."

He then confirmed that only one flare had been fired. He could not read the ship's name. There seemed some marks on the bow where he would have expected a name to be but he could make no sense of it, and he would not be able to see anything on the ship's stern until she had passed them. At the coast guard's request he gave them his mobile number. They told him they would try to radio the ship but were likely to have problems unless they knew the ship's name. Vaila and Ellis could not even make out the ensign, which just looked like a dirty rag.

In the shelter of the tower they sat watching the ship, and in around twenty minutes it had passed them sufficiently that they could see the stern but although they both tried to see a name, they still could not make out either name or register port. The ship was obviously old as there were streaks of rust at various points on the upper decks. On closer inspection with the binoculars they could make out other signs of neglect, but they saw nothing that might identify the ship, nor anything that might suggest a reason for firing the rocket.

The coastguard rang back to say that whilst they had been unable to get a response, a separate radio signal had been picked up on the emergency frequency, which appeared to come from the same ship. There were two injured men on board, the ship's Captain had explained. When the coastguard had asked for the ship's position, the Captain had been a bit vague, as if he did not want to broadcast their position to any other radio operator who might be listening. But he did say that they were passing a high cliff with 'with castle on top.' The coast guard thought it must the ship Ellis and Vaila could see. They had suggested she should turn round and dock in Hamnavoe, Stromness, which would only take an hour or so. The Captain had refused on the grounds that they had to meet a tight timetable, and asked for a helicopter to take off the injured crew.

"Off ship the two must be." The captain had said in his very poor English.

"There's something odd about all this" the coast guard on the phone told Ellis, "The Captain spoke as if he really disliked the men who were injured. He said they were bad men, though that could mean several things from a man with limited English and a strong accent. He might be implying that the real emergency was to remove them from his ship. Or he might have meant they could not cope with the men's injuries because they were very serious, as 'bad' might be either the men themselves or their injuries. Is the ship continuing to steam north?"

"Yes. There still isn't much sign of life on it, but I did think I saw someone on the bridge through my binoculars not long after my first call."

"OK. Anyway I have requested a 'medivac' by the Sumburgh Search and Rescue service. As it happens one of their helicopters is at Kirkwall airport just now so you should see it shortly. Keep watching. I don't suppose they realize they're being watched!"

After little more than five minutes they heard a helicopter approaching. They watched as it hovered over the ship, which was still steaming northward.

The winch man was lowered to the deck forward of the central bridge, with a stretcher. Ellis and Vaila were full of admiration for the helicopter crew, as not only were the masts, derricks and rigging to be avoided but none of the ship's crew appeared on deck to help.

However in a few minutes they saw a man being carried out to the stretcher, which had been left on deck whilst arrangements were made. He was strapped into it and winched a few feet into the air with the winchman. The helicopter then moved sideways over the sea and quickly dropped as the winch reeled in the line, so that the stretcher was in the helicopter in seconds. The winchman was again lowered onto the deck for the second man who was able to walk between two of the crew and again was winched into the helicopter. Ellis had given the binoculars to Vaila and she told him that she felt the second man was not so much helped to the helicopter, as treated as if he was a captive. She gave him the binoculars and he had a brief look before the second man and the winchman were lifted from the deck. As the helicopter took them in through the door it started to move up and away.

Once it had flown towards Kirkwall over the hill and the wind had carried the din of the helicopter's engine away, the seabirds reclaimed their territories and resumed their business, whilst the ship continued steaming north as if nothing had happened. It was not long before it was out of Vaila and Ellis' sight. They had tried again to read a name on the stern, but were still unsuccessful.

By this time they felt cold, even out of the wind, so they walked briskly back to the car. They had just reached it when Hal, Vaila's brother, phoned her. He was at the Balfour Hospital where he had gone to pick up his fiancée Inga, who was a senior nurse, after her shift. He told them that there was a great fuss going on over two men brought in by helicopter, and when Vaila explained that they had seen them lifted from a ship Hal suggested they came to the hospital. They had no sooner told him they were on their way and ended the call, than the Coastguard phoned back to ask them to come as well. The police were asking for anyone who had witnessed what had happened on the ship to speak to them.

When Vaila and Ellis reached the hospital they met Hal, who was trying to support Inga in a very crowded little reception area. Inga was pleased to see friendly faces.

"How am I meant to ensure patients can rest with this circus going on? We have the police, the coastguard, two people who saw the helicopter but not the ship, another who saw a ship but doesn't know if it was the right ship, and last, though far from the least demanding, two reporters, from the 'Orcadian' and BBC Radio Orkney, who won't stop asking questions. But there's nothing to know. The doctor has refused to allow any of them to see the men who were brought in, and having helped the doctor treat them, I agree. They're exhausted and one is badly hurt and anyway they can't tell anyone anything as they don't have a word of English, French or any other language anyone here can speak."

"Anything we can do?"

"How good are you at languages?"

"Lousy!"

"Pity! Well as you saw something perhaps you could at least talk to the police and hopefully also get the press off my back. They speak to me as if I am a naughty schoolgirl who won't own up to eating sweets in class!"

Ellis and Vaila spoke to a constable they knew, giving a statement describing what they had seen from Marwick Head, during which Inga reacted to a call from a patient. She told an over eager journalist that it was just one of the local patients, although she knew it was the help button of one of the rescued men, but at least it enabled her to slip into the ward without being accompanied by any of the throng in reception.

When she emerged again she saw that Detective Inspector Simmons had just arrived and went straight to him. She spoke briefly and quietly to him. He nodded and she returned to the ward. The two reporters pushed forward, suspicious that something was happening. But Simmonds brushed them off. When Inga came out of the ward a second time about ten minutes later and had spoken to Simmons again, he turned to the journalists.

"We have been able to find someone who can, I understand, speak with the men in their own language, which is Arabic. However he is in Lerwick. He will catch the 18.30 flight from Sumburgh tomorrow – it's the only Sunday flight – and then it's bound to take some time to interview the men here, as doubtless doing so through a translator will be a slow process. You'll have to wait until Monday morning when we hope to be in a position to tell you all about it. So provisionally I will hold a press conference at noon on Monday at the police station in Kirkwall."

"That's a long time to wait. News goes stale very quickly, why not tell us tomorrow evening?"

"I can't help that, Steve. I am leaving one constable here to ensure peace, as all the patients need rest."

"Why do you need to do that? What do you suspect?"

"I have no more to tell you, as doubtless you anticipated, Steve. You'll have to be patient or maybe you'll become one!"

This was met with good humour and the reception area soon cleared leaving Hal, Ellis and Vaila with Inga. Simmons, who they all knew well, said   "Inga, that was a neat way to make progress. We ought to discover more on Monday at the latest. Well done" and he left.

Inga explained to her friends that the less injured man had indicated that he wanted to use a phone. Simmons had agreed so she had given the man the patient phone, and he had wasted no time in making a call to a number he had in a small notebook.

When he had finished and returned the phone, which was a cordless instrument kept on a small trolley, she took it to an adjoining unoccupied side ward. She then looked up the number the man had called from the redial list, made a note of it, and seeing that the call was to Lerwick, had dialled it herself. When it was answered she found that it was a Shetland shipping agent. They had been surprised at her call but she had told them who she was and, as if she did not know that one of the men had just rung them, told them that they had in the hospital two injured men lifted off a ship near Marwick Head. It was proving difficult to treat them due to the rescued men having no English. The only word she had understood when they spoke to her was 'Lerwick' so, guessing the ship was going there, she wondered if the agent could help; they needed a translator but they were not even sure what language the men spoke.

She had to hang on for a short while, but then they told her that they had someone staying in Lerwick who had been waiting for the ship which had come from Qariat in Albysia, the ship's home port. The agent told her that the man appeared to know who the men in the Kirkwall hospital were, and to be concerned for them. His name was Hassan and he would fly to Kirkwall. He had missed the last flight that day so he would have to come to Kirkwall by the 18.30 flight on Sunday evening.

"Where's Albysia?" asked Vaila.

"I've not the foggiest" replied Hal, "but I don't suppose we are needed here anymore so if we go home we can see what we can find on the internet."

"It's in North Africa," said Ellis "though I'm not sure exactly where, but the remains of a Roman city called Si'pelium is, if I'm not mistaken, in Albysia. Someone mentioned it when we were in Edinburgh, and we studied it at college."

"You'd know that better than the rest of us, Ellis, but that hardly helps us know what's happening here and now."

"But it's getting interesting!" said Hal. "Why was a ship from a place we've never heard of going to Lerwick? Why, when it's so difficult for the police, do they want to go to so much trouble to discover what went on aboard? Why is the Coastguard so suspicious? I mean, if the ship was beyond the three mile limit whatever happened surely occurred outwith the country on a foreign ship. So why bother?"

"My shift is due to finish in quarter of an hour, Hal, my love. If you could all hang on for the next shift to arrive we can go together."

Their research showed that Albysia was a small country on the North African coast. It had few assets, just a small agricultural industry which exported dates, bred camels and produced more or less sufficient other food to satisfy its modest population. It also mined and exported some second quality precious and a few semi-precious stones, the best known of which was carnelian. It did however have one archeological site which is considered important, the Roman city of Si'pelium. That was, of course, of special interest to Ellis who was pleased to have his memory confirmed.

He told the others that it had been a Roman colony, developed by Emperor Lucius Septimius Severus, who had been born in the far better known North African Roman city of Leptis Magna. Ellis had not been there of course, and only knew about it from text books – and knew nothing at all about Albysia.

As Inga had Sunday off and Vaila and Ellis had their own interests to pursue, and because nothing was expected to happen concerning the two men until Monday, it was only on the Monday evening that

Hal, Vaila, and Ellis had been able to meet Inga. She had an interesting tale to tell them.

Simmons had arranged that the translator, who had given his name as Hassan - he gave no other name - would be met when his plane arrived on Sunday evening. He was taken to a hotel for the night, the plan being that Simmons himself would take him to the hospital first thing next morning, Monday, to translate, both to help their treatment and so that Simmons could interview them to discover what had happened on the ship.

However, unknown to Simmons, Hassan had hired a car by phone from Lerwick and had gone to the hospital within half an hour of arriving at the hotel.

By chance, the constable on duty at the hospital had been asked to help with a minor road incident just outside the hospital, just as Hassan arrived and the nurse on duty saw no reason why he should not see the men. After all, it was visiting time and other patients had visitors. The men had been moved to the small side ward, and it had only taken moments for Hassan to find them. He was with them for some time. The constable did not know that the men had had a visitor because Hassan had left by the time he had sorted out the accident, and the nurse on duty had not thought to tell anyone. She had at least noted it for the night shift, hence Inga had read about this visit when she came on duty on Monday morning.

Simmons arrived the next morning with Hassan about ten. They went straight into the small ward to carry out the interview. When they had finished, both Simmons and Hassan spoke to the Doctor who was doing his rounds and as Inga was with the doctor she heard the whole story.

The ship was called the *Camel Prince*. She belonged to a small company in Albysia and was on her way to Norway for a cargo of timber and timber products, to be taken to Qariat, the Capital and port city of the country. Hassan had joked about the ship's name, and said that this 'ship of the desert' still floated on water, not sand. It was the only merchant ship registered in Qariat. The men now in hospital were brothers, Bashir & Anai Tassilah.

The *Camel Prince's* intended course was to sail north of Fair Isle, briefly into Lerwick for supplies which Hassan had arranged as he was to have joined the ship there, and then to Norway. On the way home it would call into Aberdeen to refuel and for a small container loaded with luxuries for their President, General Ghedir Rezza. Hassan had looked disgusted when he had had to speak of that.

According to Hassan the brothers in the hospital had come on watch at six. Shortly afterwards they had called the Captain because they thought their position was too far south – they thought they were heading for the Pentland Firth, judging by the Strathy and Holborn lighthouses. He told them to change course to the north and to reduce speed so that they could check their position from landmarks on Orkney at dawn. It appears that their radar, never mind their navigational competence, was not working properly. Simmons commented that it seemed to him the ship and the crew were a shambles, and joked that they had doubtless refused the coastguard's advice to sail into Hamnavoe because they didn't know where it was, let alone their own position!

Anyway they were in sight of Hoy by around nine, still steaming at little more than ten knots, and in sight of Marwick Head by eleven when Ellis and Vaila had seen them.

As they were approaching Marwick Head three crew members suddenly burst into the bridge, threatened the two brothers on watch with knives and a small revolver, saying they were taking over the ship. The three locked themselves into the bridge so that it would be very difficult for the rest of the crew to retake it, and had then locked the brothers into a small cabin behind the bridge.

The brothers, so Hassan said, were loyal to their country's President General Ghedir Rezza and their Captain, Osama Daserk. They wanted to return command to the Captain, but they thought the Captain might not know that the three mutineers had captured the bridge. They decided they must make as much noise as they could in the hope that it would make the Captain come to see what was happening. They also found one flare, so opened a porthole to fire it. The mutineers were very angry and came into the cabin and beat them up, hence their injuries, but this enabled the Captain, who luckily had a duplicate key to the bridge, and the loyal crew to retake the ship. The mutineers were locked into a secure cabin to be taken back to Albysia, and the Captain, grateful for what the brothers had done, decided to call for the helicopter so that they should get the best treatment for their injuries.

Having told their story, Hassan had told Simmons he had praised the men for their courage and had promised them that he would get them back to the ship when it got to Aberdeen. He himself, of course, was unable to join the *Camel Prince*, as he had thought he should come to Kirkwall to support the brothers. He had asked the doctor what their injuries were and when they would be fit to travel, and the Doctor had confirmed they just had cuts and bruises. The problem suffered by Anai Tassilah, the younger brother, was a particularly deep stab wound, and serious bruising, but as nothing vital had been damaged he should make a full recovery especially if he could keep the arm that was knifed reasonably still for a while. The Doctor said that if they really wished to discharge themselves, the arm could be put in a sling. While this discussion was going on a call for Simmons to return to his office came in. Apparently there was an urgent and important call for him, so he had left.

After further discussion Hassan told the doctor that he had to start his journey home, but did not want to leave the men to get to Aberdeen by themselves when they had no word of English. He suggested that he would take responsibility for them if they were discharged at once. That was agreed, and Inga had noted that Hassan and the two men left shortly after the Doctor.

A couple of hours later, at the end of her shift, Inga was handing over to the next shift when the phone rang. It was Simmons to ask what the Doctor had agreed with Hassan, and if the men were still there. Inga told him what the Doctor and Hassan had agreed and explained that they had gone to catch the ferry.

"No they haven't. I've just checked with both Stromness and St Margaret's, and there is no booking for Hassan. Anyway Hassan's hire car agreement did not permit him to take the car on the ferries. Nor can they fly this afternoon, the flight is fully booked. Where are they?"

Of course Inga did not know but asked if it mattered now they had gone.

"Not really, not now. I do not need to know." Simmons explained that the Albysian Embassy in London had rung. They angrily told him that Hassan and the Tassilah brothers were wanted in Albysia because they were terrorists and murderers. According to the Embassy Official, he had spoken to the ship's Captain by radio, who told them the mutineers were the two brothers lifted off the ship, not three of the crew still on board. It had been the three crew who had regained control of the ship from the two mutineers after a fight. The brothers had then been locked in the cabin behind the bridge to stop them causing more trouble. The Captain had thought the two remained a danger to his ship, so had wanted them taken off in case they tried again. He had used the injuries they had in the fight as the reason to call for the SAR helicopter. The Captain was unaware that the brothers had fired a rocket flare, and when told about it suggested the two fired it to try to escape by alerting anyone who saw it that they were on the ship.

The Embassy angrily complained that Simmons and his police force were grossly inefficient. They should have arrested Hassan and the two brothers the moment they had got to the hospital. They seemed unable to understand that without any evidence of a crime the police could not arrest anyone. Things were, the embassy implied darkly, different in Albysia. Simmons told Inga that they calmed down a little when he had told the Official that Hassan was only with the two men when he also had been present.

He was taken aback when Inga told him that Hassan had in fact visited the men the evening before by himself.

Simmonds had thought about this for a moment before laughing. Although there were now two contradictory stories as to what had happened on the ship, neither was corroborated by evidence, nor had either Hassan or the Consulate even suggested why either group should want to mutiny. He could do nothing about it now, at least until he could interview those on board, perhaps when the ship called at Aberdeen. At that point the Embassy spokesman had told him that the ambassador himself had ruled that it was an internal matter for Albysia. Simmons felt he might as well accept the situation and find better things to do.

In any event, when Simmons had added that they had now left Orkney and were therefore outwith his jurisdiction, the Consul's spokesman had said

"You're useless," and had put the phone down.

Having taken advice from the Chief Constable, the upshot was that the matter was closed as far as Orkney was concerned and was recorded as an incident at sea, in international waters, on an Albysian ship, which had been accepted as an Albysian internal matter at their own Consulate's request.

The D.I.'s final comment to Inga was that, however fishy the whole thing was, and though he couldn't help wondering who this mystery murderer Hassan was, and especially wondered how he had managed to leave Orkney without being seen, it was unlikely that they'd ever hear of Albysia again, for which he was grateful. Inga finished her story.

"So we can now return to normal."

"Yes." Ellis paused, "Inga, what did Hassan look like?"

"Oh, dark skinned, small mustache, around six feet tall, and he wore a light coat that was totally inadequate for our weather. Under his coat he actually had a Fair Isle sweater, mainly red and green. He must have bought it in Lerwick. It looked a bit odd on him, perhaps because he could never pass as a Shetlander!" Ellis looked at Vaila,

"Could it have been him?" She nodded and he turned to Inga.

"Sounds as if he could be a man we saw today and if so, of course Simmons couldn't find out how he had left. He hasn't left, not yet! We were at the Hatson Ferry Terminal this morning getting next year's timetable for the overnight ferries to Aberdeen, just before coming to see you. There was a man buying tickets to travel overnight tonight to Aberdeen. When he pushed his coat aside to reach for the wallet in his back pocket I saw the sweater. I think he paid cash for the tickets."

"Yes, Inga," confirmed Vaila, "I didn't see the sweater Ellis saw, but the man certainly was tall, and could well have been Middle Eastern by complexion. He had a rather long nose and a very black mustache too." Ellis continued,

"He dropped his wallet trying to put it back in his pocket and I picked it up. For a moment he looked as if he thought I was pinching it, but when I gave it to him he thanked me."

"What about the other two? Did you see them? You'd know one at least, he would've had his arm in a sling. They both have beards."

"They must have been the two sitting quietly in the waiting area, one had a sling. Those black beards are not easily missed anyway!"

"We were only in the check in office long enough to pick up a timetable for next year while we were passing on the way to the Ness of Brodgar. I didn't make the connection at the time, as we didn't see any of them in the hospital. Should we tell Simmons?"

"You could, I suppose, but he said the case was closed so I shouldn't think he wants to know. After all Hassan is free to do as he wishes now."

"I don't think I will forget his face," added Vaila. "Quite distinctive I would say. The look he gave us as he turned to go was a bit scary, as if he was memorizing our faces in case we meet again. I could believe he is a ruthless man."

Italy

In later years Ellis would claim that he only remembered four incidents at their wedding; one funny, one reassuring, another a blessing, and the last unforgettable. Four images etched in his memory, moments standing out from a very happy, busy day and a mind reeling from being introduced to so many people at a time on such an occasion.

The first was when he was walking to the Cathedral with Jeff, his best man, dressed in their kilts and as smart as they'd ever been. The weather was just as they might have ordered, a sunny day, warm in spite of a brisk westerly breeze. As they walked through Kirkwall they passed a small group of teenage girls, one of whom gave them a wolf whistle. Jeff had pointed at Ellis.

"Last chance before he's married today!"

"You'll give us a kiss then," one of them shouted, urged on by her friends.

Ellis, full of *joie de vivre*, smiled, waved and blew them a kiss, which caused a gale of giggles.

The second was meeting Hal and his best man, Andrew, outside St Magnus Cathedral. They greeted each other, reassured that they were at the right place on the right day, and even at the right time for their double wedding. One less thing to be nervous about Hal had said. Andrew had joked, "Now all Jeff and I have to do is to make sure you each marry the right girl!"

Then they met Aunt Minnie, Ellis' father's sister, at the Cathedral door. She was wearing a flamboyant brilliant orange dress with a hat to match. At her age, so Ellis thought, she ought to have looked ridiculous, but she didn't. For a start she was nearly as tall as Ellis, and still in good shape, so her choice of an orange dress for the occasion, matched by a smile as bright as the day which she bestowed on everyone, complimented the shaft of sunlight falling on the ancient stone of the building. It felt like a blessing.

He greeted her with a hug and thanked her for bringing the sunshine with her, and was rewarded when she told him that he looked the image of his Father. He had felt so proud of that. Later, at the reception, he had told Vaila that she was his favourite relative, eccentric, full of fun, but also one of the kindest and most thoughtful people he knew. He had taken Vaila across the room especially to introduce them to each other at the start of the ceilidh, and as he had hoped, they became instant friends, in spite of their age difference.

The fourth picture was simply wonderful, special, and unforgettable. When Vaila arrived beside him, on her father's arm, he had turned to greet her. She took his breath away. He knew he'd never forget that moment. He whispered to her,

"You look marvellous, my stunning Piddie Maid." She'd smiled at him and whispered back,

"You're not so bad yourself, my handsome Magic Monster!"

After the service, reception and ceilidh the two couples left together, to the confusion of guests in opposite directions, both their cars well decorated by their friends.

Ellis and Vaila, now Mr. and Mrs. Mackenzie, were booked on the overnight ferry to Aberdeen, leaving late evening from the Hatson terminal, as they were to fly from Dyce airport to Naples the next day. As Jeff was acting as chauffeur in Ellis' car, taking them to the ferry, he had plenty of time to tease them about spending their wedding night at sea.

"What with the ship rocking you and the gentle lullaby of the engines, you've no excuse for not sleeping well!"

"What else could we do in bed?!" replied Vaila, trying to put on an innocent expression, although she actually just looked mischievous.

"Ah, such innocent children! Would you like me to explain?"

"Behave Jeff! Anyway how do we know they haven't been practicing?" Vaila laughed.

"Just this once, the pair of you, get lost!"

*   *   *

The Grand Hotel Capodimonte in Sorrento proved to be at the top of a low cliff, overlooking the sea. It was an elegant building with all the amenities they could have wished for. Neither of them had ever stayed in a four star hotel before but Uncle John, who had given them the holiday as a wedding present, had said he hoped it would make the start to their life together really memorable.

Their room had a spacious balcony with views over the hotel gardens and across the Bay of Naples beyond. Vaila was entranced by the series of five swimming pools cascading down its steep semi tropical gardens below the terrace. Beyond the pools the gardens flowed down to the edge of the low cliff. A path invitingly led down to the top of a flight of steps.

The journey had been hot and stuffy, and as soon as they had unpacked they went to the highest pool for a swim, relaxing afterwards with a glass of lemoncello recommended by the bartender, at the Bougainvillea terrace bar. They could see their own room's balcony just a floor above them.

"We must go down there to explore, Vaila." Ellis pointed to the gardens. "The countryside round here is full of lush plants, lemon orchards and trees. It looks as if we can get down to the sea too. There's a marina, and a harbour with boats going to Capri in the lower part of the town near the beach it says in the brochure. I think there are some interesting old buildings there too."

"Not now, Ellis." She smiled at him.

"No, not now darling."

Sometime later they sat out on their balcony enjoying the heady Mediterranean air laced with the scent of the colourful flowering plants in the garden below. They looked across the gardens to the Bay of Naples, and quietly appreciated the warmth of it all to Orcadians more used to cold, rain and wind. Ellis pointed to the brooding grey bulk of Vesuvius in the distance. A small plume of smoke from the summit was a reminder of its power even now, and he remarked that, whilst it had caused the terrifying destruction of Pompeii and Herculaneum lying at its foot, now nearly two thousand years later that same disaster provided endless interesting information about Roman life and more or less all that was known about Roman art of the time. He started to talk about the contrasts and mysteries this world provided, when Vaila interrupted, pointing to three men walking up the path towards the hotel.

"Ellis, I'm sure I recognize the man on the left, but I can't think where I've seen him before." The man wore a long plain white shirt outside his trousers, a small bright orange badge, and had a thick black beard.

Ellis' 'yes' was drawn out as he looked carefully at the men. "I see what you mean. He does look familiar, we must have seen him before somewhere. The one on the right is staying at this hotel. He checked in just ahead of us. I think he's by himself. He's looking nervous, unless I'm imagining it."

"You'll be doing a Sherlock Holmes on him next! Was he in the army, fighting in the desert with Laurence of Arabia? Was he bitten by a blind camel?"

"Elementary my dear Watson. You can deduce that from the shape of his boots and because he has a strange haircut!" They laughed.

The men sat down at a table in the Bougainvillea bar below their balcony. They were soon in an earnest conversation, speaking quietly, and drinking coffee. Vaila said no more, her interest now taken by the view. Ellis too, thinking of what had happened in October '79, took no further notice of them until he heard one say 'Pompeii' which naturally drew his attention, but it was the only word he understood. Quickly again losing interest, he went back to thinking about Pompeii. He just retained a feeling that there was something odd about the murmur of voices below. After twenty minutes or so the men left.

Dozing, part way between sleep and wakefulness, his mind wandered. He thought about Vaila, how they'd met, and their adventures in Orkney. How marvellous she was, and how lucky he felt to be her husband. He thought about the interview and how Rosemarie had tried to wreck his chances for the Orkney job, and his hopes that he'd make a good job of it now he had it. He remembered the excitement of searching for a house in Kirkwall during his visit the previous October, a wonderful week, starting with their walk up to the Kitchener Memorial.

He sat up suddenly. Of course, that's where we saw the man, the one that Vaila had just pointed out. It had been at the Hatson ferry terminal. He was with that mystery man Hassan. He and another man had been lifted off the ship they had seen from Marwick Head. The *Camel Prince* he remembered was her name. He turned to Vaila to tell her, but she was lying on a lounger fast asleep. Then he dozed off himself and forgot about it.

After a few days relaxing by the pools, reading, walking in the gardens and exploring the town, and generally ignoring any distraction but each other, Ellis tentatively suggested that they should visit Pompeii. Vaila laughed.

"Well I've kept all your attention longer than I expected, so why not? If I feel neglected at least I have discovered just what gets your attention!"

They opted for the coach trip the hotel offered. It would not give them nearly enough time at Pompeii, but Ellis thought it would at least give them an idea of the site and provide a reconnaissance for a second visit later in the holiday, when they could take the train which ran from Sorrento, via Pompeii to Naples.
The coach was nearly full, so that they were seated in the very back.

Seeing Ellis so eager to get there, Vaila teased him by cuddling up to him.

"Aren't I to be the centre of your thoughts today? Wouldn't you prefer a cuddle in the back seat with me than staring out of the window?"

"I'm quite able to do both at once - see!" and he tickled her which caused a few turned heads.

They were met at the Porta Marina, the main entrance to Pompeii, by their guide.

"Ciao. Buon giorno, mi chiamo Francesco. Good morning, my name is Francesco. I am your guide today."

He first took them through the Porta Marina and to the right into the Antiquarium, which displayed several of the casts of bodies of those who died in the eruption. He explained how they had been made and told them something of the building, which had had to be reconstructed after Second World War shelling.

When they left the Antiquarium, Francesco led the group to the Civic Forum. There he explained the large public buildings that had been around it, this being the centre of the city. Francesco called them together by holding up a little blue flag on a short stick, and gave the party a good summary of all that Pompeii was and is.

Vaila wanted to learn what she could as she knew Ellis would talk about it and would expect her to give an intelligent response. Between following the guide and looking at the buildings she was soon fully absorbed by Pompeii.

She especially took pleasure in watching Ellis, who was full of eager concentration on all they saw. He seemed to know exactly where to look for details he wanted to see, details others missed or ignored. He listened to the guide and on frequent occasions he asked, even directed, Vaila to take photos as she had the camera. She did not always understand why he wanted some close ups of parts of the buildings, shapes and marks on stones and spaces where something appeared to have been removed. He made notes as they went and marked his guidebook from time to time, all the while champing at the bit to go everywhere at once. He wanted to miss nothing, as if the purpose of this visit was as a professional archaeologist, working on an important project, rather than as her husband on their honeymoon. Vaila realized she had never seen him at work before and enjoyed watching his enthusiasm and admired his thoroughness. She didn't doubt that even from this rushed tour his knowledge of Pompeii would be considerable.

So she listened both to Francesco and Ellis as they explained what they were seeing, until she reached the stage of being confused by what was to her far more than she could take in at one time. Consequently as they continued their tour she increasingly watched Ellis and the other members of their group more than the ruins of the city.

The group left the Forum, walking past the Temple of Jupiter and the Forum Baths, shortly reaching the Via di Nola, a long street sloping down to the Porta Nola. Crossing it they went to the House of the Tragic Poet to see the famous mosaic of a dog, inscribed *Cave Canem*, 'beware of the dog', which delighted Vaila. Ellis also wanted to see the important decoration showing Ariadne abandoned by Theseus on Naxos in the room east of the peristyle hall. He knew it showed a ship setting sail in some detail. However to get into the house visitors had to use a side entrance to avoid walking on the canine mosaic, and Francesco wanted the group to move on.

Definitely one place, he had told Vaila, that they should see next time as it was an important picture not only in artistic terms but also for an understanding of ships of the period.

"Darling, it's all a puzzle to me how you know all these things. I just feel for the poor people who suffered the eruption. They must have thought the world was coming to an end, and so it proved for them. Those casts of the dead are so sad."

"Yes. There's so much here. I could happily spend a year here."

"Please don't. I'd miss you!"

The next building on Francesco's route was House of the Faun, the home of an unidentified aristocrat, he informed them. She admired the sculptures and the art work. There seemed to be wonderful paintings, decorations and mosaics here and in so many houses. They seemed to be everywhere. When she asked Francesco about the pictures he explained how four styles of decoration could be identified and took from his bag a small leaflet that explained the four artistic periods so she could work them out for herself, and gave her a copy.

At the House of the Vetii, which had been owned by two successful merchant brothers, Ellis particularly pointed out a painting of a naval battle with a galley in the foreground. She would remember it sometime later, and Ellis' description of it together with its significance in ancient Greece.

She was less enthusiastic about other decorative illustrations here and in many other houses.

Francesco's "Va bene" and little flag called them together to move on as it did at each building they visited. They left the house and he led them on a zigzag route, without mentioning where they were going. When he stopped at a bakery Francesco explained it to the group, while Ellis took a moment to check his plan. He smiled but said nothing. "Va bene."

They walked on down the small street beside the bakery.

"Ellis, I'm trying to work out what that man in the red checked shirt is doing?" Vaila nodded in the direction of a man of just above medium height with rather pale features, whose longish straight dark brown forelock kept falling over his face. He kept pushing it back with his hand, a gesture that had become an unconscious habit. He appeared to be alone.

"Why? What's special about him? He's looking around like the rest isn't he?"

"Firstly, wasn't he the man we saw from our balcony the day we arrived? He was walking up to the hotel on the path by the pools with two others, one of which was the man we thought we'd seen before?"

"Oh yes. I told you who I thought your bearded mystery man was, but then realized you were asleep! I think he was from the ship we saw from Marwick Head."

"Really? Anyway Red Check Shirt seems to be peering round as if looking for something or someone. Everyone else is looking into the houses, trying to work out which is which, admiring the mosaics and frescos and so on, never mind being determined to photograph everything they see. But he keeps looking down the street, apparently more interested in what's happening somewhere else than here."

"He certainly belongs to our coach party, and he's staying in our hotel. He got on the coach with us. I think he's alone."

They watched him for a moment, but Ellis soon lost interest in him, he was too focused on all that there was to see of Pompeii. "Perhaps there's some particular building he wants to find?"

"It's not so much that he's ignoring the guide. He seems to be interested in something quite different. It's as if he's looking for someone or something. At the House of the Faun he pretended to be listening and looking, but when everyone one else went into the house, he never even looked through the doorway, he stayed outside. I get the impression that his mind is elsewhere." Ellis said

"We'll soon find out. I bet no one will want to miss the next house if they're paying attention enough to know what it is! We'll see what he does." Vaila looked puzzled.

"Why?" Ellis grinned and nodded towards the guide, who held up his little flag to encourage the group to gather round and then announced

"Perhaps you English no want to see sexy pictures Amici?" and he laughed. "This is Lupinar, the brothel!" Ellis wasn't surprised that a number of those on the tour pressed forward to see what the guide was talking about, but the man in the red checked shirt was not one of them.

"See what I mean?" said Vaila, as Red Check Shirt took advantage of everyone's attention being on the Lupinar, and turned to the guide. They could see he was asking about something, and when Francesco replied they saw him point down the street.

"Grazie." Red Check Shirt then re-joined the group in the Lupinar. When they had all looked inside, Francesco held up his little flag again and told them. "Va bene. Now we go to Stabian Baths. After that it will be lunchtime where our tour ends. I will explain after you see the baths. People of Pompeii were very clean. Evero." He laughed.

Vaila said to Ellis as they walked,

"These Romans may have washed a lot, but their fondness for dirty pictures is hardly clean!"

"Maybe, but when you see erotic art everywhere, it surely just shows that they had different ideas as to what is moral and decent. One should treat it as evidence as to how they thought. No need to moralize from our perspective. Anyway we're all sinners." He laughed, but said no more. Vaila, like Queen Victoria, was not amused.

After they had explored the Stabian Baths, Francesco told them

"Va bene. Per finire, finally we go to Horttus Porta Marina Ristorante & garden bar, just outside the Porta Marina, where we came in. There is tables reserved for this party, just say 'Hotel Capodimonte'. Is recommended for pasta and fresh salads. A piu tardi. I'll see you later, after lunch."

Someone asked what they could do after lunch, and Francesco replied to the whole group,

"After lunch you will have two hours to go where you want. If you like I could take a group if you agree what you want to see. Remember for lunch and for leaving we go to Porta Marina, follow signs 'Uscita' in lots places. Remember depart at four, alle quattro. Va bene."

As they had coffee after a light lunch taken in the sunshine at an outside table, Ellis said he was keen to see more, but Vaila interrupted.

"I wonder where Red Check Shirt is going now?" She nodded towards him as he stood up and again started looking around as he had during the tour.

"The loo?"

"Then he's blind. There's a notice right beside him! Throughout our tour he seemed to be looking for someone, now he's doing it again."

Red Check Shirt didn't have to look for long this time. A man appeared, saw him and they met.

"Ellis. It's that man we saw from our balcony, the one with the black beard. He's got the same long shirt and a little orange badge."

"I meant to tell you. While you were asleep the other afternoon I worked it out." He told her that he thought he was one of those lifted off the *Camel Prince*. He had the distinctive dark beard they had had. They had seen him at the Hatson terminal. He paused. "Oh, that's what it was. I heard them from our balcony and thought there was something odd in their conversation; the third man was translating, he'd have to, the beard couldn't speak English."

The meeting was brief. The newcomer didn't stay long, he just gave Red Check Shirt a note, smiled and walked away. Red Check Shirt read it and then got out his leaflet on Pompeii and was studying the plan.

"He's looking for somewhere on the plan."

"We could follow him."

"Aren't we just being nosy? Why waste time better spent on Pompeii?" Vaila looked disappointed, then laughed at him.

"You just want to look at the sexy pictures!"

"Of course not, I have my own passionate Piddie Maid!"

"That'll do Monster!" She chuckled. "Anyway it's your fault if I'm passionate! Seriously darling, I'm curious about what he's up to." Ellis softened.

"I'd not like him to think we're following him everywhere, but we don't have to follow him, we saw which way the guide pointed. The plan shows that the two theatres, a couple of temples, and the Gladiators barracks are in that direction. I had intended to go that way to see those buildings in any event. I expect he'll go along the Via Abbondanza, to reach the street Francesco pointed to. If we go to the Civic Forum there's a little street at the south east corner which looks as if it's a shortcut. It goes direct to the Triangular Forum, and the Doric Temple. The theatres are beyond it. You can look for him, while I study the buildings. Let's go, we'll get there before him if we leave now, then he's following us!"

Once they had reached the Triangular Forum, they went into the Doric temple. There Ellis happily looked at it in detail, whilst Vaila kept watch for Red Check Shirt. Ten minutes later he appeared as Ellis had anticipated, and walked to the large theatre and went into it so, at Vaila's urging, they walked across to it too. Red Check Shirt stood in the middle of the open part of the stage, waiting. They found it easy enough to find a darkly shaded place in the entrance by the stage in a short tunnel. Shade from the sun was not only welcome at the warmest part of the day, but they felt they were where it would be difficult for someone in strong sunlight to see them. They were however wrong. They heard footsteps behind them almost as soon as they reached the tunnel.

Someone was coming, and realizing that whoever it was would be right by them Vaila whispered to Ellis,

"Quick, cuddle me to hide our faces." Ellis faced the wall and Vaila buried her face in his shoulder. The newcomer walked by them with a little laugh, out onto the stage and said to Red Check Shirt, "We must walk. Others are here." He jumped off the raised area and led Red Check Shirt out of the theatre by the tunnel on the far side. Vaila relaxed.

"Did you get any clue as to who that was or what they are up to?"

"Yes, I took a sneaky look. You'll hardly believe it, it's Hassan. Do you remember him?

"Yes I do. We saw him at Hatson. He gave us a look that suggested he wanted to remember us, and I felt I'd certainly remember him. "

"That proves my memory was right, the bearded man was a friend of Hassan's wasn't he? We'd better be careful, especially if he knows what we look like."

"I'm sure he would remember us if he saw us properly. We recognized him after all. On this occasion we were in the shade and had hidden our faces but I can't help remembering Simmons saying he could be a murderer. Come on! There's lots more to see so let's look at some of the other places in the time left before we have to be at the Porta Marina to get the bus. We've come to see Pompeii, not to play at being Hercule Poirot! We can have an amusing time inventing reasons for him being here over dinner."

They only saw Hassan and Red Check Shirt once more before they got back to the coach. They were talking, standing in the centre of the Civic Forum. Vaila thought it an odd place to meet, but Ellis suggested it was ideal in many ways. No one would be able to be near enough to overhear them so long as they stayed in the middle, a good distance from where anyone could hide.

That evening they enjoyed dinner out of the hotel, taking advantage of a special offer their tour company included in their package to go to O'Parrucchiano restaurant, by the harbour. As Ellis said, they could talk about their adventures in Pompeii to their hearts content there, as no one would interrupt or overhear them, and Vaila added especially about Red Check Shirt and the mystery men.

It was a wonderful restaurant, full of character and serving a number of local dishes as well as the better known Italian cuisine, and the wine their waiter recommended was an excellent accompaniment to their dinner. They loved dining in the open in the warm balmy evening watching the activity in the harbour. Over coffee they decided that the next day could be a lazy one and then they'd visit Naples the day after that. Ellis especially wanted to visit the Museo Archeologico Nazionale. They would catch the train in the morning and return when they had had enough of the city.

So on the first Friday of their holiday they caught a train arriving in Naples around 9.45. As they got off the train there were a number of people waiting for one due to come in on the other side of the island platform. They could see it approaching, still about a couple of hundred metres from the station, when there was an anguished cry

"Giuseppe!" from a women who was standing apart from the other waiting passengers. Vaila wondered why all the passengers seemed to be shunning her, but Ellis immediately saw what had caused her distress. Her small boy, little more than a toddler, had wandered a short distance away from her, dropping the ball he had been holding. It had rolled to the edge of the low platform and fallen onto the track and the little boy had jumped down after it, oblivious of the approaching train. Ellis, without thinking what he was doing ran over, jumped onto the track, swept up the child, gave him to Vaila, who had run after him, and jumped back onto the platform himself just in time to avoid the oncoming train.

Vaila turned to his mother, and with a smile handed the little boy to her. By this time he was howling, more upset at having been picked up by a stranger so suddenly than of the train, and still unhappy at having lost his ball.

The mother was full of thanks, but her torrent of Italian was beyond anything that either Ellis or Vaila could understand, so they just smiled at her. They had no common language. All Ellis could think to say was the couple of words Francesco had kept using in Pompeii "Va bene."

They turned away and walked down the platform through the onlookers and out into the street. As they walked towards the museum Vaila made just two comments. Why did the watching crowd seem strangely surprised, even a touch hostile, at what he had done? She then took Ellis arm and turned him towards her.

"Much as I admire and am proud of what you did, you gave me a nasty fright. Please, please don't be too brave my darling husband, I don't fancy being a widow quite yet."

They were soon at the Museo Archeologico Nazionale. Ellis bought a guide book, and they noted that virtually all the ground and mezzanine floors were devoted to items from Pompeii and Herculaneum. The art and sculpture, including several mosaics, were on the ground floor as well as the Farnese collection of classical sculpture. The other more domestic items from the two cities were on the mezzanine level.

Vaila thoroughly enjoyed the art works and spent a little time trying to decide if her favourite was 'The sacrifice of Iphigenia, daughter of Agamemnon' because it seemed an echo of the story of Abraham and Isaac, or a fresco, 'Spring' because it was a delicate dreamy picture of a young girl picking flowers. She told Ellis she thought it a nice change from the erotic pictures both in Pompeiian houses and on many artefacts in the museum.

However interesting, and in spite of wanting Ellis to see all he needed, she had had enough archaeology, and even art, after a couple of hours and started to drop hints about lunch.

"Okay darling, I get the hint. Its time I treated you to lunch!"

"I hope my hints weren't too obvious! But I am getting archaeological indigestion, a bit hungry and my feet wouldn't mind a breather! I hope you have at least seen what you most wanted to see. Maybe we could just stop for lunch and come back later?"

"Well, I think it's your turn to choose what we should do!"

"Okay. Lunch. Definitely. A Neapolitan long lunch! Isn't this where they invented pizza? That would be just the thing."

They saw what looked to be the ideal place to get what they hoped would be the real thing in a small square down a short side street quite close to the museum. It had outside tables with the sun shining on them. There were a number of people eating there, local people judging by the animated conversations in progress. They were welcomed by a waiter with a large smile, a large apron and a large menu. It was in Italian but with the help of a phrase book, they were soon able to choose a pizza to both their tastes and a carafe of local wine with it. It proved to be excellent in every way except perhaps that it was as large as the menu, but none the less they enjoyed it. They had taken their time, as the waiter said, trying out his very limited English, as he served them,

"Best Pizza in Napoli. Enjoy lente!"

"Va bene, eccellente!" Vaila wondered how far they could get with Francesco's two little words and the limited phrase book.

Ellis paid the bill when they had eventually finished and they started to walk slowly back towards the station to catch a train back to Sorrento. They had not even reached the end of the little street when a man came running as fast as he could though the little square they had just left, passed them and stopped at the main road, panting hard. He turned round, and said something in Italian they could not understand. "Sorry, we're British, Non Capisco."

"Thank goodness. I only know a little Italian." He looked back the way he had come and seeing no one explained, "I was doing a quiet bit of business a couple of streets up there, when a couple of locals started arguing with the guys I was negotiating with. It got heated, and all of a sudden my two guys took off in a hurry. They were funny sort of people, certainly not locals, they just ran away. I went to my hire car and unlocked it, only to find the two locals were now after me. They snatched the car keys, threw them to a mate who just appeared from nowhere who drove it away. Right under my nose. Then they got aggressive to me and all the time I didn't understand them, and they took no notice of what I said. One grabbed my arm and pushed me up against a wall. When I saw another guy coming to join them I thought it was time to vanish, so wriggled my arm free and ran for it. I hope I've lost them, but how am I going to get back?"

"Aren't you at our hotel in Sorrento?" Vaila asked.

"Oh, oh yes, now I look at you yes, of course. And you were on the bus trip to Pompeii." He paused.   "Can you give me a lift back? Incidentally I'm Gerry Jones"

"We don't have a car, we came by train. You could get back the same way." they then introduced themselves. Gerry again looked back, saw no one and suggested they went to the station at once so they walked out of the little street and turned right.

Almost as soon as they set out a car came to a screeching stop beside them. Two men jumped out and gestured for them to get in the car. The order was reinforced by the small pistols they held. The three of them had no choice, protest was clearly pointless even if they could have been understood. The car drove away at high speed until clear of the immediate area, and then slowed to a less conspicuous pace.

They didn't have far to go. The car slowed down before a gate in a high wall, which opened at the touch of a remote control and the car drove in, down a short drive and stopped in front of a large villa overlooking the sea. Their captors jumped out and indicated that they should come with them into the villa. They were taken into a large office-like room. One man stayed with them while the other went out of the room.

The wait was short. A large man of around thirty years old, Ellis guessed, came into the room. He looked at the three of them for a moment, then made up his mind.

"I suppose you know who I am." He spoke in excellent public school English with an Italian inflexion, but it had a hard edge.

Gerry Jones said he had heard of him.

"You head the Mafia here? I think you are called 'Capo'." Vaila looked at Ellis nervously and asked,

"What have we got caught up in?"

"You," the man said looking at Gerry, "have been doing business with the wrong people. Those men are Albysians. You should not have attempted business with anyone but us. I am told you knew that."

"Why shouldn't I deal with whoever I like? Those people are refugees. It's good to help them through trading with them isn't it?"

The Capo thumped the desk he was standing beside, "No. If you are told not to buy from them round here I expect you to respect that order. Also for your own good. They have fooled you, they are not refugees." He turned to Ellis.

"Who are you and why are you helping this man to defy my order?"

"I don't know who you are. We are British citizens on holiday. We are not doing any business with anyone, I'm an archaeologist not a businessman. We met this man, only a couple of minutes before being bundled into a car. He stays at the same hotel, and he asked for our help because, he told us, someone, your men it seems, stole his hire car. He asked if he could come back to Sorrento with us by train. Naturally we agreed."

"A good story. I wonder if I can believe it? Three Brits, two stories." He paused. "We'll see if there's a little proof." He spoke to the guard in Italian. The guard then left the room. The Capo, as Ellis presumed he must call him, then picked up the phone on the desk, again speaking in Italian which none of them understood. Then he turned back to them.

"If you are English then you will like tea, and it's teatime. I acquired a taste for it at that silly school I was sent to. I have asked my wife to bring some tea herself, as I am wondering."

The room was silent while they waited. Vaila looked at Ellis with a worried expression on her face. She mouthed "Scots." to him, but it seemed best to remain silent.

There was a knock on the door, and it was opened for a lady to carry in a tea tray. She set the tray down on the desk and only then looked up. She smiled and spoke in a torrent of Italian to her husband, and as she did so a toddler ran into the room. The Capo bent down and lifted the boy into his arms, talking to him in Italian. He turned to Ellis.

"I gather you met my wife Gina and Giuseppe at the station this morning. Perhaps it proves your story."

The phone rang and after answering, listening for a short while and replacing it, he said to Ellis,

"You will be glad to hear that your story about being on holiday is proven too. So I must apologise for bringing you and your wife here in such a fashion, and more to the point I must thank you on behalf of my wife and myself for rescuing our lovely bambino. My wife says you took a considerable risk in doing so. I will arrange for you and your charming wife to be taken back to your hotel by car. It's the least I can do."

"And me too?" asked Jones.

"Well, you are different. I am not so sure."

"It would be kind of you to do so. We have no idea what his problem is, but he is a fellow countryman." Ellis hoped Vaila wasn't pushing their luck too far for a man they did not know, but it worked.

"Very well. But understand this, Jones. You will not be forgiven a third time. If the Albysians approach you again you must tell them you have another source from which to buy."

Gerry Jones was clearly frightened by the implied threat, and agreed, even thanking his captor. The three of them arrived back at the Hotel Capodimonte in style, the car that took them being the biggest limo Ellis had ever seen, far too big to fit down most of the streets in Kirkwall!

Gerry Jones said nothing all the way back. It was as if he feared the driver might overhear him. But once the limo had dropped them and they were inside the hotel, he thanked Vaila and Ellis.

He smiled and joked that at least it had saved him a train fare.

"Sounds as if your business is a bit risky?"

"Yeah, well you don't want to know about that. Know what I mean?"

"Very well, but be careful. Incidentally we came across a few Albysians at home. They didn't seem refugees then. What do you really know about them?"

"Not much. Seem desperate for cash and fanatical about something. Their leader is a guy called Hassan. I don't ask questions, it's better that way."

He laughed again before wishing them good afternoon and going back to his room. He said nothing about what his business was that had apparently upset the Mafia. As Ellis said,

"At last we know who Red Check Shirt is. He seems a pleasant enough rogue. Let's now talk about where else we might go tomorrow. You wanted to go on a boat trip to Capri, and I want to see Herculaneum so there's lots to do. We're on honeymoon and that was not the sort of adventure we're supposed to be having!"

An invitation

Ellis and Vaila had only been back from their honeymoon a few days when he had a call from the Ness of Brodgar Team Leader.

"We have a problem with the volunteer accommodation, over which we would really appreciate your help. We're in a bit of a jam. Can I call in your office after lunch and talk to you about it?"

"Of course, say about 2.30? I'll ask Magnus to be with us. It sounds serious."

"Perfect. I think it'll need us all. See you later."

With the UHI team leader and the accommodation caretaker, as well as Magnus and Vaila, who Ellis asked to take minutes of the meeting, Ellis' office was a bit crowded. Once Vaila had brought them coffee, Team Leader told them he was short of staff to prepare for the volunteers who were to open up the site for the fieldwork season just at the moment they had found a serious problem with the buildings in which volunteer groups stayed and had their workshop and store.

He went on to explain that the winter's gales had damaged the wooden buildings the volunteers used. When the caretaker had gone to start opening them up she had found that there was a serious problem to the structure of all three of them. As it's was now April and the first volunteer camp was in early May he feared there was hardly time to repair them.

"Won't your usual contractors fix that for you?"

"Normally yes, but they have told us that they couldn't do anything for at least a month, having other contracts to finish first. What's worse is that we have unfortunately already overspent our maintenance budget. We're expected to work on a shoe string and UHI are not at all happy about any sudden extra costs, even for emergency repairs. I think they have their own financial problems."

He continued to explain why he could not use volunteers either. Theoretically, he explained, it was an ideal job for volunteers, and they would normally organize a special work party for it, but there's no time to do that, nor could we ask the first planned work party to do the job.

"They've volunteered to help the archeological work, not to repair buildings. That's what they want to do, why they come and is what they are good at. I am concerned that it might put volunteers off in future if we asked them to deal with these repairs and in any case where would they stay whilst the work is done?"

Ellis asked what exactly was required, and Vaila noted the items as the Team Leader listed them.

There were three wooden buildings. They were designed in a similar way to flat pack furniture.

The walls consisted of complete units, roughly two meters long by two and a half high, with windows and doors built in, which were just bolted together, and the joints sealed and covered with an internal insulated lining. Photos of the damage had been emailed to the manufacturer, who had replied that it was easier to replace the units rather than repair them. A total of six panels needed to be replaced, two window panels, and four solid ones. The company could supply everything required within a week, but someone on Orkney must fit them, for as little cost as possible.

The Team Leader then explained that there was also, on two buildings, unfortunately the ones volunteers slept in, problems with the tarred felt roofing, which the gales had so damaged as to let in quite a lot of water during the winter. The roofs needed to be repaired with another layer of tarred felt. There could be other problems from the ingress of water. The bedding was stored there during the winter and some items had been spoilt and would need replacing.

"So you can see that we can neither get a contractor nor volunteers to repair the buildings or even sort out the soft furnishings in time. I'm hoping you can help us, otherwise we may have to cancel the summer's work."

Magnus' remarked that experience suggested snags always arise with this sort of thing too. Someone used to repair work and with a knack of solving unexpected difficulties was needed.

"Can you help? Have Treasures of Scotland any resources for the job?" the Team Leader asked.

Magnus replied that they did not have any more funding than the UHI team for such work, and for a couple of minutes there was a worried silence in the room. Then Ellis suggested a possible solution.

"You'd need at least two men, and although there's no time for a whole volunteer squad, perhaps the work could be done by just one skilled employed man and one volunteer? That would ensure you have both expertize and yet can get the work done for the minimum cost."

"Who have you in mind?"

"What about Hal, my brother in law, Vaila's brother? He makes a living by mending and repairing things. Although he mainly works with machinery he has a part time job with the Flotta Terminal carrying out and organizing all sorts of repairs there. If he is free and you employed him for the job, I would be happy to act as his 'mate', which would cost nothing as I am already employed by Treasures of Scotland. I could surely justify a few days working with Hal, even if it's not archeology. Enabling important research on the Ness of Brodgar to proceed must count as well within my remit."

With Magnus' enthusiastic support, it was agreed that Ellis would discuss the matter with Hal and they would sort out a cost and timetable to complete the repairs. The UHI team would order the materials.

By the time they had agreed arrangements with Hal and the materials had arrived, there were only five working days and two weekends left to complete the work.

Hal had said he thought that if the two of them worked through the weekends and as late each evening as daylight allowed they could manage the repairs in time. In the event they completed the building repairs with two days to spare. The worst problem was lining up the new panels, which Hal solved with his usual ingenuity.

Ellis really enjoyed working with Hal, who was cheerful, competent, and always clear when explaining to Ellis how to do the job and generally a good man to work with.

Internally the main problem was in the floor coverings, and some of the soft furnishings, including six mattresses and about a third of the bed coverings in the two bunk houses. These had suffered from the damp that had got into them to a greater or lesser extent, due to the leaking roof. Vaila took charge of this problem. Working with the lady caretaker, they sorted out the items that could be rescued, and cleaned and dried them. For those which had to be replaced, Vaila went to a house clearance sale, the result of several holiday houses being converted to permanent housing, accompanied by Inga, Hal's wife, who loved the excitement of an auction and proved expert at getting good bargains. Between them they had secured most of the items needed at a reasonable price, and even those items that were not available through the auction proved reasonably easy to buy locally.

All was ready just in time for the arrival of the first archeological volunteer party. To Ellis' amusement, several of them who had been before were full of how good the improvements to their accommodation were.

With the crisis over, Ellis felt that it was important that he learnt all he could about the Ness of Brodgar and to that end he decided to spend a fortnight working with them on site.

Having tea with the volunteers towards the end of their stay, discussing what they had found and what it revealed of the site, Bob, who led the volunteer group, asked Ellis if he really had to mend the buildings with his own bare hands.

"I was just mate to my brother-in-law. I'd never have thought I was the slightest good at that sort of thing, but Hal seems to be able to mend anything! Both our wives played a part too. From Treasures of Scotland's point of view, I feel it's good that we're doing something which was important to the project even if in an unexpected way!"

"Well between you it really was an excellent job."

"Thank you. The main thing is that you have had a successful couple of weeks."

"Ellis we've really enjoyed our time here, and working with you. We are extremely grateful for making our accommodation so comfortable. In return we would like to invite you to our farewell party. The Team Leader will also be with us and it's usually a great end to our fortnight."

"That's very kind, I'll look forward to it. Can my wife, Vaila, and above all her brother and his wife come too? A bit of a cheek, but they were the really important part of our squad; I was just the assistant chief to the chief assistant."

"Yes of course, we'd all like to meet them. They might be interested in the little film that's been made of the site and all we have found – it will be shown at the party for the first time."

The main building was fairly full of people for the party. With the drinks, a buffet had been prepared. Vaila and Ellis enjoyed talking to the volunteers about the work they had been doing. One even asked Vaila where she had got her archeological experience and she had laughingly pointed at Ellis. "I didn't need to take a degree or get any experience – I married it!"

They had seen the 10 minute film and were thinking of going home when the Team Leader came over and asked if he could have a word before they left the party.

"Ellis, we really are so grateful for all you and your family did for us, so in return you might be interested in an invitation I have just received from Carnelian Cruises to lecture on one of their voyages. I get sea sick, and none of us in the UHI staff team are keen to go away in the last month of the fieldwork season anyway. So I wondered if you would enjoy a bit of lecturing afloat. Here's a copy of the letter."

CARNELIAN CRUISES

BLUE RIBBON HOUSE

MARINE ROAD

SOUTHAMPTON

SN10 8NS

Phone 033 232 4321 fax 033 232 4322

telex; cruises

www carnelian. com

e mail cruises@carnelian. net

'Roman World' Cruise 4th to the 19th September

Dear Sir

I have been given your name by Professor Edward Gerald who was to have lectured on this cruise.

Carnelian Cruises operate themed cruises which have an excellent reputation for itineraries which, together with lectures on board of the highest academic standard, provide our passengers, even if they have no previous knowledge of the subject, with an instructive and enjoyable cruise programme.

Professor Gerald has sailed with us on several occasions. However he has had to withdraw from his role on the above cruise to take part in an international conference in San Francisco at that time. We would therefore like to invite you, or one of your senior archaeologists, to take his place.

Professor Gerald was to have given three lectures. The first, on his own subject, was to have been about the Historic Environment Service of Cornwall which he runs and especially Trethevy Quoit, the Hurlers (three stone rings at Minions north of Liskeard) and Restormel Castle, near Lostwithiel.

We appreciate that you would want to speak about your own work on the Ness of Brodgar, and The heart of Neolithic Orkney World Heritage site, instead. That would of course be entirely appropriate.

We also would like you speak about Rome and the three other major Roman sites the ship will visit, Pompeii, Herculaneum and Si'pelium in Albysia, prior to the cruise visiting each of these places. Some of our lecturers prepare an extra talk on a subject of their own choosing as there can be times while at sea when an extra item is appreciated.

It is our normal practice to ask lecturers to take on some other appropriate duties such as acting as escort for excursions. Our lecturers particularly enjoy the contact with passengers this gives them, and, of course, it gives lecturers the chance to explain the places their excursions visit.

The contract with you would give you the cruise itself, including a D grade outside cabin, and full board, travel to and from the ship, which sails from Dover, insurance and we would reimburse you for other costs which you might incur.

We are not in a position to offer lecturers a standard fee in addition but our lecturers regard the cruise as a holiday as they are free to enjoy the cruise and all the facilities on board when not carrying out the duties described above.

Lecturers may also be accompanied by their spouse, for a nominal fare, largely to cover insurance and similar expenses.

I would be glad to hear that you would accept our invitation either yourself, or one of your archeological team,

Yours faithfully

Joel F Shawshank

Cruise management Director

Enc. The brochure which includes details of the Roman World cruise.

Ellis passed the letter to Vaila to read while the Team Leader spoke to him as she read it.

"I know Treasures of Scotland are keen to help with publicity and appreciate their name being associated with the Ness of Brodgar, so this would surely be an excellent way for you to reach out to one section of the public. Not only that. Lecturing should enable you to write something which compares those Roman sites to each other and, in the case of Si'pelium in Albysia, with Skara Brae, as they both were preserved by being buried in sand. I'm sure that would interest a number of magazines."

Vaila finished reading the letter.

"That looks great. If I have remembered our last Edinburgh trip correctly, it's the cruise on which two tickets were offered as a prize in a competion?"

"You do have a good memory. Now you mention it that's right. I wonder who won the prize?"

"I particularly like the bit about taking your spouse, can we afford the cost of my coming too?"

"Well we do still have some of the money relatives gave us as wedding presents. If we postpone some of the house items we had in mind we can."

As soon as they arrived in the office the next day, Ellis sent an email to Collard, explaining that the Team Leader had been invited to lecture on Carnelian Cruises' 'Roman World' cruise, but he did not want to accept it. The company had asked him to suggest another archaeologist who had been involved in the Ness of Brodgar site. The Team Leader had suggested that Ellis took up the invitation. He emphasized its value in publicity terms, and felt that it would be an excellent way to emphasize Treasures of Scotland's role in the Ness of Brodgar project.

It did not cross Ellis' mind that his email was any more than a formality, a request for the time to be away from his usual base in Orkney. After all arranging publicity was part of his job specification.

It was therefore a nasty surprise when Collard replied later the same day to say that he could not agree that Ellis should lecture on the cruise. He believed someone from Head Office should be lecturing when there was such an important opportunity to bring Treasures of Scotland's work to the attention of the public. He had emphasized that he was not thinking of going himself, but would be talking to someone he felt more suitable.

Ellis showed it to Vaila as soon as he had opened the email. Her reaction was to ask who he thought Collard would want to send.

"It must be an archeologist, and he'd hardly ask one of the other regional archeologists, they aren't at HQ. He's ruled himself out too, and that just leaves Rosemarie."

"What does she know about Orkney, let alone the Ness of Brodgar? I suppose she's made eyes at Collard and he gave in to her. I'm beginning to really dislike that woman, she always seems to want to put you down. You know more about Orkney's archeology and the Ness than she'll ever know."

"I'll find a tactful way to find out, maybe it's someone else? But as it was the Team Leader who had the invitation, Collard's refusal to let me go might create some awkwardness between UHI and Treasures of Scotland. That's not something I'd want to be caught up in. Nor do I want to upset anyone, so I'll have to be very tactful. Just the same I don't feel like just letting it go."

"I'm keen too. Especially if that McRaven woman is at the back of Collard's refusal."

So Ellis replied to Collard asking what he should tell the Team Leader and offering to introduce Collard's choice to the Orkney team.

Later in the day Ellis had a second email from Collard. It did not say who Collard wanted to go on the cruise, but told Ellis, in what seemed to him a rather unfriendly way, that Collard would speak to the Team Leader himself. Ellis was to have nothing further to do with the matter.

"Is there no appeal, Ellis? It seems so unfair, it wasn't for Collard to decide who should go, yet he seems to want to take over the opportunity the Team Leader offered you. As your boss he may not want you to talk to the Team Leader, but why shouldn't I speak to him?"

"Darling, we should let Collard speak to the Team Leader. I don't want to be seen as plotting. I'm quite sure the Team Leader will take our side so the best tactic might be to await events. Anyway there is an Edinburgh meeting of all our archeologists next Wednesday, so I will speak to Collard then. He can hardly refuse me a hearing and a better explanation. After all I specialized in the Stone Age, which is appropriate whilst Rosemarie concentrated on ceramics, and very little has been found at the Ness of Brodgar, mainly a single pot. Even if he wants seniority, Rosemarie no more qualifies than I do, so there may be someone else involved. If by next week Collard has spoken to the Team Leader, and if he has supported me, there might be a chance to reverse his decision."

But they had heard nothing further about the cruise, before Ellis caught the afternoon flight to Glasgow the following Monday. He took this to mean that Collard had not yet spoken to the Team Leader.

He took the train to Edinburgh and the bus to his Mother's house where he was staying.

During the evening, they talked of Janet's plans for a holiday. She had already arranged to come to Orkney for a week, the first time she would visit Ellis and Vaila in their new home in Kirkwall. She naturally wanted to visit all the Treasures of Scotland monuments to know more about Ellis' work, and especially wanted to get to know Vaila's family better. He had just told her that he had been invited to lecture on the *Carnelian*, but had been refused the time of to do so, when there was a knock on the door. It was Aunt Minnie.

Minnie was delighted to find Ellis with his Mum "This is a nice surprise Ellis, what are you doing here? And what have you done with that lovely wife of yours. I did so take to her, you're a very lucky man." Ellis laughed

"Aren't I just, and she's fine. Mum and I are in the midst of planning Mum's Orcadian holiday – she's another of Vaila's fans!"

"That sounds wonderful. I've just booked my holiday too. I'm going with Millie on a cruise in September in the *Carnelian*. We're going to several Roman places – the cruise is called 'The Roman

World.' it's a pity you couldn't come too, you'd be able to explain it all to us!"

"I wish. I had an invitation to lecture on that cruise." He explained how it had come about and that he had been refused the time to accept it.

"That sounds all wrong, but life does that to you every now and again. No chance of the decision being reversed do you think?"

"Well, Minnie, I intend to ask again, but beyond that it's out of my hands. I've no real complaints; I live in a great place with the girl I love. That's pretty good. After all I am quite junior and just have to accept what my seniors decree for me, although both of us did fancy the cruise and lecturing would add something to my career. It would've been a great opportunity, but I expect there'll be others. That you were going would have been a great bonus too."

The conversation then moved away from the subject, until Minnie said good night and went home.

The meeting of the regional archeologists was not until 10.30 on Wednesday, so Ellis had taken the opportunity to arrange to see the finance department on Tuesday morning as he wanted to check over his budget, and especially to see if there would be money for a pet project he had in mind. He wanted to uncover the little underground chamber he had explored previously on Bustahead farm. In the family it had become known as 'Vaila's Folly', because when he had first looked at it with Hal and Vaila, she had got trapped in it so he had had to concentrate on rescuing her. He had not been able to do any research on it to discover what it was, and now he wanted to try to find out more about it by getting into the second chamber from above. Although it did not have a high priority, he believed it was archeologically sufficiently interesting to justify a small project.

Ellis explained this to the Finance Director, giving his justification, and the estimated costs he had prepared. However it became clear that he was most unlikely to get the funding within Treasures of Scotland.

"In the current financial year, and even next year it is extremely unlikely that we could finance your project." The Finance Director had told him, "If you want to pursue it you'll have to raise funds for it yourself. Don't forget that even then you must get your manager, William Collard, to approve it."

Although disappointed, he thought it gave the perfect excuse to see Collard, and whilst he was at it, it should not be too difficult to raise the subject of the cruise lecturer again.

As it was twelve thirty by the time his meeting with the Director of Finance finished, he thought it best to go to lunch before tackling Collard about the project and the cruise.

Afterwards he was crossing the road to return to the archeology department when he met Christine just outside the office also returning from her lunch break. She greeted him warmly and asked him what brought him to HQ a day early.

"I've a couple of issues I want to talk to Collard about. I hope he's in and can see me this afternoon. I should have made an appointment, but forgot."

"He should be back soon. He was at the Museum with Rosemarie this morning. They are supposed to be doing some special research there, but he did say he'd be back straight after lunch."

Ellis detected something in the way Christine had answered him that hinted that there was more that she might have said, but he gave it no attention, thinking about the points he wanted to make to Collard, and hoping he would be persuasive.

They walked into the office, and Christine buzzed Collard's internal phone as soon as she had hung up her coat, but there was no answer. As he thought it would be worth looking at his notes again, and was aware that he had not read all the papers he had for the meeting next day, he asked Christine if there was a spare office where he could go over them until Collard came in.

Christine told him she thought the small meeting room was free.

"It's used by several departments for confidential and private meetings, but there aren't many of those. There's a notice on the door to indicate if it's free, but I expect so. Help yourself, it's just at the end of the corridor."

He went to the room, saw the notice Christine had mentioned, a sliding affair which showed 'FREE' and opened the door to go in.

He was startled by what he saw. Collard was sitting in one of the armchairs at the end of the room. Rosemarie was on his lap, her clothing awry and the two of them in a passionate embrace. It was not possible to mistake what was happening. The three of them froze and stared at each other.

Ellis, extremely embarrassed, stuttered

"Oh I'm so sorry, the notice said the room was free. Excuse me," and rapidly retreated. He heard Rosemarie say "Alors. Ce n'est pas vrai!" and then giggle. As he closed the door he saw the look on Collard's face.

Retreating to Christine's office he sat on one of the visitor's chairs. Realizing something had happened to shake him by the look on his face, Christine asked if he was okay. He just said,

"They're busy in there. I'd better just stay here."

About ten minutes later Collard came into Christine's office, and saw Ellis. He asked Christine if there had been any calls, and when she told him that she'd only just returned from lunch herself, he asked Ellis to come into his office.

When they had sat down either side of the desk Collard asked him why he had come in a day early. He seemed reasonably composed, and so Ellis explained that he had come to ask about the project he had in mind. As Collard didn't stop him he went on to set out his case for a project to open up the underground chamber on Bustahead Farm he had first explored, unsuccessfully, on a visit the previous summer. They then discussed it as if nothing had happened, and Collard gave his approval on the same basis as the finance department had laid down. Collard then said, "About that cruise you wanted to go on. Rosemarie was keen to go as her parents are booked on that cruise, and I felt you should concentrate on developing your new role on Orkney. However I have changed my mind. There is too much for us to do in HQ to spare her for it, and if the UHI team have recommended you, and therefore can't mind your being away in September, before the fieldwork season has ended, you can go. Have you lectured before?"

"No, though I've naturally been to many lectures."

"Well if you want any hints or need material or slides I'm sure UHI or your own University will help you."

"Thank you. I do think it will be good experience for me. I should be able to give ToS plenty of publicity too. I'll report back on my return. In the meantime I'll see you at tomorrow's meeting."

"Yes – and by the way, I hope you will be discreet about what you saw earlier – a moment's madness I'm afraid." He looked a little red in the face. "I don't suppose Christine knows?"

"Not from me. Thank you for enabling me to do the lectures. Good afternoon."

In the outer office, he had just put his coat on and said cheerio to Christine, when Rosemarie came through from her office. She smiled at him and asked   "I'm available for an hour or so just now, why don't you come to the meeting room with me and tell me all about the Ness of Brodgar, I need to know more about that site. You would enjoy that *N'est-ce pas?* "

Ellis realized that Collard could not have told her of the change of plan yet, and had no doubt what she thought he would enjoy.

"Sorry, Rosemarie, some other time. Perhaps in Orkney if you feel you could survive a visit to the uncivilized wild north! I have to go to the University just now. See you tomorrow."

As he left he caught her glance at him. It mixed surprise, concern and perhaps even disappointment, but certainly not defeat.

He walked up Lothian Road on his way to the University, thinking about what he would need for his lectures. He could get all the material and pictures he might need for the Ness of Brodgar on Orkney, and he probably had enough photos on Pompeii and Herculaneum, from their honeymoon visits. Photos of Rome were easy to obtain too but he needed to research Si'pelium in some detail and think through the best approach for a lecture on the Picts, which was to be his 'spare' talk. He would have a busy summer.

As he walked, his mind was so full of his plans that he took no notice of other pedestrians. He passed the Usher Hall, and turned into Bread Street towards the University.

"Fancy seeing you here? How are you these days?" Ellis looked up to see his tutor from the time he had been at University, Professor Calum Cameron.   "I'm fine, how are you? It's great to see you."

"I hear that you are now working in Orkney. How's it going?"

"I am indeed. I work for Treasures of Scotland on Orkney, mainly helping with the UHI project on the Ness of Brodgar."

"How interesting. What are you doing here?"

Ellis explained that he was also lecturing on the *Carnelian* in September and was on his way to the University to see if he could do some research in the library, especially on Si'pelium.

"The ship's going there. It's one of my lectures but it's the one place I've never seen."

"Have you time for tea before your research? Then you can tell me all about the Ness of Brodgar project, and in return maybe I can help you find what you need for your lectures?"

"Of course. There's a likely place," Indicating the Tasty Bun Bakery just across the street.

They went in and ordered tea and a cake each and sat at a window seat.

"This looks good." said the Professor. "It's a new place, I've not been in before. So how is the Ness of Brodgar getting on?"

Ellis described the site, the most recent finds and the conclusions that the UHI team were drawing from them. When he had finished and answered as many of Professor Cameron's questions as he could, their conversation turned to how he came to be lecturing on a cruise ship and especially what research he needed to do. After discussing how Ellis might approach each lecture, the Professor explained what the University library had on Si'pelium, and also offered to look out three papers, which he had in his department and a number of photos he had been given by a colleague who had visited the site around seven years previously.

"I'll send copies of them to you and then we could discuss them, either on the phone or better still, if you'll be in Edinburgh prior to the cruise, we could meet again."

Ellis thanked him and was just writing out his Orkney address, phone number and email when the Professor, looking out of the window, asked,

"You must know those two?"

"Yes, he's my boss, William Collard, and the girl is his assistant."

"Oh I remember her all right, Rosemarie McRaven isn't she? Spent most of her time here flirting with the male students, got herself quite a reputation! You must have been in a different year, or you would be bound to have met her then?" Ellis nodded assent.

"In the end she must have done some real work as well because she did well enough for her degree. I'm fairly sure she majored in the field of ceramics. She had old Michael Kantley as tutor, it was his specialism, of course. I suppose they got on well enough. He was too old to be seduced, even by her! She must have actually listened to what he taught her! Did you know that the old boy died three or four months ago?"

"No. I didn't know him well, but I'm sorry to hear that."

"Poor man, died before his time, though I've no idea of what. He had told me, and a few others, that he was writing a definitive book on archaeological ceramics. We thought he had virtually finished it, yet no one has ever seen any of it, so I suppose we can't be sure if it was finished but there must at least be a draft. He wasn't the type of man to say he was doing something when he wasn't. Now he's passed on, no one seems to know what's happened to it. It's not altogether surprising, he was a secretive old boy. He used to fear someone else might plagiarise his ideas, and never even discussed it with colleagues."

"Perhaps he hid it?"

"Yes, quite likely, even probably I suppose. But it's frustrating; a book from him would have been a particularly useful reference, as he was unquestionably a great ceramist, a real expert. It's the University's loss too so I gather, as having no family, he left all he owned to us. I suppose it might have had a good financial value, though I don't really know about that. I never was any good with financial things."

"What a pity if it's lost. I can see that such a book of reference would have been particularly useful, especially in the field. It would've been a book all archaeologists would have wanted."

The Professor pointed to the pair in the street. "Do you know what are they doing here, Ellis?"

"No I don't. Apparently they've spent a lot of time at the Museum recently, and Collard's certainly difficult to reach on the phone these days. Maybe I'll hear about it tomorrow at the six monthly meeting of all our archaeologists."

"Hum. Come to think of it they're planning a major exhibition in the Museum next winter. Perhaps Treasures of Scotland are involved. He might well be part of it anyway as he's a Museum Trustee, as am I."

The Professor drank the last of his tea.

"Anyway, Ellis, it has been good to see you again and hear about Brodgar. I won't forget the papers and pictures, but I'd better go now."

"Thank you so much for your help. I am excited about lecturing, but a bit nervous about it too. I'll let you know when I'm next down here. Goodbye."

Kirkwall to Edinburgh

They had a busy summer. At work, apart from being on call to help the Ness of Brodgar team, Ellis took on a role as tour guide working with Andrew who had been Hal's best man. His father ran a taxi business and was delighted to discuss a partnership with Treasures of Scotland. With Magnus' enthusiastic encouragement Ellis was already discussing with colleagues in Edinburgh the potential of Treasures of Scotland tours for the following year.

Between while he had a lot to do preparing his lectures for the cruise, and had completed his draft notes for them in good time. It helped that Vaila typed them out for him, and acted as proof reader and critic. They enjoyed working together. If they made little progress in setting up their house as they wanted it to be, neither minded. That was a job that could wait for winter.

They were therefore ready to head south for the cruise in good time. That too needed preparation. As Ellis pointed out even the journey to join the ship at Dover was quite an undertaking, being nearly the whole length of Britain.

"Maybe, Ellis, but I don't mind, I'm looking forward to the cruise. It'll be a bit of luxury I never expected, and I am very excited to be able to go to a Magic Monster lecture!"

Ellis was mindful of travelling reasonably economically. He might be on expenses but Vaila was not. They chose to travel by bus via the Pentland Ferry to Inverness, then by train to Edinburgh. There they would spend three days with Janet before travelling on to Dover, also by train, to embark on the *Carnelian*. They had arranged to travel with Minnie and her friend Millie from Edinburgh to Dover.

Ellis wanted to make sure he made a really good job of his lectures. For that reason he thought he needed the three days in Edinburgh where he would have access to the University library and the Museum archives and photographs. He would make use of the train journey to Edinburgh to go over the papers Professor Cameron had lent him on Si'pelium again, before returning them. He also had several reference books he was taking with him. Whilst he had studied the Romans and the Picts at University, he was keen to leave nothing to chance.

He had his own notes too for the Pictish lecture from visits to see the Rosemarkie stone at the Groam Museum, and the stones at Portmahomack, Shandwick and elsewhere, from his time in Inverness, together with 'In Search of the Picts' by Elizabeth Sutherland.

Ellis had phoned his tutor, Professor Calum Cameron, to ask if they could meet again. He particularly wanted to talk to him about some specific points for his lecture about Pompeii, Herculaneum and Si'pelium, aware that the cruise theme was the Romans. As the archaeologist on board he felt he should be prepared for questions at any time from passengers. It had been suggested to him that on these occasions there were often awkward passengers trying to show how clever they were by asking difficult questions. He had had visions of Rosemarie's parents when he heard that and was determined to be ready for them.

Vaila said she hoped he would keep time aside for Janet and herself. She also suggested that they had an evening with Liz and Jeff.

"After all you've surely had plenty of time at Pompeii and Herculaneum. Didn't you get enough from our honeymoon visits?"

"Ah, but you were distracting me then, I couldn't concentrate!" He teased Vaila, but none the less thought she was right. ToS could surely allow him to give one day to them.

So their plans were made. They would travel to Edinburgh on the Tuesday. He had arranged that the photos of Si'pelium would be sent to him at Treasures of Scotland's Archaeology office by the Wednesday. He would spend the morning there sorting them out, and then Christine would be able to scan the ones he wanted into his power point presentation, as Collard was visiting the Aberdeen office that day. The Thursday he would keep free to take Janet and Vaila out to the Falkirk Wheel and the Selkies. That evening Janet had invited Liz and Jeff to dinner. As she told Vaila,

"If they come here I will have the chance to see all four of you."

On Friday Ellis would meet Professor Cameron at eleven thirty for coffee at the Museum, to return his papers and photos and to discuss any further points that might arise from his research. Vaila would join them there for a light lunch. He would then spend the rest of the day on his lectures, including the evening if necessary. After that Ellis hoped he would have all his lectures ready and well polished. It would leave him the train journey to Dover on Saturday to complete his reading.

The journey to Inverness was uneventful, and he spent most of the train journey to Edinburgh reading the papers on Si'pelium and then making notes from a large volume on the Romans. It proved absorbing and useful for his revision and by the time the train pulled into Waverley station he felt confident his Roman lectures were satisfactorily complete.

The next day, Wednesday, proved wet so he took the bus to Treasures of Scotland's archaeology office. He found the slides Professor Cameron had sent waiting for him.

By lunch time he had sorted out those he needed for his lectures and offered to take Christine to lunch before she set to work on them, to thank her for all she was doing for him. After all she was saving him a lot of time by scanning them in.

They went to the Cambridge in Young Street and as they ate he asked how things were going in HQ. He got the impression from her cautious reply that she was unhappy with the archaeology department. She was considering asking to transfer to another department, so he asked what was wrong.

"Well it would be good to have a change," She started. The way she looked at him suggested she was trying to decide what she should tell him.

"Well." She paused, "Perhaps I shouldn't tell you this but I am worried by things going on here that aren't quite right, two specifically."

"I hope you feel you can tell me."

"Very well, but please don't give me away."

She explained that as she had worked in the archaeology office for three years she knew the way things were done, and had been given more and more responsibility as Collard came to trust her ability and discretion. Until recently she did everything to run the office, both for Treasures of Scotland and the Museum work Collard did too. For example she arranged, managed, set agendas and minuted meetings. Arranging travel and ordering office equipment and supplies she did as part of ensuring the departmental budget was adhered to. Naturally she also did the filing and typing, including all the confidential correspondence.

"For example I did all the typing concerning your interview and contract, the lot. I, er," and she paused again as if worried about saying more. He smiled to encourage her so she continued.

"I saw the horrible anonymous letter about you and Vaila. I hadn't heard of any rumour, and I wouldn't have believed a word of it even if I had. I asked afterwards what had happened. Collard had no

81

hesitation telling me how you squashed it at the interview, in fact he told me how all the interviews went, even that he had wanted someone else to have the Orkney job. He probably shouldn't have told me that, but it demonstrates my involvement in even the most confidential matters. Incidentally I was so relieved you squashed that rumour, Ellis."

"So was I. Vaila was furious, but we now think there never was a rumour in the first place. What's happened now?"

Christine told him there was something Collard was doing that he didn't want her to know about.

"Now, Ellis, all of a sudden he has decided all the Museum business must be done by Rosemarie, and all I had to do was to arrange that the filing cabinet with all the Museum files was moved to Rosemarie's office. All incoming post from or about the Museum is now to be given to Rosemarie unopened. She is to do all the typing herself and even her own posting. It is of course up to him how things are done, and he reassured me that it was not that I had done a bad job, so what's it all about?"

"That is odd. You said there was another matter that disturbed you?"

Christine hesitated. "Yes, well, it may be nothing, but it's very strange."

She went on to explain that she had gone into Rosemarie's office looking for a missing file one afternoon when Rosemarie and Collard were at the Museum and found her desk was clear of papers, and when she tried to look in the filing cabinet it was locked.

"Usually her desk is covered in papers, she's quite untidy, and we normally never lock filing cabinets, nobody does in ToS. I wondered if she's working on something secret. Then I noticed there was a lot of paper in her waste bin, and took a couple of pages out. They were full of French writing, and a lot of notes in English. She swears in French sometimes but it was news to me that she can speak or write it well enough to use it for her work."

"Did you keep any of the binned papers?"

"No."

"It doesn't matter, you wouldn't understand them any more than I would. Does ToS have any French partnerships?"

"Not in this department, no."

"Maybe she was sneakily doing a little private correspondence, naughty but I suppose we all do it occasionally."

Christine then wanted to ask him about Orkney and by the time they had finished lunch she was warming to the idea of coming to the islands for a holiday. She told Ellis that he'd given her plenty of good reasons to persuade her husband to take her, and Ellis had promised to help them have an interesting visit.

It was only later in the evening when he was telling Vaila what Christine had said that it occurred to Ellis that he should have asked what sort of relationship Rosemarie had with Collard.

The power point presentations complete, he took the bus back to his Mother's house, and felt he could confidently take Vaila and his mother to the Wheel and the Kelpies the next day.

The weather had given them a relaxing visit and Liz and Jeff arrived in good time for an excellent dinner Janet and Vaila had cooked. During a convivial meal they mainly talked about where Ellis and Vaila were going on the cruise. It was not until they were enjoying coffee that Jeff said.

"I've just remembered I've got a note for you."

"Who from?"

"Ritchie. I had a drink with him the other evening after work. I started to tell him about your lecturing afloat when he said he knew all about it. He had met Rosemarie by chance the previous weekend, and she had been full of ire about an upstart archaeologist in Treasures of Scotland, called Ellis Mackenzie, who had pinched two jobs she had wanted, Orkney and the cruise of course. She had been especially cross about the cruise because her parents were going on it, and had hoped they could get a substantial discount if she was lecturer.

"It didn't seem to occur to Rosemarie that Ritchie might know you, so he didn't enlighten her. Nor did he tell her that he had been told about her parents. Here is his scribbled note about that. It's hilarious!"

Hi, Ellis. Hope the lecture preparations are going well. Sorry I'll not see you before you float away, but you'll be amused to hear what an old college friend, another guy nearly ensnared by Rosemarie, has just told me about the McRavens. Seeing you are bound to meet them on the cruise I'm sure you'll be interested!

John, R's Father, met her mother, Danielle, in France when he was a junior military attaché in the British embassy in Paris around 25 years ago. She was a Parisienne socialite who had just had a scandalous affair with a French politician. She needed a husband to regain her social position, and chose John. Whilst he wasn't very bright, he and his family had valuable social connections. He wasn't difficult to seduce, as she was as attractive as her daughter now is, and would do whatever it took to get what she wanted for her own interests and ambitions.

There was some disquiet about their relationship by both the French and the Brits. The French weren't bothered about the steamy side of it, so much as fearful about what pillow talk secrets she might know and let slip. The Brits worried about a diplomatic *faux pas* because he is an idiot and would do anything she asked of him. Maybe some of his influential high society friends thought their own indiscretions might come to light too. So the Foreign office were persuaded to move them and they were sent to Moscow of all places. To make it look like promotion and nothing to do with his marriage to Danielle, he was given the rank of Colonel for the purpose. She of course went with him and to show she had become a loyal wife was now pregnant. Rosemarie of course.

But he was still an idiot and got caught in a honey trap in Moscow. The Foreign office had to do something about that, so he was persuaded to 'retire' with an offer of a good pension.

Danielle was furious with him but could hardly complain seeing she had been the honey in France. None the less she apparently sent him to Coventry (or whatever the French call it) and still speaks little. Doubtless she stays with him for his money and high society connections.

So he claims to have retired with honour, still calls himself colonel, and tries to ingratiate himself with those who he likes to call 'the people who matter' and is generally an unrepentant snob.

I do hope you enjoy cruising with them!

Give my love to Vaila.   Ritchie.

P.S. Rosemarie ended her diatribe about you by telling me she had another job, which 'that irritating man' would not be able to do, unless he's as fluent as she was. I suppose she meant fluent in French. Of course she's bilingual.

"Well, well well! I wonder if the job she told Ritchie about is linked in any way with the confidential thing she's doing for Collard that so bothers Christine?" Jeff laughed,

"I must remember that you are an irritating man!"

"I can see the advantage of you being irritating to *la belle Rosemarie*!" added Vaila.

"Have you done all your homework for your lectures Ellis?" asked Liz.

He explained that he had apart from going to see his old tutor at the University the next day.

"Prof Cameron has been very helpful, lending me some unpublished papers on Si'pelium and loads of photos that I must return."

"Talking about the University, Ellis, is that dear old Prof. Kantley still around?"

"No Liz, he died several months ago. How did you know him?"

"That's sad. I thought he was lovely old man. I used to have a job with a travel agent. He regularly came to me to book his visits to France. He was always going there, mainly a place called Carnac in Brittany. It apparently has a spectacular collection of standing stones. He went to the south, too, several times, something to do with the Cathars, so he told me though I'm not sure who or what they are. I didn't like to show my ignorance and never asked him. Come to think of it he could have pinched Rosemarie's new job if he was still around, if he spoke as good French as I think he did."

Ellis told them about Carnac and the Cathars, until Vaila gave him a big hint that they should talk about something - anything - else. Jeff picked up her hint and teased him about his archaeological obsession.

It was altogether a great evening and after Jeff and Liz had gone home, Ellis said he wanted to be at the Museum as soon as it opened in the morning.

"I'd like to see the display and whatever else they have on the Picts, before Cameron comes at eleven. We're meeting in the café there for coffee. You might like to join us for lunch, darling?"

Vaila agreed and said she'd come on the bus with him as she wanted to go into town anyway, the attraction being the opportunity to shop for some smart clothes for the cruise. She told him

"I want to ensure you will be proud of me." He had laughed at that.

"I'm proud of you anyway, and that sounds expensive, just as we've set up a joint account too! D'you think you'll get away with spending all our money my Piddie Maid? Your Magic Monster is watching!"

"Well if you ask me difficult questions, I may confess that I really want to be my most beautiful to seduce one - or even several - of the handsome officers on the ship, just to prove that anything Rosemarie can do I can do better! And, of course I need to make sure you don't take too much interest in the dancing girls!"

"Would I ever do such a thing?"

They caught an early bus, Ellis getting off near the Museum, leaving Vaila to carry on to Princes Street. Having had an interesting visit to the Pictish displays on the top floor of the Museum and made notes on a number of points to check with his lecture notes, Ellis went down to the café where the Professor shortly joined him. Over coffee Ellis returned the papers and photos he had borrowed, confirmed that Cameron had no problem with his using any of the material he had copied for his lectures and then discussed each of the lectures he was to give. The Professor was very encouraging.

After that they turned to the Ness of Brodgar and were about to move on to the question of what the Bustahead structure was when the Depute Museum Curator, David Singleton, approached them.

"Professor, I'm sorry to interrupt but I've just had a rather strange report from one of our volunteer guides related to next winter's exhibition. I feel I must tell you about it at once." Looking doubtfully at Ellis he continued, "It's a little delicate but it could be important so I wonder if I could interrupt your meeting for five minutes or so to seek advice? I just don't know what to do about it." He turned to Ellis "Would you mind terribly? It won't take long."

"Of course not. I have until lunch time." The Professor excused himself but promised to come back as soon as he could

"I'm keen to hear about your little underground find at Bustahead farm." He gave Ellis a file adding "Have a look at this while you wait, it's the draft programme for the winter's exhibition here. I hope I'll not be long."

Almost as soon as the Professor had left with the Depute Curator, Rosemarie came into the café, as smart as ever in green this time. She seemed to be looking for someone, and as Ellis was near to the door, he was the first person she saw. She seemed quite put out to see him.

"*Merde*. Not you again! You're bad luck for me. You're the last person I want to meet just now; you never know, you might see too much again! Must dash."

Before Ellis could reply she turned, took a step towards the door, stopped and turned back to him.

 "You must be on your way to the cruise ship, it sails tomorrow doesn't it? As you play clever clogs lecturing, remember, my Mum and Dad are on the cruise. I'll get a report on your performance when they get home." She smiled and looked cross at the same time and immediately walked out of the café. He could see her through the open door. She hurriedly went straight back out into the street. He wondered why she seemed so flustered, it wasn't like her at all. He couldn't believe she had been embarrassed by being caught with Collard on his previous visit to Edinburgh. It made him wonder what she was up to. He wasn't concerned about her Father. He didn't need Rosemarie or her parents to make him nervous, he knew he'd manage that all by himself, but he did start to wonder what they were like.

Cameron returned about fifteen minutes later.   "Sorry about that." He sat down. "Tell me about the Bustahead find."

Having described it and shown Cameron the photos he had taken of it when he had first explored it, Ellis asked the Professor what he thought it might be. The Professor looked through them again. He commented that from Ellis' description it was perfectly possible that his Bustahead find was a puzzle because it was never finished.

If you think of the process of building something like that, and consider how long it would take just to complete the basic structure, some unexpected event could easily have prevented its being put to the intended use."

They finished their business just as Vaila came into the café. She looked very pleased with herself. Ellis and the Professor stood up to greet her.

Ellis introduced them and greetings having been exchanged Professor Cameron asked her about Orkney. He said how much he had enjoyed his visits, not least the amazing archaeology.

"Now I expect you're looking forward to the cruise. Ellis had better look out, wives are usually a lecturer's harshest critics! Anyway, if you've been shopping you're probably hungry, so let's get lunch and perhaps you can persuade Ellis and me to talk about something other than archaeology. My wife gets to the stage where she demands archaeology free days!"

With lunch on the table Vaila said,

"You'll never guess who I saw just now. Your boss Collard, he was meeting Rosemarie."

She explained that she had seen Collard walking towards the Museum, but before he got to the door, Rosemarie came out of it. They had had a brief conversation as if she was asking Collard something. He pointed at the pub at the end of the street, and they went into it.

"After all you have told me, Ellis, I wanted to see what they were doing, so I went into the public bar. They were in the snug bar but I found I could see them from where I sat through a staff doorway connecting the two bars."

She told them that she could not hear what was said, and because the door was sometimes open and sometimes closed as the barman moved between customers in both bars, she could only get a general impression. Collard and Rosemarie were looking very conspiratorial. He took several blue files from his brief case and gave them to Rosemarie. It looked as if he was explaining something he wanted her to do. They seemed quite excited by what they were discussing. The door shut at that point, and when it opened again a few minutes later, she had seen Rosemarie get up to go. When she had gone, Collard seemed to be checking that no one had seen them.

"So I moved quickly from his line of sight." She concluded. "What do you think they were doing?"

"I saw her too only twenty five minutes ago, it must've been just before you saw them outside. She came in here, clearly not keen to see me, and went straight out again."

Cameron asked why Vaila thought their meeting unusual.

"She's his assistant, you would expect them to discuss what they're doing wouldn't you?"

"Yes, but yesterday Ellis told me that Christine, their secretary, was worried that Rosemarie was doing something for Collard that he appeared to want to keep secret. That's why I was curious."

Cameron paused a moment.

"I wonder. There is a coincidence here, between what you have just seen, Vaila, and what David has just told me. He didn't want to say anything in front of you, Ellis, as he knew you worked with Collard, but maybe you can help."

The Professor then explained that once the Museum Trustees had decided on the winter exhibition theme a couple of months back, each Trustee who had the appropriate contacts was to approach them to ask for loans of items the Curator recommended should be included in the exhibition.

Collard had little to offer, Treasures of Scotland did not hold much that fitted into the exhibition theme. As he was keen to be part of the preparations to emphasize Treasures of Scotland's involvement in the Museum, he had volunteered to take charge of the reception and safe storage of items as they arrived. The Curators would then unpack and prepare exhibits prior to arranging their display.

"That work requires space, but at the moment none of our workrooms are available, so it was proposed that we clear a large basement room which was full of odds and ends dumped there over several years, and several large cupboards stuffed full of old papers, mainly duplicate minutes and so on of old and long forgotten Trustee and committee meetings. As staff were in the midst of all that goes on here in the Music Festival, including some fringe events held in the Museum, Collard said he'd deal with as much as he could himself."

Cameron then described what was bothering David. He had asked one of their volunteer guides, when he had a spare moment, to take some bin bags down to the basement where Collard was working because he was not sure if Collard knew that the redundant papers in the basement would need to be ready for the recycle collection next day.

What had troubled the volunteer was that Collard was stuffing several blue files into a large brief case when he opened the door. Collard had been very cross with the volunteer for interrupting him, and told him to get out of room. He didn't want to be disturbed, and so on. He was very rude. The man was one of the Museum's longest standing helpers, so had told David about it because he was so upset by the way Collard had spoken to him. David felt he could not say anything himself to a Trustee such as Collard, but had asked Cameron what he should do. The Professor had told David that he'd deal with it; volunteers were very important to the Museum. He intended to ask Collard to apologise, although, of course, he had not yet been able to do so.

"Are the papers written in French, by any chance?"

"I don't know. Why do you ask, Vaila?"

"Christine thought French had something to do with Rosemarie's mysterious project. That's what she told you, Ellis, didn't she?"

"Yes." He looked at Vaila, and was not surprised when she added. "What about Ritchie's note too?" Ellis turned to Professor Cameron,

"We keep hearing things, all of which have French in common. Is there any way to find out if any of the papers in the basement are in French?"

The Professor stood up and waved to David who he had seen in the entrance hall. When he came through the Professor asked

"David, your volunteer. Is he still here?"

"I'm afraid not. He's just left to go on a week's camping holiday. We can't even phone him, he has no mobile and I've no idea where he's going."

"Pity. I'd like to see him when he gets back. Another, different, question for you. "How well did you know Kantley? Did he come in much?" David laughed

"So you've guessed his secret! He was also a Trustee of course. He loved the Museum, he spent hours here. He used that basement room, though not many people knew. I cleared about a quarter of the room, arranged for a desk and reading light and so on for him. He wanted to work there. He said it was the only place in all Edinburgh where he could have peace; no one went down there. There was no phone, no computer spitting out emails, nothing to interrupt him. I used to get him everything he needed, including his sandwich lunch. He always had prawn cocktail on brown bread, a chocolate brownie and coffee. I was sworn to secrecy, yet even I had no idea what he was doing. He never said, and I never asked. A wonderful man, so self-sufficient, I really think he was happiest when working here!"

"Thank you." David had to get back to other duties and left them.

"Hum. Poor old Kantley, that's his cat out of the bag. But what is your boss up to Ellis? It's tempting to wonder if he was enjoying assignations with his glamorous assistant here, but it's hardly a suitable place for a love nest is it!" Ellis laughed,

"I could offer a little evidence on that score, but it doesn't fit with the strange French connection."

"Nor blue files neither."

"We have, in random order," Ellis ticked off each point on his fingers, "Rosemarie is bilingual in French as our friend Ritchie told us. Christine found that her secret project involved working in French, perhaps translating." He paused. "Collard spent an unusual amount of time in the basement when some of it had already been cleared; the Volunteer saw Collard taking blue files from there and Vaila saw him give them to Rosemarie." He ran out of fingers and had to change hands.

"Liz, another friend of ours knew Kantley was a fluent French speaker. He worked alone in the basement. But what … " He stopped, and looked at the Professor.

"Kantley's missing draft?"

"Good gracious." The professor looked from Ellis to Vaila and back again. "You always were a bright student! Let's order more coffee and think this through."

With the coffee Cameron spoke as if thinking aloud.

"Yes. I'd forgotten, until you reminded me, how much of a Francophile Kantley was. So what are Collard and his pretty assistant up to?" He drank half his coffee in silence, and then continued, slowly,

"I really don't want to think what I am thinking. Its implications are disgraceful, unethical and probably illegal. I hope my imagination is leading me astray but I have a nasty suspicion."

He drank the rest of his coffee and looked at them both. When he spoke he had made a decision.

"I think you two should go on your cruise and I will make more enquiries when the volunteer gets back next week. We mustn't start accusing Collard and his glamour girl of anything until we're sure."

Ellis thanked his mentor for all the help he had given so generously as they got up from the table. He collected his notes together and put them in his shoulder bag as the Professor wished him good luck with his lectures.

"Just enjoy it all! If there is any firm news I can get in touch one way or another. Perhaps I won't even have to."

As they left the museum Ellis was wondering what Cameron meant by his last remark and then remembered to ask Vaila.

"How did your shopping go?"

"I'll show you at home. I'll need to try the dress on again anyway."

When they left they walked up to the Royal mile and towards North Bridge to find a bus stop to go back to Janet's house. On the corner they literally bumped into Peter Keise walking towards them, with a woman beside him, holding the hand of a small boy. They greeted each other with enthusiasm, and Peter introduced Chrissie, his wife, and their son, Jamie. Vaila with a bright smile, shook the boy's hand, "Hello, I'm Vaila."

"I'm Jamie and I'm five."

"So where have you been today."

"Mummy took me shopping. I got a blazer. I'm going to school next term. Daddy says it'll be fun and I'll learn lots of things." Chrissie interrupted,

 "Jamie you mustn't chatter on. You should be introducing yourself to Ellis too!"

Jamie eyed Ellis as if he was not so sure of him, so Ellis smiled, and bending down shook Jamie's hand. "I'm Ellis, how d'you do Master Jamie." As he did so his shoulder bag slipped and fell on the pavement and a book slid out of it. Jamie rescued it and offered it to Ellis without a word.

"Thank you, Jamie, that was very kind of you." He smiled and stood up, and complimented Chrissie and Peter on their helpful boy. Looking at Jamie again "I think that deserves an ice cream, if Mummy and Daddy agree."

"We were going to the Pizza Express over there", Chrissie pointed across the street. "Why don't you join us?"

"Come on!" Jamie grabbed Vaila's hand.

Jamie kept them all entertained, during which Ellis was able to ask Peter about his application to play on a cruise ship.

"He got it. I wish he wasn't going," Chrissie answered for him, "But we need the money. Jamie and I will miss him but perhaps we will be able to have a little outing on his return."

"To the Zoo" said Jamie firmly. Peter laughed, "Yes the Zoo, I promise Jamie!" He turned to Ellis and explained that he had been contracted to be the resident pianist on the *Carnelian* for a probationary period of a month, starting with a cruise departing the next day. Clearly neither Chrissie nor Peter were very happy at his being away, but, as Peter put it, it was difficult to judge whether the income was worth his absences without trying it.

Ellis asked if the cruise was the 'Roman World' one, and they were delighted to find they would both be working on the same cruise. Ellis and Vaila were going to Dover by train and Peter by the night bus, because it was the cheapest way to go, so they'd meet again on board.

Whilst the men were talking Jamie had pointed to Vaila's bag, because he had spotted the little dog mascot attached to the strap.

"What's the dog's name?"

"I haven't given him a name Jamie. What do think it should be?"

"Lassie. Definitely. She must be a girl as she's on your bag."

"Then Lassie she shall be!"

"Excuse me." Ellis said and went to the counter and paid the bill. When he returned Peter, who had seen what he had done, protested that he wanted to share it, but Ellis just smiled

"We've had a great time, and Jamie has been a most entertaining host." Turning to Jamie, Ellis continued "One day, Jamie, perhaps your Dad will play in our music festival in Orkney and you could come too on a big ship like the one Daddy, Vaila and I are going on."

"Do you have ice creams where you live?"

"Yes Jamie and lovely cheese, and best of all fudge. Lots of flavours of wonderful sweet fudge!"

Jamie looked at his parents again. He wasn't sure he understood. "Can we?"

"We'll see, but now we really must go as Daddy has to get ready to catch his overnight bus."

Chrissie agreed they should keep in touch, and gave Vaila her phone number which she wrote in her diary.

"See you on the ship." Ellis and Peter said to each other, and they went their separate ways.

The *Carnelian*

Their train left Waverley at 6.20am on Saturday. Janet took them to the station, leaving the house just after five.

At that time the city still awaited dawn, the first hint of which showed in the eastern sky. There had been overnight rain. The street lights reflected in the wet road surface so that they looked as if they had been polished.

A few delivery vans, the occasional early pedestrian and a couple of men running in streets free of traffic were the only hint of the city awakening.

With so little traffic they arrived at Waverley half an hour before really necessary although they did not mind. As Vaila put it, misquoting;

"For want of an early start the train would be lost. For the want of a train the cruise would be lost."

Janet risked parking on Market Street and came with them to meet Minnie and Millie at platform 19 as they had arranged, and to see them off. If the rest of the city was not fully awake, the station certainly was. It had already started the day, and was busy preparing trains and gathering passengers for their journeys.

They wheeled their luggage along the platform to their train. Janet spotted the carriage where their reserved table seats were. They quickly stowed their luggage, and having done so got off again to say good bye to Janet. Having plenty of time they stood by the train for several minutes talking to her.

About ten minutes prior to departure Vaila suggested Janet might like to go home without waiting for the train to leave, as the early morning was a bit chilly. But Janet wanted to see them off, and Vaila thought she looked a little sad. She gave her a warm hug. After Janet wished them *bon voyage*, Vaila and Ellis climbed back into the train with Minnie and Millie.

Sitting in their seats they smiled to each other through the window and as the train started to move, they waved until they could no longer see each other.

"Your Mum seemed sad, and a bit reluctant to leave us, Ellis."

"She always is. She took Dad to the airport to catch the flight on which he died, but left him there rather than wait for it with him. I don't think she's ever forgiven herself for not staying with him until the last minute."

They settled into their seats around the table and Vaila talked of many things with Minnie and Millie whilst Ellis reread 'In Search of the Picts' as he had planned. The journey went quickly and agreeably. Vaila felt she had soon got to know Millie almost as well as Minnie.

Unlike Minnie, Millie was quite short. She had dark hair tied back tightly, and whilst at first she seemed rather serious, her underlying bubbly sense of humour constantly rose to the surface. Each of the ladies claimed the other was the eccentric one to Vaila's amusement. They had both been teachers and loved being with children, although neither had had children of their own. To travel Millie wore a tweed skirt and a warm jumper, which she was already finding a lot too hot in the train.

Their carriage was nearly full by the time they reached York, and looking out of the window as the train came to a halt Ellis saw a man in a smart overcoat with a very large suitcase hurrying down the platform looking through the windows for his seat. He got into the carriage they were in just before the whistle was blown, the doors shut, and the train started to move. His next problem was to find a space for the large suitcase. When he had done that, he walked towards them, ticket and reservation in hand, searching for his reserved seat, which turned out to be opposite and just in front of their own table seats.

However a thickset man in a scruffy sweater and jeans, was sitting in it. The new arrival pointed out politely that the seat was reserved for him, and showed his reservation, but the man refused to move. He said it was his seat, and would not even show his reservation. He became quite aggressive over it. There seemed no other free seat, the only one not actually occupied was directly opposite Ellis and Vaila but it was covered by a number of bags belonging to an elderly lady who was fast asleep next to it.

Whilst the newcomer stood wondering what to do next, the ticket inspector came into the carriage asking for tickets from York. The newcomer showed his ticket and reservation and told him that the man occupying it would not give him his seat.

The ticket inspector asked the seated man where he was going, and for his ticket and reservation. The grunted reply was

"Manchester."

"I'm terribly sorry Sir, but this is the London train." He looked at the ticket and reservation. "The seat number is correct but this is the London train."

"So what? I will leave this seat only when the train stops at Manchester."

"Sir, you have got on the wrong train. This one goes nowhere near Manchester. It goes nonstop to London Kings Cross. Your only option is to get another train from Euston back to Manchester."

"You bloody people just can't run a railway properly can you? Well I'm still staying in this seat. As for you in the posh coat, you're stupid if you think you can make me move."

There was a tense pause. The ticket inspector looked down the carriage for free seats, and was about to speak when the man in the overcoat started laughing. He looked at the man in his seat

"Me? Stupid? That's wonderful, coming from a man who can't even get on the right train!"

Ellis couldn't help himself, he burst out laughing too, shortly joined by the ladies, Vaila and several others in the coach who had heard what had been said. The seated men went red in the face, he looked furious. The ticket inspector held up his hand to try to bring peace to the situation. He spoke to the old lady with the bags, who had been woken by the laughter.

"Can I put your bags in the rack for you so this gentleman can use the seat? Maybe you would find him a congenial neighbour?"

"Oh, Yes, but I can't reach up there and I'll not be able to get them down again."

"I'll do that for you," the overcoated man replied, smiling at her.

When the seat was cleared the newcomer removed his overcoat to reveal the uniform of a two striped merchant navy officer and, sitting down beside the elderly lady, they soon started a conversation.

At that the coach settled down to enjoy the rest of the journey. Ellis returned to 'In Search of the Picts' until he overheard the officer mention the *Carnelian*. In a pause in his conversation, Ellis leaned across and asked if by any chance he was on his way to the cruise ship *Carnelian*.

"Yes, I am returning from leave. I'm one of her watch officers, Second Officer Paul Unwin. Why do you ask?"

Ellis told him they were also on their way to join the same ship for the Roman World cruise,

"I am Ellis Mackenzie, and I'm giving the archaeological lectures. This is my wife, Vaila, and my aunt, Minette Mackenzie, and her friend Mildred Stone."

"Paul Unwin." He repeated, smiling, and got up to shake their hands. They promised to look out for each other and then the officer resumed his conversation with the elderly lady, who clearly enjoyed his company.

When the train pulled into Kings Cross, Second Officer Unwin got up and retrieved the lady's bags from the rack and put them on his seat. He put on his coat, and offered to help her off the train. He turned to Ellis with a smile.

"See you on board. I'm sure we'll have a pleasant cruise, the forecast is excellent for the Med during our voyage, though I'm not so sure about the Bay of Biscay! Not to worry, she's a good ship."

Paul Unwin helped the old lady off the train with her bags, which he put on a trolley with his own case, and he walked towards the exit with her.

Ellis got their cases onto a second trolley, and the ladies carried the smaller items they had. It was a simple change of trains. They just had to cross the road to St Pancras, and they were soon settled in the Dover train watching London give way to the Kent countryside.

As they passed Ashford and Eurostar had flashed by, the contrast with Orkney struck Ellis.

"Isn't it amazing how different this countryside is to Orkney."

"Yes, It all looks so soft, and it would seem gentle too if it wasn't that there's yet another town round each bend." Vaila commented.

Ellis closed his book having finished it and replied

"That's really why Orkney has so much archaeology for us to study. There must have been at least as many folk living here 6000 years ago as in Orkney, yet very little remains here now. Coupled with the abundance of timber, which of course only rarely survives that long, and little or no stone to build with, settlements just kept being rebuilt. Nothing was kept. In Orkney they built to last as stone is hard to work, and it has survived because it's durable and there was not a lot to disturb it."

"Ellis, please Darling, enough lessons in archaeology! I want to see what there is to see. We must be getting close?"

"Sorry! Yes, we should pass the Channel Tunnel terminal soon, I should think."

Shortly after they passed the Tunnel Terminal they went through Folkestone station without stopping and plunged into a short tunnel. They emerged with the sea beside them to the right of the train. They were amazed to see so much shipping. Some, judging from their course, were cross channel ferries, but most were cargo vessels passing through the Straights. But there was not much time to look before another short tunnel. When they next could see, Millie spotted the end of the breakwater protecting Dover harbour.

They looked for their ship, with its bright orange funnel pictured in the cruise brochure. Before they could see it a third tunnel blacked out the view again. This time, when they emerged they could not only see the end of the harbour breakwater but much of the harbour, marked by large buildings, cranes and ships, but there was not enough time to look for their ship. A moment later they were in a fourth, longer, tunnel and the train slowed. When daylight returned the train was drawing into Dover Priory Station.

A taxi was waiting for Paul and the other four took another from several waiting by a board with 'Carnelian' on it. It was a tight fit for them all and their luggage but it was only a short journey to the docks.

As the taxi turned a corner they saw a gateway signed 'Cruise Terminal'. They passed through it and then saw a ships funnel painted bright orange, towering above the surrounding buildings and the clutter of the dockyard. Ellis saw Vaila's excitement. It matched his own eagerness. They all looked to see what they could of the ship. She looked enormous from the road, confusing memories of the brochure's description of the *Carnelian* as a small cruise ship.

Everything that had led to this moment, the interview and the rumour that never was, their wedding and Italian honeymoon, the Ness of Brodgar and the invitation at first denied, and all that had happened on their way to the ship, all these events were over.

The *Carnelian* was waiting for them.

*   *   *   *   *

The Cruise

At Sea

The hall in which passengers checked in for the cruise was busy. As passengers arrived their luggage was taken by porters who told them it would be delivered direct to their cabin.

The staff were all wearing orange coloured blazers, and one approached them asking for their cabin numbers. They were directed to one of the desks where their tickets and passports were processed, and once these formalities were completed they were given an embarkation number, and asked to wait where there were a large number of seats near a refreshment counter. Ellis bought four coffees and biscuits and they sat down to await their boarding number being called. It enabled them to look around at their fellow passengers.

On seats just in front of them sat a very smart couple. The man was not tall, and he wore a Barbour jacket, under which Ellis saw, when he removed his jacket, a blazer with a regimental tie. He had beside him a fashionable and expensive hand case. Vaila could see on his face a permanent look of superiority, as if he was uncomfortable to be with the common herd. His voice similarly revealed a cut glass accent that defined his belief in his superiority, not that they spoke much. His wife was an elegant woman of perhaps fifty, who sat looking around with the ghost of a smile. They were near enough that her subtle expensive perfume reached Ellis and Vaila.

There was an announcement over the Tannoy "If Mr and Mrs Ellis Mackenzie are here, could they please make themselves known to the staff."

Ellis got up and spoke to a girl in an orange blazer nearby who said,

"Would you and your wife come with me. The Cruise Director would like to meet you."

They told Minnie and Millie to carry on and board when their turn came, and picked up their hand luggage. As they went Ellis saw out of the corner of his eye, the smart man's look of surprise.

"Excuse me," he said to the girl "We should be meeting the Director surely, we're first class?"

"No, Sir. The meeting is just for staff." The man looked happier at that, but he still seemed put out that he was not getting special treatment.

The Cruise Director introduced himself as Jonny Wirth. He warmly welcomed them to the *Carnelian* and gave Ellis an envelope, explaining that it contained details of a meeting that evening for the entertainment, lecture and shore excursions teams. He told them they could go on board as soon as they liked.

To do so they walked up a zigzag passage similar to an aircraft air bridge though much larger. At the top a photographer was taking souvenir photos of all who were boarding. On the ship they had their photos taken again for the ship's security system, and they were each given a credit card sized 'cruise card' with which they would be checked on and off the ship at every port they visited. The card was also used to buy any extras on board. Cash was not used on the ship. They were then shown to their cabin.

They were delighted with it. Whilst not especially large, it had all they needed for the cruise. It was warm, cosy and had a window (port hole, Ellis said) with a wide view. Ellis put his document case on the desk/dressing table and in the next hour or so they went through the routine of unpacking, lifeboat drill and reading all the information in the cabin about the ship and things they could do aboard.

The most useful paper was the day's programme, which was contained in a newsletter called 'The *Carnelian* Daily.' It was packed with information about the facilities on board, when meals were served, and especially the events of the day. It even had a schedule for the various channels they could watch on the cabin TV. A copy for the following day would be delivered after dinner each evening.
'Britain today' was a separate summary of home news, and they were glad to see it included some Scottish items.

The 'Daily' told them that afternoon tea was about to be served in the Ocean lounge.

It was their first taste of on board dining, comprising a large table laden with sandwiches, little hot snacks and a tempting display of scones, cakes and pastries, from which they were to help themselves.

"If this happens every afternoon I'm going to end up tons heavier by the time we get home." Vaila laughed. As they finished tea, they felt the vibration as the engines started to ease the *Carnelian* from the quayside and then set sail from Dover harbour, so they went on deck to watch.

Immediately outside the harbour the cruiseship was enveloped in a light sea mist. The mist meant that they could not see anything much further than half a mile away, and then only as shadows. To Vaila's especial disappointment they could not see the famous White Cliffs of Dover at all, but there was compensation. As the sun gently penetrated the light mist around the ship, it sparkled on the wave tops their bow wave created, making patterns which came and went as the wave spread out away from the ship.

Vaila remarked that it was beautiful yet ephemeral, the sort of beauty that could never be captured, never be reproduced, it was there just to light up the start of their cruise.

They returned to their cabin just before Ellis was to go to his meeting, so Vaila said she would spend the time exploring the ship. When they met again later Vaila was full of what a beautiful ship the *Carnelian* was.

"Do you remember that scruffy ship we saw from Marwick Head? I think it was called the *Camel Prince* but it couldn't have been more different to this ship!" Ellis nodded,

"That's right if my little grey cells are working properly. Such a strange name for a ship."

Vaila continued to describe how impressed she was at the wide range of facilities available. Two pools, one on the lowest passenger deck, the other on the open deck, a fitness room, several spaces devoted to different games, and a well stocked library in which Wi-Fi was available. There were several computers you could use. Apart from the main dining room, called the Equator Restaurant, there was the Island Cafeteria, from which diners could go out onto the open deck in good weather. It was referred to as the Quarterdeck.

She had even been up to the highest point passengers could reach, the Sun Deck. There were two wings to it overlooking the Quarterdeck, and forward, one could look over the rail at the wings of the bridge. The sea mist had cleared by that time and she told Ellis what a great view she had had there, in all directions, though she was a bit cold by that time so she had come down again.

Ellis then told her the arrangements agreed at the staff meeting, His first lecture was the following morning, billed as 'Orkney, the Centre of Britain.' His second lecture, on Pompeii and Herculaneum, had also been scheduled.

A fellow lecturer, David Grey, who would be giving the talks about each port visited, had suggested Ellis might like to link his lecture about Si'pelium to the one he would give on Albysia, this talk being scheduled for the morning after they left Naples. David was concerned that there wasn't much to say about the country so hoped that if they made it a joint lecture it would be much more interesting. Ellis thought it an excellent idea so had agreed. His lecture on the Picts was, of course held in reserve, although Jonny Wirth had said that it might be needed after they had left Naples.

Ellis commented on what a pleasant group of staff he thought they were.

He had also met Peter, who had told him that he would be playing each afternoon at tea, and in the evening before dinner in the Seafarer's Bar, and that later in the cruise he had been asked to give a classical recital.

Ellis suggested to Vaila that they should have a drink there with Minnie and Millie before dinner. "Come to think of it, we've yet to hear Peter play!"

Back in their cabin they worked out what to wear to match the 'casual' dress code described in 'The *Carnelian* Daily'. They phoned Minnie and Millie's cabin and arranged to meet them at six thirty at the Seafarer's Bar.

Peter was already playing when they arrived, so Ellis ordered drinks and they all sat at a table by a window as the evening light, reflecting the smooth calm sea, faded into night.

Peter saw them and smiled as he played, a gentle smile as much to himself as to them. He looked comfortable, totally absorbed and happy in his love of the music. They were all impressed by the way he played from memory, effortlessly moving from one number to the next, improvising interesting modulations of key and time. The range of music amazed them too. Bach to boogie, Mantovani to Mozart, Elgar to Ellington. Peter played them in random order and never wavered whatever requests he received.

Minnie sat next to Vaila. She plunged in by asking Vaila how she had first met Ellis, if she didn't mind talking about it. Vaila was so relaxed in Minnie's company that she found herself telling the whole story of their adventures in Orkney together just the previous year. She ended,

"For once my big brother approved. He always told me what he thought of my boyfriends and certainly didn't hesitate to tell me how dreadful my previous boyfriend was. I ignored him and suffered for it, so I was relieved when he said he liked Ellis. Now Hal and Ellis are good friends."

"I was just as critical when my brother Charles, Ellis' Dad, started to go out with his Mum. I was a terrible little sister and teased him mercilessly about their romance. I'm so glad they ignored me or Ellis would never have been born! But I wondered once or twice whether Charles put my best boyfriend off, by telling him about it."

"He was far too nice a man to do that." Millie joined in, then laughed "Come on Minnie, it's your cooking that must have put them off! No man would tolerate your dreadful cooking! Even on the rare occasions, like last week, when you make a half decent cake you go and ruin it."

"It wasn't my fault it rained."

"It was you who put it in the garden to cool down."

"Well I was trying to impress you, and it was too hot!" They both thought the incident hilarious, but Vaila sensed the wistfulness in Minnie's voice. Vaila changed the subject.

"Isn't Peter good," forgetting for a moment that the ladies had not met him. Millie looked at the floor and quietly said she must go to the Powder room. When she was out of earshot Minnie said,

"Poor Millie. I should have told you. Peter was her husband's name. He died of cancer when they had only been married two or three years. They had no children and every now and again a memory sort of catches her out. She'll soon recover. She was a wonderful teacher, so kind, so good to the children, she really cared about them. Losing her Peter and having no children of her own must really hurt. Life can be so cruel. She's a wonderful friend, and very observant." Minnie did not seem to think that she was herself in a similar situation.

Dinner was at seven so after they had enjoyed Peter's playing for a while, they made their way to the Equator restaurant. On the way they came across a large display of the photos the ship's photographer had taken of passengers as they came aboard. Vaila wanted to see if they were on it so the four of them looked through the pictures. Minnie and Millie quickly spotted theirs, But Vaila drew Ellis attention to a different picture.

"Look, that's Red Check Shirt isn't it?"

"It's certainly like him. If so he's come on this trip alone again, by the look of it. I hope he'll not get into bother at Naples this time. What's his name again?" Neither of them could remember.

They were taken to a table for eight where two couples were already seated. They introduced themselves, by Christian name. On Vaila's left was Mark, and beyond him his wife Heather. Helen and Jim sat to Ellis' right, and they were soon in conversation. Minnie and Millie sat between the couples on the far side of the table.

Jim and Helen had cruised before many times, and were full of all they had done previously. But they soon embarrassed themselves in their enthusiasm to play the old hands.

Helen said to Ellis, "Carnelian Cruises are good so long as the lecturers are good. Apparently they have had to get some new archaeologist this time. Someone Scottish. He apparently comes from Orkney, which is so remote that we're a bit doubtful if he'll be any good or could have anything interesting to say. The place is right up in the North of Scotland, somewhere miles away."

Vaila overheard, and nudged Ellis with her foot under the table. She looked a bit put out although Ellis just chuckled, and turned back to Helen.

"Where are you from?"

"Old Brompton Road. In London of course."

"Orkney isn't far from London, though London is a very long way from Orkney. But then London's miles from any place real isn't it?"

She looked at him surprised and puzzled, so he thought he'd better tell her. He smiled broadly

"I'm afraid I'm the substitute lecturer, the Orcadian archaeologist you have doubts about. My wife Vaila is an Orcadian born and bred, although she has a Shetland name, and we live in Kirkwall. To an archaeologist Orkney is as near heaven as can be on earth, and was probably the very centre of British culture five or six thousand years ago, before London was invented. That's what I shall be lecturing about tomorrow. I hope you'll both come and I'll do my best to persuade you to come to Orkney and see for yourselves – as well as entertain you!"

"Oh, so sorry, I wasn't very tactful was I?" She was clearly worried that Ellis would think badly of her, and was relieved when he laughed.

"I'll forgive you! Don't worry, I'm not the slightest bit offended. It's quite funny really. I just hope I can put your doubts to rest tomorrow. Now, tell me about some of your favourite ports, and what you think is the best thing about cruising."

So they developed an interesting conversation on a large range of places and what each offered to visitors. It lasted most of the meal. He thought they were a very pleasant couple, yet had a feeling that Jim, Helen's husband, looked a bit uncomfortable, as if he was not entirely happy in the company of strangers.

Vaila, once sure Ellis had gently corrected Helen about Orkney, asked Mark, sitting next to her, what he did.

"I'm a civil servant, just a Sir Humphry. Not always a popular thing to be but fascinating much of the time. I work in the Ministry of Transport."

She noticed that he was strictly vegetarian and fussy that everything should be just right. The white wine was not cold enough, the fish a bit over cooked and the cream on his apple tart was, as he described it, artificial. He obviously wanted everything to be 'just so'. For all that she found him interesting, as he clearly knew many famous politicians. He described how Whitehall worked and said,

"It really is a bit like 'Yes Minister'!"

Heather also had a good Whitehall job in a different section of the same ministry, and had an extraordinarily detailed interest and knowledge of what to Vaila were useless statistics. Although she looked rather severe, and seemed uncomfortable with things or ideas beyond those which could be proven and were within the rules and conventions, underneath she did reflect a kindness of spirit. She was the sort that felt a duty to help anyone remain within the bounds of her rather rigid world. Vaila wondered if either of the Meads had much of an imagination.

At ten the next morning, Ellis was in the Ocean Lounge speaking to Norrie, who dealt with projection sound and lights. Norrie sorted out Ellis' power point programme and showed him the controls for it on the podium, so that by the time his audience was seated he was ready. Vaila took a seat to the right of the stage and thought he looked a bit nervous. At least he had a large audience.

The Cruise Director, Jonny Wirth, acted as chairman and introduced Ellis as 'Our Archaeologist from the far North of Scotland'.

Ellis started with a wonderful photo of Skara Brae with the Bay of Skail in the background on a bright sunny day, explaining that Skara Brae was unique. A stone age village which is so well preserved that it is possible to imagine the life of the inhabitants. It had been covered in sand, until revealed after a severe storm in 1850, similar, it is believed, to the storm that must have covered it around 2600 BC. Radiocarbon dating suggested that it was built and first occupied before 3100 BC thus was a working village for around 600 years.

Accompanied by his Power Point presentation he described the seven houses and a workshop, how they were connected by a covered close, and the way all the buildings had been kept warm by being buried to the tops of the walls by a clay-like mix of refuse, ashes, shells, bones, sand and other domestic detritus which helped protect the village from the elements.

"Did you know that damp-proof courses were invented over 5,000 years ago? The foundations and floors of the houses have a layer of blue clay under them which would have worked as well as polythene does today."

He described the surrounding landscape as it would have been then, including a freshwater loch behind the sand dunes above the beach. It too might have been filled by sand in the same storm that buried the village. It appeared that some villagers tried to use the houses for a while after the big storm but eventually it was totally abandoned, defeated by sand. Speaking of the construction of the houses he commented that they were of roughly the same design,

"Look too at the dressers and the beds, all much the same and made of stone. Perhaps there was an Orcadian Wimpey house builder and stone age Ikea flat pack furniture in those days!"

He explained the archaeological evidence by which they could work out how Neolithic folk lived, especially picking out details of the artefacts uncovered in the village, things like the use of bone. Even the roof rafters were whale bone; a large whale stranding would provide many of their needs.

"Some of the Skara Brae houses have small cells, possibly toilets, as they have drains. Interestingly they are very similar to the cells in chambered burial cairns, which conveniently leads us to the amazing public structures the people of those days built. Neolithic Orcadians had big ideas, original and ambitious."

He illustrated three structures, part of the 'Heart of Neolithic Orkney World Heritage site', Maeshowe, the Stones of Stenness, and the Ring of Brodgar. Between the latter two was the most remarkable site of all, the recent find at the Ness of Brodgar.

Describing the spread of stone circles, he projected a map of Britain on the screen.

"There are a large number of stone circles in Britain. From Orkney they can be found all the way to Cornwall, including the Hurlers, a group of three, possibly four rings at Minions, near Liskeard, which Professor Gerald was to have spoken about.

"Carbon dating shows that, whilst Stonehenge is the best known and most spectacular, those on Orkney such as Stenness and Brodgar were the first. By itself that suggests that the ideas that led to their building must have been formulated in Orkney. The evidence for Orkney being the origin of the beliefs that motivated people to build stone circles, is becoming even stronger with the current excavation and research at the Ness of Brodgar. These ideas appear to have been exported to the south, indeed there is enough evidence to say that there was not only extensive trade with the south but also pilgrimage in some form."

He went on to speak about the Ness of Brodgar, and the UHI partnership project in which he was involved on behalf of Treasures of Scotland.

"The site contains the remains of both the largest group of Neolithic stone buildings, and undoubtedly the biggest single Neolithic building known to have existed anywhere."

He described the buildings, their construction and the evidence of their use, the trade they must have involved and the conclusions the team drew from all the site's discoveries in other ways.

"If that is not spectacular enough, the evidence suggests that during a grand event over four hundred cattle were slaughtered for a feast, after which all the buildings were systematically destroyed. We have yet to discover why, but it does suggest Orkney was a very wealthy place 5000 years ago." He ended his lecture,   "The research goes on. The more we explore the site, the more fascinating it becomes. Maybe the team, me included, will end up being buried there although we might be lonely; only one other human skeleton has been found, another mystery to solve!"

He sat down to enthusiastic applause, wondering if he really deserved it. Vaila looked pleased.

Jonny Wirth asked if there were any questions, and the first one was how did stone age people cross the Pentland Firth, one of the most treacherous stretches of sea around Britain.

Ellis, in a frivolous moment replied, "Not in stone boats I assure you!" a joke that went down well, and he then described the sort of boats it was believed that the people built. He had been part of a group that had made a replica and had paddled it across the Firth.

"It proved reasonably seaworthy but extremely wet and uncomfortable, not at all like the *Carnelian*!"

Mark, who they had met the previous evening, asked if there was any sign of what the people at Skara Brae did and made.

Ellis explained that building eight at Skara Brae was believed to have been a workshop, as it had no beds.

"It contained quite a lot of chert, some of which had been heated. This stone, when split, is quite sharp so was used to make cutting and scraping tools. Local domestic pottery was made too, some decorated with geometric patterns. It is called Grooved Ware. It is thought unlikely that they could spin wool. But clothing must have been made, and wool and sheepskin were the best and easiest materials for the purpose. There would have been some timber washed up and whale bone from beached animals, as I mentioned earlier."

The last question came from the smart man who had sat in front of them at check in.

"You have said little or nothing about the ceramics found at Ness of Brodgar, but then, of course, you are not an expert in that field."

A warning bell rang in Ellis' mind. He replied with care.

"Those of us who study the stone age cover the pottery of the period too. In the case of the Ness of Brodgar there have been very few pottery shards found so far, and only a single whole pot. This suggests that the buildings at the Ness were not dwellings, but were for public and probably religious purposes which is consistent with other evidence. The pot is in a style called ring wear. It would probably have been imported." He saw but did not hear what the man said to his wife. It looked like criticism.

Jonny Wirth thanked Ellis, and with a further round of applause his first lecture was complete. Several passengers gathered round to ask more questions, until they had to clear the lounge for the next item. As they made their way to the Island cafeteria for coffee, Vaila just smiled and said

"Well done. How did that last questioner know that you weren't a ceramicist?"

"I suppose it's obvious that my subject is the Neolithic. The question came from the man we saw at check in who asked for first class treatment. Could the couple be the McRavens, Rosemarie's parents? Ceramics are her subject."

"Could be."

That evening, so 'The *Carnelian* Daily' told them, was the Captain's welcome cocktail party at six in the Ocean Lounge, followed by the first formal dinner. Ellis had decided to wear the kilt and jacket he had worn at their wedding, and Vaila wore her bright red long dress, the one she had bought in Edinburgh on the way to the ship.

When they arrived at the door to the lounge they found a long queue waiting to enter. Captain Robert Brewer stood by the door welcoming passengers, whilst the photographer took photos of each passenger who wished to have a picture of themselves with him.

Vaila pointed out the man who had told him he was not expert in ceramics, and his glamorous wife, next but one ahead of them in the queue.

"Colonel John McRaven, and Mrs Danielle McRaven," announced the Cruise Director, who was introducing guests to the Captain.

"Very pleased to meet you, Robert. We must have a longer conversation perhaps at the Captain's table one evening. I was in the diplomatic service so I'm sure it would be most interesting."

"Pleased to meet you." The Captain replied as he nodded towards the photographer "Would you like a picture?"

"Oh, we don't go in for that sort of thing."
The Captain smiled and said,

"Well. Do have a drink, I expect you'd like to circulate." And he turned to the next couple.

When it was Vaila and Ellis' turn to be announced, the Captain said,

"I'm so pleased to meet you. Jonny tells me your lecture this morning went well. I've visited Orkney a number of times and have a good friend there, Mike Jamieson. He's Captain on the Pentland ferry these days."

"Yes, we've met him. He was very kind when we had a problem last year."

"I must hear more about that. We must find a suitable time."

Ellis and Vaila then walked into the lounge having taken a drink offered by staff and met Paul Unwin who was amongst the officers also welcoming passengers. They greeted each other warmly and Paul hoped they liked their cabin.

"Yes. It's very comfortable."

"I hear your lecture was well received this morning. It's tantalising that nearly all my time is spent on the bridge, as a watch officer. One day maybe I'll get the chance to hear the lectures!"

The lounge was quite crowded and noisy, even the dance band was playing. Vaila saw Minnie on the right side of the ship and when she told Ellis he laughed.

"You mean starboard darling!"

"Good idea." She hadn't heard him properly and thought he was promising to steer her in Minnie's direction. He tried gently to lead them through the crowd. Several passengers who had been at his lecture wanted to talk to Ellis, to ask further questions. He did his best to be gracious and to answer their questions but it was difficult to be heard against the sound of so many simultaneous conversations in the crowded room. For a few moments Vaila listened to the general hubbub, without hearing what anyone actually said. She found it a strangely compelling sound.

Before they had reached Minnie the Captain took the microphone and said a few words of welcome before introducing a number of the staff and, introductions finished, they went into dinner.

They found themselves at a table for eight again. Six people, two couples, a single man and one of the staff were already seated, so Minnie and Millie joined the next table. Vaila immediately realised that the couple she had thought must be the McRavens were at the table, but at least she was glad to see they were on the opposite side. She induced herself to the couple on her right. She was next to Fred Lightfoot who gestured to his right and said to Vaila,

"My wife Susan." He laughed. "Of course, Sharon." She did not look pleased.

Ellis sat next to Sophie, one of the excursion's team who he had met at the staff meeting the previous day. She was a blond about his own age who wore a smart white dress uniform and was a lively companion. He wondered if Vaila would tease him for sitting next to such an attractive girl.

Beyond her was the man whose photo they had seen. When he introduced himself as Gerry, Ellis had his few remaining doubts resolved that this was the man they had met on honeymoon in Naples, 'Red Check Shirt', and Vaila's nudge under the table showed him she thought so too.

"We've met before, Gerry, haven't we?"

"Have we? I don't remember." He then started talking to Sophie, forgetting that the remaining couple, sitting next to him, had yet to introduce themselves, so eager was he get her attention. He also seemed keen to avoid Ellis' question.

Gerry's neighbour said "Colonel McRaven, and Mrs McRaven of course."

He looked across the table at Ellis. "I believe you work for Treasures of Scotland and know our daughter Rosemarie." He looked disapproving, as if Ellis was not really good enough to work with his daughter.

"Yes, of course. I heard you were coming on this cruise. Rosemarie teased me that you would be giving her a report on my performance."

"Did she? She's such a sweet girl, she never complained but did say she was disappointed that you denied her the opportunity to give these lectures. She wouldn't say why, and I still don't understand what happened. She should have been here, being senior to you. We think she would have given fascinating talks."

"I was invited by the UHI Team Leader, not by Treasures of Scotland, partly because my special subject is the Neolithic, whilst hers is ceramics. I expect that was why Mr Collard agreed to my accepting the invitation. But our dinner companions don't want to hear about that."

Vaila noticed that the Colonel was not mollified by what Ellis had said, and thought it was just as well that the waiter came to take their orders, thus ending that line of conversation.

As the meal progressed a little uncomfortably, Ellis and Vaila, together with Sophie, tried to create more cheerful conversation. Danielle stayed silent most of the time, although she was interested in what others said and prompted her husband to take part from time to time. She hardly replied to Gerry, when he asked her if her accent was French. In any case he clearly wanted to talk to Sophie who was polite and cheerful but did not encourage him. When he tried to ask more personal questions, she turned to Ellis for conversation. Ellis took the hint and asked if she would explain how excursions were organised, enabling her to give him a long enough description for Gerry to get her message.

The Lightfoots on the other hand responded willingly to Vaila's conversation. Fred, sitting next to her, explained that they were enthusiastic about doing all they could to live a green lifestyle. Sharon, who had a rather sharp voice, and perhaps appropriately wore a bright green dress, joined in, talking more to Vaila than to the Colonel next to her. By the time the main course was being cleared away, she was animated in support of her principles.

"We always live green, use little of the world's resources, and vote green at every election."

That brought a reaction from the Colonel.

"Pah! That's a waste of a vote. They're virtually communist, total no hopers. You should vote Conservative or not at all."
Fred wanted to support his wife.

"You lot will just destroy the planet for everyone. What are you and your Tories contributing to reducing global warming? What do you yourself do to reduce waste, do you recycle?"

It was, Ellis thought, an argument that threatened the evening. It contrasted with the laughter from the next table where Minnie and Millie were, and when Gerry joined in he made it worse,

"I see no point in voting. No one listens. I don't like the Tories and I think the Greens make no sense." He laughed, "Fred, you should be careful or the secret you must keep from your friends will come out!"

"What secret?" Fred first looked puzzled and then anxious, almost guilty. "We've no more secrets than anyone else." He spoke a little too quickly. "I bet you have a secret too Gerry."

Sophie looked at Ellis, who understood.   "Whatever secrets we all may have Fred, I don't think this is a good time to try and get confessions!"

Gerry thought he was winning so did not want to drop the subject,

"Okay, but you must admit, Fred, that coming on this cruise is not very green."

Ellis was surprised to see Fred now looking a touch relieved.

"That's not a secret, and I need have no conscience about it. We won the cruise in a raffle, and as the cruise would use as much fossil fuel whether we came or stayed at home, we saw no reason to turn it down."

Vaila congratulated him on his having the winning tickets and asked if it was the raffle in support of a new Edinburgh Hospice. Sharon confirmed it was. Ellis added,

"Let's just agree that everyone – most people anyway - have secrets, private things they wish to keep to themselves, and if we all do then it's in everyone's interest to allow sleeping dogs to lie." He looked at the Colonel but could not read the expression on his face.

'Of course' Ellis thought to himself, 'He wouldn't want me to know his secrets, and doesn't realise we already know all about them.'

Danielle broke her silence.

"*Vous avez de la chance, Monsieur Fred*. Let the dogs lie, I agree with Ellis. One day, Ellis, maybe we can talk of what my daughter is really up to! She'll not be sleeping like the dogs I think." She smiled at him. The Colonel frowned at her.

As they arose to leave the table, Vaila said   "Thank you all for your company. We'll see what's happening tomorrow. Perhaps we'll see you at Ellis' other lectures." Gerry Jones said

"See you around," smiled at Sophie and hurried away. The Lightfoot's,

"Yes. Nice to meet you, good night." was spoken to Ellis and Vaila, rather pointedly excluding the McRavens, who said nothing as they left.

Sophie, when she was sure no one else could hear, said to Ellis

"A funny collection of folk. It's always a bit like that. Thanks for rescuing me from Gerry. Single men of a certain age can be a bit of a problem. Maybe that's his secret!"

*   *   *

The sky was heavily overcast when Ellis looked out of their porthole next morning. He turned on the TV with the sound off, as Vaila was still asleep. Channel one, the view from the bridge, also showed dark clouds. Then, on channel two he checked the ships position, it showed the *Carnelian* to be just south of Pointe du Raz, Finistere, about fifty miles from land at the northern edge of the Bay of Biscay. He wondered if they were sailing into bad weather. He turned off the TV and went into the bathroom to shave. As he shaved he remembered Paul Unwin, on the train, saying he was not sure what the Bay of Biscay would be like. He thought it would be worth going to have a look from the open deck.

He was just finishing dressing when Vaila woke up, yawned, put her arm over to his side of the bed and realizing he was up, opened her eyes.

"Good morning darling, sleep well?"

He told her he wanted to go on deck to see properly what sort of a day it was going to be, and promised to come back by the time she was ready for breakfast.

On deck the weather did not seem so bad, it was reasonably warm even if there was no sign of the sun, and more importantly, dry. The wind was steady from the west, perhaps around force four or five, a moderate breeze, with few white horses and no more than a metre high swell.

He was amused by the early morning walkers. They were so earnest, so determined. They were not out for a stroll just to fill their lungs with sea air, but for serious exercise, and they dressed for the part, shorts or track suits and trainers. 'The Carnelian Daily' said that one needed 6 circuits of the Promenade deck for a mile, and there could be no doubt, a mile they would do.

He was about to return to the cabin to see if Vaila was ready when one of the walkers came round the corner and stopped and wished him a cheerful good morning. It was Fred Lightfoot.

"Yes it's a nice morning, though I'd like to see the sun. Do you walk round the deck every morning?"

"I should. Susan doesn't come with me, she thinks it boring, walking round and round. What did you make of that Colonel last night? Why didn't he like you knowing his daughter?" Ellis laughed

"I was preferred for a new post last year that she wanted and I was invited to lecture on the ship when she wanted to do that too. It's a long story. I suppose it's only natural that he should think I have obstructed his 'sweet girl's' career!

"But he said she was senior to you."

"We're both on the same grade. Maybe he meant that she's held her post in HQ for three years whilst I started in Orkney, the post she wanted, only last January? He certainly needn't worry that I've designs on her!"

"If she's like him no one would want to have designs on her, as you put it."

"Actually she's very attractive, very smart. But..... Well, Vaila calls her clever, glamorous, and dangerous. Perhaps she's more like her Mother than her Father? Anyway I promised Vaila I'd not stay here long. We've yet to have breakfast. Enjoy your walk."

As Ellis waited for the lift down to B deck he realized what was odd about his conversation with Fred. Last night his wife was Sharon, this morning she's Susan.

'Doesn't he know if his wife is Susan or Sharon?'

Vaila brought 'The Carnelian Daily' with her to breakfast. As it was to be the second day at sea, and Ellis had no duties, they were free to enjoy the ship and entertainment programme.

They would call into Lisbon the next morning, so they went to David Grey's talk about the city and the countryside around it.

Vaila made notes on what David told them and Ellis said he would get tickets for a morning excursion around the city, perhaps the one on a tram. She was impressed by David's knowledge of so many places. He was a man a little above average height who, she was to discover, looked at everything they saw with a quizzical expression, as if he had to know about everything and anything.

Having settled their visit to Lisbon they went to the Island Cafeteria for lunch. They had hoped to be able to eat on the open Quarter Deck, but the weather spoilt the idea. The clouds were rather darker than Ellis had noticed before breakfast, and there was no doubt that the wind was a bit stronger. However they chose a couple of dishes from the buffet and sat by a window discussing the ship as well as all David had told them.

After coffee they went on deck to try the deck games on offer, but only stayed fifteen minutes or so. The wind was definitely stronger than they had expected and, as they went inside, they realized that the ship had acquired a slight but permanent list to port. Ellis thought it funny,

"It's like being in a sailing boat!"

In the library Ellis spotted a book on the battle of Salamis. He explained to Vaila what an important naval battle it was, one that had had long term consequences.

"Western civilization would not have been the same if Xerxes and his Persians had won." He explained the background to one of the world's most important naval battles. He reminded her of the picture they had seen on honeymoon. It was in the House of the Vetii in Pompeii and showed a magnificent trireme, the sort of galley used in the battle by both sides. She smiled at him, proud of him she might be but she wanted to think of the present. She left him to his book and found a book about Italy for herself and they spent a happy afternoon reading.

When they got up to go to the Ocean Lounge for tea, they felt the increased motion of the ship. It was becoming difficult to walk in a straight line. Some passengers, especially the older ones, were clinging on to every solid object they could find. But the motion still did not dampen any one's spirits, most found staggering from side to side funny. One elderly lady very nearly fell as the chair she grabbed slid away from her. Ellis took her arm to steady her and then found they both wove an unsteady course, so Vaila took her other arm and all three of them burst out laughing.

They noticed that some sick bags had been put out in a number of places, so the announcement, coming over the loudspeakers throughout the ship just as they reached the lounge was no surprise.

"This is the Captain speaking. We are running into a bit of a storm. The ship will be quite lively for the next twelve hours or so. Please be careful as you move around the ship. Use the hand rails as much as you can. You will also find in a number of places life lines are being rigged to help ensure you do not fall. I recommend no one goes onto the open deck."

Several passengers looked rather alarmed and wondered how they would manage. The Captain continued:

"Staff are there to help you. Let them serve you in the Equator restaurant, rather than try to serve yourselves in the Island Cafeteria, unless you are experienced sailors. If you are at all anxious about going to the dining room this evening, why don't you order a meal from room service and stay in your cabin? You will be most at ease with the motion when lying down, so an early night could also be a good idea. Last, the good news. You will be glad to hear that the storm should have blown itself out by the time you get up in the morning. Good afternoon."

A number of passengers went to the table to enjoy the scones savouries and cakes available. Vaila heard in passing a man say "Best stock up now. You should face motion sickness with a full tummy!"

Seeing Minnie and Millie seated near a window, they joined them with the lady they had been helping, and Vaila and Ellis got a selection from the buffet for all five of them. Being so much younger than the majority of passengers they were able to carry their plates to their table without too much difficulty, although for those less secure on their feet the staff willingly carried their choice to a table. Dora, the lady they had been helping was already in a lively discussion with Minnie and Millie, when Ellis and Vaila returned to the table.

The first thing Millie said when Vaila and Ellis sat down was,

"Isn't this exciting? I've never been in a storm before. "

"It is isn't it? I bet you'll be seasick before me!"

"You're on! I bet you'll succumb first Minnie!"

"I'll not want to have an early night, I want to see what happens."

Vaila told Ellis later that she was full of admiration for them. Dora remained a bit uncertain but the incident cheered her up. Ellis asked Vaila how she felt.

"I'm an Orcadian, remember, and survived the old *St Ola* many times, never mind the *Hamnavoe*, and you're a sailor."

"That's no guarantee. It wasn't for Nelson, but I'm okay now and for dinner too. But I don't want to sit anywhere near that Colonel." Vaila agreed with him.

But when they sat down to dinner at a table for four, the other two places were at first unoccupied.

At a small table near them were an elderly lady in a wheelchair and a woman who appeared to be her daughter. The lady looked thoroughly miserable. The daughter did her best for her demanding mother but it was hard to tell whether the mother appreciated her efforts. She certainly never smiled.

Beyond them the Colonel and his wife were on their own at a table for two. They clearly saw Ellis, who was well within the Colonel's line of sight, but he did not acknowledge Ellis' smile and nodded recognition. Vaila noticed that they hardly spoke to each other throughout the meal. When he spoke to the waiters it was as if to his servants.

"Which is worse, Ellis. That miserable old woman who must make her daughter's life hard, or the stuffy colonel?"

"The daughter has something to complain about. McRaven has no excuse for not being kinder to the staff. Remember Ritchie's friend said he was only concerned with 'the people who matter'. I suppose they don't matter to him.

"Nor us either presumably!"

"No, and I'll do my best never to matter to him!"

They were relieved when a couple came to fill the two empty seats at their table. Rachel & George Redman introduced themselves and proved to be very interesting companions. They complemented Ellis on his lecture the previous day.

George had travelled all over the world during his working life, and on many occasions Rachel had gone with him. Vaila asked what George did that took him globetrotting.

"Originally I bought tea for one of the big tea companies in the UK. But it became such a ruthless business. I saw how the workers in the plantations lived. So I quit. Now I work with Traidcraft, promoting and organizing fair trade including, believe it or not, tea!" He described it as a Christian organization.

"We live just outside Gateshead. Rachel works as a legal secretary now the children have left the nest, which enables us to afford a holiday like this each year. I love working with Traidcraft but it doesn't pay much. I just look at it as giving something back."

As the four of them were served coffee, the McRavens got up to leave. By now the movement of the ship was much greater than it had been when they had started their dinner, but the Colonel clearly considered it demeaning to accept a member of the staff offering him an arm to steady his walk out of the room. He haughtily started to walk towards the door.

The ship hit a wave and lurched in response. The Colonel staggered, grabbed a chair back which rocked uncertainly, lost his balance and fell to the floor right beside Ellis, who got up to offer help, only to be sworn at. Staff again rushed to help, by which time he had realized that he needed their help after all. He grumpily accepted an arm, but showed no gratitude for it. Danielle however thanked the staff and, before following him, smiled at Ellis.

"You are very kind. He can be a complete fool."

"Did you see the look he gave you?" George asked when Danielle was out of earshot.

"No, but I heard what he thought of me."

"What a rude man. Wasn't he the man who said you knew nothing about ceramics at your lecture yesterday? Why doesn't he like you?"

"I am definitely not his flavour of the cruise! I expect he still resents my lecturing instead of his 'sweet' daughter. She doubtless has told him that I cheated her out of that job. He said something about it yesterday. But he probably doesn't realize that the invitation came from the UHI team who have never met his daughter."

The meal over, Vaila said she'd like to go to the show in the Ocean lounge, so after wishing the Redmans good night they made their way there.

Several passengers were trying to dance to the ship's three piece band whilst waiting for the show to start, which was funny to watch as the movement of the ship, although not so bad as to prevent them attempting the appropriate steps, caught several of them out when the ship rolled. The couples had to cling to each other to stay upright.

"It's like a funfair ride!" laughed Vaila.

The Cruise Director was watching and as soon as the dance finished he went to the microphone on its stand to the left of the stage.

"Ladies and Gentlemen. I'm afraid we have decided to cancel the dance routine as this poor weather makes it hazardous for the *Carnelian*'s Dynamite Dancers to perform the billed Glen Miller show. We hope to bring it to you later on our cruise. However our resident pianist, Peter, has volunteered to play for you, and the Carnelian orchestra will also play so we hope you will enjoy that. Our dancers had already dressed for their show so I have suggested to them that they join you for Peter's impromptu recital."

Peter came onto the stage and sat at the piano. He seemed unaffected by the ship's gyrations. Vaila dug Ellis with her elbow and pointed with a nod of her head. Gerry was doing his best to chat to one of the girls in the dance troop, which didn't surprise Ellis as she was very attractive. But her magnificent costume included a large bonnet with several long feathers in it, and whenever she turned her head they brushed his face. It was clearly impossible for him to get too serious with her, but laughing together showed that he was not being totally unsuccessful in attracting her attention.

117

When Peter's impromptu performance was over, Vaila said she was excited by the storm and wanted to see it from the highest point on the ship. Ellis said they should take the Captain's advice and avoid going on deck. He suggested going to the Sunset Bar on the bridge deck.

They were the only passengers there, and were chatting to the barman as they enjoyed their nightcap, when there was the sound of raised voices in the passage outside the bar. They could hear a woman's voice pleading

"Darling don't go out there, the weather's wet and cold, and it's dangerous."

"I must. It's the only answer. I must, the nightmare keeps returning. It was my fault. Its time I paid the penalty for what I did."

"No! Please No! You don't have to. Your nightmares are more than enough punishment. Please Jim. Please Jim for my sake. I need you."

"I must. The nightmares are worse than death. I nearly killed him and maimed him for life. I'm dogged by what I did. There's only one way to end it."

They heard the door that led from the passage to the open deck slam shut on its spring, as the woman again pleaded. "If you go I'll go too."

As they could not hear his reply they thought the couple must have gone onto the open deck.

Ellis put down his glass and went to the window to look out.

"Oh no!" He ran to the sliding glass door from the bar onto the same open deck and pulled it across to go out.

"Vaila, I think he's threatening to jump over board." She was just behind him.

They were greeted by a strong blast of wind and rain, but there was enough light to see a man with his foot on the first bar of the deck rail on the port side. There was nothing but the sea below him whenever the ship rolled to port. The woman, unrecognisable, her rain soaked hair blown over her face, was behind him crying and still pleading with him to stop.

"Please darling, I love you. I don't care what you did. It was long ago darling, I want you with me now. Please."

"I must. It was my fault. I love you but you are too good for me."

He climbed up on the next rail and started to try to swing his other leg over the top rail. Ellis rushed forward to stop him, but before he could reach the man the ship crashed down on a wave with a thud, followed by the hiss of sea water flung away from the bows. The deck suddenly lurched to starboard. The man, taken by surprise, fell off the rail onto the deck, and the woman fell down beside him with her arm over him, trying to pin him down.

He lay still as Vaila crouched down beside them. He was shaking. Vaila laid her hand on the woman's shoulder in support but said nothing. Ellis stood beside them ready to help should the man try again, but he was calmer now. They stayed without moving for several minutes buffeted by the wind and rain. Then the woman gasped "Thank you, oh thank you!"

Ellis knelt down beside the man

"Can I help you up now? We're all getting wet and cold. The deck is slippery. Let's go inside and get a warm drink."

When the man looked up, and Ellis could see his face he realised it was Jim Blackwood. Jim was calm now. He rolled towards Ellis and put out his arm and Ellis helped him to his feet.

"I wish it wouldn't come on me like that. Thank you." He sounded quite rational. Then he turned to Helen, his wife.

"What would I do without you?" and the four of them went into the bar. In the warm bar with a hot chocolate in his hand, he turned to Ellis

"I have never told anyone what happened that dreadful day."

"Would it help to tell us? In confidence of course."

"Do you think so? Perhaps I should."

He told them that at school, when he was fourteen, he had been a bit of a bully. He especially picked on a boy who was not strong, and had a prominent broken tooth. His name was Colin. He teased him, telling him that no boy would pick him for his team because he was stupid, weak and no one liked him. The girls would think him ugly. He had kept on doing it as he got a kick out of making the boy cry. But one day, when he had taunted him in the playground Colin had burst into tears and run out of the school gate straight into the road. He was knocked down by a car and both his legs were broken. Jim ran away, his part in the accident had not been seen and he had kept quiet. Colin was off school for months, and when he had returned he was on crutches. What had completely shattered Jim was that Colin never gave him away. In fact he had been very pleasant towards him, although they had never got as far as being friends.

The accident had changed Jim's life. He had had bouts of depression and gone from being an extrovert to a complete introvert.

"I can't forgive myself. Helen has been wonderful, I don't deserve her but she stays by me. Tonight the storm did something to me. I suppose I need help."

"Yes you do. You can't live your life worrying about things you did years ago, especially as you can't do anything about them. I hope you'll be okay now."

"Helen" added Vaila, "Can you manage now?"

"Yes thank you. We are on an early excursion in the morning, so ought to get some rest. Come on Jim."

"Good night. See you tomorrow in the calm of Lisbon."

"Good night."

Lisbon

The Captain's prediction was correct. They woke next morning to a bright sunny day. 'The *Carnelian* daily' said they would be picking up the Tagus estuary pilot about nine, and described their approach as one of the finest to a maritime city in the world, so the two of them got up promptly, had a quick breakfast and were on the Sun Deck as they passed Cascais. They picked out the Belem Tower and the only sculpture of a seaplane neither of them had ever heard about, celebrating the first crossing of the South Atlantic by air.

Beyond it lay the Monument of the Discoveries, a surprisingly modern marking of Henry the Navigator's achievements, and, as Vaila put it, the courage of the Portuguese sailors he sent on voyages of discovery. They soon came to the double bridge carrying both road and rail across the Tagus. It gave out a loud hum as the wind blew through it, so loudly that it could not be ignored.

On the South bank was the statue of Christ the Redeemer. It looked huge but the commentary from the bridge pointed out that it is a half size copy of the one in Rio de Janeiro in Brazil.

Not long after that the ship slowed as it approached the berth allotted to her. Ellis was much more interested in the operation than Vaila, but in any event it was, for them, time to go below to prepare for the excursion. David Grey had suggested that Ellis came with him as assistant escort so that he'd be able to act as escort at ports they would be visiting later. Vaila opted to go with him.

David first took them to the Ocean lounge so Ellis could see how the staff checked tickets. Each ticket was issued with a coloured sticker which indicated which coach a passenger was to take. The *Carnelian* was a relatively small ship, carrying no more than four hundred and fifty passengers, but if three quarters of them were on an excursion, that still meant over three hundred people who needed to be sent on their way within an hour or less.

The staff in the lounge checked with the team who were waiting by the coaches by radio and when the coaches were ready the passengers with the appropriate coloured sticker were told that they should disembark and were offered a small bottle of water if the weather was warm. Those on the excursion then made their way to the gangway, which was usually on C deck, had their cruise cards swiped and went ashore.

"The system means folk go for their excursions in small groups and there is not too much of a crush on the gangway."
Vaila and Ellis then went ashore with David who checked with Sophie who acted as dispatcher, ensured the coaches had reserved seats for

disabled passengers, met the local guide and driver and got ready to receive passengers.

Once everyone booked was on the coach, and the count they expected tallied with the list Sophie had she ticked her list and the coach went on its way.

The broad dual carriageway from the ships berth soon brought them into the centre of the city. They saw the main central areas and some of the east of the city, the history and places of interest all being described by their guide. "Lisbon is a warm sort of place set off by the Tagus." Their guide told them.

"There are comparatively few old buildings in the city due to the major earthquake that destroyed much of it three centuries ago." By the water the city had several large open squares and the more modern commercial and administrative buildings. It gave passengers a general impression of the city which was helpful to those with limited mobility.

The coach then drove to a slightly higher and older area. The coach stopped in a small square where they could see two trams waiting and David and Ellis helped passengers exchange their comfortable coach seats for hard wooden ones on the historic wooden bodied trams. Vaila noticed an elderly couple finding the coach steps difficult and helped them. The tram ride went through the Alfama and Bairro Alto districts, the trams twisting and turning through old streets to the top of the hill from where there were glimpses of the estuary between the buildings.

As they went they saw narrow side streets either side of them, some too narrow for any vehicle. They were lined by whitewashed houses with colourful flowers filling balconies defined by beautiful iron work. At the top they stopped to see the view for a short while before the trams descended again to a wider street for the promised port wine tasting and lunch.

From the trams they were taken into a very large bar and once seated, passengers were given generous glasses of both white and tawny port and offered Pastel del Nata cakes, the traditional accompaniment to the wine.

Having enjoyed the wine, the guide said that the Portuguese equivalent to the Spanish tapas would now be served in the garden behind the restaurant. To get to the garden they had to pass a small shop selling souvenirs.

The moment David saw it he said to Ellis and Vaila in a quiet aside "Here's trouble. Why do tourists find shops so irresistible? We could get delayed here."

The delay whilst a number of the passengers looked at the stall was however mercifully short, perhaps because everyone was a little hungry, and they were soon sitting at garden tables in the sunshine. The tapas was brought to them by two local ladies who looked as if they had sampled the snacks many times before. There was a little quiet banter about that, and Ellis felt it was as well that their servers had no English.

The guide told them they had forty five minutes, where the toilets were and then left them to enjoy the break.

Ellis and Vaila found themselves at a table with the Lightfoots. Another couple, whose name neither of them knew, had bought a small pendant of an orange stone. It was semitransparent and they were holding it up to the light. They could all see what an attractive stone it was. Mrs Lightfoot quoted,

"'As the unexpected fire of a sunset, or the first flash of autumn brilliance.' It's a carnelian, a most appropriate souvenir of the cruise, a good choice for several reasons." And Susan went on to explain its properties in the art of Reiki.

"Reiki teaches that carnelian brings a rush of warmth and joy. It is stimulating, energising and empowering." She was quite lyrical in her enthusiasm.

"There are other legendry powers associated with it too. There is a tradition for example, that one of the three wise men who followed the star to Bethlehem, Caspar, had a box of healing stones, one of which was a carnelian because in his eyes it was proof against all evil and envy."

"Do you really believe all that?" asked the lady who had bought the pendant. She said her name was Amanda.

"Oh yes. I understand your doubt. Ignorant folk will exaggerate or belittle Reiki. If they are persuasive others will believe whatever they're told by the cynics. They give a bad name to Reiki, but if one studies the power of certain types of stone, as observed and developed over centuries, one can see and understand their meaning, power and value."

"I wonder how they came to call our ship *Carnelian*?" someone else wanted to know,

"I've no idea but as some of the stone's qualities were said, in ancient Egypt, to attract prosperity and good luck, rather like a talisman for success, I can imagine the directors of Carnelian Cruises favouring it! For ourselves, other sources say it stimulates appetite." Vaila joined in, "I don't need my appetite stimulating, I'm tempted beyond my resistance already with the wonderful food on the ship!"

At that point their driver appeared and they reluctantly returned to the coach. Several passengers wanted to hear more, although whether their enquiries were due to genuine interest or not Vaila was not sure.

After a good lunch, including another glass of wine, the passengers were happy to relax as they were given a panoramic tour of the west of city. They drove to the St Geronimo's monastery and the adjacent boat museum. On the way they stopped above the sloping King Edward VII Park, named to celebrate the King's visit. Ellis was disappointed that their tour did not allow time to see the boat museum, but understood the wish to return to the ship as scheduled.

David said that it had all been easy this time. He explained that the most difficult task was usually to get everyone back to the coach when leaving somewhere and then onto the ship on time.

"Not always as easy as it sounds," he warned. "The trick is to keep counting! We don't want to lose anyone, the paperwork involved if someone is left behind is horrific!"

On this occasion however there were no problems, perhaps, Vaila suggested, because the white and tawny port glasses had been of a satisfactory size!

As the coach turned into the dockyard beside the *Carnelian*, David asked Ellis if he had any questions, Ellis said he didn't think so.

"It all looks easy enough, but there's probably a snag I haven't spotted yet!"

They walked across the concrete quayside with the Redmans. Vaila asked how many cruises they had done and was amazed that it was their eighth cruise on the *Carnelian*. She wondered if they approved of Ellis as a lecturer and by the time they reached the gangway to the ship, she had heard that Ellis was already popular.

David, Ellis and Vaila let the passengers board first and then followed them, having their cruise cards electronically swiped again. After returning to their Cabin to leave their things they were just in time for tea so went to the Ocean Lounge where it was served, took a scone, clotted cream and jam each from the buffet and sat at a table for four by the window to enjoy the view as the ship sailed down the Tagus estuary.

As they discussed all they had seen in Lisbon, Vaila noticed a couple looking at their tablet intently. She guessed by their expressions that they were extremely unhappy about what it told them. It must be bad news, she thought, and was sorry that anyone should get news that spoilt their holiday. She was sure she recognized the couple but could not think of their names, so asked Ellis if he remembered them. He looked at them.

"Yes I think so, aren't they the couple who are high heid'yuns in the Civil Service? We were at the same table on the first night. But I can't remember their names."

Neither of them could recall their names, and when another couple they had not met before asked if they could join them they welcomed them, and then enjoyed a conversation with them as the ship sailed down the estuary. They thought no more about the unhappy couple with the tablet.

Gibraltar

The *Carnelian* was scheduled to arrive alongside the cruise berth at Gibraltar, the next port of call, at midday for a half day visit, so in the morning Ellis and Vaila enjoyed David's talk about the Rock at ten thirty. Afterwards they went for coffee on the Quarterdeck, the open deck reached through the Island Cafeteria, enabling passengers to eat meals, or enjoy coffee and other refreshments in the fresh air sheltered from the wind. It was very popular, not only because it was a pleasant place to sit in good weather but also because it offered good views, each side and astern. From it there were two stairways leading up to the Sun Deck above.

"Isn't Trafalgar around here somewhere?" Vaila asked.

"I think the ship will have passed that before breakfast. I looked it up on the map, it is about 65 miles from Gibraltar. There's nothing to see but sea anyway!"

Idly watching the coast go by Ellis became aware of the couple they had seen with their tablet at tea time the previous day, after the tram excursion. They were looking at their tablet again, but as they were sitting at a table out of the sun, whilst Ellis had the sun in his eyes and as his mind was on other things he took little notice of them.

Vaila just relaxed with her coffee in the warm morning air, watching the coast on the port side. Ellis hadn't intended to bring the duty free list, but had unintentionally picked it up with the news sheet 'Britain today', but now he casually looked through it. He wasn't sure if the discounts on whisky and other spirits were really worth the effort of carrying bottles home, when it was rather like coals to Newcastle, and he knew too little about wine to know if he really wanted what the list offered. He noted Drambuie in the liqueur list, together with Benedictine and Mead.

He turned to the news sheet. The main headline from home covered another row about rail franchising. According to a brief article the Ministry of Transport had made another blunder in the latest round of tendering, this time for the London Scottish Railway. A company called the Great North British Partnership had won the franchise but another company, the London Highland Railway, run by the charismatic Sir Rollo Branscomb, had appealed on the grounds of a faulty brief and process. Now it appeared that Sir Rollo was right, his complaint was valid. Reading between the lines, Ellis felt the reporter did not understand the detail any more than he did, but because the cost of tendering alone amounted to millions of pounds it was a serious matter, never mind that it meant that the franchising could not be settled in time to allow the trains to run normally.

'Oh well' he thought, 'no railways on Orkney.' He didn't need to worry about it. But as he put the news sheet down something struck him, a coincidence.

"Vaila, I've just remembered the name of those people we saw at tea yesterday with the tablet. They're over there, and their name is Mead, Mark and Heather. The duty free list jogged my memory and the news sheet confirmed it, well I think it did."

He explained that he thought he remembered Mark and Heather telling them that they worked in the Ministry of Transport. He was involved with railway policy, and Heather was in the statistics section where they worked out things such as the proportion of trains that are late. He showed her the item in the news sheet.

"Are you suggesting he's made a mess of the franchise?"

"No I'm not, I only know what the papers say, but they imply someone in the Transport Ministry messed things up. They've not named whoever might be to blame."

The Captain announced throughout the ship that they would shortly turn to port around the point into Algeciras bay when the Rock of Gibraltar would come into view. It was much more interesting than the news from home so they finished their coffee, picked up the papers and went up the stairway to the Sun Deck to see it.

As the bay of Algeciras opened to their view, they saw the famous Rock dominating the scene. It looked over the straights in a way that made it easy to understand why, in the Roman world, it was one of the Pillars of Hercules. Below it the harbour and the town seemed squeezed into a fringe between sea and rock.

In front of it the bay was full of shipping, cargo vessels from all parts of the world mostly at anchor. Some seemed just to have paused on passage to their destinations. A few looked deserted as if they had no voyage to make, but the ferries between African and European ports were never short of passengers and goods, running backwards and forwards with little time wasted between crossings. Many much smaller boats crisscrossed the anchorage busily too, and for those who were looking for them dolphins could be spotted. It was a very busy bay.

As they sailed towards the berth allocated to the *Carnelia*n they could see the end of the airport runway. Through binoculars they saw the traffic lights, the airport being perhaps the only one where road traffic and aircraft taking off and landing were controlled by traffic lights because they shared the same tarmac. Their berth was not far from the end of the runway, but then nothing in Gibraltar is far from anywhere else.

Ellis had no duties that day so they decided to take a taxi with Peter to the cable car so they could go up to the top of the rock. They thought they might have to queue but in the event were able to get on the cable car as soon as they had bought tickets.

The view from the top was magnificent. The ships in the bay were like toys below them to the west. Beyond they could see the industrial town of Algeciras, with its prominent factory chimneys. To the East they could follow the coast line until the Costa de Sol faded into the haze. To the south Europa Point, the southernmost point of Europe, was in the foreground and was backed by the coast of Morocco about twenty five miles away.

A small family of Gibraltar's Barbary apes was sitting in a corner of the viewing platform. Peter took several photos to show to Jamie when he got home. Vaila thought they looked sweet, until another a couple with a small girl were unwise enough to ignore notices requesting visitors not to feed them. In a moment there were three animals competing for whatever scraps they could get. They became quite aggressive, not only to each other but to the couple and their child too, which scared their small girl. She tried to hide behind her father's legs.

Peter walked calmly over, looked into the eyes of the largest of the apes and spoke quietly to the animal. It hesitated, and then backed off. The incident lasted only a minute or so, but was a lesson to the couple.

"They do look friendly animals, but they can be aggressive, especially over food." Peter smiled at the girl and her parents, "Just like some humans."

"How did you do that?"

"No idea, Ellis. It just happens, it always has. On my uncle's farm even when I was quite small the animals and I got on well. Perhaps I'm a bit of a monkey too!"

Returning to the bottom cable car station, the three of them came onto the street looking for a taxi back to the ship but no taxi appeared. Asking one of the cable car staff they learnt that many of the taxis were on strike and that there was no other form of transport. It seemed that they were stranded. Even walking might not solve their problem as they did not have the time. They had been told that 'All aboard' was at six and it was already nearly five.

Vaila commented,

"It's strange how one becomes quite affectionate towards our floating home when you are stranded on shore."

They tried a small hotel at the end of the street, but there was no one at the reception desk to speak to. They walked down to the main road but for all the traffic, there were no taxis.

It was Peter's resourcefulness that solved the problem. He had brought a copy of the Carnelian Daily which gave a phone number for the ship. He called the number given and the ship's staff were able to arrange for one of the working taxis to come and fetch them.

While they waited they speculated on what they would do if they could not get back to the ship and were relieved when the taxi arrived. It was not a prospect they wanted to face. Ellis said how glad he was that the ship connected to the local phone landline system whenever they were in port.

Once back on board, Vaila went with Peter straight to the Ocean lounge for tea, whilst Ellis returned to the cabin to leave the rucksack he had been carrying. When he opened the door he found a large envelope awaiting him. It had a postmark showing it to have come by airmail from Edinburgh and was addressed to him care of the ship. It was marked, rather enigmatically 'Open soon.'

Wanting to join the others for tea he left it on the dressing table and went to the lounge. He was only just in time to get tea as staff were starting to clear away the tea things. Peter shortly said he needed to prepare for his usual evening stint in the Seafarers Bar, so had a hurried cup of tea and left them to enjoy the scones. Vaila being keen to go on deck to watch both their departure and to look for dolphins urged Ellis to finish his tea promptly. They then went straight up to the Sun deck.

They watched as the *Carnelian* threaded her way through the shipping at anchor. The dolphins gave them a magnificent display, jumping out of the water around their ship's bows. The excited passengers watching, including themselves, were full of what a wonderful experience the display was. In their enthusiasm for the dolphins Ellis gave no thought to the envelope and it was only when they went back to their cabin that Vaila saw it. She picked it up and asked him what it was.

"I've no idea, I'd better open it."

In the envelope he found a letter on university notepaper from Professor Calum Cameron. He read it, and then passed it to Vaila.

THE UNIVERSITY
Edinburgh
Memorandum.
18th September.

Dear Ellis,

After your good detective work on the mystery of Kantley's draft I thought you'd be keen to know what has happened. It has proved quite a drama, threatening to disgrace the University, the Museum and Treasures of Scotland, and has almost certainly finished both William C and his beautiful assistant as archaeologists.

When David's volunteer returned from holiday I went to see him. Having apologised on Collards behalf, I asked him if he knew what the papers were that he had seen Collard putting in his brief case.

He told me that he didn't see the papers themselves, as they were in blue files. But each file had a sticky label in the corner with a number and title. He said the labels were written in French. The only clue to the papers was a photograph that had fallen on the floor. He recognised it. It was of a pot on display in the archaeological section of the museum. Next I rang Christine, Collard's secretary, as you had mentioned her concerns. She was a little worried about being disloyal but I said that you had suggested I spoke to her. All she said seemed to confirm our suspicions.

It was enough for me. I put our story to the other Trustees at a special, confidential, meeting I called, omitting Collard. It was decided Collard be confronted by three of us, so I arranged a meeting with him that afternoon.

He came with Rosemarie at my suggestion, and when we told him what we knew and asked for an explanation, he started to say that he was having the draft translated to be sure it really was Kantley's work. He was doing it for the museum. But when I asked him why he had told no one about it, and had treated it as a confidential project even in his own office, he lost his nerve went red in the face and muttered a reply which dodged the question. Rosemarie realised much more quickly than he did that the game was up. No doubt wanting to distance herself from him she said Collard had asked her to translate it, and he had said he would pay her for doing it too. She claimed to be unaware of what it was that she was translating and told us that she thought what Collard wanted was entirely legitimate. They started to blame each other, yet at that point we hadn't accused them of anything.

Flustered, Collard could not maintain his story and, with such clear writing on the wall as it were, he eventually admitted the whole thing. He said no harm had been done, he would give the draft and translation to the museum and that he would resign as a trustee.

Rosemarie swore at him volubly in French and walked out. She had lost her share in the plot of course. She realised that as she was herself a ceramics student of Kantleys she would not get away with her claim to be unaware of what she was working on.

The story went round Edinburgh in a flash. Someone started a rumour that the Museum, the University and goodness knows who else would sue, and/or that the police were involved. Then the press got wind of it. It became national news if only briefly. James Chisholm rang me to check the story and once I had confirmed it told me he *felt he had little option but to sack both Collard and his assistant, for damaging ToS' reputation. Rosemarie had the sense to resign first, but Collard had to be persuaded, so James told me later.*

There was concern that one of the miscreants might try to remove the files, but their secretary Christine had beaten them to it. She had remembered my asking her about it, drew the correct conclusions and had the whole filing cabinet safely removed to another office the moment she heard that C and R were in trouble over it. James was so impressed with her initiative that she has been promised promotion, so at least there's one heroine. Now we just need to let the dust settle.

The good news is that we now have the draft and a small team is working on it, so the university and museum will publish it. I told James of your and your wife's smart work over it all but we decided to say nothing publicly about it until you return. I know the University and Museum will be grateful to you both, and doubtless James will be too.

Hope you are both enjoying yourselves!

Calum.

"Wow! You were right, Ellis. It must have caused quite a stir in ToS."

"I'm delighted that Christine's contribution is appreciated. It goes to show you can't keep a secret from your secretary!"

"But can a secretary keep a secret from her principal?" Ellis was so intent on the end of Calum's story he missed the mischievous grin that went with h*er question.*

"Let's see if there is anything in my work emails about it."

They went to the library, logged into one of the computers and Ellis then entered his office user name and personal password and the first email in his office inbox was the answer. He read it to her.

"To all staff. I regret to inform all staff that Mr W Collard, chief archaeologist, and Miss R McRaven, assistant archaeologist, have resigned with immediate effect at my suggestion. The reasons are in the public domain, and I need not repeat them.

As it will take some time to appoint a replacement I have discussed the situation with Professor Cameron and the Chairman as a result of which the Professor kindly volunteered to be available to our regional archaeologists for advice and help. They will therefore report to him on professional matters and to me on all other issues until the problem is resolved.

It is essential that whatever your role in ToS you are mindful that the organisation depends on keeping to the highest standards of integrity. I am confident that I do not need to spell out what I mean to staff, especially in the current circumstances. James Chisholm. Director."

Vaila said she was not surprised.

"You won't have to bother about them again."

"Yes, I'll enjoy working with the Prof even if it's just in the interim. I wonder who they will appoint? I'm not sure if any of the other regional archaeologists will be interested."

"You?"

"You're joking. I'm far too junior and anyway I don't want to leave the Ness of Brodgar site. Much more exciting than being stuck in HQ."

"I'm relieved. I have my own good reasons for not wanting to move from Orkney anytime soon."

Ellis did not notice the look on her face, nor did it occur to him to wonder what her good reasons might be. He switched to his home emails and opened one from Jeff who put the whole issue succinctly.

'Hi, I'm sure you'll have heard the news that Holy Willie and Lucretia Borgia have had to get on their bikes. It's all round the town. Richie thinks Rosemarie will find another warm bed soon enough, but said it definitely won't be his! Don't suppose we'll ever hear of your former boss again.

Hope the lectures are going well. Jeff & Liz.
PS Doubtless your famous beautiful wife is nursing you through your seasickness. Ha Ha. Give her our love.

"I wonder if Rosemarie has told her parents?" Vaila chuckled. "In spite of everything I feel a bit sorry for her Dad. All his illusions about her will be shattered. He'll surely have to stop calling her his 'sweet girl'. Nonetheless I don't think it's our place to tell them if she hasn't."

"No. Perhaps we'd better watch to see if they give any sign of knowing what's happened as he might blame me for corrupting his sweet girl!"

At sea to Ajaccio

It was to take two days at sea for the *Carnelian* to reach Corsica, where she was scheduled to berth alongside the pier next to the ferry terminal at Ajaccio. The sea days went by very pleasantly, the Mediterranean being calm and the hot sun being matched by a cool breeze. In such weather Vaila thought none of the passengers would be interested in lectures, soaking up the sun was surely more attractive, but that turned out not to be quite true.

During the first day they saw the Meads twice. During the morning Vaila went to the library to change her book and get a magazine she had seen on display there. She found the magazine and as she turned to go saw the Meads again deep in research on line, using one of the computers available to passengers. Once more the two of them were pouring over the screen. Their expressions suggested it was for something serious, apparently requiring on line research. Heather was making notes from their work. Vaila still wondered why they needed to spend such a sunny day working, never mind that they were on holiday.

Ellis had asked her to discover from Damien, the ship's computer assistant, if they would have net access all the way to Corsica as he wanted to reply to Calum's letter and Jeff's email.

When Damien told her that he doubted if the connection would last long, probably only until they passed the Balearic islands, she felt it might explain why whatever the Meads were doing would need to be done without delay, and it also meant that if Ellis wanted to congratulate Calum Cameron particularly on his new role, and to invite him to come and stay with them in Kirkwall to see the Ness of Brodgar for himself it must be done at once. Apart from her liking Calum, as they now felt able to call him, Vaila was well aware of the value of a friend who could do so much more for Ellis' career than Collard ever could.

So she typed a suitable email and sent it from another of the available computers. She was lucky. The connection was broken almost as soon as she had done so.

The Meads looked disappointed and frustrated at having to close their computer. They collected the notes they had made into a file, binned the other papers and went out of the library. Vaila too closed the computer she had used, put her own draft with the magazine, and turned to go, inadvertently kicking over the waste bin as she did so, spilling the papers across the room. She picked them up knocked them into shape on the magazine at the nearest desk and put them back in the bin.

She returned to the lounge, where Ellis and David had just finished working out a schedule which fitted their talks together covering the next three ports, Ajaccio, Rome and Naples. Because there were no sea days between the three ports, they would give the talks that afternoon and the following morning, the second sea day, covering all three.

Ellis wanted to take all his notes back to the cabin before they had lunch and Vaila went with him.

"I've replied to Calum by email for you, as Damien told me the connection was about to be lost. I hope you approve." She put the magazine down on the bed,

"Here's the draft of it." She handed the paper to him.

"Funny sort of shorthand, darling." What he was looking at was not her draft. Looking over his shoulder she laughed.

"Sorry, wrong bit of paper." She swopped it for the right one and as Ellis read her draft she glanced at the sheet she held and knew at once that it was one out of the library bin. It could only be Heather Mead's scribbled notes on their research, which she must have accidentally picked up when tidying up the waste bin.

"Thanks Vaila, what's that you have?"

She explained what had happened and what it must be, spread it out on the dressing table and they looked at it.

Heather had scribbled a whole lot of miscellaneous names, dates, numbers and initials. Doubtless she would have known what they meant, but neither of them could make anything of it.

LSR 15 or 7. Means after 28 weeks???
Release of ITT feb   Prospectus - after prequel. Must be wrong, or Was Consultation claim right – 41% + pass no.??? Can't be!
They definitely are wrong. / An Error crept in / May be it was miscalculated Class 800/801 sets. Seats?? Calc odd. Not the same.
GNBP 25th March, 15th April, 13th May 28th May
Not within p rules surely. 3 sat 1 sun. Equiv. for LHR???

Vaila laughed and pointed at the first of the dates.

"Look, our wedding day, and the second date is when you were working with Hal on the huts."

"How do you remember the exact dates when I started working with Hal?"

"I'm your secretary aren't I? Anyway, we missed out on Andrew's party because of it."

"So they're all Saturdays?"

"Except for one Sunday, yes."

"Anyway, it's nothing to do with us is it? None of it makes sense to me anyway."

"I've no idea either. Its rubbish to them, they threw it away, and double rubbish to us." She scrunched it up and threw it into the bin.

"On a totally different subject, Vaila, I see from 'The *Carnelian* daily' that there are bridge visits for passengers just after lunch at two. David and I start our series of talks at three thirty. We have everything prepared so let's book for the two o'clock tour. I'd love to see what goes on there and we might see Paul." He rang reception and put their names down as requested in the 'Daily'.

The group met at reception and were taken up to the bridge by one of the excursions staff. The first impression of the bridge was the excellent view forward and to Port and starboard. To see astern the officers would have to go out onto the open bridge wing.

Vaila was delighted that Paul was there to explain everything.

He started by pointing out the two main computer screens, one an electronic chart and the other the radar screen. There were a large number of gauges and buttons, including a computer keyboard by which all aspects of the ship could be displayed. The engines, electrical and other systems were run by the engineering department of course, but the properties and state of them could also be monitored from the bridge too.

Paul explained that they planned their course from one port to another. The plan was plotted on the electronic chart and together with the current measurement of their position speed and distance, the electronic chart showed both. The smallest deviation from the plan was instantly and continuously shown.

The radar screen showed what was around the ship and Paul showed his little audience how it could be set to cover just nearby ships and land, or to give a wider, more distant, view. Paper charts were not needed at all.

The ship was steered by an autopilot if she was steaming above seven knots. All these systems were duplicated. It was a reassuringly sophisticated little talk.

Paul, in answer to a question, said there were three watch officers, the first and two seconds, working six watches twenty four hours a day, one being on duty on the bridge at all times whether the ship was at sea or in port, together with at least one other lookout. When the ship came out, or went into port was different. The Captain would be on the bridge, the ship would be steered by the coxswain and apart from watch officers they would have a pilot to provide local knowledge and advice.

This description led to a question about the crew and officers.

Immediately under the Captain was the Staff Captain, Paul explained,

"Our Staff Captain is Larry Frew and he also has a master's ticket. He is in charge of all aspects of the ship's crew. For example he organizes the men on the winches dealing with their lines, the ropes that held the ship safely to her berth.

"You won't see him much; he works in the background to ensure the efficient running of the ship and its crew.

"The officer of the watch spends most of his time simply checking that all is well with the many aspects of the ship that made for a comfortable voyage. The only concession to former days was a small wooden wheel. As the ship was currently on autopilot, no one was actually steering, so Paul said that it was a good moment to get a photo.

"The ship's photographer is here, so you can take home a picture showing you steering the ship!"

Whilst several people had a photo taken, Paul answered further questions, before going out onto the wing of the bridge. From there they could appreciate how the officers could bring the ship into a berth. At one point Paul looked through the binoculars at a small cargo ship sailing a roughly parallel course some distance away on their starboard side. Someone asked why he bothered.

"You have radar and so on to track a ship on a collision course?"

"Of course, but it is always good to double check. The 'mark one eyeball' is still important! At the opposite extreme we can 'acquire' a lot of details of other ships too. I'll show you."

Back inside the bridge he pressed some keys on the computer keyboard and said "There you are. That ship to starboard is called the *Camel Prince,* 6000 tons. She has come from Barcelona and is going to Naples with a mixed cargo, and is steaming at 9 knots, so we are overtaking her as we are at thirteen knots. She's registered in Qariat, where we are going after Naples and belongs to the Albysian Trading Company."

"Can you get any other details about her, like her captain's name?" Ellis was curious.

"No. If we needed that we would have to use the radio. Actually we're lucky to know that much. Ships like that often fail to turn on the equipment that allows us to know so much about her."

Ellis looked at Vaila.

"Quite a coincidence. We should look out for her in Naples."

The visit over they went to the Ocean Lounge where David was ready to give the first of his port talks about Corsica and especially Ajaccio.

He spoke of its background and a little of the island's history. He spelt out the practical details and described the excursions on offer, three of which still had vacancies. The excursion for which Ellis was to be escort was however fully booked.

When he had been asked to go with the coach tour called 'Vizzavona and Spuntinu' at the staff meeting that morning and had asked where these two places were, David had roared with laughter.

"You can't eat Vizzavona, it's a mountain pass, and you can't visit spuntinu, it's a sort of snack! But don't worry about knowing anything about the places you'll see. The local guides usually know their stuff. Just keep counting and ensure you return to the ship with the same folk you started with! If you are asked a question refer it to the guide or just answer confidently whatever comes to mind. Most folk are happy with that.

In his talk, however, David did describe something of the background. He told his audience that Ajaccio was Napoleon's birthplace, and thus the island's most famous son. It had some British historical connections. It was considered the model for Shakespeare's 'The Tempest' too.

Ellis felt glad that he had also said that the island was never really Roman, and thus not usually thought of as part of the 'Roman World', the cruise theme. The Romans must have been to the island, he said, but say little about it. Since their time it had been Genoese, and is now French, though I think Corsicans think it is and has always been nothing but Corsican.

Discussing what David had said in his lecture with Vaila over tea he said he felt he had a good excuse for leaving everything to the guide.

"You'll come into your own with the next three ports, the Roman ones. I want to come on the Spuntinu trip. It'll be something new, a change from all those Romans!" was Vaila's comment.

On the second day at sea on passage to Corsica Ellis gave the lecture he had prepared on 'The Roman World', an overview of the Roman Empire and all that it had bequeathed to Europe even after 2000 and more years. His slides concentrated on Rome. Vaila spoke to him afterwards as she was a bit critical of him taking a rather too wide a view. She thought his audience would have wanted him to concentrate on Rome itself, but accepted that no one seemed to take that view when it came to questions.

He was not sure if the McRavens had come to his lecture, as it was well attended and he had better things to do than look for them. Vaila wanted to support Ellis, and gave no thought to the McRavens either. She did not even think about the Meads.

The only time they discussed Cameron's letter further was briefly as they were getting up the next morning, when they had wondered again if the McRavens were aware of what had happened in Edinburgh to their 'sweet girl'. Ellis had dismissed the question.

"Why spoil a cruise worrying about all that. We'll catch up when we get home."

"They'll perhaps forget about telling her how dreadful your lectures have been when she tells them she's been sacked!"

At ten thirty after the coffee break David spoke about the various excursions from Cittiavechia but kept it short as they were all sold out. He concentrated on what independent passengers might do in the city.

After lunch David continued his talks, speaking about what there was to do in Naples, and the available excursions. After a short break Ellis spoke about Pompeii and Herculaneum, feeling on much safer ground than for any other places the ship was visiting.

He illustrated his lecture on Pompeii and Herculanium with the photos Vaila and he had taken. He had joked that he hoped they were all right.

"I had trouble concentrating as we were on honeymoon at the time they were taken," he had joked. Vaila was not sure she approved of his joke but it certainly put the audience in a good mood.

At dinner that night they were at a table with Minnie and Millie and two other couples, and enjoyed a convivial evening. The two couples were full of questions about the visit to Naples in a couple of days' time.

Vaila noticed that the Meads had taken a table for two and were again in a serious discussion as if it was a sort of working dinner. She felt a bit concerned for them, as she interpreted their demeanour as suggesting they were in some sort of crisis.

In the morning shortly after they docked Ellis collected the usual items from the cruise office and was given the number of passengers booked on his coach. There were two coaches for the excursion and it was as well to ensure his passengers did not get confused. His was to be number two, with a red coach sticker to match the sticker on the tickets. Then, with Vaila, he went ashore. He was relieved to find that the guide was a British woman who had married a Corsican. Her name was Karen and she was welcoming and friendly.

The road they followed climbed through forest and maquis, an attractive fragrant shrub, in the sunshine. As they went Karen gave an interesting description of Corsica and its history. She had a wonderfully wide knowledge of the island and a very clear voice, an ideal guide.

At one point she asked if there were any questions, and as no one spoke up Ellis asked about the British connection. She was obviously impressed that he would even know there was one and by the time they reached their refreshment stop, she had given an interesting talk, broadcast to everyone on the coach about it. Vaila remarked that the British had an interest at various times with several Mediterranean Islands. Certainly Corfu, Mallorca, Minorca, and Malta as well as Corsica.

The building in which their spuntinu was laid out was part of a railway station. Vizzavona was one of the highest stations on the Corsican narrow gauge line. Ellis was curious about it but first wanted to go with the guide to see the building so that he could help passengers.

He had not reached the building when there was a cry from behind, and looking back he saw that a lady had fallen from the bottom step of the coach. Her husband was trying to lift her. Vaila was trying to help but the lady was too heavy for them so Ellis left the guide to deal with the rest of the coach party and ran back to see if he could help.

When the man looked up he saw it was George, the Traidcraft man. The lady on the ground was his wife. He crouched down and she told him that she had twisted her ankle and was concerned that even if she stood up she would still be unable to walk on it. With George on one side of her and Ellis on the other they lifted her sufficiently that she could sit on the step from which she had fallen and after a short rest they got her to her feet.

She was clearly determined to get to the railway station, not least because she did not want George to miss anything. Between the men she hobbled to the building where Vaila and the guide had arranged a seat for her at the nearest table to the entrance, and could take part in the refreshments. Vaila stayed with them while Ellis went round to see how everyone else was getting on.

The snack consisted of cold meats, cheese, local bread with various salad items all washed down by Corsican wine. Red or white it was a pleasant drink, which Vaila thought deceptively strong. It was nice to enjoy it without thinking of who would drive home.

The guide, talking to those who had arranged the spuntinu, discovered that a train was due in about fifteen minutes, so it was decided to wait so they could see it. It was a pleasant interlude in the sunshine, and a contented group enjoyed wandering round the platform. Ellis himself was sitting on a platform wall, confident that Vaila would keep an eye on the Redmans.

In due course they all heard a whistle in the distance and through the dense woodland and maquis the train appeared.

It stopped at the station and a Girl Guide troop got out. It seemed to Ellis that the stream of children, rucksacks, their adult leaders and equipment getting off the train would never end. There was hardly anyone on the train by the time it moved off towards Corte, the ancient capital of Corsica, the train's next stop.

That excitement over the passengers returned to their coach. When Ellis arrived having checked so far as he could that no one was being left behind, he found that Vaila and their guide had organized a change of seats so that Rachel could sit in the front rather than having to walk to the back, and between them and with the help of the driver, she was already on board.

The drive back to the ship offered dramatic views, as the road wound through the maquis on the edge of cliffs, occasionally giving glimpses of the railway and once they were lower down the hill side they could also start to see the sea.

Once back at the ship Ellis and Vaila returned to their cabin to freshen up before tea.

"How did you get on with the Redmans, darling? It was so good of you to stay with them."

"It was a pleasure, they are such a delightful couple. I learnt a great deal more about the company George works for. There was one other thing too. It could be nothing but it could be an interesting coincidence."

She told him what the Redmans had told her about Traidcraft and the way it set out to help the third world by developing fair trade.

"It seemed to me Ellis, the sort of organization that attracts some very nice folk, such as George and his wife. The Redmans are great folk."

"What's the coincidence?"

"They know a man called Colin, who walks with crutches and uses a scooter. They told me how much they admired his spirit, he is always cheerful and never refers to his injuries. He is married and has two children who he adores. I was wondering if it could possibly be the same guy Jim Blackwood knew. Do you think we should introduce them to each other?"

They discussed the possibility for some time and decided to speak to both couples again, especially to see if Jim really would like to meet and compare notes. After all it might not be the same Colin, and if it was it could be disturbing to Jim.

That evening they again found themselves at a table with the Lightfoots, and of course Minnie and Millie, who had had an excellent day, having taken the tour to Napoleons birthplace. They had enjoyed Ajaccio and its tree lined streets and as the tour went down the coast to the Filatosa standing stones, they were anxious to talk to Ellis about them, so Vaila spoke mainly to Fred and Sharon.

By the time the sweet course had arrived Vaila had become even more curious about why Fred occasionally called his wife Susan, but try as she might she could find no tactful way to ask without being seen as nosy, and thought she would have to leave the question for another time.

They went to the Ocean Lounge after the meal. Minnie and Millie opted for an early night and had gone to their cabin. They had hardly sat down when Fred and Sharon asked if they could join them around the low table. The show was not to start for another fifteen minutes, and Fred stopped one of the bar waitresses and offered Ellis and Vaila a drink. The order having been given Fred said Susan and he wanted to talk to them.

"You must be puzzled as to why I sometimes call   her Sharon and sometimes Susan, and we felt we should explain. You see Susan is not really my wife."

He went on to tell their story. His wife Sharon, Susan and himself were members of a club trying to save the planet in as much as it's possible for individuals to do.

"Sort of giving a local example if you understand the idea."
They campaigned for more recycling points. They switched to a renewable energy supplier and installed solar panels. They sold their petrol cars for electric or hybrid ones, and made a point of using their bikes or public transport whenever practicable and so on. Four of the group volunteered with the Woodland Trust to plant a new wood and they and others did similar voluntary work, Fred, Sharon and Susan usually working together.

The three of them founded a local Transition group mainly to encourage folk to grow their own veg and they organized a shared transport scheme. As they had said at the beginning of the cruise they actively supported the Green Party and were all members.

"We were all close friends, so we thought." Fred continued. "Then I won this cruise in the raffle and all the trouble started. At first Sharon didn't know I'd bought a ticket; she regards raffles as gambling. I told her I thought of it as a contribution to the hospice and I had never expected to win. But she told me I wasn't being true to the green movement."

He explained that the Green Party branch heard about it because she told Oscar, the local chair, who said they must not go. The party consider cruises a waste of fossil fuel and damaging to the environment, generally unsound and they would be setting a bad example. He had argued that as the cruise would sail with or without them it would make no difference to global warming whether they went or not. It caused quite a split in the local branch and from Fred's viewpoint the fact that his wife Sharon was on the 'don't go' side and had said she would refuse to go with him was a big blow. She told him she had hidden his passport to make sure he stayed at home. He thought it a really mean and unloving thing to do. They had a major row about it. He had felt she was putting green issues before their marriage.

So it had become a personal row as well as splitting the local party. When he said he was going to go whether she came or not and demanded that she gave him his passport back, Sharon stormed out of the house. He discovered she was living with the branch chairman a week later.

Susan took up the story. "When I saw Sharon she had got angry with me too for backing Fred and that was the last straw."

She had resigned from the Green party and from Transition and had gone to see Fred.

"I was so sorry for him. It was rotten of Sharon to leave him over it, and when I heard she'd left him for Oscar, who I never liked much, I felt all our little team was ruined. I started to wonder whether Sharon and Oscar had been having an affair under our noses all along." Fred turned to her.

"You were so kind, Susan, so understanding. Sharon is a fanatical green, it mattered more than people to her and Oscar's the same. Sharon didn't want to understand my views. I believe in green things because I think they are good for people. Susan's the same."

She told Ellis and Vaila that through it all she'd admired all that Fred did and she'd always liked him, and had similar views. She had been to see him, to see if he was okay and to ask if she could help. One thing led to another until in a rash moment she had asked Fred if he would take her on the cruise. He had been delighted. He really wanted to come, to try an unfamiliar life style, but to have Susan with him encouraged him to go.

Their only difficulty was that by now there were only three days before the cruise sailed.

Fred had searched his house and found both Sharon's and his own passport, but Susan had not got one. They were discussing it at a vegetarian restaurant when Sharon and Oscar, the chairman, came in together holding hands.

"To cut a long story short," Susan said "we icily stared at each other, from tables at different sides of the restaurant, until Fred asked me eat up so we could leave well before they did." He had an idea.

"Sharon and I are similar enough in height and so on. We quickly got back to Fred's house where we checked to see if Sharon's passport would contain anything to give us away. The usual passport type photos look pretty vague so I took it to her flat with Fred's, in case Sharon tried to remove one or both of them, and all I had to do was dye my hair the same colour as Sharon's and, sure enough, we had had no problem with passport control when we turned up at Dover for the cruise."

They both looked at Ellis and Vaila,

"I hope you won't give us away. I keep forgetting, and call Susan Sharon. When we get home Susan will eventually truly become my wife and we have already decided that we will move somewhere different, and start again." Ellis laughed.

"That's an amazing story. It would be difficult to invent it. So long as you try to remember to call Susan Sharon in front of people you may well get away with it, and I doubt if anyone will ask us. I'm afraid I'm an archeologist and think much more about the past than the future of the planet."

The Band now struck up the opening tune for the show, as the Dynamite Dancers came forward. Vaila nudged Ellis and whispered,

"Look over there by the pillar near the front. Gerry's got himself a front seat, to watch Sandie. Another romance in the making!"

Rome

"Docking in Civitavecchia, nearly fifty miles from Rome seems illogical until one realises that anywhere else would be even further from the Eternal City." David had told his audience in his talk about their visit to Rome. All the excursions therefore faced an hour or more on a coach before they even arrived in Rome.

Ellis and Vaila had been asked to act as escorts for the walking tour of the centre of the city, a tour which was one of the first to set off. Their coach was a bit big for their group, as the fifteen booked for it only filled around half the seats.

Vaila had asked Minnie and Millie if they were coming with them but they had said they didn't think they could cope with so much walking and had opted for the panoramic coach tour. They told Ellis that they were glad to find that Peter was one of the escorts for their tour and hoped they would be on his coach.

Ellis had only met one couple amongst the passengers on their excursion, Heather and Mark Mead. They exchanged greetings when they arrived at the coach. The Meads had spoken rather briefly as if they were preoccupied by something else. While Vaila and Ellis waited for the last few passengers Vaila commented on it and resolved to do what she could to help them.

Their Italian guide introduced himself as Bruno and in Vaila's eyes he looked just as a Caesar should, a real Roman emperor. He was not especially tall but had wide strong shoulders and a thick neck which made him look as powerful as a bull. His face was alert, an impression given by the way he constantly looked around him. Ellis, as escort, had a seat at the front with Vaila, who whispered to Ellis as they travelled the autostrada that she would look out for statues with which to compare him. He laughed at that.

However Bruno proved an excellent guide and able to answer almost any question, so that even at the Roman sites there was little for Ellis to do but ensure they lost no one. That was not quite as easy as it might have been; the city was very crowded.

Bruno had started his commentary as soon as the coach began to move, pointing out that Civitavecchia itself had ancient walls and interesting buildings. It had been the port for Rome for nearly two millennia so that was not surprising. The coach however swept past the town and onto the autostrada, so the group only had a quick glimpse of it.

The autostrada went through flat rural countryside with occasional views of the sea. Bruno appreciated this was not especially interesting and filled the journey with a potted history of Italy, starting with the Etruscans, right up to the present day. He explained the Greek influences on many areas in the country and how, in Roman times, the whole of the Italian peninsular had been united under the 'Pax Romana'. Emperor Constantine made Rome the centre of western Christianity, and in some ways and for all its sometimes turbulent history it still was.

After the fall of the Roman Empire the Italian peninsular divided into a large number of states. They were mainly ruled by powerful families, or in some cases, such as Venice, became republics under city leaders. Several Popes too owned large areas of the Italian peninsular and even had their own armies.

Many states became wealthy before and after the Renaissance, places like Florence, Venice, Genoa, and Naples. He suggested the group held this history in mind because it had a considerable influence on later architecture. He covered the influence of external powers, such as the Holy Roman Empire in the north and the Vikings and later Spain and Napoleon in the South. All these changes and rivalries conspired to discourage any form of unification until the nineteenth century when Italy was finally unified once more in 1870, under a number of influential leaders from Cavour to Garibaldi.

Bruno touched on the twentieth Century pointing to Italy's ambition to have its own empire. "We didn't get far with it but our brief and modest empire included Albysia, for the second time. I think it is one of the ports you are visiting. It had been part of the Roman Empire. Our disastrous flirtation with fascism under Mussolini lost all that."

He suggested that fundamentally Italians these days were a people more concerned with the arts than politics. He spoke of artists such as Michelangelo, and composers like Verdi, still admired everywhere, but in contrast settled government and politicians eluded the country much of the time.

"For example our recent leader, Berlusconi. He's no longer thought a good politian even if Italian men might envy his success with the ladies." He laughed. "It was different once, when we were good at everything. You will see what I mean in Rome."

He then spoke about Rome itself, its past and present. The influence in many ways it still had today in Europe culturally and in other ways. By the time the coach entered the city passengers had had a first class foundation for their visit.

Their exploration of Rome started when they drove past the Circus Maximus. It was now little more than a large depression in the ground but it was easy to make out the shape of the Roman chariot race track in the hollow, with sloped sides from which Roman race goers could watch the action. The Aventine hill followed, and then the Palatine Hill, where Romulus and Remus were said to have been nurtured by a wolf and later founded the city. Everywhere there were Roman ruins, interspersed with churches, each decorated elaborately with statuary from every age.

Leaving the coach, they walked first to the remains of the forum which Bruno described as the centre of life in Imperial Rome. Beyond it, still dominating the view today stood the Colosseum. They walked to it through crowds of tourists where Bruno explained its architectural features, including the differing columns and tiers which had such an influence on later Renaissance architecture.

Returning to the coach, they drove to the centre of the city so that they could compare a different, later, side to the city. Whilst on the way Ellis heard Vaila ask Bruno about the Vestal Virgins, remembering the conversation with Jeff and the others in Edinburgh. She was a bit put out to learn that if they didn't remain virgins they were likely to be put to death by being buried alive.

Their second walk started at the Spanish steps, a baroque meeting place always popular with students and tourists. What surprised Ellis was how large the steps were. He thought they could have been thirty metres side to side, with around ten flights of marble steps. Dozens of people still met there, sitting on the steps.

From there they walked to the Trevi fountain where some of them threw in a coin to ensure, so legend promised, that they would return to Rome. Bruno said that anyone who threw in three coins would marry a Roman girl. Vaila told Ellis she'd prefer he only threw one.

"Mmm, I don't know. You could get buried alive and the girls here are very pretty." he teased. He saw the fleeting look on her face and quickly added "But perhaps I'd be safer to stick to my own Orcadian Piddie Maid, mischievous though she is!"

Nearby a stall sold flowers and in a fit of gallantry Ellis bought Vaila a carnation to pin to her escort T shirt, to the amusement of the other passengers. She thanked him.

"I might even forgive your teasing!"

They walked on to the Pantheon, frequently stopping to allow Bruno to point out buildings, their significance and sometimes important detail. By the time they had had a good look round the Pantheon they were all starting to tire.

The walk was hard on the feet and the whole city was full of people and very hot. They were ready for a breather and were glad when it was time for lunch. Bruno took them to the Piazza Novona, an oblong baroque piazza which, he explained, was built over Domitian's stadium for athletics and chariot races and which still reflected its original purpose in its oblong shape. They walked to the centre of the piazza to see the large Fontana del Quatro Fiumi, sculpted by Bernini, representing the four great rivers of the Nile, the Plate, the Ganges and the Danube. Pope Innocent X had commissioned it because his family palace was on the piazza.

"Such was the ability of seventeenth century Popes to use their wealth," someone commented, whilst another replied "Or spend the Church's money."

It seemed tactful to end that conversation so Ellis asked Bruno where they were to have lunch. He pointed across the piazza to where an outside table had been booked for them at Pizzera Tucci.

The excursion party sat together at a long table in the warm sunshine, drinking in the atmosphere as much as the wine the waiter brought unasked, relaxing and people watching. They talked happily together trying to remember all Bruno had told them of the wonderful places they had seen. They were also anticipating the climax of their tour, the Vatican, which they would visit after lunch, not least as they had seen glimpses of the massive dome of St Peter's in the distance across the river from the end of many streets and between buildings.

There was an exception to the group's cheerful conversation. Vaila happened to be sitting opposite Heather with Ellis at the end of the table between them. Mark was next to his wife. They were not joining in the conversation. At first Vaila thought Heather must be finding the walking, the crowds and the heat too much for her, yet as she had had no difficulty keeping up that seemed unlikely.

During the morning Vaila had also noticed that Mark was not always paying attention as if he was extremely worried about something, or at least trying to think through a problem. She wondered if it was the same matter which they had been researching on the ship's computers ever since Gibraltar. Whatever it was must be serious for them, and she remembered that they had thought the Meads had had bad news when they were in Lisbon. Twice since she had seen the Meads working on something on the ship's computers or their own tablet.

There were a couple of moments when Heather seemed to be comforting him. She too was distracted and concerned. Vaila had had to offer to pour Heather a glass of wine from the carafe three times before she responded. Mark, sitting next to her just looked down at his plate and said nothing. Vaila did not like to ask what was troubling them, nor could she ask Ellis what he thought when they were all sitting so close to each other. But there was little she could do to help unless they asked.

Ellis was unaware of Vaila's concern, partly because he had concentrated on keeping the party together when walking through the crowded city streets and partly because now that he could relax for a few minutes he was enjoying simply being there. Looking around the piazza he saw a news stand on the corner next to the restaurant and while they waited for their order to be brought to them he wandered over. The stand carried a wide range of papers from a number of European countries and amongst them he spotted a Daily Mail with a large headline.

"Whitehall accused of carelessness and cover up. The Ministry of Transport is a shambles, says MP, calling for a public enquiry."

He bought the paper, which was twenty four hours old, and returned to their table. He had only just sat down when their orders arrived, together with another large carafe of Frascati, the local wine and, being hungry after walking around the city the group attended to an excellent lunch. Even the Meads seemed to put aside their problem to appreciate the meal. They were still talking of all they had seen and still full of questions for Bruno as they enjoyed the meal, the rest and the warm atmosphere of their surroundings.

As they rounded off their lunch with coffee as only Italians can make it, Ellis picked up his newspaper and opened it, then held it up to fold it to read an inside page. There was a quiet "Oh" from Mark. Ellis realised that he must have seen the front page, and wondered what had caused his reaction. He did not like to turn it over to look but remembered it concerned a rail franchise.

The rest of the party, deep in their own discussions, took no notice.

Mark asked Ellis if he could borrow his paper.

"Of course," he replied, and passed it to him.

Mark put aside his knife and fork and read the front page. He said nothing and when he had finished it he passed it to Heather who had just finished her lunch, and he resumed his meal.

She passed it back to Ellis just as Bruno got up from his seat at the other end of the table and came to Ellis to suggest they now continued their tour. He rang the coach driver and confirmed that they would be picked up in ten minutes and Bruno guided them to where the coach would stop for the party to board. Vaila saw Mark whisper something to Heather as he got up ready to go.

The coach dropped them off near the Vatican. They walked to the huge Piazza San Pietro in front of the Basilica. Inside the scale of the building was even more overwhelming than the exterior, never mind the sheer quantity of art and sculpture throughout as if no space could remain unadorned.

The group spread out, having been given thirty minutes to look at whatever most interested them. Ellis and Vaila started with the papal altar in the centre of the church, itself magnificent and set above the place where St Peter is allegedly buried. Admiring it Vaila commented that it wasn't at all bad for a fisherman. Next they crossed the Basilica to admire Michelangelo's Pieta. As they looked at it they heard whispering from behind them. Turning round they saw Mark and Heather. They appeared to be in an animated discussion about something which certainly had nothing to do with the Basilica.

Vaila wanted to offer them help, but Ellis suggested they should be left alone.

"If there was something causing you so much anguish you'd want me to help you and vice versa rather than a tour escort you hardly knew wouldn't you?"

Accepting that he was right, she reluctantly walked away. She was beginning to feel sorry for them, they were normally so controlled, so confident. Not only that but in her head she was trying to catch an elusive memory. She was sure that she should know what had happened to Mark and Heather but could not bring out the clue her head told her was there. She saw them take a seat together and wondered if they were offering a prayer.

The group reassembled outside below the library window from which the Pope blesses the faithful on special occasions. Vaila was pleased to see Heather looking a little better as if they had thought of a solution to their problem.

The others in the group were full of all they had seen, but were now ready to return to the coach for the journey back to their floating home.

As they waited for a straggler, Ellis' phone rang. It was Peter. He had quite a long conversation with him and then spoke to Bruno, who nodded and called the group to gather round so Ellis could explain.

"I have just had a call from Peter, our pianist, who is escorting one of the coaches on the panoramic tour. There were two coaches on that tour, and the first left to return to the ship half an hour ago, but his coach has broken down not far from here. The coach company is trying to replace it but say that it will be at least a couple of hours before they can do so, and by then it will be rush hour."

He wondered how many of the group would guess what was coming next.

"If Peter's group are so late that it badly delays the ship's departure, there could be a knock on effect at our next port. Peter asks us if we can take his passengers on this coach. Having spoken to Bruno, we think we can, if only just. Bruno and his colleague in Peter's coach have agreed the best way to make the transfer bearing in mind traffic problems. We can't drive to the other coach as their breakdown has caused a traffic jam around them already. But Bruno suggests a place where this coach could probably wait not too far away. The guides suggest it might take them fifteen minutes or so to walk to our coach." He paused. "Can I ask if that's a problem for anyone?"

Vaila saw an anxious look in Heather's face as she looked at Mark, but could not hear what was whispered between them. Neither of them said anything aloud nor did anyone else have an objection.

Luckily Bruno knew the area well so they soon found the place where Ellis' coach could wait, and then he walked the couple of blocks to where the broken down coach was. His colleague and Peter had explained the plan to their passengers who then got off their coach and the guides brought them on foot to Ellis' coach. Considering Peter had two wheel chair passengers and most had limited mobility the transfer went smoothly and did not take too long.

Ellis' passengers, being entirely fit, cheerfully made room at the front of the coach and having settled the panoramic passengers found there were still three seats short. Bruno spoke to the guide from Peter's coach, and then to Ellis who told passengers through the microphone that their guides would go home to free two seats as both tours had been completed. Peter took the guide's seat leaving one aisle seat for Ellis and Vaila who had given up their seats for passengers.

With a cheerful "Arrivederci!" everyone clapped and the guides got off the coach and Ellis and Peter took charge. Ellis sat in the remaining aisle seat next to a man travelling alone. Vaila sat on his lap, Ellis just joking that he wished she had not had so large a lunch!

Having solved the seating problem, probably illegally as they could not use the seat belt, the coach set off, everyone hoping that the journey back would create no further problems.

Peter in the guide's seat with the microphone, announced that he had phoned the ship to tell them what had happened, and so could reassure everyone on the coach that all was well. The ship was waiting for them. The coach settled down to the journey.

While they had been waiting for the panoramic group to come to the coach, Vaila had noticed Mark and Heather again quietly talking together. Now they were in the seats just in front of Ellis and Vaila. Being higher in the seat on Ellis' knee Vaila occasionally heard snatches of their conversation.

They were clearly discussing their problem and continued to do so all the way back to Civitavecchia. The occasional phrases she heard told her little but it was enough to realise the issue was the rail franchise story that had been on the front page of the paper Ellis had bought. She heard Mark speak of GNBP, and realised these initials had been in Heather's discarded rough notes that Vaila had accidently picked up. It was what she had half remembered earlier but she still did not know what the letters stood for. The only complete sentence she picked up was *"I wish I knew for sure that my email reached the Chief Secretary. There's a chance it hasn't yet."* But then she felt a little ashamed of herself for listening to the Mead's discussion and just looked out of the window.

In all the business of transferring passengers Ellis had not at first realised that the man in the window seat next to them was Gerry Jones.

Gerry laughed when Vaila settled on Ellis' lap.

"Pity Sandie isn't escort on this trip, or I could have offered her a seat on my lap. Lucky you!" Ellis thought for a moment,

"Oh I remember, she's one of the dancers isn't she?"

"That's right. She's a super girl. She doesn't get ashore much but she's hoping Chloe, leader of the Dynamite Productions team, will let her come ashore with me at Naples. She has a day off when we're there." He did not seem to want to take the conversation further and Vaila was hinting that Ellis should be quiet, so after that they just watched the scenery and Ellis thought back to what he knew about the man as they were driven along the autostrada.

In their brief brush with the Mafia in Naples on honeymoon the issue was that he was doing some sort of business. The Mafia 'Capo' had been very cross with him because Gerry had been dealing with some Albysian refugees of whom he disapproved, but Gerry never said what his business was. Earlier, with Vaila, he had seen Gerry meet Hassan at Pompeii, presumably the same business. That was on their honeymoon when they called him Red check shirt because they didn't know his name. Hassan was undoubtedly Albysian, they'd known that since the Orcadian incident with the *Camel Prince*. What had the mafia to do with Albysia? For that matter what had Gerry to do with that little country? What had Hassan been doing in Naples? It gave Ellis two reasons to be especially interested in what would happen in Naples. Perhaps they would discover what Gerry's business and Hassans activities were.

Then it struck him, what about the *Camel Prince*? When they had been on the bridge visit before Ajaccio they had discovered that the scruffy little ship was also going to Naples and wondered if that was significant. All these mysteries might come together tomorrow in Naples. He might even be able to work out how you could call a Camel Prince 'she'!

Gerry himself seemed comparatively young, especially relative to most passengers and he'd come on his own. That also made Ellis wonder. Did anyone do legitimate deals with the Mafia? Lots of people did come alone on cruises but he still seemed an unlikely sort of person to be on this sort of holiday. Ellis decided he'd better watch him when they got to Naples, preferably at a distance. He didn't want to get tangled up with the Mafia a second time. Yet Gerry was the sort of man one found oneself liking even if his business appeared likely to be a bit dodgy.

Naples and beyond

Ellis was unsurprisingly asked to be escort to the excursion to Pompeii from Naples and Vaila would come with him as his assistant. By now they had become familiar with the process and having visited the famous site twice on honeymoon only five months before, felt confident that they could make a good job of the task, and Ellis felt he would be on home territory, professionally speaking, and confident that he could even help the guiding too if necessary. He expected questions anyway from the lecture he gave when at sea prior to Ajaccio.

They had not seen Minnie and Millie after returning to the ship following the Rome excursion on the previous day, as the ladies had been on the first panoramic tour coach rather than Peter's, the one that had broken down. Their coach had returned without incident. As they walked into the dining room for breakfast they saw the ladies at a nearby table and joined them.

They were all glad that today the ladies were to be going on the same excursion to Pompeii, and asked Ellis to ensure they would be on his coach, as there were no less than four coaches for this excursion.

The waitress had just brought their order when the Redmans also asked if they could join them at the table. Vaila introduced the ladies to them, explaining that they had met on the Vizzavona trip from Ajaccio.

Ellis remembered the coincidence about a man called Colin in both George Redman's description of his work with Traidcraft and in the Blackwood's story in the Bay of Biscay storm. He did not think Helen and Jim would be offended that they talked to the Redmans about Colin in order to see if it really might be the same Colin in both cases.

So having told the Redmans Jim Blackwood's story, and how even after so many years it still troubled Jim that he had been responsible for the accident that had crippled Colin, the six of them around the table discussed whether they should tell Jim and Helen about it. It was Millie who suggested that they should tell just Helen. Because as Jim's wife she was in the best position to decide if he should be told and she was certainly the best person to tell Jim, if she thought it would help. Their hope was that Jim might feel better about it if he knew how Colin had made a good life for himself, with his family and a satisfying job.

Having finished breakfast Ellis went to arrange for the ladies and the Redmans, who were also coming on the Pompeii excursion, to be on his coach. Then he went to get ready for it, to discover which coach he was to escort and which coloured sticker he would be given.

He met the Redmans and Minnie and Millie at nine thirty in the Ocean lounge where passengers were allotted coloured stickers. He had spoken to the staff and had taken four red stickers, the colour for his coach, and now put them on their tickets, smiled and left with Vaila to find the coach.

There was a short delay before the passengers were sent down to the coaches during which Ellis took the opportunity to look around the port with the binoculars he had brought with him. He saw the *Camel Prince* with her distinctive orange bridge tied up not far from the *Carnelian* across the harbour beyond the ferry terminals and a dry dock. She was at one of the commercial piers. He had a good look at her. There was some activity on her pier, but all the cranes, small buildings and other things on the pier obscured much of the view so he could not see from where he was what the activity was. He thought it would be a reasonable guess that she would be going to Qariat next just as the *Carnelian* was, Qariat was after all her home port. He thought she would be loading imports for Albysia after unloading whatever she had brought from Barcelona. He soon forgot about her as the passengers started to arrive at the coach.

Apart from the ladies and the Redmans, amongst the passengers on Ellis' coach were the McRavens. Vaila, who was checking tickets, greeted them cheerfully and got a grunted "Good morning" in reply, which did not feel to her to be very friendly.

She wondered if the grunt indicated that they now knew about Rosemarie but she could give them no further attention whilst she continued cheerfully greeting passengers and checking tickets as they arrived. Ellis, helping passengers onto the coach, was glad to see the Blackwoods, and when he got on the coach himself to check numbers saw that they were seated on the opposite side of the coach to Minnie and Millie. If they could get an opportunity to introduce them maybe they could manage a quiet word with Helen.

It had been arranged that a guide from Pompeii would join the coach at the ship and Ellis was delighted to find that the guide allotted to his coach was Francesco, who they had met when they visited Pompeii on honeymoon, but he didn't expect Francesco would recognise them. However Francesco looked at Vaila and Ellis for a moment and said

"You were with us in the spring I think?"

"How did you recognise us? You must see hundreds of visitors?" Francesco laughed.

"You were very obviously just married, and equally obviously you knew what you were looking at here Ellis. An archaeologist I think? A mixture not to be forgotten!" He shook their hands enthusiastically.

"Were we that obvious?" And Francesco laughed again.

On the coach and the usual introductions over, they set off, the coach threading its way round the busy dockyard towards the main gate. There they came to a standstill. The traffic on the main road immediately outside the dock gates was heavy and only crawling along.

Francesco took the traffic jam as normal and spoke to the passengers about the city's history as they waited.

Vaila nudged Ellis and pointed to the pier nearest them. From the stationary coach they had a clear view of the *Camel Prince* alongside. They saw that the ship was being loaded with three large wooden crates from a lorry. There were several men helping or watching as if the crates were both heavy and perhaps fragile. He still had the binoculars around his neck so trained them on the scene whilst the coach was at a standstill. Carefully adjusting the focus he found himself looking at Hassan. What was even more surprising was that a short distance from them was the large limo, which he was sure was the same one that had returned them to Sorrento when they had had their brush with the Mafia. He gave the binoculars to Vaila and suggested she looked too, and she confirmed it.

Hassan was with the local Mafia boss they had met. It was as if the Mafia was delivering the crates to Hassan for shipment. Ellis wondered what was in them. As she watched Vaila exclaimed

"Oh ho! What's this? Ellis, Gerry is there too. He's approaching them and he has a girl with him. I hope he won't get himself into deeper water than he did in April with both the Albysians and the Mafia." She passed the glasses back to Ellis. He watched for a moment and laughed. "My guess is that he has got into plenty of deep water but not with the locals! The girl is Sandie, the dancer who he has become fond of, and she's appears to be having a major row with him!"

As the coach at last joined the traffic, the last he saw, or rather thought he saw because as the coach drove away from the scene he was unable to use the binoculars, was the Mafia boss shrug his shoulders and turn away. Sandie, if it was her, also turned and walked quickly away in the direction of the *Carnelian* with Gerry chasing after her. Ellis told Vaila what he had seen, put the binoculars away and turned his attention back to Francesco.

The tour round Pompeii followed the same route around the Roman city as it had on their honeymoon visit, but this time their group was much larger.

Ellis stayed towards the back of the group as they walked and was able to help those who were not near enough to Francesco to hear him properly. He felt confident he could tell them nearly as much about the city and what had happened in the eruption of Vesuvius in AD 79 as could their guide. He asked Vaila to keep her eyes out for stragglers, so he could concentrate on helping with the guiding.

This time there was no red check shirt, as Gerry had not, of course come on the excursion, nor were there any close encounters with Albysians. But Ellis did have to gently calm the ladies' and the Redmans' horror over the erotic art. At least he had Vaila with him to try to avoid as much of it as possible.

But there was much wonderful art and decoration that they could point to and, as Vaila had also learned about the four styles described in the leaflet Francesco had given her on their honeymoon visit, so she could identify which was which. For Vaila the one picture that was to stay in her mind was of the galley in the house of the Vetii, and she remembered Ellis' enthusiasm for it.

Both the ladies and the Redmans were clearly tiring after so much walking by the time they got to the Horttus Porta Marina Ristorante and Garden bar at lunchtime and were relieved to be able to sit down.

As he had on their previous visit, Francesco said that they would be free to look around further after the meal and that he would take a group to wherever they wished to go. It would mean, of course, that they would have to agree what they wanted him to show them.

The ladies and the Redmans said that they really did not want to walk far after lunch and the majority of those who did were keen to see the two theatres. But not Colonel McRaven. He said he wished to see The Villa of the Mysteries because their daughter had recommended it. She had told them that it was important that her parents should not miss it.

"She's a firstclass archaeologist herself, of course, and told us the villa has the famous decoration telling the story of the mysteries in the second-style and is considered the best in Pompeii in terms of size and quality."

Francesco agreed but pointed out that he could not go with both groups, the two places were in opposite directions. The Colonel's reply was sour and selfish, though Vaila thought she could not deny it was true,

"Mackenzie can take the group to the theatres, he surely knows enough about them to do that?" Vaila read into his suggestion that he wanted to imply that his daughter was a better archaeologist than Ellis.

Francesco looked at Ellis who simply said

"No problem, of course I will." He paused, "I suppose you are aware, Colonel, that it's outside the city itself, a bit of a walk?"

"Of course. Walking is no trouble to me." He made no attempt to ask his wife but Ellis felt it was not for him to interfere. One other couple asked if they could go to the villa too so it seemed everyone was able to do what they had hoped to do.

Turning to the group Ellis said

"I'll stand just over there by the Porta Marina. Those of you who want to come with me, join me there. Could I remind all of you that the coach will leave at four o'clock from where it deposited us this morning?" He pointed. "I hope that's okay Francesco?"

"Yes." And he quietly added "You have the better party I think. See you at the coach."

Apart from the Redmans and the ladies, one other passenger opted to stay by the restaurant, Helen Blackwood. She had twisted her ankle on a stone in the civic forum as they had walked back to the restaurant and although not too serious she didn't want to risk aggravating it. Jim however wanted to go with Ellis.

As soon as the two groups had left Minnie grasped the unexpected opportunity she fortuitously now had to bring up the subject of Colin with Helen. She explained that there seemed to be a coincidence between Jim's Colin and the one now working at Traidcraft and asked George to tell Helen about the Colin he knew.

The Redmans did so and Helen was surprised and very interested in what they said. As they discussed whether both Colins could be the same, Helen pointed out that she had not actually met the one Jim had known but by the time they had had another coffee all of them agreed that it did seem highly likely. Helen said she thought she should tell Jim.

"Somehow, things do seem to be coming to a head on this cruise. If Jim was convinced that the Colin he knew was now happily married with a family and a job he enjoyed, it might convince Jim that he need not think about it again."

The two groups met at the restaurant and moved together to the coach. As Ellis and Vaila stood by the coach with Francesco helping folk get onto it, one man complemented Ellis on how he had taken the role of an expert guide to Pompeii as if he had done it hundreds of times.

"You certainly must know this site well. It can't be easy to step in without warning and make such a good job of it. Well done."

"Thank you. It was certainly a surprise, but archaeology is both my passion and profession. I'm glad you enjoyed it."

Francesco laughed, and said he was surprised that Ellis could do it at all, teasing him by saying to the man,

"It's amazing your escort knew anything. When he was here before he was on his honeymoon. An Italian would have been thinking of something else!" The man spread the story throughout the coach, and as they moved off Vaila whispered in Ellis ear "We'll not live that down now."

The only other thing Ellis noticed on their drive back to the ship was that the *Camel Prince* had sailed, but it didn't seem important enough to tell Vaila.

After Ellis had been to the staff meeting at six, they met with Minnie and Millie in the Seafarers bar at seven as usual. As they had a drink with the ladies they told Ellis and Vaila that they had spoken to Helen at the Pompeii restaurant. Helen had been most interested and would tell Jim about it at a suitable moment. It had, the ladies felt, tied up that issue as as well as could be expected.

Dinner was at a table of folk they had not previously met. The conversation around the table confirmed how impressed they had all been with Ellis' impromptu guiding. He shrugged off their praise.

"You'll be giving me a big head." He laughed and told them that the next day, at sea on the way to Qariat, he would be lecturing on the Picts, as well as giving a joint talk on Albysia and Si'pelium with David Grey. He hoped they would join him for it. Much later Vaila told Ellis what she thought of the Colonel's idea that Ellis should guide at Pompeii.

"I'm sure he suggested you took a group partly because he wanted Francesco to take him to the Villa of the Mysteries, 'We're first class don't you know'" she mimicked, "and partly to try to catch you out. I hope he gets to hear that the party who went with us thought you had made a really good job of it, 'a first class job of it.'" Again mimicking the Colonel. Ellis laughed and again just shrugged it off.

"It is my profession, darling. It's not all that clever."

Ellis' lecture on the Picts, set for ten the next morning, went down quite well although he wondered if he had chosen the right subject. He explained to Vaila over coffee,

"Most passengers are English, and I wasn't sure that they were very interested in the ancient history of the north of Scotland. At least I think they liked the photos of the stones."

There had been one amusing incident however. When Jonny Wirth, chairing the lecture, asked if there were any questions, the first came from the Colonel. Ellis was curious as to where he got the question from as Rosemarie would undoubtedly have known and disliked the answer.

"You say that there is much evidence of the Picts from place names, but what about people's names? I believe my name, McRaven to be Pictish, proving my aristocratic lineage goes back over a thousand years. Do you know anything about that?"

"I'm not sure that you would want to explore your name too deeply. In Pictish mythology the raven is the bird of death. A raven is depicted on the Aberlemno stone pecking at the dead after a battle, not a comfortable thought. 'Mac' however spelt usually indicates 'the son of' so if you are descended from the Picts it sounds as if you must have had a very unpopular ancestor. I'm sorry to give you bad news."

There was laughter at that and, as his talk ended, applause. Ellis hoped the Colonel would not be too offended by his teasing reply. Vaila was becoming irritated by the Colonel's attempts to find questions Ellis would be seen to be unable to answer, even though he had not yet been caught out.

After lunch he joined forces with David to speak about Albysia and of course, Si'pelium. David started by saying that he had to admit that he did not know much about the little country. But he explained that it did had two claims to fame, and there were excursions to each.

"Si'pelium, the recently found remains of a Roman city, which Ellis Mackenzie will tell you about, and Albysia's famous camels. The excursion to see them means going into the desert.

"The camels are claimed to run faster and have greater stamina in desert conditions than any other camels. Albysians are very proud of them."

He did not think there was much to see in Qariat for those going ashore independently, although as it was the one port he had never visited before he could not be sure of that. He only warned that few if any of the locals would be able to speak English.

He then spoke of the Italian involvement in the early twentieth century.

"They built a large breakwater in order to create an outer harbour. Doubtless you will see that once we arrive. But they did little more here. I gather that at least once the guides in Rome referred to it."

He then handed over to Ellis.

"Thank you David. I am looking forward to seeing Si'pelium as I have never been there before either. The pictures being projected were taken about seven years ago and show that there is a limited amount of the site so far uncovered from the large sand dune system that had covered and protected it for nearly two millennia. It's not nearly as old as Skara Brae but there is a parallel in that both were covered by sand. Hopefully the sand has protected this site as well as it protected Skara Brae, but what we will see is limited. Nonetheless what you do see is a North African Roman colonial City which very few Europeans have ever seen, making the visit an amazing first for all of us on our excursion. With any luck we will be able to make some discoveries of our own. You never know we might find a new Villa that no one has seen since Roman times, and it could then be called after the ship, perhaps the Villa of Carnelian!"

He explained that recently the Albysian Government had approved a visit by a team of archaeologists but no one had so far been able to raise the funds to organise anything.

"One feature is interesting, the remains of a Roman harbour. In other Roman coastal cities, harbours make use of natural features such as at Leptis Magna. At Si'pelium there is no useful natural feature to speak of and the Romans attempted to create a sheltered harbour where there was the minimum help from the lie the land. The probable reason why the city was abandoned was that the harbour they tried to build was not very successful. The harbour where the *Carnelian* will berth is at Qariat only about five miles away, a much better site for the purpose so it is a mystery why the Romans put their city where they did. The remains of their attempt at building a harbour can however be seen. One hopes that excavation will help us to find an answer to these questions.

"One thing is certain, at least from an archaeological perspective, the fact that we know so little about it makes for a very exciting visit. A local guide will no doubt explain to you its history and what there is to see. To me the excitement is that I am reasonably sure there is much interesting material to find that no one else has yet discovered."

Beyond that Ellis did not try to expand his description of the site further than the power point presentation he had prepared in Edinburgh with the slides Calum had lent him. That now seemed a very long time ago.

At lunch they found themselves at a table for four on the Quarterdeck, in the open air, where the Meads joined them. They looked extremely happy to Ellis' surprise and the surprise grew when Mark ordered drinks and asked Ellis and Vaila to join them.

"It's a celebration." Mark said "Much better to celebrate with friends than alone."

"What's happened to celebrate?" Vaila asked, and the couple told their story.

Mark had worked on the latest rail franchise for the LSR and there had been two bidders, the GNBP and the LHR when the ITT went out last February Mark explained. As sometimes happens the whole project seemed to go wrong from the start.

"The Minister put us under pressure to push the matter ahead as fast as we could because he had not authorised certain parts of it as soon as he should have done. The work is always complicated, but there were changes required in this case which were especially complex." Heather stopped him. "They'll never understand unless you tell them what all the initials mean."

"Sorry. LSR is the London Scottish Railway franchise. GNBP is the Great British Rail Partnership, the company who hold the current franchise which is about to expire, LHR is the London Highland Railway company and ITT is just the Invitation to Tender." Heather looked pleased. She would want everything in the story correct, clear and in the right order, Vaila thought.

"Things got tangled up." Mark continued. "The prospectus was printed after the pre-qualification stage instead of before because of the rush. My team had to work out some of the detailed calculations and statements on numbers of passengers and the number of seats we would need on certain trains and what extra provision would be required at set busy times. It was important to make the right calculations. Civil servants worked late and into weekends to try to analyse the information that wasn't complete because of the rush." Heather interjected

"I'm sure they don't want all the fine detail." Ellis smiled and nodded. He was lost already.

Mark explained how it came to a head a couple of weeks before they were due to leave to come on the cruise. He was working with Heather in the statistical section to extract some statistical information about the sizes of trains, to ensure everything was accurate and every detail correct when they realised that there were a number of straightforward mistakes in the prospectus other staff had inserted.

"All very technical but they were details that might well make a difference to who won the franchise. I went to my line manager about it who said he would deal with it. I was not to worry about it, 'just enjoy your leave' he said."

Mark paused as if trying to be quite sure he had the story in the right order.

"When we were in Lisbon I had an email telling me that the franchise had been let to GNBP but that Sir Rollo Branscomb on behalf of LHR had complained about the process and faulty prospectus. To me, it was obvious that Connor, my line manager, hadn't done anything about the mistakes I had brought to his attention. It seemed likely he was trying to cover up the mistakes. At that point my worry was that cover ups rarely work, and I might get the blame.

"In Gibraltar, there was a short item in 'Britain today' saying that the Department had blundered, and that Sir Rollo was right. It wasn't hard for me to work out what that meant. Connor had indeed left the contract on the prospectus without correcting the mistakes. LHR had spotted the mistakes, complained and been proved right.

"Later in the day I checked my emails to discover that I had been suspended for being responsible for the mistakes. Worse, and a nasty surprise, I was also being blamed for the press getting hold of the story. Of course that was totally untrue, but it meant I faced an enquiry into my conduct. But then Heather reminded me of the list of dates I had seen in Connor's diary. We realised something else was going on. The dates were all weekend ones with GNBP."

Vaila looked at Ellis and they both realised that was what they had seen on Heather's binned rough notes.

"While we were crossing the Med to Ajaccio Heather and I researched the whole business and wrote a statement in my defence, something our rules allowed as an opportunity to clear my name and avoid an enquiry. I couldn't send it until Ajaccio, and then I decided to send a copy of it to Sir John Guthrie, the chief secretary because describing myself as a whistle blower might in the current climate put me on the side of the angels. In Rome it was a bitter disappointment to see from the paper you had that nothing had changed, the paper just emphasized the wasted public money. It looked as if my position was worse than ever."

"Yes," said Heather, "but it wasn't. I couldn't believe that the Ministry had read Mark's statement. They would be properly concerned at ignoring a whistle blower."

Mark took up the story again.

"Today I had an email acknowledging that I had been the one who had spotted the mistakes. The suspension was lifted. I was right. Sir John would want to avoid the accusation that the Ministry had not only ignored a whistle blower, but had suspended him too." He smiled. "Better still, the journalist who'd written the earlier story had also discovered something about the weekend meetings which he had uncovered via a leak from GNBP, not the DoT, and therefore there could be no case against me for any leak either." He continued to say that he thought Connor must have been trying to get GNBP to say that they had spotted the mistakes, and had bid accordingly. It was in both Connor's and GNBP's interests to take that line. The meetings were to ensure that argument was watertight, and thus provide a solid reason why GNBP should keep the contract that they had just been awarded.

"But of course it was totally out of order to do that and unfair to LHR. Thank goodness Sir Rollo Branscomb and the LHR team spotted the mistakes as it not only meant that they will have a second opportunity to win the contract but also ensured I was exonerated, hence this celebration."

"Congratulations. I saw the news in 'Britain Today' at Gibraltar but took little notice. No railways in Orkney."

Ellis and Vaila spent a lazy afternoon on deck in the sunshine. At one point Ellis said

"It's nice to feel that all those secrets we have heard have, in one way or another, been resolved."

A little sleepily Vaila, who wanted to get the sort of tan she would never be able to achieve in Orkney laughed.

"I don't think so, there are a couple left."

"Which ones?"

"Gerry, for a start. I'm still curious about what we saw from the coach yesterday. Then what about..."

She was interrupted by Helen and Jim. They were looking relaxed and happy.

"We just wanted to thank you and your aunts for making the connection over Colin." Jim said. "I think it must be the same Colin, and although I will always regret what I did, Colin is clearly a wonderful man. I've asked George to speak to Colin when they get home. I want him to know that I am truly sorry for what happened. I don't think I ever had a chance to do that properly. If Colin wishes, I'll go to Gateshead to see him myself."

As they moved away Ellis said he hoped that two couples at least would go home happier than when they came.

It was a formal night that evening and as usual they arranged to meet Minnie and Millie in the Seafarer's bar before dinner. It was as usual quite busy, but only one thing surprised Vaila. Gerry sat at the bar by himself. He looked miserable.

"I think poor Gerry has lost his girlfriend."

"Yes darling, I wonder what happened on the pier in Naples."

It was however time to go to the dining room, and afterwards they decided not to go to the show in the Ocean lounge that night. Instead settled for having a nightcap back in the Seafarer's bar. To their surprise Gerry was still there, at the bar. Ellis was beside him when he went to order drinks, so he asked Gerry if had had dinner yet.

"Oh hello. Oh yes, I eat in the Island cafeteria. I didn't feel like talking to anyone."

"Okay, but if you feel like company why not join us now?" He nodded in the direction of the table where Vaila was sitting.

Ellis returned to their table and not long after the waiter brought their drinks across Gerry did come to them. He said

"Everything went wrong for me yesterday. I suppose it's all my own fault. The worst thing is that Sandie doesn't want to see me again."

"I'm sorry to hear that. You two seemed to be getting on so well."

"Yes. I had an opportunity to conclude my business yesterday, just as Sandie and me walked towards the gate to explore Naples. I'd promised to take her out to lunch and had in mind that café where I met you in the spring, I expect you remember. But there was the Mafia guy, talking to that Albysian man so I thought I couldn't miss the opportunity to make a deal with both of them there. I told Sandie that it wouldn't take long. They'd either agree to sell to me or they wouldn't. When the Capo chap asked me exactly what I wanted, Sandie heard that it was drugs and got very angry with me. She hates drugs. She said she knew someone ruined by them. I told the Capo and the Albysian that I'd changed my mind. I didn't want to buy after all because Sandie didn't want me to.   "They didn't seem to mind, but it was too late for Sandie. She walked away, and when I caught up with her she was still furious with me. She told me to get lost, she wouldn't see me again and a load of other stuff. So I lost both the business and Sandie. I've decided to keep to legit stuff from now on whatever happens. Sandie's contract ends after this cruise and we had already agreed to meet at home, so I know where she lives. I'll try to persuade her I mean it, if she'll listen. I don't know she will even meet me but I'm really keen on her. I'll certainly not touch drugs again."

"She's right. I'm glad you'll forget the drugs Gerry, and good luck with Sandie, if she's knows you mean it I'm sure she'll be able to forgive you. Anyway we have an early start tomorrow so we must turn in now. Good night."

The Excursion

The *Carnelian* arrived at the pilot station off the port of Qariat at the scheduled time on Tuesday morning.

Having slept well, Ellis had got up at seven. He was keen to see what he could of Qariat as, for him, this was to be an especially exciting day.

He would be leading two excursions to Si'pelium, one in the morning and the other in the afternoon. The Roman city had recently been uncovered from the sand dunes that had protected it for centuries. Now he would see it and put, as it were, life into what he had read and studied of this little explored, and possibly particularly important site, where he might be, if not the first archaeologist to see it, then certainly the first for many years. That he should be working on sites at home that had been preserved by burial in sand like this Roman city was an exciting parallel, even if the Roman city was much younger than the Orcadian sites.

The photos Calum Cameron had lent him suggested that it was not in nearly so good a state of preservation as Skara Brae, but part of its attraction for Ellis was that it was a site on which no one had previously done much work.

That it might be difficult for a layman to understand only concerned him to the extent he might need to explain why it was important. The passengers would find it much harder to understand than Pompeii which they had just seen and he hoped the local guide would be good at his job.

His duties might limit what he could see, but of course he had no idea whether he could ever come again. For all these reasons he wanted to be well prepared.

He hastily shaved and dressed. He saw that Vaila was still asleep, looking peaceful. He smiled to himself thinking of her as his own Sleeping Beauty, but thought he would not be her Prince Charming quite yet, he would let her sleep a bit longer. He wrote a note to say he had gone on deck and would be back shortly in case she woke before he came back, and put it against her bedside clock, picked up the binoculars provided in the cabin and crept out as quietly as he could.

He reached the Sun Deck just as the *Carnelian* was picking up the pilot, still a mile or so from the port. About twenty other passengers were also curious enough to be on deck early to watch what was happening. Ellis had been told that some passengers did so at every port.

The open Sun Deck was the highest part of the ship for passengers. At each side of the forward end of the deck it was possible to look over the rail and have a grandstand view of the whole operation, because on the *Carnelian* the bridge was just below the Sun Deck, and the Captain, the pilot and officers would be guiding the ship from a wing of the bridge.

The calm giving of orders regulating the ship's speed and direction gave an air of competence which reinforced the passengers' confidence in the way the ship was handled. They were able to watch the ship's progress as it came into the outer harbor, through the north entrance of the breakwater into the outer harbour.

From 'The *Carnelian* Daily' Ellis knew that the ship's berth in the inner harbour was to be against the quay on their port side, and he could see several men waiting to take her lines as she edged towards the berth allocated to her, gently assisted by a small tug.

The passengers did not know it, but the Captain was unhappy about the tug, as it was not large or powerful enough to be much help, and he thought it might get in the way rather than be of use. The *Carnelian* had, after all, bow thrusters which enabled her both to come alongside and depart unaided. The Qariat harbourmaster had however insisted that the tug was used, and as neither the *Carnelian* nor her Captain had been into Qariat before, and friendly relations with local officials were highly desirable to ensure smooth arrangements in all the various aspects of their short stay, he had accepted it. Doubtless the accountants at the company's headquarters would grouse about the cost, but that was just what accountants did.

Nevertheless the operation of docking was completed just as it should be. The pilot had recommended they lay alongside with the bow towards the town, rather than turning the ship prior to docking, because it would be more comfortable, as there was often an onshore breeze by midday which, it was suggested, would keep the ship cool. Again this was not the Captain's normal practice and he thought the northerly sirocco was likely to be a bit too much, but he could see no reason to refuse local advice. Much later he came to realise that the passengers were safer with the bows to the town.

The quayside where the *Carnelian* was berthed had a large open concrete area by the ship, perhaps a hundred metres by seventy, surrounded by a high fence. He wondered why the enclosure was so large. To get from the ship to the dockyard and town beyond, involved a walk across this large open space and through a small building about the size of a single garage. It had a large and newly painted sign 'Customs' over the door facing the cruise ship. Four coaches were already parked by the customs shed. There was also a large gate in the fence near the ship's bow, but it was shut. It was presumably the way supplies could be delivered.

Ellis noted that Qariat was much smaller than many other port cities, certainly smaller than he had expected, perhaps not much bigger than Inverness. The ship would be very close to the town centre, a feature which many passengers would appreciate as it would enable them to walk into it without the need for transport if they wished.

There were no buildings over two floors high near the port, so the *Carnelian* dominated the dockyard and sea front of the town, being higher than the buildings on the road just outside the dock.

Most of the city was built on flat land a little higher than the dock road, as if on a geological raised beach. The view over the city from the ship was therefore limited.

Already several townspeople had come out to see the ship with as much curiosity as the passengers showed looking at the town. The *Carnelian* was the first cruise ship to visit Albysia for a considerable number of years, maybe the first ever.

The street immediately outside the port was lined with shops, a few cafes and other businesses. None of the buildings were particularly distinguished. Through binoculars they did not look at all well cared for either and many were dark and dirty. Ellis wondered if this reflected poverty or just plain neglect. Beyond them the minaret of a mosque formed a prominent part of the skyline and from it their arrival was greeted by the morning call to prayer.

There was some mixed traffic moving on the adjacent street, and a couple of buses of uncertain age went by as Ellis watched. One had a broken window. He hoped the coaches provided for the excursions would be better than the buses or the escorts would never hear the last of it. They looked all right but he could not see them clearly.

Within the dockyard area there were three small cranes, one of which was finishing unloading the cargo from a small coaster into a couple of lorries, though it was not possible to tell what the cargo was. It looked as if the coaster was preparing to leave. To their right, to westward across the dock from the *Carnelian*, there was a small gunboat alongside a naval quay at the foot of the low cliff which protected the port from the west. The gunboat looked old, and although they were trying hard, the crew who were scrubbing the deck could not disguise her obsolescence. At the bow it had a large newly repainted "2" in white on the rusty grey hull, and as she had no other name displayed maybe they just called her *Number 2*. At the stern she proudly flew the Albysian colours of yellow and orange, as James Grey had described in his lecture the previous day. The dock between the *Carnelian*'s berth and the naval quay was quite narrow, little wider than the length of the cruise ship, and it crossed Ellis' mind that the ship would have to go astern to leave Qariat as there was not nearly enough room for her to turn round within the dock.

Looking astern he could see the large outer harbour which enclosed and sheltered the inner harbour and dockyard. The long and fairly high breakwater had two entrances, one directly astern, through which they had just come, and one at the eastern side. He remembered David Grey explaining that this had been built by the Italians at a time when they had had ambitions to have a North African empire. They wanted to support it by a small naval base at Qariat.

Beyond the harbour the coast to the west was hidden by the low cliff. To the east the country behind the beach was flat, dry, and marked in several places by single or small groups of scrub like trees and the occasional palm. He could see a small minaret presumably marking a village not more than five miles away and a little inland

At sea some distance from him Ellis could see a few sailing craft, characteristic of this coast. He presumed they were fishing boats, going gently out to sea for a day's catch, but how odd, and how interesting, that they should be sailing craft, presumably without an engine. He speculated that that this must mean a small harbor, or perhaps an inlet, but if so it was not visible from where he stood. They might even be using the remains of the Roman harbour at Si'pelium. He looked for Si'pelium. It should be somewhere in view but to his disappointment Ellis could see nothing of it even through his binoculars.

Closer was a small cargo ship at anchor. He had no difficulty recognising it, with its distinctive orange painted bridge. It was the *Camel Prince*. It was the third time they had seen her on the cruise.

He wondered what she was doing anchored off instead of tied up in Qariat harbour. Perhaps she was waiting for the coaster to leave, or she just might already have unloaded the crates he had seen in Naples and be awaiting orders for her next voyage.

Ellis was much more interested in Si'pelium, and forgot about her. After twenty minutes or so he thought he had left Vaila long enough. If she wasn't up yet, then she should be, so he returned to their cabin. He found that she was having a shower. When she came into the bedroom he asked her if she was coming on the Si'pelium morning excursion he was to lead. They had not discussed it the previous evening but as Peter had wanted go with Ellis as his assistant, it was entirely her decision.

"I'm sorry Ellis, I don't feel too good this morning. I think it must be something I've eaten, as I feel quite queasy. Would you mind if I stayed on the ship this morning?"

"Are you all right? If you're not well you should see the doctor" he suggested anxiously, as she had never shown the slightest sign of any illness in all the time he had known her.

She reassured him. She said she just needed a quiet morning.

"Maybe I could come on the afternoon excursion." He laughed

"Oh dear I hope your queasiness is not the result of my giving you archaeological indigestion!"

She smiled, a knowing sort of smile, and continued dressing.

"Are you okay for breakfast?"

"Queasy as I am, I am still a bit hungry. I fancy a kipper. Just one! Isn't that ridiculous when I'm not too well? I'll be with you in a moment."

"Fine." He put the binoculars on the table and picked up the day's programme to check the time of his first excursion had not changed, and noted it was the last tour to leave the ship at 10 o'clock, so there was plenty of time. It would also be the last to return. He was to pick up the items he would need from the cruise office at 9.30, which gave him half an hour for breakfast.

"Who else is going with you as escort?"

"Just Peter. We only have one coach load this morning, as many passengers have opted for the drive into the desert as they not only get a ride on one of the Albysian champion camels but also refreshments in a Berber tent. Even if I haven't given you indigestion with all that archaeology in Italy and my Ness of Brodgar lecture, maybe I gave it to the passengers!"

"No you didn't. You have quite a following on the ship. They enjoyed your talk on the Romans and your talk on the Ness of Brodgar went down well and would have won you a medal from the Orkney Tourist Board. Folk also loved the way you dealt with that Colonel in the Pictish talk. I wasn't the only one who had a good laugh at that."

"Well, there may be three coaches for the afternoon trip to Si'pelium they tell me, as there's no second desert excursion, so maybe you're right! I hope the old buffer is not on either trip, but I'll bet he is. Sometimes I wonder if he is trying to exact revenge for my lecturing on this cruise instead of his precious daughter. I feel sure he still doesn't know she's been sacked and why. Anyway I hope you'll feel better by the time I get back. Si'pelium should be worth seeing, darling, so hopefully you'll be up to coming this afternoon."

As they left for breakfast she laughed

"So do I. Your Piddie Maid doesn't like being away from her Magic Monster! You'll be back for lunch then?"

"Oh yes. Much as I would enjoy an hour or two there on my own to explore, my job includes getting the first lot back safely and gathering up the second. So I'll see you at lunchtime anyway. If you want to check up on me, just ask at reception."

He just had a light breakfast, as in his excitement at the prospect of going to Si'pelium he was in a hurry. Nor did he say good bye to Vaila properly, something which he would regret later as much as she did.

He left Vaila having a second cup of coffee in the dining room and after briefly returning to the cabin to change into his 'Excursion Escort' purple tee shirt, was at the excursion office by reception just before 9.30. There he met Peter as they had arranged the previous evening. The Excursions manager gave them the final briefing and the numbers booked to go with him, together with cold hand wipes and sweets which traditionally the *Carnelian* handed out to passengers as they returned to the ship after an excursion.

"There's only one thing I can't give you. The radio for your excursion is broken," the Excursions manager told them, "But Si'pelium is hardly five miles away so I doubt you'll need it."

They left the office and went down to the gangway, which was on the lowest passenger deck. This had the advantage of enabling the gangway onto the quayside to be nearly flat, instead of being the steep stair it would have been from the Reception deck.

It didn't take them long to cross the wide expanse of the concrete quay and pass through the customs shed, where the two officials took little notice of them, and to identify the right coach.

Presuming the two men standing beside their coach were the guide and driver, Ellis said

"as-salaamu; alaykum"

"wa-: alaykum as-salaam"

"I'm afraid that is all the Arabic I know!"

Ellis and Peter then introduced themselves, and in turn the guide introduced Mustafa, the driver, who, he explained, spoke no English, and gave his own name as Hosni. Ellis thought Hosni's English was somewhat limited, but there was little he could do about that.

They stowed the items the excursions office had given them in the overhead locker above the front seats they would take, and put a reserved card on the seat behind the driver in case they had a couple of disabled passengers. Ellis wondered what was in the large bag Hosni had with him, which he stowed in the small space behind the driver, but he quickly forgot about it as the first passengers were already approaching the coach. He put the large blue coach sticker in the windscreen by the coach door, quickly established that the coach appeared in reasonable order and got off to join Peter welcoming their passengers. Hosni just stood by the coach chatting to Mustafa.

Peter collected the tickets and Ellis greeted the passengers, helping those who needed it to get up the steep steps. Nine of the passengers he already knew by name, including his aunt Minnie and Millie of course. They took the double seat on the right or, as Ellis joked, on the starboard side, three rows behind Ellis' and Peter's seats. The next couple were Fred Lightfoot and Susan. They took the seats behind the two reserved for the disabled.

Next to arrive at the coach, at which Ellis gave a silent groan, were Colonel John McRaven and his wife Danielle. He seemed to have forgiven Ellis for teasing him about his name. He said

"Morning old boy. Here we are very much alive." Ellis laughed for the sake of politeness,

"I'm glad to hear it, Colonel."

They, of course, sat in the front seat behind the driver as if by right, in spite of the seat being reserved for the disabled. They would be nearly opposite his own seat. Ellis said nothing, as he had not been told of any passengers who had booked as disabled, but he wondered if he'd have difficulty moving them if one turned up.

The Meads arrived just after the McRavens and Ellis was glad to see them so relaxed. They greeted each other cheerfully.

Once it appeared that all their passengers were aboard Ellis and Peter counted them, checking that the numbers tallied with the figure the excursion team had given them, and told Sophie, who ticked their excursion off on her clip board confirming that everything was correct. Ellis nodded to the guide that they were ready to go, and in turn Hosni spoke to the driver. He then took the fold down seat in front of Ellis and Peter. The engine was started and they drove out of the port. As they went Ellis took the microphone, waved to Sophie and announced, to the coach passengers,

"Good morning. Everyone is aboard so we're off to Si'pelium. First can I introduce our driver, Mustapha and our Albysian guide Hosni."

Mustafa wore a white uniform with a badge on the breast pocket in yellow with an orange border. It seemed to Ellis that everything in Albysia was in these two colours, although Hosni was an exception. He wore undistinguished casual clothes.

He passed the microphone to Hosni, and took his seat beside Peter.

As they drove onto the street, to Ellis' and Peter's surprise, Hosni gave neither a welcome, nor even said 'Good Morning' as all the guides they had met at other Ports had done.

Instead he spoke passionately about what a special day this was going to be.

"How lucky you are. You will see important thing today. Romans, Italians, lots of peoples invade us. Rulers come and away go. You'll see." He seemed very excited about it.

He then changed the subject to that of Albysian industry and economy, not a big subject, and anyway one David Grey had lectured about the previous day. He was especially enthusiastic about Albysian camels. "Best in world. Run faster, carry more. They have special place also today."

Less than fifty metres from the dock gate, Mustafa turned right, up a short steep street into the central square, and past the mosque. Hosni took no notice of where they were, his commentary carrying on with a dull list of facts and statistics, delivered in a monotone as if he had learnt them by heart or spoke from a script. With his limited English it was not always easy to understand what he said in any case. He said nothing about the square, the mosque, not even the monument with its statue and Arabic inscription when it was right beside the coach, as they were held up by traffic. He seemed unaware that no one was listening, not least because it was a great deal more interesting to watch all that was going on in the city as they passed through it. So Ellis leaned forward and asked him to tell passengers about the statue and the mosque.

"That put there by President. We not like him. Mosque is city mosque." He resumed his monologue.

Ellis was still not sure who 'him' was celebrating, and wondered if Hosni knew anything about the mosque, but as he doubted if it would interest anyone on the coach anyway, he made no comment.

Because Hosni had so little grasp of what would interest tourists, Ellis and Peter looked at each other with puzzled frowns. Peter whispered

"This guy doesn't seem to have much clue."

"Maybe Hosni didn't know what else to say. He can't have acted as a guide before. Of course we are the first cruise ship to come here."

"He sounds as if he is speaking from a script learnt by heart."

"If he doesn't know what to do, what's he doing on the bus?"

"I hope we won't get complaints, but there's nothing we can do about it just now." They then did as the other passengers were doing, they ignored Hosni and looked at the scene outside the coach.

Their progress was slow. It was mainly due to the traffic, as local drivers seemed to take little notice of traffic signs and lights, let alone keep to their own side of the road. The ensuing chaos helped no one and was frustrating. The one benefit for passengers was that they had plenty of time to watch all the activity going on in the streets.

Down one sidestreet they watched a group of children kicking a football around. Ellis thought they would know the final score if the coach didn't move any faster.

The small and densely packed houses, shops and cafes at least provided a glimpse of the life in the city. A little further on Peter pointed out a shop keeper setting out vegetables in front of his shop, which had a bright red painted door, window frames and even a bright red sign board.

"He must have got a cheap tin of red paint!" Peter commented.

At several cafes they could see the older men drinking tiny cups of coffee and smoking hooker pipes, while they leisurely discussed the latest news and gossip. One area of wasteland, near the edge of the city, had a couple of enormous hoardings advertising, of all things, holidays in Europe.

By this time Ellis was getting impatient, as he wanted to get to Si'pelium, so he was relieved when at last they left the city.

The countryside through which they passed was arid, the plants in the dusty fields seemed exhausted by the heat and most of the trees were little more than scrub. Only the few palm trees seemed happy in their environment. Ellis looked out to sea, and saw the *Camel Prince* again still anchored off shore, just as he had seen her on his early visit to the Sun Deck. They went through a small village and shortly after that the coach turned into a car park by a sign that proclaimed in Arabic and four European languages that this was Si'pelium, the greatest Roman city in North Africa. Ellis smiled at that. Leptis Magna would dispute such a boast, but he said nothing. In any case he was keen to get started.

There were no other vehicles in the car park so Mustafa drove the coach in a large circle so that it was facing the exit, and stopped about twenty five metres from the end of a two storey building the size of a large house. Over the door near to the left hand end, the end nearest Si'pelium, was a sign in English that amused them all. It read 'Ticket Sails'. It triggered another elusive memory he could not quite identify, but again he put it aside to concentrate on his duties.

As soon as the coach stopped, Ellis asked Hosni where the local expert was to take the passengers round the site, as he could see no one waiting for them. Hosni seemed surprised by the question. He spoke to Mustafa, who just shrugged his shoulders.

"Aren't you guide to ruin, Mr Ellis, you expert?"

"I am an archaeologist, but this is my first visit. I understood there was to be someone who would take us round and explain the site."

"No people spoke me about other guide. I know nothing. Only bus guide."

"I see. Please give me the microphone." He then announced to the passengers,

"I am very sorry to say that the local guide that Carnelian Cruises had booked to take us round the site is apparently not now available. I have not been here before but I have studied the site as an archaeologist when at home, and have some information with me. I will therefore do my best to tell you what I can of Si'pelium. I shall take you to the central area of the Roman city, the forum, and point out the main buildings and their purposes, and do my best to make our visit interesting. You can either come with me or explore on your own. The important thing is to be back at the coach by 12.30. This should give you a reasonable time here, and still ensure you return to the ship for lunch as scheduled, and so the coach is ready to pick up the passengers booked for this afternoon."

A voice from the rear of the coach called,

"Can we stay all day and return on the afternoon coach?"

Before Ellis could answer, Hosni took the microphone and replied loudly, as if quite anxious about the question.

"No you must go 12.30. Is important, very important, is meeting in area. You not allowed to go to buildings." He pointed towards the ticket office, "Just to ruins. Nowhere else. Is not allowed. I shall be there, and then will meet at coach. 12.30. No delay please."

It seemed a strange thing to say, and confirmed in Ellis' mind that Hosni was either a very poor guide or maybe no guide at all. But Ellis gave it no further thought in his enthusiasm to get into the Roman city. He took the microphone back.

"So to answer your question, I'm afraid not. The afternoon excursion here is fully booked with a waiting list anyway, and there is no public transport to get back to Qariat. It would be a long hot walk back to the ship! Please remember 12.30 at the coach."

With that, the passengers filed out of the coach. Ellis and Peter led them to the entrance to the site. The gate was open and there were no staff, in fact nobody at all, at the gate or within the site either, so far as he could see. The whole place seemed deserted. It did not worry Ellis but Peter said quietly to him,

"This place is unnaturally quiet. Or am I getting jittery because I don't really trust our so called guide?"

"Yes it's odd. Please don't give the passengers any hint of our disquiet, better not to worry them. But Peter, can you keep an eye out for any passengers exploring on their own and note which way they go in case we have to search for them later."

In front of them was a wide straight Roman street. The ruins of a number of buildings lay each side of it, and most of them were surrounded by large and small pieces of stone where they had been partly destroyed. In Ellis' judgment many of these seemed likely to have been thrown down much more recently than Roman times. In one or two cases stones had been laid out as if to tidy the site or perhaps to start to identify or even replace them. It concerned Ellis that the standard of care was well below the standard that he was used to seeing, but he thought it would be tactless let alone pointless to say so. As he had warned the passengers in his lecture the previous day, none of the buildings had any paintings or decoration so far as was known, partly as Si'pelium had a far shorter life and was far less sophisticated a city than Pompeii, and partly because none of the buildings were in as good a condition as those in Pompeii, but Ellis felt sure that there would be several mosaics that would have survived under the sand. He told passengers this.

"It'll be exciting to see if we can find some of them, I should be able to find a few for you."

"This main street leads to the forum. It was called Navonum. The buildings either side would have mainly been shops and workshops of the more successful businesses. Behind each are likely to have been the houses of the owners of the businesses. I'll show you those which can still be identified."

He hoped he would be able to identify what those businesses were, depending on what he could see.

"At the end of the street we will arrive at the forum. As in most Roman cities, the more important public buildings are clustered around it."

He felt lucky to be able to identify the bakery, from a carving on a stone, and a wine shop from an amphora marked on another. He took the group through the bakery to where there had been a door into the house. The floor of the entrance hall was covered in three or four centimetres of sand. He swept an area clear with his shoe and was delighted to reveal a mosaic, though it was a poor thing compared with the House of the Tragic Poet in Pompeii. Several of the group also cleared what they could with their shoes, and gave Ellis the credit of knowing that it was there. He felt they would have something to make them feel their visit worthwhile.

When they reached the forum he gathered the passengers around and pointed out each building around the square space.

"On the right of us is the Basilica, originally used as a type of court house. This was a city founded before the Roman Christian era, but it was at its zenith during the early Roman Christian times. We really know too little about Roman ambitions for the city. One might presume that the Romans wanted carnelian and other such stones and, who knows, maybe the camels here were valued even then. Until there can be a proper exploration of the site the city's importance cannot be fully assessed." He looked around. He could see that to a layman none of what he said would relate closely enough for them to understand.

"It is however reasonable to conjecture that its rulers would have been encouraged by Emperor Septimus Severus to convert it to an important religious site. This would, of course have been after Pompeii was buried. Perhaps it would also be somewhere for survivors from Pompeii to settle well away from a volcano?"

In answer to a question he explained that a basilica was usually defined much as a cathedral but not the seat of a bishop. Prior to the Christian era in Rome, it was just a term for a building used for a variety of public purposes. He knew his answers were a bit simplistic, but he hoped it was enough.

He showed them the features of other buildings which remained standing, including the Senate, the bath house and the market, and then he explained that a mix of villas, shops and other smaller businesses lay in the streets leading away from the forum. He ended by saying that although it might be somewhat disappointing to see that little conservation work appeared to have been carried out, as long as all the original stones were left alone, there was a great deal that could be achieved when funds were available. He hoped that if an Albysian heard what he said they would at least not be offended.

Looking around thinking about what to do next he remembered his fleeting thought about sails.

"It's now eleven, so we have an hour or so to explore. I now intend to walk to the Roman harbour down there," and he pointed, "Those who would prefer to stay in a group might like to come with me. On our other Roman excursions we have yet to see a Roman harbour, though I'm not sure what's left of this one. Alternatively you can stay in the city. Even by Roman standards, it's quite small and you might be able to find another mosaic. I will be back here at noon. At that time I will answer what questions I can and then will lead you back to the coach in good time for our return trip."

A few couples chose to stay within the city ruins, including the Lightfoots and the McRavens, so Ellis suggested that Peter remained with them.

The Roman harbour was immediately outside the city wall and was reached through the Porta Marina. It must, he thought, have been quite grand when first built and even now was more or less complete, although much of the carvings which Ellis thought would have decorated it had gone.

The other city walls were in a poor state, but at least delineated the city, suggesting that the Porta Marina was the busiest entrance to the city. Scrub and desert were once all there was around the other sides of the city. He noted a much more recent building, the same size as the ticket office, on his right with only one small door into it from the site.

It was only when they got to the Porta Marina that they could see the sea below them, and as they walked through the archway they got a good view of the harbour just below them.

Originally, he remembered from his studies, the way to the sea was a paved road although it now looked like a sandy track, but it was at least easy to follow. It went in a zigzag down the small cliff not unlike that which protected Qariat's harbour, although not so large. However, unlike Qariat, there was no inlet in which a harbour could be constructed. Instead the low cliff formed the westward side of a bay, roughly five miles wide. There were two lines of rocks just showing above the sea. One about a hundred metres long running diagonally from the point between the bay and the coast towards Qariat, and the other, perhaps a hundred metres from the first, straight out from the cliff at right angles to it. Together with a sandy beach below the cliff they formed a natural harbour roughly triangular in shape. The only weakness of it as a safe haven was that many of the rocks hardly showed above water, which explained the squared stones to be seen, especially at the landward end of both lines of natural rock.

Built using the natural rock as foundations, these stones would have made the harbour both useful and well protected from the weather. It seemed to Ellis that the jetties must be Roman by the way the blocks of stone had been shaped, but over the sixteen centuries or so since, wind and water had largely destroyed most of the manmade additions to the natural rock.

However the rocks still offered sufficient shelter to enable some use to be made of the harbour, the proof being in the group of seven sailing fishing boats pulled up out of the water on the sandy beach under the cliff.

Each had a long lateen yard, slung on a relatively short mast with a sail already bent on ready for the boats to be launched. In use the sail would unfurl into a single long triangular shape. The crafts themselves were fairly small, perhaps six or seven metres long with a shallow draft. They were fairly wide in the beam, with narrow side decks. Ellis thought this shape would make them reasonably stable and quite strong, but more akin to cart horses than race horses. They had long keels, and carvel planking. In spite of their construction being crudely executed, they appeared strongly built workboats with a distinct shape and rig. The design over all displayed their ancestry as traditional craft of the North African coast. None of them had an engine.

The boats were not especially well maintained. However there were two exceptions, which looked to have been recently painted; one red and the other green. They were undoubtedly the best maintained of the little fleet. Even the standing rigging looked new.

He noted that there was no village, and wondered where the fishermen lived. Probably, he thought, in the village they had passed shortly before turning into the Si'pelium car park. In a number of the boats he saw nets and other items for fishing.

"There's not much to see, is there?" asked one of the passengers. Another added,

"I'd not like to sail very far from land in those boats."

Ellis briefly described the way the cut of the stone blocks on the reefs suggested Roman influence, and shortly said that they should now return to the forum to collect the rest of the group so that they could get back to the coach by 12.30. He did not mention how much he would have loved to have stayed much longer himself as the combination of Roman remains and the boats was exceptionally interesting to an archaeologist keen on sailing. It was only as he reached the top that he noticed tyre marks in the sand as if vehicles had recently been driven up from the harbour. He supposed it could have been the fishermen, but he was beginning to feel that there were a lot of strange things about Albysia in general, and Si'pelium in particular.

Rather to his surprise, Peter was in the forum with nearly all the other passengers. Comparing notes the only exceptions were the Lightfoots and the McRavens.

"Have you seen them, Peter?"

"The McRavens are over there. The old boy was taking notes. I saw the Lightfoots ten minutes ago, they looked as if they were going straight back to the coach."

"Okay. We'll do the same, but in case they stopped somewhere on the way we'd best keep looking around." Ellis called to the McRavens as he began to walk with the group back to the coach, discussing what they had seen as they went. Inevitably, so Ellis thought, the Colonel complaining that there was not much to see of Si'pelium.

"It's disgraceful that this place is in such a state. So little to see and all so unkempt, uncared for. I don't understand how Carnelian Cruises could charge for an excursion to a place in such a neglected state. They should at least tidy the place up and repair it so that visitors can see how it appeared in Roman times. You, Mackenzie, should have known what it was like even if you've not been here before."

Ellis soothed him a little by saying that it was not considered good archaeological conservation to rebuild a place like Si'pelium. He added,

"But of course, Rosemarie will have explained that principle to you."

"Huh!" The Colonel moved away without further comment. Peter, with a grin on his face, whispered to Ellis,

"Checkmate, well done!"

When they got to the coach they found the Lightfoots and the driver standing beside it. The McRavens had disappeared and there was no sign of Hosni. While the other passengers got back on the coach, Ellis and Peter took a moment while they waited to answer the Lightfoots' ideas about life in Si'pelium. They were full of ire about Rome, or any country, having colonies and enslaving the native inhabitants. Peter remarked that the Italians held the country for a short while in the twentieth century, which made them all the more outraged. Ellis could see that to some extent Peter was winding them up because he thought they were being unnecessarily hot under the collar about two thousand year old problems and politics. While they were talking Danielle McRaven came back and got on the coach followed by the Lightfoots.

Ellis and Peter got onto the coach to count the passengers to discover that only the Colonel was still missing, and there was still no sign of Hosni. Danielle said her husband wanted to look behind the building.

The door of the ticket office opened and Hosni came out with the Colonel pointing to the coach and furiously castigating him, presumably for going behind the building against Hosni's demand that they did not do so.

Another man then came out of the door and, with Hosni, marched the Colonel over to the coach. Ellis got off to see if he could help, as it looked as if Hosni and the newcomer thought the Colonel's trespass was a serious offence, and were very angry about it. He was astonished when he recognised the newcomer. It was Hassan, and he was giving the orders.

The Colonel was about to climb onto the coach when Hassan stopped him.

"Stand there, by the coach."

The Colonel was about to refuse when Hosni, having already boarded the coach himself and picked up the bag he had stowed behind the driver's seat, pulled a gun out of it and pointed it at the Colonel. Without a murmur the Colonel moved to do as he had been ordered. Perhaps thinking that it might make him look to be in charge, he gestured to Ellis to stand beside him. Ellis however ignored him. He asked Hassan what he was doing.

"This is not the way to treat passengers on an excursion." Hassan told him to get all the passengers off and stand back to the coach by the old man, adding,

"You will see."

Ellis hesitated as Hassan spoke to Hosni who immediately ran to the ticket office, opened the door and shouted something through it. Ellis waited; he was not going to tell the passengers to do anything until he understood what was happening.

Almost immediately three other men emerged, each armed with the same sort of automatic weapon that Hosni held, and they ran over to the coach. Ellis realised they would have to do as Hassan demanded, so climbed on the coach, and picking his words carefully, said through the microphone.

"Hassan, the man in charge of whatever's going on here, says he will explain what is happening if we get off and stand beside the coach. We appear to have no choice. I am sorry we find ourselves in a distressing situation, but I will do all I can to sort out what is surely a misunderstanding."

Once they were all standing together in an untidy group with their backs to the coach, Hassan addressed them. Ellis noted that his English was far better than Hosni's.

"What is happening here is important for my country. That old man has disobeyed my order which Hosni carefully explained to you all on the coach. He is lucky, our Fezzan revolution has already started. If it had not, he would have had to be prevented from revealing our preparations and our headquarters. He would have been shot."

He paused to let the point sink in.

"I have no intention of harming you if you obey my orders, but I will have no hesitation in doing whatever is necessary for the good of the Fezzan and our future in Albysia. It suits my purpose to allow you to return to your ship in a short while, so you can tell the Captain I mean what I say. You are to tell your Captain that he is to stay in Qariat harbour. Meantime I shall hold two of you as hostages here to be sure you all obey my orders this time. They will be kept to ensure you do as you are told and so long as the ship makes no attempt to leave. They will be returned to the ship only if you and your ship obey my commands. They will be shot if you don't!"

Ellis looked along the line of passengers. Some looked frightened, others seemed determined to be British, to keep 'a stiff upper lip'. All wondered what the Colonel had done.

Hassan looked carefully at the passengers. They stood nervously trying to look anywhere but at him. If he was choosing his hostages then each hoped to be inconspicuous, if not invisible, so they would not the ones to be picked.

"I shall keep the youngest and oldest men – you, you who disobeyed me, and you." He pointed to the Colonel and to Peter.

"You can't pick me." The Colonel protested. "I have a weak heart. I'm not fit enough. I'm ill and no longer young. I misunderstood which building and did no harm."

Ellis thought he looked frightened more than ill and it was news to him that he had a weak heart. He had after all been fit enough to walk right round Pompeii only a couple of days previously. His wife, Danielle, Ellis noted, maintained her usual silence. She even took a short step away from him.

"I'm a passenger" continued the Colonel. "That's the man you should take, he's staff. It's his duty" He pointed to Ellis and paused as if to judge if he needed to say more to be allowed back to the ship.

"You're scared witless. Funny sort of Colonel." It wasn't obvious who had spoken, but it gave Ellis a moment to think. He could not assume the Colonel was lying, maybe he did have a weak heart. If he had a heart attack whilst held hostage after Ellis, the excursion escort, went safely back to the ship he would feel responsible, whether he was or not. It would be on his conscience for the rest of his life. Anyway he would feel uncomfortable going back to the ship leaving Peter with such a companion.

"Hassan, let the old man go. I'll stay."

"If you wish. Now the rest of you get back on the coach. You will wait there until I give the order for your release. Please do not make the mistake of taking my decision to let you go as weakness. Ensure your Captain understands that I mean what I say. If he doesn't obey the hostages will be shot."

Ellis smiled at Minnie as she passed him to get on the coach.

"Give my love to Vaila, and tell her not to worry, I'll be back soon." He spoke to each passenger as they passed him to get on the coach, "See you soon." He smiled encouragingly at each of them. Even to Colonel MacRaven, who said

"I expect to be called 'Colonel', not the 'old man'." He did not even thank Ellis for taking his place. Danielle at least said "Merci."

Hosni got back on the coach after the passengers. Hassan gave orders to the men with him, and returned to the ticket office with one of them, whilst the remaining two men marched Ellis and Peter round the building at gun point until they were no longer in sight of those on the coach.

The Revolution

The passengers on the coach remained in their seats. They had little choice, and some at least hoped that by accepting the situation they would encourage their release a bit sooner and ensure Hosni, their guide, now their guard, was given no excuse to shoot anyone. No one commented on the Colonel's extraordinary behaviour. He seemed oblivious of their reaction to it.

Except for him they all in their different ways, worried about Peter and Ellis. In ignorance of what was happening to them, each passenger had to contend with the fears their imaginations conjured up. From that concern, they tended to turn to worrying about what would happen to themselves.

Why should their captor, who Ellis had called Hassan, want to hold the ship in Qariat? His message to the Captain suggested that they might not be any better off back on the ship. Would Hassan keep his word to release their escorts?

Some remembered other hostage situations. The media made many of them sound dramatic and dangerous. They remembered that they did not always end happily. Could Hassan change his mind and want to hold them all? What could those on the ship do about it? Cruise ships are not equipped for such contingencies were they? There was no communication with the ship anyway. With Hosni watching them they felt unable even to discuss their position between themselves.

As the coach's engine had been switched off, the air conditioning was also off. As the minutes ticked by the temperature rose under the North African sun, and they all felt more and more uncomfortable. The men tried to loosen their shirts whilst the women fanned themselves as best they could. The bottles of water they had been given when setting out from the ship soon ran dry.

A fly, which must have come into the coach by the door, flew around them, irritating every passenger it visited. No one dared to try to swat it in case their guard took it as resistance and shot someone.

Tension rose. The silence grew oppressive. Hosni said nothing, not even to Mustafa. He stood back to the windscreen, looking down the aisle of the coach with his gun held ready cradled in the crook of his arm. His expression was impossible to read. Uncertainty about him and his reaction to them was another thing to worry about.

After a quarter of an hour Gerry Jones, sitting in the fourth seat back, called to Hosni,

"There are cool towels in the locker above Mackenzie's seat. Please can I distribute them?"

Hosni, holding his gun ready for use stood up, went to the locker and opened it. He saw Mackenzie's bag, and returned to his secure position back to the windscreen.

"Okay. You find in bag. Take round. No take other thing from bag. No talk, keep quiet or I shoot."

Gerry got up, came forward gingerly so he did not provoke Hosni, took the bag down from the locker and rummaged in it. He found the box of towels, put it on the seat, and replaced the bag in the locker as Hosni had demanded. He then started to take the towels round to the passengers. Each took one and wiped their faces and hands, and found relief for a short while from the heat. He walked the length of the coach, giving towels to everyone on one side, and then returning from the back to the front on the other. This meant that he got to the Colonel and his wife last.

The Colonel looked at him in silent fury, and Gerry smiled at him, silently winding him up. There could be no doubt that they understood each other. The Colonel had expected to have had his towel first, and Gerry was expressing his disgust at the Colonel's cowardly behaviour by coming to him last. Not many of the passengers saw the exchange of mimed dislike, and those who did, even though they might agree with Gerry, just felt the further rise in tension it caused.

As they continued to wait for their captors, they tried to pass the time, thinking of other times and places, of family and friends, of anything, occasionally wiping their heads with towels that had rapidly lost the refreshingly cool scented moisture they had had when given out.

Time passed slowly.

The heat also seemed to contaminate the air. Many felt the sweat on their bodies contradict their increasingly dry throats. Even swallowing was becoming uncomfortable. Troubled minds mingled with the troubled bodies of passengers unused to, and unprepared for either.

Minnie and Millie felt especially concerned. They whispered together in some distress as to what they would say to Vaila. Now Ellis and Peter were out of sight the ladies had no idea as to what was happening to them. It was all very well that Ellis had shown such selfless courage and cheerfulness in contrast to the Colonel, but however proud of him Vaila might be it would be no substitute to him returning to her. They thought it could not get worse for her.

But it did.

They all heard it. Gunfire. A short loud burst by a number of guns firing as if to an order. It might sound like a riff on a snare drum, but it was unmistakably gunfire, just a short burst and then no more. It caused a ripple of shocked exclamation up and down the coach, despite the Hosni's gun pointing at them.

"Good God. A firing squad." The Colonel forgot his caution for a moment.

"You've shot and killed them, murdering savages," snarled Fred Lightfoot from his seat behind the Colonel. He reflected the other passengers' feelings although the Colonel, regaining his instinct of self-preservation, told him.

"Shut up, or they'll shoot us next."

Their guard laughed, and said

"Is you worry for two less Westerners? Is very funny!"

"For goodness sake. Do you have no respect for human life?" It was Susan who spoke in support of Fred, reflecting what they all felt.

"You talk silly thing. It is our way, is good for leader to do shooting. You people soft, silly. People shot for Good leader shows respect, that we ready shoot for him people who not obey him. You see? You very funny!"

He laughed then frowned, his mood instantly changing.

"Now stop talk." He held up his gun to be sure they did not ignore his order. He was obviously excited which did nothing to calm the passengers' nerves.

The whole coach had heard what was said. Some remained silent for fear of being shot, others were too shocked to speak. The coach lapsed into silence again until, a short time afterwards, they saw a man with a coloured armband come out of the ticket office and wave towards the entrance.

"You go now." Hosni smiled at them, and turning to the driver said something in Arabic. The driver quickly started the engine, and immediately put the coach in gear, wasting no time. The coach was already moving as Hosni jumped off it. Mustafa then drove out of the car park and turned right towards Qariat.

He took little care of others on the road. He overtook regardless of traffic coming the other way. He drove as fast as he could, continuously blasting the horn, demanding to be let past anything that impeded the coach's mad dash back to the ship. None of the passengers spoke, partly because they were still in shock, partly as the way the driver was weaving through the traffic had them all hanging on, concerned that the driver's recklessness created a new risk to their lives. Their only consolation was that the air con started to work again.

As the coach entered the outskirts of Qariat, where the traffic was heavier, the driver was forced to reduce speed, but those near enough to the front could see how anxious he was, fretting at every delay. He seemed as frightened as the passengers.

They now started to see indications that much had changed since their outward drive. People in the street were talking excitedly, gesticulating, pointing, and passing the news. Others came running out of buildings all along the road, gathering in ever growing groups. The old men who had sat relaxing at tables outside the cafes had gone.

They passed the shop with the red door. A young man, perhaps the assistant, was just finishing taking in the displays of vegetables and the proprietor was shuttering the window. Reminded of what they had spotted as they drove to Si'Pelium, some looked to see what had happened to the boys playing football, but none were to be seen down the side streets, just a few women hastily hurrying into their houses. Doors were slammed behind them. Older men hurried home, younger folk seemed to be coming out to see what was happening.

Most of the cars on the road seemed to be leaving the city, whilst there were some pickup trucks coming into the city carrying young men, all of them wearing an armband in orange and yellow, with something black on it. At one point two pickup trucks were having something fitted to them just behind the cab, which, the Colonel said, loudly and confidently, as if to counter his earlier behaviour by acting the professional soldier, were mountings for machine guns. There were several pickup trucks on the plot of waste land with the large advertising boards, assembling to form a unit of armed pickup trucks, and men milling around with determined faces, a bizarre contrast to the posters of smiling holidaymakers above them.

As the coach passed the next block, they saw other men building temporary barricades made of whatever they could find, including cars that had been parked nearby. It looked as if they were trying to prevent access to some areas lying to one side of the main road. The coach was brought to a standstill by traffic beside one of them, which enabled thepassengers to see their armbands more clearly, orange and yellow, Albysia's colours, with a black silhouette of a camel superimposed on it.

The men were all well armed and several of the groups had completed their barrier. One even had a flag matching the armbands waving gently over it.

By now the traffic was down to a crawl, and as they came round a corner, it became clear why. Fifty metres or so in front of them some soldiers had set up a check point. They were stopping every vehicle as it came to them. Some vehicles were waved aside and these were being searched by soldiers. Other soldiers stood by, their weapons held ready. As they edged closer, the coach passengers at the front could see that these men were in proper uniform, and did not wear armbands.

A small van two vehicles in front of the coach was stopped amid a great deal of shouting. It looked as if the driver was refusing to pull over as instructed. After a short argument, it was however waved through and its driver wasted no time in driving away as fast as he dared.

The one car remaining in front of the coach tried to follow but in the driver's panic he stalled the engine. When he started it again with a loud grinding of gears it leapt forward, so that one of the soldiers had to jump aside to avoid being run over. A second soldier fired into the cars radiator stopping it and a cloud of steam came from under the bonnet.

More shouting followed around the immobile car. Mustafa had fortunately reacted more slowly, and now not wanting the soldiers to do the same to the coach, Mustafa did not move.

There was a blare of a horn from behind the coach and a pickup truck, with five men in the back, one of which was operating the machine gun fitted to fire over the cab, pulled out of the traffic and accelerated past the coach. The half dozen soldiers manning the check point lifted their guns ready to fire but the machine gunner was quicker. He fired a burst over the heads of the soldiers, stray bullets shattering windows on the far side of the street. The soldiers promptly accepted defeat, dropped their guns and, surrendering, fell to the ground themselves to avoid being shot.

Those coach passengers who could see were thankful that none of the soldiers had returned fire, as it was extremely likely that the coach would have been hit had they done so. The pickup truck that had so intimidated the soldiers had stopped so suddenly that tyre marks were made on the road. The four men in the back jumped down onto the ground and covered the six soldiers with their guns and indicated that they should stand against a wall at the back of the pavement on the right. They then could be seen talking to the soldiers and it was not difficult from the gestures the four made that they were persuading the soldiers to change sides. They must have been successful because a fifth man got out of the pickup truck with a handful of arm bands, the same as the four were wearing, and handed them out to the soldiers. Whether they willingly switched sides it was hard to tell, but it looked as if theirs was the wise choice, at least for the moment.

Having completed this gunpoint conversion, the men from the pickup truck waved the traffic through as if nothing had happened. The coach driver needed no persuasion. But his difficulty was that the damaged car with the radiator destroyed by gun fire could not drive away. The coach had to manoeuvre past it which was difficult with traffic in both directions. It was a surprise that he managed it without hitting anything in his haste, but he did, and Mustafa was not the only one in the coach to be glad to be moving again. A collective sigh of relief rippled from front to back.

Their relief was premature. As they got to the town centre they saw more uniformed soldiers on street corners and especially in front of public buildings, where they seemed to be nervously guarding both the buildings and their own lorries. It could be seen that here at least some soldiers were preparing for a confrontation from a group of men with armbands a short distance away. It looked as if it was a stalemate.

The coach was able to move on only because neither side stopped them, if only slowly because of the other traffic and Mustafa was at last being cautious, warily trying to ensure they would not be a provocation to either side. All the passengers could do is hope their neutrality would be recognised.

As the driver signalled right, towards the harbour, three men with armbands did however stop the coach, and demanded something from the driver. What they wanted the passengers could not tell, but the driver opened the coach door and two of the men climbed onto the coach. They shouted something down the coach which, of course, none of the passengers could understand, so no one spoke. The driver said something to the men, and one of them walked the full length of the aisle of the coach looking at each of the passengers carefully.

He called something to the man who had remained by Mustafa, at the front. Judging by their actions they had completed their inspection and were satisfied whoever or whatever they were looking for was not on the coach. The first man spoke briefly to Mustafa and they jumped off the coach and waved them on, directing him to turn left.

Now that the coach seemed at least temporarily safe, passengers carefully searched for streets and buildings they recognised in an attempt to judge how far from the ship they were. They had become as anxious as the driver to reach what they hoped would be safety. Those with a good sense of direction soon realised however that, having had to turn left, they were going in the wrong direction for the harbour. Mustafa, however, drove on with the confidence of a man who knew where he was going.

They saw fewer groups of men with the arm bands, and even fewer soldiers as they went. Feeling that they were being taken out of the area where there was fighting gave some relief, but no one relaxed.

There was an audible sigh of relief when they turned a corner and found themselves overlooking the port a little below them. The route the coach had taken had brought them to the harbour from the opposite side to the one on which they had left. Now that they could understand why they had been sent on the diversion they could feel their ordeal would shortly be over.

As the coach drove down the hill towards the harbour they could see that much had changed since they had left on the excursion, just as it had in the city.

Instead of the usual bustling business of loading and unloading cargo the port seemed to be at a standstill. The only people in sight were a few groups of men who were either leaving or standing together as if waiting, although it was not clear what they were waiting for.

When they reached the entrance to the harbour area, and could start to believe their frightening journey was over, there was another problem. The dock gates were closed and guarded by several soldiers. Mustafa turned left to stop in front of the gate and shouted something to the nearest soldier, who took no notice. Mustafa shouted again, but the soldier had different ideas and started a shouted argument, but it did not lead to the gates being opened. Because the coach had had to turn across oncoming traffic to go into the docks, and was now stopped it entirely blocked the road in both directions.

After a couple of minutes of incomprehensible shouting, Colonel McRaven got up from his seat, indicated to Mustafa to open the doors, and got out. He went round to the driver's side and spoke loudly to the soldiers.

"I am Colonel McRaven. Please call your superior officer and I will sort this out."

It was an absurd gesture. The soldiers did not understand a word he said. The Lightfoots were not the only passengers unsure whether to laugh at his intervention or to urge him to leave alone in case it made things worse. They wondered where he had suddenly got some courage from until they realised that the soldiers guarding the gate had their guns slung over their shoulders. He must have felt it safe so he was again attempting to cover up his previous actions and once more play the man in charge. He showed no sign of being ill.

The soldiers however must have thought he was just being difficult and one unslung his rifle and pointed it at the Colonel, nodding his head at the coach. The effect was immediate, the Colonel quickly obeyed the unspoken order and fled back to the coach and resumed his seat.

Next, passengers saw two elderly but large cars coming rapidly towards them. They were overloaded with people and luggage and looked to be families fleeing the city.

As the coach was blocking the whole road, they stopped twenty metres from it. Two of the soldiers waved them forward, but for whatever reason the first car pulled right across the road trying to make a three point turn. The second car saw the soldiers waving them forward and started to drive past the first as it reversed and they met with a crunch. It was not a serious bump, it did little more than make an extra dent in the second car, which was far from new anyway, but the drivers, nerves already taught, and frightened of the soldiers and their guns, started their own argument accompanied by blaring horns. The coach was now sandwiched between the gate and the furiously arguing men and could not move. Fred Lightfoot later told anyone who would listen that it would have made a comic film, but at the time those on the coach found it disturbing and frustrating because it prevented them reaching the sanctuary of the *Carnelian*.

One of the soldiers had a radio, which he now used. It was not a long call, and after it he came across and spoke to Mustafa. Other soldiers now made some attempt at sorting out the two cars.

Several of the passengers were getting increasingly anxious again at the frustrating delays, not least as they now heard sounds of gunfire coming from the city much nearer than previously. In their nervousness they were only mirroring the driver, and could do even less about it than he could. The impasse was however eventually resolved without explanation, though perhaps because the soldier with the radio received orders to let the coach go.

When the gate was opened for them to go into the dock Mustafa wasted no time driving to the customs shed and parking right beside it.

He opened the door. He had no need to tell anyone to get off the coach, but Minnie and Millie, who usually stood back to let others get off first, this time got to their feet immediately. They stood in the aisle blocking the exit and as loudly as they could asked passengers to say nothing of what had happened until they had had an opportunity to speak to Mrs Vaila MacKenzie. Most understood and nodded assent, if only to avoid further delay.

 There were no good byes, no reminder to take their belongings with them, not even a hand held out for tips. Mustafa just waved his hands to urge them all to leave the coach as soon as they could. The last passenger had hardly set foot on the ground when Mustafa put the coach in gear and drove quickly away.

They went through the customs shed, where again the two officials urged them to hurry and waved them through without asking to see their cards. The passengers walked as fast as they could across the open concrete dockside, onto the gangway and into the ship.

Once aboard they were greeted by a ship's officer who asked what had happened. He had some difficulty understanding what he was being told because everyone spoke at once, until Millie and

Minnie reached him and they recognised each other. The officer was Paul Unwin. He waved the others through and Minnie and Millie took him aside and quietly told him their story. Just as she had on the coach, Minnie said that as Ellis Mackenzie's aunt, she felt she should break the news to Vaila Mackenzie and asked that nothing was said publicly until she had done so.

"Very well, I will tell the Captain. He might want to make an announcement of this sort fairly quickly but I will pass on your request. Please stay here until I have spoken to him."

He then phoned the bridge, reported briefly what had happened to the Si'pelium excursion and to Peter and Ellis, while they waited. He then said that the ladies had asked to be allowed to break the news to Vaila Mackenzie personally, one of them being a relative.

The Colonel, who had held back so that, so he said, he could be sure all those on the coach had got onto the ship, now arrived on board and announced, oblivious of the call the ship's officer was making,   "I'm the senior passenger so I'll take matters from here. I'll go to the bridge to discuss it with the Captain. I have checked everyone is off the coach."

Second Officer Unwin put the phone down, thanked the Colonel and told him that everyone was checked on board electronically and other matters would be settled by the Captain and the officers so they did not need to take up his offer, and added, "Please do not go up to the bridge. They are very busy up there."

Turning to the ladies Paul Unwin told them that the Captain had agreed to their request but asked that they spoke to Mrs Mackenzie, asking her to pass a message back to the Captain as soon as possible via any member of staff or crew.

The Colonel listened to them without comment, turned away and walked to the stairs.

The ladies took the lift to the Ocean Lounge, as they thought that it was where Vaila would be. They dreaded telling her what had happened, but the sooner it was done the better. Minnie had told Millie that she thought Vaila was a brave and feisty girl, but what she now faced was well beyond anything she'd experienced, and no one could doubt how close the couple were.

They saw her sitting by a window which looked over the concrete dockside that they had just walked across.

The ladies had not reached her when the Colonel cut in front of them and sat in the vacant chair beside Vaila, whilst his wife, silent as usual, stood beside him. Vaila initially took no notice of them. She was concentrating on trying to spot Ellis through the window. The ladies reached the table as the Colonel without any attempt to break the news gently, said   "Mrs MacKenzie, I'm really frightfully sorry old girl. He did his duty, and I will certainly recommend him for a medal. He did it for his passengers, in the best tradition of the British, fulfilling his duty and all that, as we all naturally expected."

Vaila looked blankly at him, as he added,

"Hard to know why these foreigners should shoot him and that pianist fellow."

Minnie and Millie were horrified at the unsympathetic way the Colonel had told Vaila of the death of her husband. Minnie said sharply,

"Colonel, please move away, right now, as I must speak to my niece," and she glared at him and Millie looked at him as might an avenging angel, almost daring him to stay. She even elbowed Danielle out of her way.

For once he realised he must do as he was asked but said to Vaila as he got up to go. "It was my duty to tell you, as the senior man involved of course." He walked away looking self-satisfied and apparently oblivious of how unnecessary and unkind his intervention had been for Vaila.

The ladies sat down, Minnie beside her, and Millie opposite, waved away a waitress with a coffee pot and turned to Vaila, whose face showed that it was dawning on her that something serious had happened to Ellis. Minnie took her hand and spoke gently to her.

"You must be very brave, dear Vaila, as we have terrible news to give you. I can think of no way to disguise something so horrible for you. The bus we were on was hijacked by a group of armed men led by a man called Hassan, in Si'pelium's car park, just as we were about to leave."

She continued to tell Vaila the story, bringing out Ellis' unselfishness, bravery and cheerfulness. At that stage she made no mention of the Colonel's behaviour.   "Ellis asked us to give you his love and to say he'd be back soon."

She continued to describe how Peter and Ellis had been marched away at gunpoint as hostages to ensure the coach went straight back to the ship and told the Captain that the ship must stay harbour. He emphasised that he meant what he said. The last they had seen was the two of them being taken round the end of the nearest building.

Then, to the horror of all the passengers, they had heard the sound of gunfire. The Colonel had told them that a short burst of gunfire like that could only be a firing squad. He had said that there could be little doubt that they had shot Ellis and Peter. None of the passengers was in a position to contradict him, and it certainly sounded as if they were shot.

None of them had imagined that their captors would kill them, there had been no opportunity to help Ellis and Peter or protest, and no explanation had been given for their being shot. It had come to as a complete and shocking surprise, especially as Hassan had said that they were to be kept as hostages to show that he meant what he said.

Minnie explained their guide turned guard had dismissed their protests with a laugh as if he was pleased they had been shot. He had just said 'Two less Westerners,' and made the passengers on the coach wait in silence by threatening to shoot them too, until the leader had given an order that the coach could return to the ship.

"I am so sorry Vaila, we all grieve for such a wonderful man. But it will be so much worse for you. We would so like to do what we can for you, and I'm sure you know we are here for you. Perhaps a prayer would help?"

"Yes." Her voice was flat, as if it had been an effort to speak at all. She looked out of the window again, perhaps still looking for him, perhaps not looking at all, as if she couldn't take it in. She nodded, tears forming in her eyes. All she said was "But we haven't been married even a year yet, not even a year. Yes pray for him – and Peter too."

Minnie's prayer was not long. She felt this was not the time for more. When she had finished she put her arm around Vaila.

Suddenly Vaila sat up straight

"Who is going to tell Chrissie, Peter's wife? Yes, you can do something. I must go to our cabin and phone them. I must, no one else knows them and she shouldn't have some poor police woman she doesn't know going round. I must do it. And what about Janet? Please tell whoever would deal with such things I am going to phone. Excuse me." Resolutely she got up and walked swiftly out of the lounge.

She did not see the sympathetic looks from the coach passengers who knew what she had had to be told, nor the puzzled expressions of those who did not yet know what had happened. She did not see anything. She came close to running, she only knew she was descending into despair. She must be alone, must be away from them, from anyone, she didn't want to be comforted, what was the point? There could never be any comfort. She just wanted to be alone to think of him, weep for him without having to pretend to be brave. She must be alone. Out of sight. Alone.

But first she must phone.

Vaila

Vaila reached their cabin, fumbled with the key and let herself in, shut the door behind her and leaned back on it, relieved to be there, out of view.

She looked around the cabin. He was everywhere she looked. His slippers under a chair and a shirt over its back. Ellis' shirt, one she had bought for him.

She saw the phone on the bedside table. His side of the bed with his alarm clock, everything as he had left it. She looked round the cabin again, thinking of how excited she'd been about coming. It had turned into a nightmare.

She told herself she must phone. Now. Before it became impossible. It's what he would want me to do, she repeated to herself.

She found her diary with Chrissie's number, and checked how to get an outside line, which was explained on the phone itself, and with dread in her heart rang the number. Slightly to her surprise the call went straight through.

"Hello. Mummy's busy. Who's there?" It was Jamie, Peter and Chrissie's five year old.

"Hello Jamie. It's Vaila. Do you remember meeting us at the Pizza Express a fortnight ago – two weeks ago. Ellis was with me."

"Yes. I ate a whole pizza. You had a brown dog. It was all furry. I called her Lassie."

"That's right. Now what's Mummy doing?"

"Brenda's here. They are talking. Have you still got Lassie?"

"Yes, Jamie, but she's asleep just now. I would like to talk to Mummy please."

She heard him put the phone down and call to his Mother, her asking who it was, and his reply, and a few moments later, Chrissie picked up the phone.

"Is that really you, Vaila. Are you still on the ship; is it all going well?"

"No. Peter is with Ellis ashore, but I have to tell you what's happened to them. It's terrible, awful."

"Oh" Chrissie paused. "I'd better see Brenda to the door."

"No Chrissie, ask her to stay awhile. Please. Before I go on."

She heard them speak, she felt rather than heard anxiety in their voices. When Chrissie returned to the phone she told her what had happened. Peter and Ellis. Shot. She tried to be gentle, but it was impossible. Chrissie was silent for what seemed hours to Vaila.

"Both of them? Shot? Dead? No. No." She pleaded. "Please say it's not true, please. It mustn't be true. Are you sure? Not Peter."

Vaila heard another voice, Brenda she assumed, who must have heard what was said.

"Chrissie, he was so good, such a nice man, so kind too. But he would surely want you to be strong for Jamie's sake."

Vaila heard Chrissie starting to cry. Shortly she heard movement and Jamie said down the phone "Mummy's crying. Poor Mummy. Is Daddy there? He always cuddles us and makes crying go away."

"Your Daddy's not here just now, Jamie. Will you do something for me? Will you look after Mummy? You're the man in the house just now, so how about you go and give Mummy a cuddle, perhaps you can make her crying go away?"

She next heard Brenda on the phone, obviously a very practical lady.

"Is there any chance that the information is wrong?"

"Thank you for asking that, but there's only this Brenda. No one actually saw them shot." Vaila then briefly explained to Brenda what had happened. "It's true too that they have no bodies. We could cling to that I suppose, but there's a Colonel on the trip who is sure they were shot. All the coach passengers think so too, because one of the hijackers said so. I don't dare to let myself think there might be a chance, because I fear it'll make it worse. I can't bear to think of it. I'm trying to think of what to do, even though that's horrid too. Sorry. I can't go on. I've got to ring his Mum, while I still can. I'll ring again if there's more news. The Captain said he is speaking to the British Ambassador, so maybe we'll know more soon."

"I'm so sorry Mrs Mackenzie, we're forgetting you've lost your husband too. I will do all I can for Chrissie, but perhaps you should both not give up hope yet. Miracles do still happen. Thank you for ringing. That was very courageous of you. Good bye."

Vaila had no sooner put the phone down when there was a knock at the door. She didn't want to answer it, but it came again and it did sound a gentle knock somehow.

When she opened it, she saw Minnie.

"Can I come in Vaila?"

"Yes."

Minnie sat on the bed, encouraging Vaila to sit beside her. With an arm round her she said,

"Have you rung Janet?"

"No I've just rung Chrissie. It was terrible, their little boy, Jamie, answered. Poor wee boy, he's only five. After I told Chrissie, Jamie came on the phone again, wanting me to put his Daddy on the line, because he said his Mummy was crying and Daddy could stop crying. Poor wee lad, it breaks my heart to think of his anguish when he realises that he'll not see his Daddy again."

"Shall we ring Janet together?"

In fact it was Minnie who rang, while Vaila listened. Janet was clearly stunned, but would not accept that it was true. She said, in a voice full of emotion, that she would never accept the loss of her son, as well as her husband, until someone proved it. Minnie did not argue.

Janet then asked Minnie how Vaila was.

"She's with me now, sitting next to me. She's been amazingly brave. She rang Chrissie, Peter's wife. Peter's the man Ellis was with. It's all so harrowing for her. But Millie and I will do all we can for her."

Minnie asked Vaila if she'd like to speak to Janet. Vaila silently held out her hand for the phone.

"Hello Janet. I'm so sorry you have had to hear such dreadful news. I'm so sorry. I can't really take it in."

"Darling Vaila. It is such a terrible loss for you, and I naturally understand. Don't give up hope yet. You've had far too little time with him, and he loved you so much. His love will endure Vaila. Remember 'Many waters cannot quench love.' Let's stick together. However strong the evidence, it doesn't sound conclusive. I am with you in spirit at all times. Ring me anytime, day or night, and Vaila, don't give up."

"Thank you, I .... I'm sorry."

Minnie took the phone back, offered Janet what comfort she could and rang off.

They were both drained by the time the call ended. Vaila just sat on the bed saying nothing. But there was one more event for her to endure. It came at once, the Captain's message to all passengers broadcast all over the ship, including in every cabin.

He explained what had happened, and with deep regret, told passengers of the loss of two of the staff, Ellis Mackenzie, the lecturer, and Peter Keise, the pianist. He said that he did not yet know exactly what had happened or why. The passengers on the excursion had seen them being marched behind a building at gun point, and then shots were heard. A retired Colonel, who was on the excursion, said that the shots could only have been a firing squad, and the hijackers had confirmed it. Yet the leader of the men who had held up the coach had initially said they would be hostages, and would be only held for a short while, apparently just to ensure the coach went straight back to the ship without speaking to anyone. We don't know why they changed their minds and shot them.

Neither the Foreign Office advisory service nor any other sources of information had suggested that Albysia was not a peaceful, stable and safe port of call. The hijack came out of the blue, a complete and shocking surprise.

"With my senior officers, I am endeavouring to discover more through the British Embassy in Albysia. They in turn are speaking to the British foreign office but as communication is poor and difficult, it might take some time. Meanwhile it is increasingly clear that a revolution is in progress, and there is fighting in some parts of the city.

There has been just one development in the last hour affecting the ship. We have had a message to say that neither pilot nor tug will be available to us, and that the *Carnelian* is ordered to remain in her present berth, and would be unharmed if she did so.

"Whilst I would not normally accept such orders, especially as I can't be sure who was giving them, it would be difficult to leave without the pilot, coupled with my wish to stay until I am quite sure what has happened to our two staff, and as there appears no threat to the ship, I propose to stay at this berth for the time being.

"My officers, crew, staff and myself are deeply shocked at our loss. I am sure all passengers will feel the same way. Our hearts go out to Mrs Keise and Mrs Mackenzie. Mrs Vaila Mackenzie, as many of you will know, is on the ship, and I am sure everyone will do what they can to ease the pain she must feel.

"I will keep passengers informed of developments. In the meantime there are a few practical matters I must tell you about.

"First, in the interests of their own safety, and that of all on board, no one is permitted to leave the ship for any reason without my express consent. All excursions here are cancelled and refunds will be given. The gangway is still in place for emergency use, but will be fully manned until we leave port. The officers on duty there have orders to allow no one off the ship.

"Second, as we do not know how long we will be here, and it seems unlikely that we can be resupplied, I have ordered the catering department to find ways of cutting waste, and therefore meals will offer a very limited choice. I deeply regret this necessity but I am sure you will all understand. Similarly please be careful with your use of water, especially drinking water. We have equipment to purify sea water, but it is designed for use at sea away from possible pollution and is not usually used in port.

"Third, whilst I am sure you will all be anxious to speak to family and friends, there is no mobile coverage in Albysia, and the satellite phone and radio we have on the ship will be in high demand. Therefore I must ask that you limit individual calls in number and duration. I will be ensuring our company and home shipping agent is kept up to date. They will ensure next of kin of everyone on board are kept informed.

"I regret these limitations but they are obviously essential. I am confident you will all want to support the ships company in a very tricky situation. I will keep you all informed of developments. Good Night."

Throughout the Captain's talk Vaila had said nothing, she continued to look at her feet as if she couldn't take it in. After ten minutes or so, Minnie asked Vaila if she would like her to stay with her for the night. Vaila thanked her but refused the offer. Minnie judged she meant it so just said before leaving that Vaila was to call on her any time, day or night if she wanted.

When Minnie had gone, Vaila looked at her clock, trying to think.

"Where's my feisty Vaila?" It was Ellis. She looked around the cabin, but he wasn't there. Feeling a bit foolish she said "I'm here, darling, where are you?" Yes it was foolish, of course it was. He wasn't there, it was just his voice in her head, and the will power by which she had held back her anguish burst, and she fell on the bed sobbing.

She had no idea how long she lay there, but gradually she felt, if not better, then a little relieved because she had been able to express her grief. She tried to be positive by remembering some of the wonderful times they had spent together.

Her memories were interrupted by the phone. She moved across the bed to reach it, again aware that she was lying where Ellis had lain the previous night and picked it up.

"Hello."

"Mrs. Mackenzie?"

"Yes."

"It's Annie at Reception. I have Mrs. Flett on the phone for you. It's a poor line I'm afraid. I'll put you through."

"Mum?"

"Vaila, darling. Janet kindly rang just now and told me your dreadful news. I'm so sorry, I know how devastated you will be. I had to ring to find out how you are, and to be with you for a few moments."

Vaila explained to her how she had heard that Ellis had been shot.

"I don't know what to do Mum. It's so unfair. We've hardly been married, and I've never even told him.... What can I do now, Mum? I wasn't on the coach when they took him. I wish I had gone with him. We didn't even say good bye properly."

"Vaila, Janet said that no one actually saw him shot, nor have the local authorities admitted that they have his body, so surely there is no proof that he was shot?"

"Yes Mum, but there's a revolution in progress, and an army man who was on the excursion said that the gunfire they heard could only be from a firing squad. He was quite certain they were shot. Then a hijacker on the coach confirmed it, he said 'Two less Westerners.' The coach passengers are sure, they said that there could be no doubt."

"You at least have Ellis' Aunt Minnie with you on the ship. I expect she is helping you?"

"Yes. She and her friend have been wonderful. They prayed with me for Ellis. But I am so twisted up inside...."

"We are praying for you too, and for Ellis. I gather your pianist friend was with him?"

"Yes. We had met him, his wife Chrissie and their little boy, Jamie, when we were in Edinburgh. I expect you remember me telling you. We became even better friends on board. I rang his wife. It was terrible, it was piddie Jamie who answered the phone. He's a lovely child, and I hate to think of his reaction when he fully understands what has happened to his Dad. Poor Chrissie, I don't think she could take it in at first, but at least she had a friend with her."

"You are such a kind, brave girl, Vaila, to do that. How I wish I was with you. I can't even talk to you for long as I was asked to be fairly brief on the phone. Is there anything we can do from here?"

"It's a nightmare. There's nothing anyone can do unless you can bring him back."

"How I wish we could. Dad and I will pray, and we think of you day and night. Hal and Inga send their love and sympathy and are thinking of you too. Remember we all love you. We all loved and admired Ellis. If anyone could survive, it would be him. I'm sure of it. I'll ring again. Don't give up hope darling."

"Thanks, Mum. Love to all of you too. Good bye."

She now felt exhausted. It seemed a huge effort even to go to bed so she just climbed into it.

*   *   *   *   *

Vaila felt that she had not slept that night, at least not until she dozed off from exhaustion in the early hours. At 8 o'clock she was woken by the phone from a wonderful dream. She was with Ellis on a trireme called Carnelian, it was beautiful. She had admired it as Ellis described it to her. A long, narrow, fast and beautifully built galley painted orange. Carved illustrations of life in ancient Greece decorated it. It had a sharp ram at the bow and three banks of oars. Ellis told her of its role at Salamis in the Greek and Persian wars with enthusiasm, and she knew she'd seen it before somewhere, yet it was manned by all her friends and many of the friendly folk she had got to know on the cruise, and they were all smiling happily as they rowed to a drum beat given them by Minnie.

The phone kept ringing, but it was on his side of the bed, so she rolled across the bed and picked it up.

"Hello Vaila, I hope I haven't woken you but Millie and I thought you probably hadn't slept much anyway, and were concerned about you. How do you feel?"

"As well as could be expected I suppose. You're right I didn't sleep much and I'm glad it's day again."

"Do you feel strong enough to come to have breakfast with us, if we call for you?"

"I think so. I am a bit hungry. I forgot about lunch and dinner last night, and I'll have to face folk sometime. But I'm still in bed. Would it be all right if you came in half an hour? I need a shower, I must look a mess."

"Of course. See you about eight thirty then."

She got up and sat on the edge of the bed, shut her eyes and told herself, aloud, that she must pull herself together. She must be strong. She prayed for Peter and Chrissie, and for Ellis and herself, and repeated to herself 'I must be strong so he would be proud of me', and then went to the bathroom. Looking in the mirror she thought she might manage to look and feel better once she had had a shower.

As she turned away from the mirror she saw his shaving brush, just as he had left it twenty four hours before on the glass shelf below the mirror. It still had a small wisp of shaving soap on it and she remembered he'd been in a hurry. She picked it up, gently put it against her cheek and an incident vividly came to life in her mind.

It was about the third or fourth morning of their honeymoon. She had woken to find that Ellis was already up, and she could hear him moving about in the bathroom. She had got up, and after a moment's hesitation, because she was not yet used to being in the bathroom with him, she went in. He was in the midst of lathering his face with shaving soap using the brush. She had laughed and told him how funny he looked with his soapy beard. He had turned to her and tried to put soap on her face with the brush. She had dodged and run back into the bedroom with him in hot pursuit with the shaving brush. She ran round the bed, and jumped on to it where he had caught her, both of them in a fit of giggles and shortly covered in shaving soap.

By the time they went down to the hotel dining room, breakfast had been cleared away and the room was being cleaned.

As the memory faded she feared her resolve would fade with it. But it seemed to have the opposite effect. She felt stronger, and in a strange way began to have a tiny glimmer of hope, to be just a little optimistic, as if the shaving brush held some sort of promise, or even as if it was a little bit of him that had already come back to her. He spoke to her again, 'So there you are, my Piddie Maid, your Magic Monster was wondering where you'd got to.'

Unlike the previous evening, she had no illusions this time, she knew it was just in her head, but it didn't matter. It was real to her, it still felt as if it was Ellis, her Magic Monster, and she had no doubt that if he had been there it was the sort of thing he would have said.

She replaced the brush on the shelf and got into the shower, and as she stood under the comforting hot water, she resolved again to do all she could to make him proud of her. As she dressed, with her energy slowly recovering, she also started to wonder. Dare she question the story that the coach party brought back? Was it unkind of her to doubt what the Colonel said? She remembered Rosemarie on the first occasion she had met her. She'd understood well enough that Rosemarie had tried to upset her – perhaps just for amusement - and then Ellis had thought that Rosemarie had invented that nasty rumour in an attempt to spoil his chances of the Orkney post. All she had discovered in the office supported that view. There had never been a rumour, it was a lie, an underhand attempt to get Rosemarie what she wanted. Was the Colonel a liar, like his daughter? Did he want revenge because Ellis had poked fun at him? Even if he was not being malicious he was only guessing anyway, how could he possibly know that Ellis was dead from the sound of a few rifles? Who knows what that hijacker had meant, his English wasn't very good, Millie had said so.

She suppressed these thoughts, as luxuries in her present circumstances, for which she knew she might pay a terrible price if he didn't return. A horrible thought tried to get her attention, what if she had to identify his body?

She pushed the thought away trying to remember Millie's description of the excursion to Si'pelium, and Minnie's telling her what Hassan had said.

By the time she was ready for Minnie and Millie, she thought she might have balanced enough optimism to help her keep her dignity, as Ellis would expect, with sufficient realism to ward off any shocks she might still have to face. Promptly at 8.30 they knocked on her door and she went to breakfast with them.

She noticed, as they entered the dining room, several sympathetic looks, and a few folk spoke to her as she passed saying how sorry they were. Others were a bit embarrassed, not knowing what to say. She was glad to be able to accept them all sufficiently graciously that she felt she was doing as she had resolved to do.

Having ordered, she asked Millie and Minnie.

"Do you know anything about telepathy?"

"I have certainly heard that some folk claim to be able to communicate with loved ones miles away mentally, but I don't really believe they can. Why do you ask?"

She told them that she had heard Ellis speak to her. They looked surprised, but she continued.

"At first I really thought it was Ellis, there in the cabin with me last night. But of course it wasn't spoken out loud, it was just in my head. But why was it in my head?"

"That could just be because you know the sound of his voice so well and the sort of things you would expect him to say. It's understandable, but it isn't telepathy, Vaila." and she added "What did he say to you?"

"He said 'Where's my feisty Vaila?' last night. This morning he used the nicknames we use to each other– no one else knows those."

"If it gives you comfort, that's fine, but it does sound as if you heard what you wanted to hear."

"I expect that was it. But one thing is undeniable, it has made me feel so much better, and just a little optimistic. Tell me again as exactly as you can what happened."

Millie did so, carefully trying to remember the exact words. Vaila was silent for several moments when the story ended. But then she saw Millie's wistful expression as if she was thinking of another time, and Vaila remembered what Minnie had told her about Millie's own tragedy. Sorry for prompting an unhappy memory, she quickly moved on.

"Minnie, now you; you tell me what you saw and heard. All the details. Sorry to be a bit bossy, but please."

So Minnie told the story again as she remembered it. She told Vaila how Ellis had had to act as guide, and what a good job he made of it, even taking passengers to see the harbour. He had explained the design of the fishing boats in the harbour too.

She included the incident involving the Colonel, when Ellis had bravely taken his place as hostage, as she thought they had not told Vaila about it before. She ended where Hassan had said they should tell the Captain he meant what he had said.

As she finished the waiter came with their order, and as they ate Vaila concentrated on an idea forming in her head. She wasn't sure if she dared allow it to grow, it seemed too good to be true. So she ate in silence, and the ladies did not interrupt her thoughts.

When they had finished, Minnie asked what she wanted to do next.

"I need some air. I think I'd like to go up to the Sun Deck, up to the highest point. Would you come too?"

When they had agreed to meet there in half an hour Vaila added, "Have you got binoculars in your cabin? Could you bring them with you. I'll bring ours."

"Of course, but why?"

"I don't know. Maybe something is going to happen. I have a strange feeling it will."

She caught a glance between Minnie and Millie. They were wondering what she was thinking, and they were worried about her. Maybe they thought she was going off her head a little. She understood but didn't want to enlighten them. Not yet.

As was to be expected in a North African port, the sun was strong and by the time they had climbed up to the Sun deck it had already heated every metal surface to the point where it was uncomfortable to touch. The light too was hard on eyes unused to so strong a sun and they were grateful for hats and sunglasses. Several other passengers were there too, listening to sporadic gunfire in the distance and trying to see what was happening in the town. The fighting at least seemed to be well away from the ship for the moment.

In and around the harbour there was a notable absence of activity. The quayside next to the ship, the large concrete open space the passengers had had to cross the previous day, was empty of anything today. It somehow felt pointless. The lorries that had brought supplies to the ship yesterday before the revolution broke out had not returned. As the quay was surrounded by a high fence, no one could approach the ship except through the customs shed now that the wide vehicle gate was locked shut.

The dockyard outside the fence was deserted too. Every now and again one of the customs officials in their small shed appeared and looked at the ship. It all seemed unnaturally quiet in the port area and even in the adjacent streets. The only movement was when the wind blew some piece of litter across the concrete, but even that had a cautious feel to it. The Mosque was silent. There was no traffic. The waterfront shops and cafes remained closed. With fighting continuing from time to time elsewhere, the contrasting silence in the dockyard felt eerie.

Minnie remarked that the customs men were carrying guns today. They had not been armed the previous day when they had passed through the shed for the excursion. It added to the unease felt by some of those watching, to the extent that some began to wish something would happen to remove the anxieties they felt.

Although there were no more signs of life on the other side of the harbour or on the gunboat or the naval pier, there was something to see. Three vehicles were coming down the road to their right from the higher ground beyond the small cliff. Led by a large black

202

Mercedes car followed by two pickup trucks with some half dozen men in the back of each, they turned towards the landward entrance to the naval quay where the small gunboat was tied up. The pickup trucks had prominent guns mounted just behind and above the cab, similar to those seen elsewhere the previous day, and they were manned, ready for use. There was no guard on the open gate to the naval quay so the vehicles drove in and stopped by the gunboat. Most of the men jumped out of the trucks and before anyone on the gunboat knew they were there, they ran across the gangway onto the little warship. They heard a lot of shouting and then silence. A man in a very smart suit, an orange and yellow tie and a wide orange and yellow sash on which was a silhouette of a camel, got out of the Mercedes and, escorted by what were presumably bodyguards, walked to the gangplank and stood there, clearly waiting for his men to report back, as they shortly did.

Vaila was looking along the coast, and took little notice when Millie, after looking at the man through their binoculars, said

"Minnie, that man looks a bit like the chief hijacker we saw yesterday."

Minnie borrowed the binoculars. Speaking quietly she replied,

"I'm not sure. The man we saw yesterday didn't wear a suit like that and he certainly didn't have a Mercedes, not that we saw anyway. But it does look a bit like him." Vaila turned to the ladies,

"Is he the man who took Ellis and Peter hostage?"

"Well yes. We think he is. I'm afraid so."

Vaila looked at the man by the gunboat through the binoculars and said,

"That's Hassan. We met him in Orkney, last autumn, nearly a year ago and again briefly when on honeymoon. We also saw him by the *Camel Prince* in Naples. He met ..." She stopped, paused and then said "Was he the man who said to you that they were only to be held hostage for a short while?"

"That's right."

"So if...." Vaila seemed about to continue, but she returned to looking down the coast.

Millie turned her attention to the action at the naval pier.

"What's he doing? They all seem to be taking orders from him. I wonder what's going on." Minnie looked puzzled "I don't know, but I think we are about to find out."

It was soon clear that Hassan and his men had captured the gunboat. They changed the colours from the plain Albysian flag, flying at the boats stern, for one which had a large silhouette of a camel across it.

Hassan did not stay by the gunboat for long. Several of his men came ashore with six of the crew. The crew were taken away on one of the pickup trucks. Hassan got back into the car and the second truck, still with several men in the back, did a U turn, and followed by the Mercedes, drove out of the naval pier and came round to the quayside where the *Carnelian* was berthed. They drew up at the little customs shed, got out of their vehicles, and a moment later had taken it over. It was quickly and quietly done and although no shots were fired, it left the watching passengers uneasy. It was not clear what had happened to the two customs men. A few moments later a loud speaker broadcast a message to the ship.   "We have just changed the guard. If you stay there and no one leaves ship no harm will come to you, as we said in our message last night. These are my orders as the new President of Albysia. I am Abu Hassan bin Zilla."

Hassan, whose announcement that he was President was confusing, then left the shed and returned to his car, which left straight away with its pickup escort now with only four men in the back, and the passengers watched as they turned up the road from which they had come. The two who had been left in the shed, then pushed the original customs men out into the main dockyard amid loud shouts and laughter. They walked away as quickly as they could, while holding up their trousers, having had their belts and side arms removed. The two new guards then continued as had their predecessors, watching the cruiseship.

All the time the other passengers had been watching what was happening on the gunboat and at the customs shed, Vaila had been looking along the coast to the east through her binoculars, taking no interest whatever in the gunboat nor, to the ladies' surprise, in what Hassan did.

Millie could see her total concentration on what she was looking at. She thought Vaila must be trying to spot Si'pelium, which might be possible. It was not that far away as the crow flies. As she watched, Vaila said very quietly to herself.

"It must be, it must be!"

Millie wondered what Vaila had seen so she looked herself. There seemed nothing that could interest Vaila. All she could see was the parched landscape, the scrub and a few palm trees, no different from the landscapes they had seen from the coach the day before. Then she realized that Vaila was looking, not at the land, but at the sea. There was a small coaster with an orange painted bridge at anchor some distance from the harbour. Beyond it there were six sailing craft, perhaps fishing boats. They appeared to be sailing along the coast towards them. A pleasant scene that might have made a postcard, but not one, Millie thought, that explained Vaila's interest.

She was about to ask what 'must be' when Vaila said, in little more than a whisper, still as if to herself and rising in a gentle crescendo,

"It must be! It really must. It is! Yes it is! I'm sure it is."

She turned to the ladies who could see that she was getting excited. She pointed

"Look, look! We just have to hope and pray they can sail faster than any of the others!"

"What are you wanting us to look at? What are you talking about?"

"Look!" She was smiling, her voice rising with her excitement as she pointed again.

"That anchored ship looks like the *Camel Prince*. Ellis and I first saw her from Marwick Head, about a year ago. She was loading cargo at Naples the other day when we were there. Astern of her d'you see the sailing boats all sailing hard? That's Ellis and Peter in the leading boat."

"How can you possibly know that? They're miles away, and those are just local fishing boats."

"Of course. Look carefully at how the boats are spread out, and look at the way they are being sailed, watch the wind heel them. It is like a race, yet those boats are not designed for speed, and certainly not for racing. So they can't be racing. The others must be chasing the leading boat. Who else could be in it but Ellis and Peter?" In her excitement her voice had risen yet further. The other passengers watching could now hear all she said. Several looked where she pointed.

There was no doubt in their minds. Vaila could almost hear what they were thinking; 'poor girl clutching at straws.' She heard one couple whispering "She's going balmy. How could a few fishing boats and a small steamer possibly mean the dead can return?"

Heather Mead spoke gently but nonetheless as she might to someone confused.

"That's illogical. We know it's impossible. I'm sorry, love, but they were shot. We were there. We heard the shots and the guard said so. He said two less westerners. We all heard him." Her husband added "Vaila, I know it's hard but one can't deny the facts. We all support you but we can't do much for you if you can't accept what everyone on the coach witnessed. A third passenger added,

"The boats are too far away for us to recognize anyone."

But Vaila just repeated.

"Look, it's the two of them. They are coming back. Look!" and she pointed again.

Minnie put her arm round Vaila.

"It's fine, we understand but, dear Vaila, don't let your dreams deceive you. It's just a few local fishing boats. Maybe they are in a hurry but how could it possibly be Ellis?"

"It's much more likely that it's something to do with this revolution," added Millie.

Vaila looked through her binoculars again, as before watching the boats in the distance intently. Then she turned to the passengers, who had gathered around her. She saw in their puzzled faces sympathy, and concern. They were sorry for her but none of them believed her. She laughed,

"I've sailed with Ellis. I know how he sails hard when he wants to, right on the edge of capsizing. How he gets the most out of the wind to gain the advantage."

Seeing they still did not understand, she tried again.

"Doesn't anyone believe me? We may not have been married long but I know him, and I see what's happening, and know what it means. It's not just my imagination, as when I thought I heard his voice, it's not in my head. I am not imagining it."

Heather Mead looked a little exasperated.

"Even if by some miracle they survived being shot, how could they have got away from these revolutionary people? If they did they still had to find a boat. Then they would have had to launch it, without anyone seeing them. Then sail it. Just because your husband knows how to sail, how could he handle those boats, they aren't like ours? That's at least four reasons why it's impossible, never mind that those boats are miles away. You can't possibly identify who's in them."

Mark pointed out that anyone could be sailing them.

"I do feel, Vaila, you shouldn't allow yourself to think the impossible. Your idea is, you must admit, rather far fetched."

"But ..." Helen Blackwood let Minnie speak.

"Please, Vaila, for your own good that ...."

Vaila interrupted her.

"I know you don't believe me." She smiled, "I'll not try to persuade you. But I'll stay here to cheer him on whether he can see me or not. I must watch him come back."

Minnie was a little relieved that Vaila was now much calmer, speaking in a matter of fact way. She started to wonder if, by suggesting Vaila join Millie and herself for coffee, they could encourage her to be more rational, when there was a roaring sound from the other side of the *Carnelian*. It drew nearly everyone's attention. It was the gunboat starting its engine. One of the men amongst the passengers remarked that the gunboat's diesel engine sounded very rough, and another asked where it was going, without expecting an answer.

A lot of smoke arose from its exhaust, and then it stopped. It was restarted a couple of times but eventually it seemed to settle down. It sounded as if Number 2 gunboat had a sore throat. Someone said,

"That engine sounds positively clapped out. I wouldn't trust it to take me to sea without a complete overhaul."

The crew cast off the lines, and pushed it away from the quay. Whoever was acting captain cannot have been very competent, because in trying to turn to sail out to sea, it looked at one point as if the gunboat would collide with the ship as she turned seaward in the narrow dock. In an obvious panic she was hurriedly put into reverse at full speed creating a considerable backwash. This stopped her just before she collided with the cruise ship, but then, as her speed astern increased it looked inevitable that she would now hit the naval quay where she had been berthed. Another frantic change from astern to ahead at least meant her contact with the quay was quite gentle, and had the benefit of completing her turn so that at last she was able to sail into the outer harbour. From the *Carnelian* the watching passengers could not see the reaction of those in Number 2's small bridge, but it was easy to imagine the arguments this exercise would have caused.

The chaotic start to Number 2's voyage was over, and the only thing still to see was three of the crew sorting out ropes, covers and lashings on deck and uncovering the gun in front of the gunboats miniature bridge. The passengers on the sundeck realized that the little ship was not going to provide further entertainment. Another passenger joked that he was glad Number 2 was a little gunboat. If it had been a battleship it might have done a lot of damage!

The passengers on the Sun Deck started to lose interest and drift away as the gunboat turned to starboard to take the eastern channel through the outer breakwater. Several smiled at Vaila, as they left, but only one said anything to encourage her, Helen, Jim's wife, said as she turned to go

"I've never been sailing, so I don't really understand what it is that convinces you that it's Ellis but I really hope you are right. Would you like company, we could stay?"

"You're very kind, Helen, stay if you like, it'd be good to have company. But I'll be fine. Thank you for believing in me. If you pray then silently pray for them. They'll have to keep ahead of the others, they aren't free yet."

"Okay. Yes we'll stay and watch with you." But Helen thought Vaila might want to feel space around her, so with Jim she stood at the rail a short way from her.

Minnie and Millie anxiously looked at Vaila again. She was the only one on the Sun Deck to have taken no notice of the gunboat. Her eyes were still glued to the binoculars, watching the sailing craft in the distance.

"How about having a coffee in the lounge, or on the open Quarterdeck?" asked Minnie. "I'm sure Helen will keep watch for you."

"No thank you, I won't be able to see from there, and I must stay to do the only thing I can, silently pray and cheer them on. But you go. Choose a seat on the Quarterdeck where you can see me if I wave to you. I can't possibly abandon him. I must stay. I must, because he can only get back if the other boats don't catch him." The binoculars never left her eyes as she spoke.

Minnie and Millie looked at each other.

"I hope you are right, but wave and we'll come back up here."

Millie looked one last time through her binoculars, but saw no more than before, a few sailing boats, their crews impossible to identify at such a distance. She turned to go with Minnie. They felt quite unable to understand what had got into Vaila. If they could not persuade her out of her day dream, it was all too likely that she would sink into yet deeper despair when she realized that she had just been imagining his return. But she seemed so set on prolonging her dream that they felt that it might be best to leave her alone for the moment. Perhaps she should be allowed a few more minutes of hope. They would return to comfort her when she realized she had been fooling herself, but they dreaded it. What would anyone be able to do for the poor girl then?

The chase

Ellis and Peter were marched in front of two men and their guns round the ticket office building, and found themselves in a large square yard. There were four buildings, each two floors high, forming the sides of the square, with access into the yard between them at each corner.

It might have once been the stables of a large house, or at least a farm yard, though taken together the buildings were rather grand for a farm. Peter had a fleeting thought that it might have once been where Albysia's famous camels were bred. There were a large number of men in the yard.

The ticket office building was on the west side, hiding the yard and the other three buildings from the coach in the car park. On the yard side of it were a number of windows on both the ground and first floors, and just one door to the yard, in the centre. Their captors indicated that they should stand back to this building to the right of the door. On the left of the door were three large wooden packing cases which Ellis recognised. He had seen them previously on the pier at Naples being loaded onto the *Camel Prince*. Now the cases were open they could see that they contained guns which were being distributed to the men in the yard.

Various pieces of stone and some items of equipment lay outside the building on their left, the north side of the yard and nearest the ruins of Si'pelium. These suggested that it held the workshops and stores needed for the maintenance of the ruins of the Roman city. After seeing the state of the archaeological site Ellis was not surprised that there was no sign of any conservation work having been done for some time, or even that anyone had used the building at all in the recent past.

But that could not be said of the third building, opposite them, on the east side of the square. It also had a number of doors and windows, but all of them were open, and several men could be seen leaning out to watch what was happening in the yard.

Ellis thought it must have been used as an accommodation building for resident staff. The men in it now however did not look like the staff of an archaeological monument. Most held guns that must have come from the wooden packing cases.

The building on the south side, to their right and nearest the road, was between two guarded gates. It must have once been a stable and cart shed, judging by the series of arches facing the yard. Each arch could be closed by large double doors, but they were all open revealing a number of pickup trucks of a variety of makes. A mounting was being fitted to each vehicle, just behind the cab.

There were a number of similar vehicles already lined up in the yard, with their mountings holding machine guns. Whilst most of the men milling about in the yard held small automatic guns, others carried larger machine guns to the last of the pickups yet to be fitted with one. In contrast to all the warlike preparations, on the east side of the stable building in a small paddock they could just see a donkey. It was contentedly munching on what plants it could find. It took no notice of the activity in the yard. Against the gable wall of the southern building was a small cart.

None of the men wore uniform, but each had an armband, in yellow and orange, the Albysian colours, with a prominent black silhouette of a camel. Several men also had small round orange badges. One of the men had two armbands, and appeared to be acting rather like a sergeant major. He was doing his best to get the men to stand in ranks by shouting at them. He had had some success, but they were still, in Ellis' eyes, a bit of a rabble.

Not much notice was taken of Ellis and Peter. Their guards were clearly friends of some of the men in the yard who called out to them, perhaps light hearted questions about their prisoners which clearly amused them.

It was not long before it appeared that preparations were complete. Hassan now came out of the office building, flanked by two other men. He was now in a smart suit and wore a wide orange and yellow sash which, like the armbands the men wore, had a camel silhouette superimposed on it. The two men with him had unmistakable black beards. Once again Ellis was looking at men he had first seen in Orkney, after they had been lifted off the *Camel Prince*. They had similar sashes to Hassan's, although much narrower, and the small orange badge he remembered them wearing in Sorrento. Hassan stepped onto one of the packing cases, and stood still for a moment surveying the men before him, as they fell silent.

Hassan raised his arms in greeting.

"SabaaH al-Khayr." The men in the yard called back with enthusiasm

"SabaaH an-nuur."

Ellis had no difficulty in following the announcement even though he did not understand Arabic. Hassan was introducing himself and his two lieutenants.

The men cheered him and greeted him with a short burst of rifle fire, but Hassan immediately put his hand up to call for silence.

The men were clearly excited and it was a moment or two before Hassan could continue, which allowed Hosni to slip out of the door and come to stand between Ellis and Peter. He repeated Hassan's greeting and translated,

"'Morning of the light. Morning of the goodness.' Now you see why today so important. Listen I will tell you what our leader, Abu Hassan bin Zilla, say to wonderful Fezzan. Party of people, our leader is created the Fezzan." He pointed at the men either side of Hassan. "His friends Bashir & Anai Tassilah have been in your country."

Hassan described how he had long planned for this moment, when he would free the Albysian people from their Dictator, General Ghedir Rezza.

He spoke of their glorious cause in which everyone present, the cream of the Fezzan, had an important part, together with the many citizens who would rise against their evil Dictator. After further exhortation he explained why he had taken two hostages. Hosni translated.

"In Qariat port is British pleasure ship. Lots rich people in. Group of them wanted to see Roman ruins Si'pelium here."

Ellis saw Hassan gesture towards the site.

"We allowed bus to bring them. Our Fezzan brother, Hosni, arranged to be guide. He carried out my plan well."

Hosni's smile was as broad as his face, as he continued translating.

"One of British disobeyed my orders, and came into this area, some of you may have seen him. He see too much. Gave chance to teach silly westerners obedience to leader. Took these two useful hostages. Group sent back to ship not told my plan."

He pointed to Peter and Ellis, and all eyes turned towards them.

"These men are from ship. Westerners are sentimental, ship will not leave if Captain think these men could not come back. Tell ship that men to be unharmed, if my orders obeyed. Ship will be unharmed also, if ship does not attempt to leave Qariat port. Men go back to ship when Fezzan is government."

He explained that if the Fezzan captured Qariat quickly they would then be able to prevent the ship and all people on board leaving Qariat. They would be impounded until the British Government recognised the Fezzan government of Albysia, and gave them substantial aid.

"Albysia can be rich again, and you, the Fezzan, will be heroes."

There was a cheer.

"Is important to ensure ship stay in Qariat."

Hassan emphasised his orders about Ellis' and Peter's importance as hostages.

"Sending the rest of Westerners back to ship, Captain will get the message that we mean what say."

Then, explained Hosni, Hassan had told his men how merciful he is if obeyed, and if British Government cooperate. His conclusion was chilling.

"If British not obey, we start shooting rich passengers, starting with hostages." He pointed at Ellis and Peter as Hosni laughed.

"Ship obey or you are, bang, dead!"

Hassan ended by saying that everyone was ready.

"Go, my Fezzan brothers. Go to your vehicles, Join with our friends preparing in city. Drive into history. Take Qariat, capture coward Ghedir Rezza. Storm government buildings and harbour and navy. Then, with British ship impounded, I'll set out our demands to British on your behalf."

The men seemed inspired and happy to do as Hassan asked and took to their pickup trucks noisily cheerful and confident of a triumphant victory.

Hosni's excitement had been growing as he translated. He told Ellis and Peter that he would stay with them, together with some Fezzan, to 'look after' them.

The pickup trucks departed in small groups, until Ellis and Peter, together with Hosni and three guards were the only people left in the yard. Hosni spoke to his men, and then to Ellis and Peter.

"Come, you go to your new house!"

They were led into the southern building, the one with the arched doorways. Inside, at the back of it was a ladder up to a trap door in the loft floor and Hosni pointed up it. Incongruously there was an armchair close to the foot of the ladder.

`"You go up. The hatch has bolts, and ladder will go. If no trouble maybe we give you food tomorrow." He laughed then added.

"One always on guard in here." He nodded to the chair and then pointed his gun at them to ensure they understood. When they were both through the hatch it was shut and they could hear the bolts drawn across, and the ladder being removed.

Once in the loft they were relieved to find that at least there was a certain amount of light from four window like openings. There was one on each gable end, closed by a slatted shutter. The two small windows under the eaves on the yard side, over the arched doorways, had slats of wood fixed firmly so that they provided plenty of ventilation but otherwise were closed off.

The loft was totally bare, except that at the east end where there was a very large pile of empty sacks. They looked out of each opening. Both were of one mind. Escape.

But how were they to get out of the loft without being seen or heard? With a guard just below it was going to be extremely difficult.

They made a small pile of the sacks as a seat, sat down and spent most of the afternoon considering their options and by early evening had decided what to do, just as a new guard came into the stables to take over.

While it was light, they took turns watching through one of the windows to try to work out what their captors were doing. Both of them walked up and down the loft from time to time to see what reaction there was from their guard and to see how quietly they could move. The answer was that however hard they tried, their every step would be heard by the sentry below the hatch, although he gave no audible reaction.

Peter found that by laying sacks on the floor the sound was deadened considerably, but they thought it was not nearly quiet enough to be much help. They put out a number of the sacks by the east window opening so that when they made their move they did not have to walk across the floor. It offered a slim chance of escape.

Two other precautions were possible. First, to get the sentry used to them moving about they continued to walk up and down fairly frequently. The other was Peter's idea. There was a small gap in the floor boards by the hatch. If he put his eye to it he could see the sentry below. He told Ellis in a whisper that he had close cropped hair which was going a bit grey. It suggested their guard was too old to fight with the others.

They then needed to let time pass; ideally they should sleep on the sacks, but neither felt like sleep, so they told jokes and riddles. To follow, they sang songs Peter knew. The sentry clearly enjoyed their impromptu concert especially one round:

> 'I like the flowers, I like the daffodils
> I like the mountains, I like the rolling hills
> I like the fireside, when the lights are low,
> Singing doo wop a do wop a do wop a doodle do.'

There was the sound of clapping from below and a rush of Arabic called up to them ending la la la la! The guard laughed.

Peter repeated the song to more applause, and Ellis then sang it, but changed the words.

> 'We need to exit here, he needs his beauty   sleep,
> We like a night that's dark, oh what a splendid   lark
> We like the outside when the light is low.
> Singing doo wop a do wop a do wop a doodle do.'

Their guard clapped again. He would not have done that, they felt, had he understood the words.

Dark came about eight o'clock. It was time to be quiet in the hope the sentry would fall asleep. So they stopped singing and went through the motions of going to sleep themselves, hoping they were making appropriate sounds so that he thought they really were going to be no trouble to him.

They moved about as if making a sack bed as near the east window opening as was reasonable, and lying on it. By taking off a shoe and dropping it on the floor, and then repeating it as if it was the other shoe and then silently putting it on again they hoped their performance was believable. Then they remained quiet, except when they gently added snoring noises from time to time.

To their surprise and delight they heard the sound of snoring from below only an hour after night fall. It was helped by the guard having only a dim paraffin lamp for light himself. They gave it another hour before moving.

Ellis very quietly tried the shutter of the east gable window opening. It seemed loose. Peter kept watch through the crack in the floor. He could not see much by the light of the guard's lamp now that daylight had gone, but he also listened. When he was sure the guard was still asleep he touched Ellis arm, their agreed signal.

Ellis was delighted when the shutter opened inwards with hardly a sound. It had no hinge to squeak and simply came right out, so he laid it carefully aside.

They made a sort of rope by tying sacks together until it was long enough to tie to the rafter nearest to the opening and still reach the ground outside. After a further quick check on the guard below, and then out of the window opening, to ensure there was no one within sight able to see what they were doing, they climbed down. They were met by a curious donkey. Peter patted its head. Ellis whispered

"Come on. It's a long walk."

Peter nodded in the dim light.

"I know. I wonder if we could get the donkey to pull its cart."

As he searched around the cart, Ellis said "I've no idea how to drive a donkey cart."

"But I have! They've left the harness under the cart. Let's hitch it up." It only took five minutes and they were ready to go.

"Open the gate, Ellis." Peter tickled the donkey under the ears for moment and as he led it and the cart out of the paddock he spoke softly to it. Ellis remembered the incident at Gibraltar with the apes so just got on the cart and left the driving to Peter.

Having made their way out to the road, Peter clicked his tongue and the donkey seemed quite happy to trot along the road at a good pace. It seemed they were in luck, and congratulated themselves at having made a clean getaway. But their optimism was soon dashed.

It was not long before they got to the village through which they had passed in the coach on the way to Si'pelium. They had hoped that the inhabitants would be asleep like their guard. Instead there was a great deal going on and it was soon obvious what it was about. It was a celebration, presumably for the start of the revolution.

Several men were dancing in the main street through which they had to go to reach the road to Qariat. The dancers were accompanied by a sort of pipe. To Peter's ear it was a double reed instrument like a bombard but Ellis disliked the raucous and loud sound. It was undoubtedly ensuring everyone in the village was wide awake.

They still might just about have got away with it, but for two men. One knew his donkey, and the other knew exactly who Peter and Ellis were. Hosni.

There was a lot of unfriendly shouting. The pipe continued, but they didn't need to know what was shouted.

"Time to bail out! Come on Peter."

They did the only thing possible, jumped off the cart and ran as fast as they could back towards Si'pelium. Their pursuers had been dancing for some time, and were somewhat older than Ellis and Peter so they had a good start, but both of them soon realised that they were in strange surroundings, running from local people who knew the area well. They ran past the building in which they had been held and round a sharp bend in the road, and almost as soon as they had rounded it they came to a crossroads. There was a large area of scrub beyond it, and Peter pointed to it.

Ellis, out of breath, shook his head and indicated that they should go left, and Peter soon realised he was correct. They just managed to be out of sight by the time their pursuers were at the crossroads so instead of spreading out, their pursuers all went straight on, presumably to search the scrub so that Ellis and Peter could now slow to a walk while they got their breath back.

"What now?" asked Peter between gulps of air.

"Into Si'pelium," was Ellis' reply. "At least we'll have some idea where we are there."

It was easy enough to find their way into the ruined city. The road they had taken turned out to be the way to the harbour, so they went into the ruins by the Porta Marina, which Ellis had used only a few hours earlier with most of the excursion passengers. Once in the Roman city Ellis suggested a good hiding place while they decided what to do next. There was a small door into the north building from Si'pelium, the workshop, he remembered from their visit earlier. It was, to their relief, not locked.

By the light of the moon, which had just emerged from light cloud, they went in, and found a ladder up to a similar loft to the building from which they had just escaped. They however now had one advantage, they could pull up the ladder behind them. They didn't think they would be found, when it was such an unlikely hiding place with apparently no access to the loft.

They could hear in the distance the sound of men calling to each other as they searched for them. It went on for several hours, while they rested, alert to any sound nearby. Only once did the searchers seem to be getting on their track. This was when they searched Si'pelium itself.

Ellis and Peter could not really relax, let alone sleep. It might be unlikely that their pursuers would find them, but they would have to get away sometime, or they would be in no better a situation than when they were first made hostage.

Whispering quietly they discussed the problem. They felt they had no chance of getting back to the ship on foot now.

"I know," Ellis suddenly said, "why didn't I think of it before, it's the obvious solution."

He was about to tell Peter when they heard voices. It was not easy to work out what was happening in the dark, and without a clue as to what the voices said, but they heard a door open below them. Through cracks in the rough wood floor they could see lights; at least three torches shining round the workshop below. They held their breath for what seemed hours but in the end the searchers left, apparently satisfied they could not be in the building.

*   *   *

They waited for several hours after Ellis had explained his idea. Neither could sleep and when by the dim light of the waning moon Ellis saw on his watch that it was six in the morning he felt it was time to put his idea into operation. They had considered starting earlier but partly because Ellis would need light to work with and partly because they realised that there was little or no wind, six seemed about right.

They both knew it was the only plan that stood a chance. They were fully aware that if they were caught they would be shot. Both thought of their families, and Ellis felt heartbroken when he remembered he had not even said good bye to Vaila properly. He knew by instinct that Peter was having similar thoughts for Chrissie and Jamie. But they could not stay where they were. The risk had to be taken.

As quietly as they could they opened the hatch and checked. So far as they were able to see in the dim light there was no one in the building. They gently lowered the ladder to the floor and climbed down. They left the ladder and opened the door by which they had entered and went out into the ruins of Si'pelium. All seemed quiet. Taking a route which followed the original city wall so that they would at no point be silhouetted against the sky, they soon reached the Porta Marina.

There they waited for several minutes, listening carefully as well as looking to be as sure as possible that there was no one to see them, and then they walked quickly down the zigzag road to the harbour.

Ellis remembered that the two best maintained boats were to the left of the row, and even that the end one was red and its neighbour green. Ellis climbed into the red one.

By now the first signs of dawn were in the eastern sky. Although the better light helped Ellis as he checked the boat's equipment, it also brought a greater risk of their being seen. He was glad that he had had a good look at the boats when with the passengers on the excursion.

He removed the lashings on the lateen yard to loosen the sail. Having made sure he had correctly identified the halyard he clipped it onto the lateen yard ready to be raised. He ensured Peter also understood how it worked. For the moment however there was still virtually no wind. They would have to row.

The boat had only one set of oars, so once he was reasonably sure nothing was missing he gestured to Peter that they should now push the boat into the water.

They were pleased to discover that launching it was rather easier than Ellis had feared. The boat slid easily over the sand because it was firm enough for the keel not to dig in more than a centimetre or so. They were soon aboard. Taking an oar each they punted it towards the harbour entrance. Once in deeper water they put the oars in place and started to row.

The next concern for Ellis was the harbour entrance. He remembered from the excursion visit that the rocks were only partly above water, and indeed as they approached the entrance the boat suddenly grounded with a grating sound and stopped. They pushed off from the submerged rock and tried again, this time successfully. They resumed rowing straight out of the harbour and then turned to port. They had gained the sea.

By now it was about seven and the light of dawn was rapidly revealing their surroundings. The sun would show itself soon. They could see the harbour behind them, still little more than two hundred metres away. But what drew their eyes to it was the sound of a vehicle. It became visible as it turned the corner in the zigzag, and more importantly those in the vehicle, a large van, could see them.

It gave a couple of toots that sounded like a greeting.

"They must think we're just their friends who have started early,"said Peter.

"Wave back."

When the vehicle got to the harbour and stopped there was a moment's pause.

"Row harder Peter. Any moment now they'll know we're not fishermen, and with all the drama last night it'll not take them long to guess who we are."

Four men got out of the van and looked at the line of boats drawn up on the sand. The morning being so still Ellis heard shouting and gesticulating. One of the men ran back to the van, jumped in, started the engine and drove as fast as he reasonable could up the zigzag. He could only be going for help.

The other three went to the green painted boat getting it ready to launch in a considerable hurry.

Ellis and Peter did the only thing they could do until there was some wind, and continued rowing as hard as they could. In five minutes or so they could see the men launch the green boat, but to Ellis' surprise they then waited, presumably for more crew. It gave Ellis and Peter time to round the point towards Qariat to the west. The last thing they saw before the low cliff blocked their view was the van returning. By this time the sun was fully up revealing a bright blue sky.

"What do we do if there's no wind, Ellis?"

"Row! But you're right. Once they have one or more boats fully manned we won't stand a chance unless there's a wind."

Between gasps for breath, Ellis said "Whistle or stick a knife in the mast. That's what tradition says brings wind! Seriously, the theory is that the sun will heat the land and create an onshore wind. It's called the Sirocco round here."

They were silent after that to save breath, as they concentrated on rowing hard whilst hoping and praying the wind would come to their rescue. It was not long before they saw the green boat come round the point followed by four others. There could have only been one boat left in the harbour. All were manned by four or six oars.

Ellis was getting very worried about their position and wondering if they'd stand a better chance if they beached the boat on the sands abeam, and made a run for their lives. They were already finding the rowing difficult. How long could they carry on? The boat was heavy and beamy. Peter already was looking as if he was tiring, and Ellis wasn't feeling much better himself. After all they hadn't eaten for twenty four hours and had slept little.

Just as he felt they'd have to beach and hope they could make a run for it he felt a slight breeze. An onshore breeze, so he knew it would grow stronger. He handed his oar to Peter.

"Do what you can. I'll get the sail up."

Having prepared it carefully on shore it didn't take long, but in that short time the five boats following them were appreciably nearer, rowing hard.

Probably because they saw Ellis had made sail, the other boats did likewise. To Ellis' surprise they all stopped rowing to do so, which gave them another short breathing space. It crossed Ellis' mind that their adversaries were more used to sailing and fishing than trying to sail as fast as they could. Maybe they were not used to hurrying of any sort.

The chase changed from a rowing event to a sailing one which was now in their favour. Under oars Ellis and Peter had been at a disadvantage, but now all the boats were under sail in a gentle breeze their red boat had an advantage, as with only the two of them she carried less weight. She slipped through the water a fraction faster than the boats chasing them each with at least four men aboard.

Ellis was especially glad of this advantage at an early stage in their attempted escape as it gave him the opportunity to become more familiar with the boat and a rig that was new to him. It might not be enough to make him an expert but it was an opportunity to try to work out how best to get the most from the boat. Better still, he felt the wind slowly increasing to a steady if still light breeze.

He tried gently bringing her nearer the wind and found that there was a limit to how close to the wind she would sail. On the other hand if he put her too far up into the wind, being a relatively heavy craft, she at least carried her way well.

There was another advantage to his attempts to see how close to the wind she would sail, in that the chasing boats only made feeble attempts to do the same, so that after twenty minutes they were definitely gaining on their pursuers. Being somewhat up wind, they were also further out to sea in their red boat than those chasing them. He supposed that if these boats and their crews rarely if ever raced, such tactics were not something that they had practiced, or even thought about. But they were still far from out running their adversaries. Ellis looked around to check what further difficulties or opportunities there were.

The open sea was to their starboard side, the same direction from which the wind was coming. It was, from a sailing viewpoint, a good wind direction for, as Peter put it, it was both hare and hound. On a close reach, with the wind just forward of their beam they had plenty of opportunity to manoeuvre.

To their port or lee side was the shore, mainly a sandy beach but with an occasional outcrop of rock, rather like the rocks at the harbour from which they had set sail.

"This type of on shore wind is likely to get much stronger as the sun warms the land. Maybe up to force six." Ellis told Peter, who asked what he meant by force six.

"It's a way to describe the strength of wind and sea, called the Beaufort scale. The higher the number the stronger the wind and the higher the waves. Force six is sometimes called a yachtsman's gale. Officially a strong breeze, with lots of white horses. For us, if it does get that strong, we'll be at a disadvantage again unless we're careful, as they will be able to hold on to their sail longer than we can, having more weight to balance their boats. We can counter it a little by continuing to edge out to sea. It will enable us to turn a little away from the wind, getting some extra speed from time to time."

"What about the coaster anchored over there? It's between us and the harbour entrance. It must be a couple of miles from us. We'll be going close to it on this course."

"Yes I was wondering if there would be any advantage in dodging round her. I wish we had binoculars to see if her crew are awake!"

"Why?"

"She's the *Camel Prince*. Vaila and I first saw her off Orkney, nearly a year ago." He paused to look round.

"She was passing Marwick Head when Vaila and I were there. We saw two men taken off by the SAR helicopter. It turned out that there were two stories as to what had happened, one by Hassan and the other by the Albysian government. It seems to me that the two men, the Tassilah brothers, tried and failed to take over the ship so that Hassan, the brothers and the guns could get to Albysia to start their revolution. This time they've succeeded. Vaila and I saw the crates from which the men were taking guns loaded onto the *Camel Prince* in Naples."

Peter nodded.

"But is she Hassan's ship or has he just chartered her?"

"Let's hope the latter. I don't suppose they can or would do anything as we sail by as they won't know what's happening, but we really don't want to go aboard her and find out! Keep an eye on her as much as you can for any sign that they are launching a boat. If they do it could be trouble."

"As we saw the packing cases at Si'pelium may we assume they've delivered all the guns, and have none left on board?" Peter asked.

"I'd like to think so."

The wind was now appreciably stronger. Over force four, a moderate breeze on the Beaufort scale Ellis thought. *Red,* as they now called her, seemed happy enough in it, with both of them on the windward side balancing the force of the wind. Ellis looked astern, and thought he had been right, that as the wind strengthened the other boats would regain the advantage. *Green* appeared the fastest boat and was perhaps in the hands of the best skipper, was not only clearly leading their pursuers but getting closer to them. Of the other four chasing boats two were almost side by side so close were they to each other.

"Peter, watch the surface of the water up wind, to seaward. If you see dark patches coming our way warn me, it'll be an extra strong puff, and we're getting close to the limit already."

Only a minute later Peter pointed to a ruffle on the water. Ellis said nothing but let the sail spill a little wind.

Not so the two boats sailing together. The leeward one was nearly a length ahead of its companion, and caught the squall first. She heeled and inadvertently luffed into the wind across the bow of the windward boat which had to luff sharply herself to try to avoid a collision, though not sharply enough. As the boats touched, the leeward boat's long yard caught in a rope from the top of the yard of the other, and in panic turned sharply away from her neighbour. This made the situation much worse, with one boat slowing as the wind caught the other so that the pair twisted round, like a couple dancing, tripping and falling. The windward of the pair capsized over the other, the force of their movement pulling hard on the mast stay. Even on *Red* they heard the crack as the short mast broke and the sail went over the side. They would take some time to disentangle themselves, and the dismasted boat would drift to the shore, maybe both of them if they remained tangled together.

"Two less," was Peter's only comment.

Green however was getting much nearer. Ellis, in his attempt to keep their red boat going as fast as possible, was frequently sailing with the lee gunnel nearly awash now, so far were they heeled over. Water was inevitably beginning to accumulate in the bottom of the boat as the lee side clipped the wave tops, and from spray blown across the boat as the bows crashed into each wave. They had no time to worry about it.

The wind speed was still increasing, and soon Ellis judged it to be over force five, a fresh breeze. The waves were much higher too, with many white horses breaking over the wave tops, and Ellis was now having to spill the wind a lot of the time. The last thing they needed was for their rigging to give way, let alone to capsize. It took both of them, sitting out as far as they could, to balance the boat, but as there were no toe straps to hold their feet it was not enough. To ease the situation and increase speed a touch Ellis pointed a little downwind although this meant losing some of the up wind advantage. It was still not enough to stop *Green*. She was clearly sailing faster than *Red*, and before long she was within a length of them. One of her crew came to the bow and it was easy to see his purpose. He was intending to jump across. Peter found a small net in the bow and brought it to the stern where Ellis was steering. It took him a little while as he had to keep his weight on the windward side.

"I'm not sure what to do with this, but there's nothing else."

"It looks as if it's made of polypropylene. It floats. See if you can throw it into the water across *Green's* bow. It might slow them down for a little while."

But the potential boarder was not waiting. He took a step back and then jumped. Ellis anticipated his jump and put the helm hard over to increase the space between the boats. The man just managed to get one foot on *Red*'s gunwale, but Ellis pulled in the sail's sheet hard, and as the boat suddenly healed the boarder lost his balance and fell back into the sea. Another of *Green*'s crew managed to grab his hand in the water, but it took three of them to get him back on board, which meant that *Green* lost a number of boats lengths.

Green was not giving up and even though it took some time to catch up, she was now approaching *Red* again.

Only a length away, Peter threw the net across *Green*'s bow as Ellis had suggested and *Green* sailed right over it. The effect was not immediate, but just as she might have got within boarding distance of *Red* again, she slowed, and the gap between the boats quickly widened.

At first the men in *Green* did not seem to understand what had happened. They looked at their sail. And then in the water both sides of their boat before they realised that the net was caught around the rudder and was trailing behind them acting as a sort of sea brake.

Two of *Green*'s crew hung over the stern trying to remove the net for several minutes, until they realised that the only way to do so would be to unship the rudder. In their hurry to do this they forgot that, rudderless, the boat would uncontrollably luff into the wind. Without her rudder her skipper could not control her movements. The sudden turn into the wind caused panic, as *Green* put herself about, totally out control, lolling around as the waves struck her. But at least she freed herself of the net. Replacing the rudder in the increasingly rough sea took a little time and once they had regained control *Red* was a good distance ahead of them, and the two other chasing boats had caught up and overtaken *Green*. However they were not as fast as

Green, and as the two slower boats let *Green* past, Ellis judged that she would now start to catch up again.

The next decision Ellis and Peter had to make concerned which side of the *Camel Prince* they should sail. The ship was stern towards them, parallel to their course and directly between them and the eastern entrance to Qariat's outer harbour, which was now less than two miles away. They could, of course, sail well clear of the ship but they did not want to deviate from the shortest course to the harbour entrance with *Green* now once more gaining on them.

As Ellis considered that problem, Peter pointed to the small gunboat that had come from Qariat and was heading for them. They were not sure if she was the Government's little warship or Hassan's, although either way it seemed all too likely that she would be hostile.

"If we have to assume they are our enemy we're sandwiched between the boats behind us and the gunboat ahead." Peter looked worried.   "How on earth can we dodge both?"

Ellis said nothing for a few moments.

"I wonder. We might be able to …"

There was a sudden bang and a splash about fifty metres ahead of them, between the *Camel Prince* and themselves.

"That makes my mind up. However risky we've got to try something."

Red was getting quite a lot more water in the bottom of the boat as Ellis had concentrated on speed without concern for shipping water each time she crashed into a wave. Peter had started to bail it out as fast as he could because, not being knowledgeable about boats, he felt something had to be done about the accumulating water. Ellis asked him to leave it.

"We've more pressing problems." He explained what he had in mind, and asked Peter to look very carefully at the gunboat and the *Camel Prince* to judge how far beyond the latter the little naval boat was. The gunboat was still on a course to pass the ship to seaward, the windward side.   *Red* and *Green*, on their present course would also pass the *Camel Prince* on the seaward side. They were on a course directly towards each other. The distance between them was closing even faster than was the distance to the *Camel Prince*. *Green* was now only three lengths behind Red continuing to gain slowly on *Red*.

Peter took his time to answer Ellis' question and Ellis was beginning to be concerned that they needed to take action at once, when Peter said

"Not very far, but that ship is moving."

Having had it pointed out to him Ellis saw it too. The ship must have raised her anchor, and as she was reasonably high in the water when he looked carefully he could see the splash of the propeller turning, the blades breaking the surface at their highest point.

"That does it. Peter, I'm going to let slip a little of the sheet so as to ease the sail out and change course a couple of points downwind. Watch what *Green* and that gunboat do."

Ellis made a sudden turn to port, downwind, so that it would look as if he had decided to go to leeward of the *Camel Prince*. *Green*, close astern of them, saw what he was doing and followed his course change. The gunboat must get the same message if Ellis' plan was to work, and he silently pleaded that her captain did so. It was vital that she thought Ellis intended to go to leeward of the cargo boat.

For perhaps two long minutes, minutes that seemed to last for hours as they rushed towards the ship with Green getting slowly closer, the gunboat held her course to seaward of the ship. She fired her gun a second time, a much more accurate shot than before but still ten metres short and a little to starboard of *Red*. Then, to Ellis' relief he saw her turn sharply to go to the leeward side of the *Camel Prince*, crossing the ship's bows rather too closely.

By now they were rapidly approaching the cargo ship with *Green* now only a couple of lengths astern and slightly to *Red*'s port side, both boats sailing hard and getting very wet. Ellis had a fleeting thought that this would have been both exciting and good fun in different circumstances.

"Peter, take the sheet controlling the sail from me. When I say, pull it in tight as fast as you can and be prepared for the boat to heel violently." He was glad to see Peter get ready to do so without wasting time asking him why.

They were within no more than a boat's length of the *Camel Prince*'s lee quarter when Ellis shouted

"Now!"

He put the helm hard over as Peter pulled in the sheet. *Red* caught the wind and heeled to port nearly to the point of capsizing as she turned sharply to starboard.

Ellis saw the short mast and the lateen yard bend with the strain, but they held. He thought the high end of her long yard actually went under the *Camel Prince*'s counter. They missed her rudder and the churning propeller by a whisker and shot up into the wind. *Red*'s weight served her well as she carried her way almost straight into the wind for a few important seconds, enough so that when Ellis pulled her back onto a close reach clear and to windward of the *Camel Prince* he could ask Peter to ease the sail out a little. *Red* picked up the wind quickly and Ellis steadied her back on a course parallel to the ship on the windward side and was sailing fast again.

They could not see either the gunboat or *Green* now. *Green* had been unable or unwilling to follow them and must be on the lee side of the *Camel Prince*, as was the gunboat. Ellis was also grateful that the ship was moving, so far more slowly than they were sailing, it meant that it would cover them for a little longer. Ellis hoped that if they could remain close to the ship the gunboat would be unable to shoot at them, even if she came round the *Camel Prince's* stern. He suspected *Green* would sail along the ship's lee side hoping to catch them when they were no longer hidden. The other boats that had chased them all the way from Si'pelium were also on the other, leeward, side of the ship. Their relief at being away from them all might be temporary, but was still welcome.

They heard the crack of the gunboat's gun over the sounds of the sea and of the ship's engines, but could only wonder what the little warship was firing at.

The *Camel Prince* now started to pick up speed. Ellis considered sailing up wind to be further from *Green* and the others, but that would mean being further from the harbour too, and they would lose some speed by sailing closer to the wind. He looked ahead to try to judge how far they would need to sail to be in the relative safety of the outer harbour. If they could make it that far then they would be turning down wind towards *Carnelian*, and safety. Once there the gun boat could not shoot at them in the confined waters of the harbour.

But there could be another problem in the inner harbour because to get ashore the classic manoeuvre would be to turn into the wind, a complete U turn. He doubted if their pursuers would allow them the time and luxury to do that. He put the problem aside and looked towards the harbour and especially at the upper decks of the *Carnelian*. He wondered if they had been spotted from the ship and especially hoped Vaila was watching and took great comfort in the thought. But then those on the *Carnelian* might not even realise that it was Peter and himself in a close run bid to escape Hassan and his Fezzan.

There was no more time to consider such things. Ellis was anxious to keep sailing as fast as he could whilst they were hidden, and to be as near the harbour entrance as possible when the *Camel Prince* would no longer shield them.

Suddenly, so it seemed to them both, the ship was ahead of them as she gained speed and started to turn to starboard across their course to head out to sea. That too was an advantage to them, as he didn't want her to get in his way in the harbour. They could now see the gunboat and two of the fishing boats that had been chasing them. There appeared to be no sign of *Green*. Was she still on the leeward side of the ship? It seemed unlikely, she couldn't sail that fast especially as she must be in the wind shadow of the *Camel Prince*. She would lack a clear wind to sail by.

The scene was also unexpected in other ways. The gunboat seemed to be stopped, and one of the fishing boats too was no longer in the chase. She was hove to, pointing into the wind and appeared to be picking something out of the water. Peter stood precariously holding on to the mast in curiosity.

"I think I can see something in the water near the gunboat. I'm not sure, but could it be *Green*?"

*   *   *   *   *   *

On the *Carnelian* Vaila, who had never ceased to watch the little boats in the distance, suddenly stiffened, and cried out,

"Look, look Helen! Now they are much nearer but the second boat is dreadfully close to them." In her excitement, Vaila was jumping up and down. "Come on darling. Come on!"

As Jim joined them Vaila said

"I was right, it's them. I knew it, I knew it! They're still wearing their purple Escort T shirts! I knew it. I knew it!" She was so excited she could not contain herself. Jim looked through his binoculars and said

"Yes you are. I see the shirts even if I can't yet identify the wearers." Helen joined in.

"There's that little warship too. And what's the cargo ship doing, there are men in the bows. Are they lifting the anchor?"

They watched as the two sailing boats reached a point where they looked as if they were almost touching, and both seemed to be on a course to collide with the ship.

The leader, Vaila was already calling Ellis' boat, seemed to pull ahead quite quickly just before the second got alongside. They heard the bang of the gun, and saw the splash not far ahead of his boat. Vaila seemed to freeze for a second and then shouted in anguish,

"No, you evil bastards. No!" Then she saw the boats separate, and then slowly close again.

"They're heading straight for that ship. He'll never get past like that. What's he doing?"

They saw the gunboat turn across the bows of the *Camel Prince*. Ellis, it had to be him, suddenly turned under the stern of the cargo ship and vanished from their view. They saw the following boat hesitate, miss the chance to follow and then come on alone on the landward side of the ship. Ellis was now hidden behind the ship. They watched as the gun boat fired and hit the only boat she could see. It was a perfect shot. The boat seemed to explode into bits of wood and sail. Through binoculars they could see men in the water.

The gunboat hurried towards her victim in triumph. It reached the remains of the boat and stopped as the next sailing boat arrived, and turned into the wind to pick up men in the water whilst the gunboat stood by. She then slowly turned towards the shore and began to drift towards the beach. It seemed an odd thing to do. But Vaila was more interested in watching for Ellis.

All this time his boat had remained hidden from the watching passengers on the Sun Deck, and it was a moment or two before they realised that the ship was moving too. When at last the ship pulled ahead they saw Ellis and Peter still sailing hard, heeling gunnel to the water, spilling wind only when it was essential.   The   remaining fishing boat had kept sailing on a direct course for the harbour, ignoring the wreck of her colleague, and the gunboat. Vaila said to Helen

"I need to tell the bridge, though I'm not sure what they can do."

She went to the rail, leaned over, and seeing the officer on watch on the wing of the bridge called "Hello. Hello. That's Ellis and Peter."

The officer looked up and to Vaila's relief it was Paul Unwin. He had also been watching the drama at sea. She explained briefly why she knew Ellis and Peter were returning in the leading boat, although even through binoculars the red boat was still too far away to recognise its two man crew more than by the colour of their T shirts.

"Are you sure?"

"Yes. Entirely, absolutely certain. Is there any way to help them?"

"I'd better call the Captain." He disappeared into the bridge. Vaila turned to continue watching, then asked Helen to go to the back of the Sun Deck.   "You should be able to wave to Minnie and Millie from there. They said they would stay on the quarterdeck. Beckon them to come up."

They came quickly. Other passengers came too. The news spread fast throughout the *Carnelian* that those on deck were increasingly sure that the two missing staff were leading the chase.

Red came fast through the outer harbour entrance, with the last fishing boat not far behind them, which had caught up, seeming to sail faster having more men to steady her in the rising wind. The two boats now with a following wind made a dramatic sight. In the calmer water of the outer harbour those watching could see the white water around their bows, and the flash of buckets full of water as Peter bailed out to lighten *Red*. Much of the time Peter himself was hardly visible, while he was bailing.

Those on the Sun Deck saw the helmsman stand up to judge when to turn towards the *Carnelian*, and Vaila, her eyes still glued to the binoculars, recognised Ellis. Others who had gathered on the sundeck could also see him and made up for doubting Vaila by now cheering.

Hearing them, Ellis and Peter were heartened, although cautious. They still had to get ashore unhindered by the last 'hound', and then they had to get aboard the cruise ship.

It was the Captain who pointed out that it could be more difficult than *Red*'s crew knew, because the rebels now had possession of the customs shed. Ellis and Peter would not be aware of that. He spoke to Paul, who left the bridge.

*   *   *   *   *

The situation in *Red* was coming to a crisis point, and Ellis had to explain their next problem to Peter in somewhat of a hurry. Peter understood and went forward and standing before the mast waited, holding onto the halyard. Ellis swung *Red* hard to port to enter the inner harbour in a flying gybe. The last chase boat followed suit, and had two men ready to board *Red* if they could get alongside. Ellis banked on them knowing that *Red* would have to swing round in a U turn to stop by a ladder, and encouraged them to think that way by edging a little away from the quayside. Twenty five metres from the quayside ladder astern of the *Carnelian*, which was just outside the fenced off area by the cruise ship, Ellis turned hard to port pointing straight at the ladder and shouted

"Peter, let go the halyard!"

Peter let the halyard run through his hands to ensure it ran clear and as soon as he could reach the long yard, he threw it over the side of the boat away from the harbour wall. It helped slow the boat as Ellis had told him it would and he leapt onto the ladder as soon as he was near enough. As he did so Ellis let go the tiller and was able to jump on the ladder too behind Peter. He put one foot on *Red*'s gunnel and pushed as hard as he could, shouting after her

"Thanks for a wonderful sail, *Red*. We'll not forget you," and scrambled up the ladder after Peter, as *Red* drifted off all by herself.

Their pursuer had to choose whether to recover the boat, or to catch those who had borrowed her, and to Ellis' relief they chose to recapture *Red*. Those on *Carnelian* watching the drama in the harbour saw them transfer two of their own crew who turned *Red* into the wind, raised the wet sail again, take a couple of short tacks in the narrow inner harbour and then start their long sail home.

By now nearly everyone on the *Carnelian* was on deck. They were still cheering as if Ellis and Peter had won Olympic gold. Vaila however was off so quickly that Helen did not realise she had gone until she turned round to congratulate her.

Vaila was taking the stairs two at a time all the way to the lower deck, and arrived there as Paul was arranging to open the entry port with the officer on duty.

Peter and Ellis walked quickly round just outside the wire fence to the customs shed, and went inside.

There they saw the two men on duty were not customs men. They were wearing the same orange and yellow arm bands with a camel silhouette which, of course, they recognised, as they had seen them at Si'pelium. The men had the same sort of guns too.

They kept cool and thought that with a bit of luck these men would not realise who they were, or what had happened. Ellis said to Peter "Have you got your cruise card?" and pulled his out to show to the guards. Peter did the same but the guards did not understand. Peter gestured towards the ship, said that they belonged on board. He pulled at his soaking clothes and made a falling gesture and was delighted when his mime was understood; they had fallen overboard from the ship! The men thought it hilarious, and never gave a thought that it was a most unlikely story.

They edged towards the door to the ship. Peter even held out his hand for the cards to be returned and the obviously puzzled guards gave them to him.

"Good afternoon," said Ellis as if everything was normal, and moved to the door.

The guards still looked as if unsure of what to do. They might have stopped them, but the phone rang at that moment and as one of the guards moved to answer it, Ellis and Peter went out of the door onto the large bare concrete quayside and walked at a normal pace towards the welcoming gangway. They were about half way to the ship when one of the guards came to the door and shouted at them. Ellis thought he shouldn't ignore them entirely and turned round to see the guard beckoning him to return to the shed. Ellis waved, hoping to confuse them and then said to Peter,

"I think we'd better run for it."

As they ran the guard fired a short burst over their heads, and as Peter was much faster on his feet than Ellis and therefore a bit ahead, Ellis swerved to cover Peter and was rewarded by the next burst missing him.   Peter, several metres ahead, had now reached the gangway and ran onto the ship. The second guard fired again. Vaila saw Ellis' left leg leap forward and he fell to the ground.

"No!" She ran down the gangway before the *Carnelian*'s officers could stop her, straight to Ellis where she almost literally threw herself down beside him sobbing. Ellis exclaimed,

"Darling, what are you doing here? It's dangerous."

"I thought they'd killed you. You lay so still."

"It'd take more than that. I'm lying still so they think I'm dead, and won't shoot me again."

"But …" He explained.

"One bullet has grazed my rib. It stings a bit and I think it's bleeding, but it's okay. The other seems to have hit the heel of my shoe. It knocked my foot from under me and I must have some interesting bruises from falling on this concrete. The worst part is that they've ruined my shirt and destroyed my left shoe. I'm fine. But I wish you hadn't come out here, it's dangerous, even if it shows what a brave girl you are."

"You're sure you're okay? What now?"

The loud speakers on the ship gave a rasping sound.

"This is Captain Brewer speaking. We wish to send out a stretcher party to our man that you have just killed."

"Vaila, do you think that was for us? The guards wouldn't understand?"

"Possibly. We'll carry on pretending anyway."

Paul appeared at the entry port waving a white flag. He stood there a moment while the message was repeated. Being in English there was still no knowing if the guards understood.

Paul came out carrying his white flag and slowly walked onto the quayside. He paused. One of the guards in the customs shed came out of it, holding his gun ready for use, but he stayed by the shed watching. Ellis lay still. Vaila put on a heart rending performance, crying loudly over him, holding his head, kissing his forehead. By leaning over him she even managed to smear a little of the blood from the flesh wound by his ribs onto his face, as if it had come from his mouth.

It certainly fooled the watching passengers on the ship. They started shouting

"Murderers!" When that brought the other guard out to check what was happening, they booed him too.

The stretcher party, three men in white coats, joined Paul and his white flag, and put the stretcher down beside Ellis. He lay absolutely still to ensure the success of the play. His only communication was a slow wink. The men lifted him onto the stretcher and picked it up, and carried him up the gangway into the ship, Vaila following wailing in her distress. Ellis remembered thinking that she was a good actress.

Once on the ship the entry port was closed and Ellis got up from the stretcher and shook Peter's hand   "You can crew for me again!"

As he turned to Vaila, Peter said

"Okay but let's make it a bit more relaxing next time!" But he realised that neither Vaila nor Ellis heard him.

In jest, Peter, having both cruise cards, politely presented them to the duty officer.

"A lecturer and pianist reporting for duty," he grinned. The duty officer said

"The Captain is anxious to get your story as we know nothing of your adventures and not much of what is happening anywhere else on shore. Could you come soon? You will want to reassure your families too and will probably be hungry. He says you may call from his office, priority, and he'll have a meal there for you too." Vaila took Ellis' arm.

"How kind of him. Of course we'll come." She did not ask if she was to come too. Paul could only admire her determination. She was not going to take no for an answer, so why ask?

It took Ellis a little time to change out of his wet clothes, change his shoes and have a quick shave, and then Paul took them to the Captain's day cabin.

The relief of their families was obvious when they were told that Ellis and Peter had escaped. Vaila was so pleased when it was Jamie who answered Peter's call. The boy was so excited at hearing his Dad's voice that he danced round the room with the phone in his hand, singing so loudly that they all could hear him through the phone on the ship,

"I told you. I told you." Over and over again. Chrissie had to ask him several times who was on the phone!

Ellis rang Janet who was much calmer. She promised to ring Ingrid. She just said to Ellis, "My prayers answered." They could not of course see her tears of relief.

Having told their story the Captain congratulated them on the most remarkable sailing exploit he'd ever come across.

"Not only that but you will have discovered much about the revolutionaries, so I will need your help. In the meantime celebrations are certainly in order."

The internal phone rang, and the Captain answered it, listened to it and replaced the phone.

He continued as they ate their lunch,

"We will have a formal dinner tonight. We must keep up appearances and we have something to celebrate which will cheer everyone up. I shall host a table and you three must join me after you've had some sleep. You should have a night off Peter."

"Would it be possible for Ellis' aunt Minnie and her friend to come too? They were so helpful to me and they are also very observant." Vaila asked. The Captain smiled.

"Of course." His smile faded,

"Nonetheless the rebels have by now realised they have lost their hostages. The message was to tell me that two of their pickups with large machine guns have arrived, to remind us that we are at risk if we make any attempt to move. We mustn't forget, as we celebrate your return, that we are still impounded in Qariat."

The Decision

By the time they returned to their cabin, it was well past midday. Ellis felt so tired that he just lay on the bed and promptly fell asleep. Vaila also having had a sleepless night just managed to set her alarm, before joining him.

They slept until Vaila's alarm clock woke them about six, and reluctant as they both were they needed to change if they were to accept the Captain's invitation to join him for dinner. As he had promised Ellis rang Peter to ensure he was also awake.

Once ready they went to the Explorers bar, as they had arranged to meet Minnie and Millie there.

In spite of the Captain giving him an evening off, they found Peter playing. He smiled to himself as he played, as if nothing gave him greater pleasure, just as he always did. Everything appeared to be as it had been their first night aboard, except that they noticed there were neither ice nor nibbles with the drinks they ordered. Minnie wanted to tell Ellis about Vaila's courage in her distress. She was not sure Ellis even knew that Vaila had been told that he had been killed. She was again frustrated by Ellis' cheerful response to the stream of passengers who wanted to congratulate him on his escape. She thought it hard on Vaila that no one congratulated her too on her courage, though Vaila herself did not seem to mind. How could Ellis appreciate her bravery and belief in him if no one told him?

When it was time to go to dinner they had to persuade Peter to join them. When they reached the Equator restaurant there were two couples waiting to be allotted a table ahead of them, the first of whom were the McRavens.

The Maître d'hôtel had spotted Ellis' party and came to them smiling.

"Tonight is your night. Come with me." Turning to the couple just in front of them he added

"I'm sure you won't mind my taking the Captain's guests first tonight."

Of course not," they smiled.

One of the waiters came forward to take them straight to the Captain's table. Ellis, behind the ladies heard the Colonel say.

"Why are those staff being put on the Captain's table and not ourselves? We are far senior to them. A mistake has surely been made."

"I understand, Sir. But it's not a question of seniority, but the Captain's personal choice, because we are celebrating their return. I'm sure you'll agree with everyone else that they deserve to be with the Captain tonight after all they've been through to return to the ship."

Ellis' impression from his tone of voice was that the Colonel didn't agree at all.

Captain Robert Brewer was a good host and sat Ellis and Peter at opposite ends of the table, aware that his other guests would want to hear their story first hand. He asked Vaila to sit next to him with Minnie on his other side and Millie sat opposite. Both Peter and Ellis were a bit reluctant, but everyone wanted to hear what they had done.

Minnie listened with mounting admiration for her nephew. When the story had been told the Captain suggested that others might want to hear their story too.

"Perhaps you could give a talk about it once we are away from Qariat?" There was no doubt that the pair were admired throughout the ship.

But one burning question remained. How had everyone in the tour coach have concluded that Ellis and Peter had been killed? Ellis had pondered this – and then he remembered the greeting the men had given to Hassan when he came to address them. Such a common reaction in that part of the world that he had not thought to connect it with the conclusion of the passengers aided, it must be said, by Colonel McRaven's instant reaction. On such a passing incident had such a wrong, and terrible, conclusion been reached, and to what unnecessary anguish it had led. Ellis found himself harbouring thoughts of real hatred for the Colonel for his unthinking cruelty.

After an enjoyable dinner they went through to the Ocean Lounge where the resident band was playing for dancing. Peter said he'd join the band, but Vaila stopped him. "Peter, I do believe you just can't see a piano without wanting to play it!" she teased. He smiled,

"Is it that obvious?"

"You might ask me for a dance first."

As they danced, she told him how glad she was that he had been with Ellis.

"You seem to have made a good team."

"I wouldn't have survived without Ellis. He had the best ideas and his skill with that boat was amazing. I think he is a great guy." Vaila laughed.

"So do I, but then I would! But I wish he didn't get into such adventures."

The way she spoke suggested to Peter that she had something in mind beyond a wife's natural concern for a husband in danger, but he had no idea what it was. When the dance ended, he took her to the table close to the dance floor and to the right of the stage where Minnie, Millie and Ellis sat and he went to join the band.

At a table close to the stage opposite them they saw Colonel McRaven and his wife, talking to a couple unknown to them. Ellis laughed

"He looks as if he's recovered from his adventure. I expect he's telling them how he won the war!"

"Or maybe he's taking the credit for your return."

It reminded Minnie again that Ellis would not know what had happened on the ship. Her concern that he should be told was starting to worry her. Ellis should know of Vaila's courage even in the face of the Colonel's unsympathetic and inaccurate intervention. But she still felt it impossible. The band was a little too loud for such a conversation, nor did it seem the moment anyway, especially as they looked so relaxed and happy to be together again. She felt it would be a pity to remind them of darker times that evening. Vaila turned to Ellis,

"Never mind the McRavens. It's time you asked me to dance. I feel like dancing the night away!" He stood up and bowed to her,

"Will you do me the honour M'Lady?"

As the dance ended the Cruise Director, Jonny Wirth, acting as MC, took the cordless microphone from its stand.

"Thank you. It is time for the band to take a break. They'll be back in fifteen minutes."

As he spoke a waitress came through the server's door, stumbled and spilt the drinks she had on the tray she was carrying. Jonny hastily put the microphone on the nearest table, the one where the McRavens were sitting, and ran over to help.

Vaila did not notice. She was overcome by all she had been through, what she was told, the phone calls, the sleepless night and her struggle to be believed as she had anxiously watched Ellis being chased back to the ship, never sure if he would make it to the *Carnelian*. When he had got back, she had seen him shot. Now in contrast her relief at being in the arms that she had thought would never hold her again was overwhelming.

It seemed only natural to wrap her arms round him, oblivious of where they were, as the other dancers melted away to their seats. For a moment they were alone in the centre of the dance floor in each other's arms.

"Damned disgraceful way to behave. Just not British. Typical of them." The Colonel leant across to the other couple at their table, his voice amplified by the still live microphone for everyone to hear. Millie wondered if he actually wanted to ensure the whole room heard him.

"Y'know they had the most disgraceful torrid affair last year before they married. Probably had to marry after such blatant behaviour. I suppose he thinks he's a hero and can do anything now, and as for her, she's still a slut. Just look at her. Not like our sweet daughter to whom they've been so horrible."

Ellis froze. He disentangled himself from Vaila and without a word led her back to their table.

The room went silent as he turned and marched across the empty dance floor to the Colonel's table. Vaila felt a little frightened, she had never seen him so angry.

He picked up the microphone. The Colonel looked defiant. The whole room waited, wondering what Ellis would do.

"You will withdraw that remark. You will apologise to my wife for your false and foul accusation, and you will do it through this microphone right now to be sure that all who heard your unwarranted insult, also hear you admit publicly that you lied." He spoke quite quietly holding in his fury. Then he thrust the microphone at McRaven, who, alone in the room, seemed unaware of his anger.

"I don't apologise to people like you."

"I will give you just one more chance. If you do not do so, then in my wife's defence I am left with no option but to tell the truth about you and your daughter."

McRaven silently folded his arms. After a tense moment's silence Ellis repeated what he had said a third time.

"Apologise, John," Danielle told him.

"Of course not."

Ellis spoke into the microphone, looking around the room.

"Very well. You will all understand that I must defend my wife. Perhaps you should all know the truth anyway. It is perhaps my duty, as McRaven told me on a previous occasion." He paused as if to ensure McRaven would start to realise he meant what he said, but whether it was arrogance or ignorance that prevented him understanding, he remained stubbornly silent.

"First this man is not a proper Colonel. He should be called Mister."

That had McRaven's attention, but it was too late.

"Second, his daughter is certainly clever, but not clever enough. She and another man have been caught stealing someone else's work for their own profit. I received a letter and email at Gibraltar, describing what had happened if anyone wants proof. She no longer works for Treasures of Scotland. She has been sacked. He turned back to McRaven.

"If you still believe the rumour that never was about an affair between my wife and I before we married, then you are even more stupid than I thought you were." McRaven looked furious.

"Do I have to continue?" McRaven said nothing.

"Very well. Your daughter invented the rumour you referred to in an underhand attempt to take the post I hold for herself. I take no pleasure in describing your 'sweet girl' in this way. But I will continue if necessary. There's much more to tell. You dishonour your name and your country. I still require you to apologise to my wife."

He paused and looked at McRaven, waiting for him to respond, but whilst still stubborn he'd had enough. His pride would not let him apologise, yet it fought with his fear of what else Ellis might reveal. He just stared sullenly at the floor.

Danielle stood up and held out her hand for the microphone, which Ellis gave her.

"I apologise to Mr and Mrs Mackenzie on behalf of my husband. Nothing Mr Mackenzie says is a surprise to me."

She put the microphone on the table and walked out of the room. McRaven could only follow her in the heavy silence. He could hardly fail to understand the mood throughout the room. As he went someone rubbed it in.

"Good night, Mister McRaven."

After the McRavens had left, and the conversational buzz in the room had recovered, Ellis walked back to Vaila, took her hand, wished Minnie and Millie good night and they left too. There was no smile on his face.

*   *   *

The next morning at breakfast they were discussing what they might do and had just decided go on deck to see what the situation in the city was now, when they saw Paul Unwin looking around the dining room. He soon spotted them.

"Good Morning. I hope you both slept well?

"We slept like two logs."

"Good. Ellis, the Captain is holding a meeting of the officers and senior staff in the chart room at ten. He'd like you to describe what you learnt when held by the rebels. He says he wouldn't detain you after that. Sorry Vaila, we're taking him away again!"

"Just don't let him off the ship! I'll go up to the Sun Deck. Join me afterwards, darling."

The Captain started the meeting by telling them that there had still not been any further communication from the rebels or the General's Albysian government nor even the British Consulate.

"Our land line phone connection is still in place but I'm especially concerned that I can't get through to our Consul this morning. The calls just go to an answering machine. However I want us all to be ready to react at any moment to developments, whatever they are."

He then asked Ellis to describe what he knew of the rebels and their plans just as he had told the Captain on his return the previous day.

"Certainly. Adjacent to the Si'pelium archaeological site there are four buildings now used as the rebel HQ. The rebels, a group calling themselves the Fezzan and led by a man called Hassan, were preparing for their revolution."

The Ambassador nodded,

"Yes, a shadowy group I have heard about." Ellis continued.

"They had plenty of guns for their men, brought in by the *Camel Prince* which you will have seen anchored off to the east of us. We saw some fifteen or so pickup trucks which they armed at Si'pelium with machine guns mounted on fittings behind the cabs. They all left to go into Qariat before we were locked in the stable loft, leaving just our three guards and Hosni, the translator, to hold us prisoner. They must have similarly armed a number of other pickup trucks and sent them into the city, the ones which the excursion passengers saw. I would guess they have around thirty such vehicles altogether. Hassan must have thought it enough to take Qariat fairly quickly. That's what he said to his men. The pickups were similar to the two now covering the ship." He gestured towards the window.

"As the fighting does not appear to have resolved anything yet," the Staff Captain, Larry Frew, said. "I wonder if it's proving harder than he thought. What did he plan to do assuming he won the city?"

"In his speech to his men before they left, as translated by Hosni for us, he said that Peter and I were hostages to persuade the *Carnelian* to stay in Qariat harbour. Once they took the city and had ejected General Ghedir Rezza, the President, his idea was that the *Carnelian* and all on board should be impounded to persuade the British Government to recognise his Fezzan as the new Government of Albysia. He then proposed to demand substantial 'aid'. We were to be shot if the *Carnelian* didn't do as he ordered, and other passengers would be shot if Britain didn't give him the billions he wanted."

As he finished, the internal phone rang. It was the watch officer reporting that a small tank, or armoured car, had appeared at the dockyard gate, just as a large car flying the Union flag was approaching down the road from the west.

The Captain immediately adjourned the meeting.

"Larry, go to the bridge, broadcast a message throughout the ship asking passengers to clear all the open decks and to take cover within the ship. Jonny, get the staff to ensure everyone does so. Ellis, please can you help him? Reassure everyone that we hope it's a false alarm, just a precaution." He looked around the room.

Ellis, on second thoughts, I think your wife said she was going to the Sun Deck. Go and join her. Take one of the staff radios and keep Larry informed if you recognise any of the rebels or see anything else, especially as there are blind spots from the bridge. For example, Larry will not be able to see what is astern of us. In any case you may well get a better view from the Sun Deck. But keep down, there could be shooting." He turned to Paul.

"Come with me. We'll go to the entry port to welcome the Consul."

Ellis immediately went up to the Sun Deck and found Vaila just as Larry's message was broadcast. They spoke to the few passengers there and a moment later he and Vaila had the Sun Deck to themselves. They found a spot near the funnel where they could have some cover, yet see everything that happened in the dockyard.

The tank had stopped about twenty metres inside the dockyard gate, facing towards the customs shed and the two rebel pickup trucks. The dock gate was shut behind it. Neither side made any further move except that the pickups had turned round to face the little tank, one each side of the customs shed. Ellis wondered how evenly matched the two sides were.

The car with the Union flag had reached the dock gate and stopped. There were two soldiers in the guard post beside it, presumably General Rezza's men.

Two men got out of the car leaving, so far as Ellis could see, only the driver in it. One of them was formally dressed, presumably the British Consul, and the other must be acting as an interpreter. Ellis wondered if he was British or Albysian. They then spoke to the guards and very much to Ellis surprise the gate was opened and the car came through and stopped for the Consul and interpreter to get back into it. The car then passed the tank and came on towards the customs shed.

It was not clear whether it was the car or something else that triggered what happened next, but one of the rebel pickups fired a burst from its machine gun over the Consul's car. The car was untouched. It may not have been the intention but nonetheless some of the bullets rattled against the little tank's armour. The tank commander must have thought it was deliberate and fired the tank's main gun back, hitting the engine of one of the pickups and blowing it apart. In an instant the pickup was engulfed in flames as the men on it leapt off and ran for what cover they could find. Its companion took off at high speed and was round the end of the nearest building and out of sight before the tank could fire at it.

The two men in the customs shed fired at the tank from the door, a futile gesture to a tank, however small. It simply provoked the tank to fire back.

The shell hit the customs post and demolished it. The men inside it must have been killed, or at least severely injured.

While these things were happening the Consul's car had stopped well out of the firing line, but it now made a dash for the point beside the ruined customs shed where there was now a gap in the fence. The driver just drove over the remains of the fence. There must have been some sharp edges to the remains of the fence, because two of the car's tyres blew out, but the driver ignored the damage and managed to get the car quite close to the *Carnelian* before he was forced to stop. The three men in the car jumped out, fearful that there might be more firing, and ran up the gangway that had been hastily put in place and into the entry port even before it was totally opened. It was quickly closed again as soon as they were through it. The interpreter brought a long case with him.

Ellis then saw the tank come forward again to stop by the ruined customs shed. One man warily got out of it, looked all around to be sure no one was there to shoot at him and then searched the ruins. He moved a number of pieces of rubble. They saw him look under one large slab, part of what had been the wall, and then heave it to one side. He had found the two men who had been in it. He looked at them carefully to see their condition, shouted to the tank commander, removed a bit more of the rubble and returned to the tank.

The commander must have radioed his superior because a white van with a crudely painted red crescent on the side soon appeared. It went to the ruin and with a stretcher two men in white coats removed the rebels who had been in the shed, and drove away. It was impossible for Ellis to see whether they were alive or dead.

The tank then took up position near the remains of the shed. Its gun was pointed at the *Carnelian*, but otherwise it did not move, and matters on the dockside settled down, if uneasily.

The Captain called his officers and staff, including Ellis, together again in the chart room. He started the meeting by asking the Consul to give them what news he could about the current situation in the City.

He introduced himself as Julian Traynor and told them that the rebels were still very active, and the Government forces were still fighting back. Neither side could be said to be winning yet so far as he

240

could tell. In summary, he told them he thought the current situation was close to stalemate.

He looked round to see if anyone wanted to ask questions, but as no one spoke he continued.

"Early this morning a group of soldiers led by a Senior Officer called at the embassy. My translator, Ahmet, didn't want to let them in, but they brushed him aside threatening to arrest him for helping the British on the *Carnelian* to work with the rebels.

"I asked him what he meant, as I was unaware that there had been any contact between the ship and the rebels."

The officer had explained that the Government had a spy at the rebel base at Si'pelium. He had reported that two of *Carnelian*'s men had stayed at Si'pelium with the rebels when the coach with the rest of the excursion passengers went back to the ship. The spy's report was that the two were staying to help Hassan by arranging with the ship's Captain to stay in Qariat. The spy's report convinced the General that *Carnelian* was working with Hassan to persuade the British to recognise and support the Fezzan, in return the Fezzan and would protect the ship. Hassan had ordered a couple of pickup trucks and their men to guard *Carnelian* against the Government army. General Ghedir Rezza was furious at this unacceptable British betrayal. The Ambassador had told the officer that he simply did not believe this story and offered to come to *Carnelian* to check for himself, after which he would be able to reassure the General, if he was given free safe passage to do so.

The Officer had phoned the Presidential Palace to report while the Consul waited. The General had agreed, but had said that he should tell the Captain that one false move and he would attack the ship. He also demanded that one of the men who had stayed at Si'pelium and then had stolen a fishing boat be surrendered to the Government in the next twelve hours so he could be tried both for theft and for consorting with the rebels.

"What a mess," said the Captain. "It sounds as if we now have both Government and Fezzan rebels against us. Do you think there is any chance that the General will believe you if you tell him that the spy was wrong?"

"He is an unpredictable man. I'm afraid one can't ever be sure what he will do. In these circumstances however I think it most unlikely as he seems to trust his spy. He called him a very brave man. I've never felt he trusted me much, and at best he tolerates the British. There is little chance he'll accept my word for anything without proof. Anyway he wants at least one of your men. He might want to show how he deals with westerners who steal boats too."

"Mr Traynor, I have not introduced you to Ellis Mackenzie, who is one of the men concerned. I think he should tell you his story, then you will fully understand the truth of what happened and why no one on the ship would dream for a moment of handing him over to the General or anyone else."

When Ellis had repeated the story of his being taken hostage with Peter and of their escape, the Consul said that he was glad to know what really happened.

"Unfortunately it's not me that you would need to convince. The story as you tell it might well impress the General, but for him to let you and the *Carnelian* go, it is not enough. He will want to be able to use it to his own advantage."

"How could I do that?"

"If he captures you, Mr Mackenzie, and puts you on trial it would be a victory. I have no doubt that he would see it as great propaganda. He would look good in front of the whole of Northern Africa." He looked at Ellis.

"Effectively you not only need to convince him of the facts, but also that he would gain more glory by releasing you and the ship than he would by trying you and, inevitably, finding you guilty and imprisoning you, or worse."

"What do you think he will do if we tell him that we refuse to hand him over?"

"Unless he's too busy with the Fezzan, he will attack the ship. Everyone would be at great risk then."

"What about playing for time until the Royal Navy sends a ship."

"No, very risky. It would just increase his anger. I'm not sure how long the navy would take to get here anyway."

"But" Ellis chipped in. "If I went with you, Mr Traynor, surely that would be okay wouldn't it? You must have diplomatic immunity, would that not cover me if I was with you?"

"I'm afraid, Mr Mackenzie, they do not always play by the rules here. I have little doubt that the Government's people would take you the moment they saw you."

"Then effectively the best option is for me to go ashore voluntarily and hope I can prove I was trying to destroy Hassan not help him?"

"Yes."

"Ellis, you may be a courageous man but I fear the risk is too great, and it sounds as if the chances of success are not good enough," the Captain said. "However we have twelve hours to decide what to do. So, for now, my decision is this. We will let time pass. We will reconvene after tea at four thirty. If no one has had any better idea by then we can consider whether the risk of refusing the

242

General's demand is worse than the risk of meeting it. At that point you will have to decide, Ellis, if you really are prepared to risk your life for the ship. No one will put you under pressure. The decision must be yours and yours alone." Larry added,

"We've now got that tank holding us here, ready to shoot at any time. There must be a risk an unstable General will order it to fire on us at any moment. It would take somewhere around twenty minutes to start the engines before we could manoeuvre out of this berth. The tank could fire on us for at least thirty minutes and is so close that it couldn't miss. Whatever we do we can't put passengers at risk. It looks as if we've jumped out of the rebel pot and into the Government fire without lifting a finger. If only we could find a way to get out of Qariat without being fired on."

The meeting then broke up.

When Ellis met Peter, whilst looking for Vaila, he told him the position. Peter said that if Ellis was going to volunteer to go ashore in the way the General demanded then he ought to come too.

"No need Peter. It would be unnecessary anyway and you've a young family.

"And you should think of Vaila."

"That's different. Vaila is at risk with everyone else on board if I don't go, but Chrissie and Jamie are safe at home."

It took him sometime to find Vaila. She was on the Quarterdeck near the stern rail. Paul was there too, talking to her, and Minnie and Millie were at a table nearby listening to their conversation. When Paul saw Ellis he excused himself. He had to return to the bridge. Ellis went to Vaila

"So there you are. Have you had coffee?" As he said it he realised that she was looking at him with fury. "Are you okay?" he asked.

"Paul has just told me what you have volunteered to do. He thinks you're brave. I don't." He thought she looked like an angry tigress but he was entirely unprepared for what she did next.

"You impossible man. You uncaring, stubborn, stupid man." She hit him on the chest with the side of her fist between every word, "You unconcerned, unloving, uncaring, unthinking, dreadful man." She paused for breath and as she started again she continued pounding his chest, now with both fists. He tried to back away but found himself with his back to the rail. "You cussed, cruel, hurtful, horrid, hateful monster. Why did I have to fall in love with you?" She fell against him. "How can you do this to me? Damn you, I can't even hate you. And we need you! Damn you, damn you!" She burst into tears and clung to him sobbing.

Minnie came to them. Ellis said to her "What have I done? What have I said? I don't understand."

"I'm so sorry Ellis. I should have told you. When you were taken hostage at Si'pelium, on the coach we heard gunfire. The Colonel thought it was a firing squad and Hosni said 'two less Westerners.'" We all thought you and Peter had been shot dead. We had to tell Vaila that. She was amazing, ringing Peter's wife and your Mum. She was so brave. In the morning she saw the boats sailing this way. She said it was you, but none of us believed or supported her when she needed us to hope and pray with her. She knew that you would be both lucky and have to use all your skill as a sailor to avoid being caught. Then the gunboat also came after you. She really believed in you. I'm so sorry we let her down, we thought she was fantasising, had gone off her head. Then you were shot when trying to get back on board. I know that only lasted a moment, but even then she was there for you." She lowered her voice, not wanting others to hear and worry that the ship was in real danger. She had heard what Paul had said.

"Now, I gather, you have volunteered to risk your life again. It must really hurt, Ellis. She adores you, but you're asking too much of her."

He turned his attention back to Vaila, quietly saying how sorry he was.

"No final decision has been made yet, not until tea time darling." He held her gently until she recovered.

"What are you going to do?"

"I don't know. I suppose think of better times until the afternoon meeting if I can. But something must be done or everyone on the ship is in serious danger. The General has given the Captain an ultimatum, demanding I am surrendered to his government's so called justice by this evening. The Captain won't do that but the Consul says I might have a chance to persuade the General that I didn't side with Hassan and only borrowed the boat to escape. It's an awful situation we're in. If we stay here, whether the General or Hassan wins the battle, the *Carnelian* will be at the mercy of the winner."

"I'm coming to your meeting. I won't believe it unless I hear it from the Consul. And I don't want you to go."

"The Consul says however risky I have a better chance than anyone else. No one can think of any other way to save the *Carnelian* and everyone aboard, including you. It looks as if it's my decision."

She looked at him, clearly devastated at the thought that, after everything that had happened, all he had done to escape Hassan, he would now be risking his life again by putting himself in the General's hands. It was highly likely that he might yet be taken from her. She just wanted him alive, she didn't need him to be a hero.

The Captain welcomed her to the meeting. He started by asking if anyone had had a better idea than Ellis attempting to get the General to accept he was not on the Fezzan side and to remove the tank and let the ship leave, but no one had.

The Consul repeated what he had said earlier; there was no question that unless Ellis was prepared to take the risk of surrendering himself to the General in the hope of persuading him that he was not on the rebel side, and that he had taken the boat as the only means of escaping from Hassan it was hard to see how the *Carnelian* could get away without further loss of life. He was straightforward about the risks he would be taking if he went.

The Captain reiterated what he had said earlier, that he would never 'surrender' Ellis to the General. Only if Ellis volunteered would the plan be tried.

Vaila asked what would happen to Ellis if the General did not believe him.

"At best, he will be imprisoned for a long time, at worse he'll be shot." The Consul was gloomy. "I'm sorry, Mrs Mackenzie I cannot be optimistic, I can only tell you what the position is. The General is such a volatile character. But I am sure of one thing Ellis, only you stand any chance of success."

Ellis looked at Vaila. Tears were forming in her eyes.

"I love you, I....," she paused and looked straight at him whilst the others awaited his decision. None of them would have blamed him for refusing, nor did any of them believe there was any other way to save the ship, slim as his chances were. They all felt desperately for Vaila. "....I can't stand in your way, you must do what you think is best."

He wanted to look away from the fear and anguish he saw in her eyes. He knew in that moment exactly what she was going through. She instinctively knew his decision.

He was about to speak when the phone rang, interrupting him. The Captain picked it up and listened.

"Are you sure?" He listened again and then said. "Thank you."

He turned to the meeting.

"The officer on the bridge has just told me that things are happening on the beach where the gunboat went ashore. There is a battle going on around her. The tank that was holding us is leaving, presumably to join in. The little tug has also put to sea. He thinks it must be manned by the Fezzan men in the pickup truck that disappeared to avoid the tank, and if so, at this moment we are unguarded though perhaps not for long. The meeting is adjourned. I am going up to the bridge at once to see for myself, with the intention of giving the order for as rapid a departure as possible. Ellis

245

and Vaila, take the radio and binoculars and go to the Sun Deck as you did earlier. Let me know what you see." They saw his determination.

"I'll make a public announcement if I think there's a reasonable chance of getting out of here. All of you should be able to hear it where ever you are. Take it as my decision to go, and therefore for you to carry out my orders for leaving as quickly as we can. Just get cracking. Do what you can to keep the passengers safe, Jonny. Who knows what'll happen but if I think we can get away I'll go for it."

He picked up the phone again and dialled. The Chief engineer answered and the Captain said

"Steve, something is happening which just might enable our escape. Get everything ready to start the engines. I want you to be able to start them within a minute should I call you to do so and then I want power as soon as possible after that. We may not have much time." He put the phone down without waiting for Steve's response.

"Larry come with me, and prepare all departments for leaving port in a hurry. You'll need a squad to release the lines ashore, as well as the usual crew to operate the winches.

"Paul, open the entry port for the shore squad. They should cast off all lines except for a single stern line to help us out of our berth immediately I give the order to go. We won't drift much. They are to wait for nothing. As soon as they have cast off the lines the shore squad are to run as fast as they can to get back on the ship. Report when they are aboard. The stern line may have to be abandoned after use. Have someone check it can be released from the winch immediately it has done its job.

"Paul, don't go through the usual procedure to remove the gangway, it takes too long, just hook it up and shut the entry port the moment the shore squad is back. Hopefully we won't need it."

He looked at the man next to him.

"Mr Traynor, please stay here to man the phone and coordinate if there are difficulties, injuries and so on. If we are to risk grabbing this brief opportunity I need you to hold the fort here."

"Any questions?" They all shook their heads.

"Good luck everyone. Let's go."

The endgame

As soon as Ellis and Vaila reached the Sun Deck they took a good look round to see if there was anything that might affect the *Carnelian*'s actions, or delay their rapid exit, but the dockyard appeared deserted. No tank, no pickup, no tug and, of course, no gunboat. For the moment the cruiseship was alone. They quickly walked a complete circuit of the deck, Ellis taking the starboard side and Vaila the port side. They met at the rail nearest the stern looking over the Quarterdeck. Jonny had done a good and quick job of persuading all passengers to leave the open deck, it was as deserted as was the Sun Deck. Ellis noticed Vaila still shaking from the tension she had felt at the meeting, and took a moment to kiss her, to restore her smile.

"I'm so sorry darling. I saw what an ordeal that was for you. I feel terrible about it." He might have said more but she put her finger to his lips in a sign for silence.

"I won't ask."

"You don't need to, do you?" Then the loudspeaker crackled into life:

This is the Captain speaking. There is a battle being waged between the Government forces and the Fezzan rebels on the beach where the little gunboat went aground. The Fezzan seem to be preparing to tow the gunboat off the beach. We have to presume that they have managed to repair her engine. At the same time the tank that threatened to fire on Carnelian has left, and I believe it is going to the beach to join the fighting. Therefore Carnelian has an opportunity to escape Qariat, and officers and crew are working to enable us to do so as soon as possible. You should know...

He was interrupted by the sound of the engines starting...

...that there are risks. We have to be clear of the port before either the tank returns or the gunboat is near enough to fire on us, but the risk of staying is even greater. There is no time for me to explain just now why that is so.
I urge you all to stay within the ship. Do not go on any open deck or balcony for your own safety. The decks may become dangerous, and we need to give the crew all the space they need to work the ship without any delays.
Please go to your cabins, put on your life jackets and I will keep you informed so far as I am able. The lifeboats will be prepared in case of

problems, although it is my hope and intention to outrun any opposition. May God go with us all. Thank you.

"We've a job to do. Come on Ellis."

They returned to the bows on the port side overlooking the dockside together. They had just reached the large open part of the deck above the bridge when Vaila pointed.

"There's a pickup. It must be the one that escaped from the tank, and has been hiding somewhere."

It was being driven round the end of one of the dockyard buildings on the far side towards the ship. It would have to drive round a crane and a second building near the dock gate to reach the ruins of the customs shed from where it could use its machine gun to fire on the shore party. He doubted if the shore party was aware of the danger.

Ellis hastily spoke through the radio he had been given.

"Captain, A rebel pickup truck is coming back. I imagine it saw the tank going and now wants to stop us leaving. The shore squad is still on the dockside, removing the lines, and won't have seen it yet."

"Okay." The Captain cut the call.

As they were speaking Ahmet appeared beside Ellis and Vaila. He had the long box that he had brought on board with him.

"Trouble?" was all he said. He put the box on the deck behind them, but they took little notice in their anxiety for the shore squad.

As the pickup came out into the open near the gate and accelerated towards the ruins of the customs shed the Captain could now see for himself the danger to the shore party. He spoke through the loud speaker "Shore party return now an armed pickup is nearly on you. Return now, return now, return now."

Ellis wasn't sure why the pickup drove through the same gap in the fence as had the Ambassadors car, as it could have fired on the shore party whilst staying outside it, but it did and one of its tyres was punctured, making it lurch round in a half circle.

All three of the men in it were in the cab. Two of them jumped out before it had quite stopped. They ran round, hastily climbing onto the back to man the machine gun. Ellis could see that four of the *Carnelian*'s shore party releasing the lines furthest from the gangway had no chance once the machine gun fired, they were totally exposed without shelter of any kind. Vaila held her breath, it looked too late for the men to save themselves.

"Crack. Crack." It was so loud and sudden right beside Ellis it made him jump. It was Ahmet. Resting his elbows on the ship's rail he had calmly used just two shots to kill the two men manning the machine gun. The rifle he held had a long telescopic sight, but it was still an amazing feat. Ellis had concentrated so hard on the scene in front of him he had not realised that Ahmet had calmly assembled and armed it behind them.

They heard the pickup's engine rev as the driver tried to turn to escape Ahmet's lethal accuracy. A further shot must have just missed the driver, the bullet entering the open window of the pickup. From Ahmet's smile Ellis realised the miss must have been deliberate. Ahmet's shot was to scare the driver into turning right round to face away from the ship. At that point Ahmet put a shot into both back tyres. The pickup was no longer any threat. Facing away from the ship its gun also faced the other way. The driver realised he was now a sitting target if he did anything. Nor could he warn anyone of his hopeless situation.

The shore party realising that they were now safe, completed their task and ran back to the gangway and onto the ship. Ellis was amazed,

"Ahmet, that was remarkable marksmanship." Ahmet smiled.

"My hobby. Practise every day. Saved for years for this rifle and it never leaves my side. What we do about him?" He pointed at the pickup.

Ellis reported to the Captain who had had no idea who had saved the shore party but was equally astonished at the way it had been done when Ellis told him. He replied

"I will thank him personally when we're out of here. Please could Ahmet keep his rifle on the driver. No need for more deaths. Just so long as the driver does not attempt anything. Steve has just told me we will have power in five minutes. Please thank Ahmet for me."

Ellis told Ahmet what the Captain had said. He just smiled, and kept his eye to the telescopic sight. The driver of the pickup gave up, switched off the engine and stayed low in his seat.

"Now my life depends on your escape, especially if the Fezzan win. I stay here." Ahmet looked determined.

Ellis looked through binoculars at the beach again and Vaila asked him what he could see.

"Almost continuous flashes of gun fire."

Although the beach was two or three kilometres away, they could hear the firing too. Ellis could see four pickups lined up in front of the gunboat facing outward. Although he couldn't see any of the soldiers, clearly there was plenty of movement at the top of the beach. The pickup trucks were exchanging fire whenever the soldiers hidden in the scrub revealed their position by firing at the Fezzan protecting the gunboat. There was as yet no sign of the tank.

Turning his binoculars to the gunboat he could see plenty of activity. Number 2 had struck the sandy beach bows first and lay at around fortyfive degrees to the line of the gentle surf, half in and half out of the water. There was virtually no wind.

There were men on the stern of the little warship who had prepared a warp, and on the water other men were rowing a messenger, a light line, out to the tug. It took them only a minute or two before Ellis saw the rope passed from the gunboat to the tug. Ellis thought the water would shelve quite gently and wondered how long it would take to pull the gunboat from the sand.

Then the tank appeared at the top of the beach and wasted no time before shooting. Ellis could see the fall of shot; the tug was its target. The first shot was over and to one side. As it fired again the gunboat fired back. The duel between them was short. The gunboat's third shot hit the tank. It was pushed back, the gun pointing to the sky. Ellis saw two men hurriedly climb out of it just before it burst into flame. Now the Fezzan were ready to pull the gunboat off the sand and to Ellis' surprise it was refloated almost immediately. When he reported this to the Captain he replied

"Thanks. We are ready now too. Keep watching. I've no time to watch the beach. I won't be able to see it anyway from here, once we are free of our berth."

From their vantage point Ellis and Vaila saw the winches recovering the lines as the ship started to go astern. Guided by the one stern line, which was cast off when the ship's stern had passed the bollard to which it was attached, and dropped as soon as the Captain was sure it would be well clear of the *Carnelian*'s propellers. They saw the bow thrusters push the bow to starboard as soon as she was in clear water. Now she had to leave port before the gunboat could get near enough to fire on her.

The cruise ship now had to go astern towards the east entrance far enough to enable her to alter course to exit the outer harbour by the north opening in the breakwater. As Ellis watched the radio beeped and the Captain asked

"Can you see where the gunboat is now?"

"She's clear of the beach, and I saw smoke from her funnel as she started her engines just now. She's already turning to come this way."

"Okay. And Ellis, keep the radio open. As long as we are unable to watch astern of us, give me a running commentary of what you see."

Ellis told Vaila what the Captain had asked so they moved nearer the stern to have a clearer view of the gunboat.

It seemed to take an age before the Captain was satisfied that the *Carnelian* had gone far enough astern that she could go ahead to reach the north exit from the outer harbour. As Ellis felt the engines stop for this change he saw that the gunboat was already nearing the east entrance to the outer harbour. He noticed the little tug was following her about a hundred metres behind.

As the *Carnelian*'s engines started to go ahead the gunboat reached the point where she had to choose whether to come into the outer harbour by the east opening or follow the breakwater on the outside to catch ship at the north exit. Ellis gave the binoculars to Vaila.

"I'll give the commentary without them and you may be able to see more useful detail. Tell me the moment you can be sure which way the gunboat will go. I can't hold the binoculars and operate the radio at the same time."

In was only a minute before Vaila said she was sure the gunboat had made her decision. She was on course to sail along the outside of the breakwater. They could now only see the top of her stumpy mast because of the height of the breakwater. As Ellis continued his running commentary through the radio the Captain responded by saying that at least the gunboat would not be able to fire on them until they reached the north entrance.

Vaila said she was surprised how fast the gunboat was going. It became increasingly clear that as the *Carnelian* gathered speed the two ships would arrive at the north entrance at more or less the same time.

There was now no need for the radio. The gunboat was to starboard of the *Carnelian* and the Captain and officers on the starboard wing of the bridge were just below Ellis and Vaila, back by the rail of the Sun Deck just above them. Nor at that moment was there anything to say. All they could do was just to watch.

Paul Unwin came out onto the wing of the bridge and spoke to the Captain.

"I've calculated our speed with theirs. If neither vessel slows down, we are on collision course just outside the harbour."

"I thought that was the case. Steve is giving us all the speed he can. We're doing over seventeen knots already and still accelerating. But the gunboat's Captain is a fool anyway if he doesn't slow down or turn away. By bearing away she could fire at us any number of times before our superior speed takes us out of range. I would think any seaman would realise that. If she gets under our bows the collision will cut her in half, and even if she is very close she'll be swamped by our bow wave, and the faster we go the worse for that toy ship."

The end came suddenly. As the *Carnelian* came out into the open sea just ahead of the gunboat they could see someone behind the gun. Vaila, with the binoculars, shouted down to the Captain.

"It's Hassan himself at the gun. If he shoots he can't miss."

Whoever was at the helm of the gunboat suddenly understood their danger and put the helm hard to starboard, but far too late. The gunboat was much too close. Hassan took no notice. He had to adjust his aim which he quickly did. He was about to fire when there was the crack of a rifle. Ahmet, beside them on the Sundeck, had shot Hassan a fraction before he could fire. With both ships moving as they were it was an even more remarkable shot.

The gunboat caught the *Carnelian*'s bow wave at its highest only a metre or two from the point of collision. It threw the gunboat onto its beam ends. It looked for a moment as though she would capsize but she righted herself, and her momentum carried her forward and she hit Carnelian just under the bridge wing. From the Sun Deck and bridge they felt nothing but saw the collision immediately under them. As the *Carnelian* rushed on, the second bow wave again rolled the gunboat nearly onto her side. She did not sink immediately, but must have been full of water.   Ellis and Vaila ran along the side of the deck keeping abreast of the stricken little warship, and so saw that once she was astern she was sinking rapidly. Her crew jumped overboard. She finally sank when the cruiseship was about fifty metres ahead of her. They saw men in the water waiting for the tug to pick them up. Vaila, watching through binoculars, was not entirely certain, but she called down to the Captain on the wing of the bridge that she thought Hassan was one of them.

Ahmet beside her said,

"You are probably right, you see I aimed to hit his arm." He said it as if commenting on hitting a practice target, an everyday occurrence.

Ellis looked at him in surprise. Ahmet smiled at him.

"You see, I'd like to go home one day. If I had killed him, the Fezzan would hunt me down. If they win one day I shall say that I naturally only hit his arm in my own defence, I did not aim to kill him. But If the General wins, I shall say that I tried to kill Hassan for the glory of Albysia, but unfortunately the shot was too difficult for me and I missed."

Ellis and Vaila looked at each other and laughed. Ellis said,

"Ahmet, you'll never get away with that. No one will believe that you missed!"

*   *   *   *

Postscript

Ellis and Vaila leant on the stern rail, watching the wake pointing back to Albysia. The sun had just reached the horizon to the west, and the little country had become no more than a grey shadow across the southern horizon.

I don't suppose the General will do anything about Si'pelium." Ellis mused.

"I don't care. We are not going there again, however interesting you think Si'pelium is. Next year we're having an adventure at home."

"At least we seem to have sorted out all those secrets. Which reminds me. Why do you keep calling yourself 'we'?"

"You noticed!" she laughed. "As your piddie Princess, I must prepare you for your new title!"

"What are you talking about? What title?"
He saw her mischievous grin, the one he found so irresistible.

"Daddy!"